WHO IS PREACHER?

In 1985, William W. Johnstone's western *The Last Mountain Man* was published—and the legendary Smoke Jensen was born. The series became an immediate hit and remains to this day one of his most popular creations. In 1990, Bill was asked to create a spin-off character. He created a prequel to the Last Mountain Man series called *The First Mountain Man,* featuring another man of the frontier, known only as Preacher—a boy who left home in 1812 and became one of the most fearless men who conquered the American frontier.

But the question remained: Who Is Preacher?

To answer that question, Pinnacle Books has now released in the volume you hold in your hands—two Preacher western adventures: *Forty Guns West* and *Blackfoot Messiah.* In these pages, you will learn the legend of the first mountain man: Preacher. Solitary, smart, armed with a long gun, and as fierce as the land he calls home.

Look for These Exciting Series from
WILLIAM W. JOHNSTONE
with J. A. Johnstone

The Mountain Man

Preacher: The First Mountain Man

Matt Jensen, the Last Mountain Man

Luke Jensen, Bounty Hunter

Those Jensen Boys!

The Family Jensen

MacCallister

Flintlock

The Brothers O'Brien

The Kerrigans: A Texas Dynasty

Sixkiller, U.S. Marshal

Hell's Half Acre

Texas John Slaughter

Will Tanner, U.S. Deputy Marshal

Eagles

The Frontiersman

AVAILABLE FROM PINNACLE BOOKS

FRONTIER DESTINY

THE PREACHER EPIC CONTINUES

THE FIRST MOUNTAIN MAN:
Forty Guns West
and
Blackfoot Messiah

WILLIAM W. JOHNSTONE

PINNACLE BOOKS
Kensington Publishing Corp.
www.kensingtonbooks.com

PINNACLE BOOKS are published by

Kensington Publishing Corp.
119 West 40th Street
New York, NY 10018

Copyright © 2017 J. A. Johnstone
Forty Guns West copyright © 1993 William W. Johnstone
Blackfoot Messiah copyright © 1996 William W. Johnstone

All rights reserved. No part of this book may be reproduced in any form or by any means without the prior written consent of the publisher, excepting brief quotes used in reviews.

If you purchased this book without a cover, you should be aware that this book is stolen property. It was reported as "unsold and destroyed" to the publisher, and neither the author nor the publisher has received any payment for this "stripped book."

All Kensington titles, imprints, and distributed lines are available at special quantity discounts for bulk purchases for sales promotions, premiums, fund-raising, educational, or institutional use. Special book excerpts or customized printings can also be created to fit specific needs. For details, write or phone the office of the Kensington sales manager: Kensington Publishing Corp., 119 West 40th Street, New York, NY 10018, attn: Sales Department; phone 1-800-221-2647.

PINNACLE BOOKS, the Pinnacle logo, and the WWJ steer head logo are Reg. U.S. Pat. & TM Off.

ISBN-13: 978-0-7860-4190-9
ISBN-10: 0-7860-4190-0

First printing of *Forty Guns West*: December 1993
First printing of *Blackfoot Messiah*: February 1996
First printing of omnibus edition: October 2017

10 9 8 7 6 5 4 3 2 1

Printed in the United States of America

CONTENTS

THE FIRST MOUNTAIN MAN:
FORTY GUNS WEST

BOOK ONE

Don't tread on me!

1

The townspeople of the long-settled eastern village never really grew easy with Preacher around. The mountain man walked like a big panther, silent and sure. A few of the town and the area's bully-boys felt compelled to call him out for a tussle. They very quickly learned that Preacher fought under no rules except his own. One bully-boy lost an eye, another was abed all winter with broken ribs, and the third—and final man to challenge Preacher—was buried one cold February morning.

"I reckon," Preacher said to his pa and ma one day, "I best be thinkin' of headin' back to the High Lonesome."

"It's been so good to see you, son," his mother said, placing her hand over his. "But I fear for you here."

"You don't need to be fearful for me, Ma," Preacher said. "That bully-boy pulled a blade on me. I had no choice in the matter."

"Your mother's right, son," Preacher's father said, stuffing his old pipe full of tobacco. He knelt by the fire and picked out a lighted twig and puffed. Back in his chair, he said, "You've left us money a-plenty to last for the rest of our years. I don't want to see grief come to you. And it will come if you stay around here."

Preacher knew his parents were right. He just didn't

want to admit it. But he knew he'd out-stayed his welcome in town. He just didn't fit in. Preacher was all muscle and bone and gristle. He was tanned dark by the sun and the wind, he carried the scars of a dozen deadly battles, and he operated under no moral or legal code save that of his own. And nobody was going to make him conform to any standard except that which he considered fair. But in his own peculiar way, Preacher was a highly moral man for the time, this year of our Lord, eighteen hundred and forty. He had the utmost respect for womanhood. He loved the land and the critters on it. He could not abide injustice. He didn't like lawyers and thought the country in general was going to Hell in a handbasket.

Preacher nodded his head. "You're both right. My good brothers won't even come around whilst I'm here."

His mother smiled. "They're afraid of you, son. They belong to order and families and the clock. You belong to the wilderness. Their lives are routine. Your life is like the wind. They don't, can't, understand that."

Preacher cut his eyes to the west. "For a fact," he muttered, "I have missed the mountains."

His father's old eyes twinkled. "I see where you've packed your gear. You must have been thinking about leaving."

Preacher laughed and gently placed one strong hand on his father's stooped shoulders, bent from years of brutally hard work, clearing the land and wrestling a living from the soil. "I reckon I'll pull out come the mornin'. Ma, if you'll make me a little poke of food, I'd be obliged." He stood up.

"Where are you going, son?" his mother asked.

"Oh, I think I'll take me a little stroll through the town. Give the good folks one last look 'fore they're shut of me." He looked at this parents. "You know when I leave this go-round, I prob'ly won't be back."

They nodded their heads.

Preacher stepped out of the house into the cold early

March air of Ohio. A thin covering of new snow the past night had laid a carpet of white over the land. Preacher checked on his horse, Thunder, and then decided to stretch his legs and walk the short distance into the village. A town, actually. Darn near five hundred people lived all crowded up like ants.

Preacher still drew stares from the citizens but he paid them no heed, just walked on to the combination coach stop, hotel, and tavern and opened the door. The buzz of conversation stopped when he padded silently up to the bar, the soles of his high-topped moccasins making no more than a whisper on the floor. He leaned on the bar and ordered a whiskey with a beer chaser.

Several ladies who had stopped there for the night and were waiting on the afternoon coach began whispering behind their fancy fans. Preacher paid them no mind. From the looks of them they were city women, all gussied up to beat the band. Preacher took a sip of whiskey and a sip of beer. He hid a smile as the few locals who were lined up at the bar backed away, clear down to the end, getting as far away from Preacher as they could. It had been in this very tavern, just two weeks past, that Preacher had killed that feller who shucked out his knife during what Preacher had thought was just a friendly fistfight. Preacher had left him on the floor, cut from navel to neck.

The door opened and a frail boy of about nine or ten entered. They boy's clothing was ragged and the soles of his shoes were tied on with string. He carried a small bucket with a lid on it. The top of the boy's head just did reach the lip of the bar. He placed the bucket on the bar and said, "A bucket of beer for Mister Parks, please, sir."

The barkeep took the bucket to rinse it out and the boy looked at the free lunch on the table, hunger in his eyes. His pinched face was pale and his eyes held a strange brightness.

"You hungry, boy?" Preacher asked.

The boy's eyes were scared as they fixed on the mountain man. "Yes, sir. Some."

"Then fix you a sandwich or two."

"That food's for customers!" the barkeep hollered.

"The lad just bought a bucket of beer, didn't he?" Preacher asked. "So that entitles him to food. Fix you something to eat, boy."

"I'll slap you, boy!" the barkeep barked. "You stay away from that food, you . . . woods' colt."

Preacher gave the barkeep a disgusted look as he walked to the table and fixed two huge meat and cheese sandwiches and gave them to the boy. "You sit over there by the stove and eat and get warm, boy." He turned to the barkeep. "You want to slap me?"

The man paled. "Ah, no, sir!"

"Fine. Now you pour that lad a big glass of milk and then go on about your business and leave the boy alone."

The boy fell into a hard fit of coughing that reddened his face. Bad lungs, Preacher thought. A wonder he lived through the winter.

Hard footsteps slammed on the boards outside the coach stop and the door was flung open. The hard and big bulk of Elam Parks filled the doorway, his face mottled with rage. He held a quirt in one hand. He pointed the quirt at the boy. "What the hell do you think you're doing, Eddie?" he shouted. "I didn't give you permission to eat."

"No. But I did," Preacher said.

In the time Preacher had been in town, he'd seen enough of Elam Parks to last him two lifetimes. Parks was an important man about the community. He owned several farms, a couple of businesses, and about fifty percent of the local bank. His brother was in tight with the governor, or senator, or some damn blow-heart politician. Parks thought himself the bull of the woods around these parts. He was a bully and a slave-driver to those who had the misfortune to work for him. He gave

Preacher the same type of look he might give a roach. Then he turned to the boy.

"Get up and get back to work, you worthless whelp!"

"When he finishes his meal," Preacher said.

Parks turned to face Preacher. He was a big'un, all right. Preacher guessed him at about six feet, one inch, with the weight to go with it. A big man with hard packed muscle. "This is none of your affair, Mountain Man," Parks said, contempt dripping from each word. "So stay out of it. The boy is bound to me and does what I tell him to do."

"Bound, huh? I thought that practice stopped a long time ago. I never did hold with it. It's just a fancy word for slavery. I don't hold with that either. You eat your meal, Eddie. This big mouth can wait."

Elam started stuttering and sputtering, his face beet red. People just didn't talk to him in such a manner. He pointed the quirt at the Preacher and shouted, "I'll have you run out of town, you, you . . . *trash!*"

Preacher smiled and finished his whiskey. He sat the cup on the bar and said, "You figure on doin' that all by yourself, or you gonna call some boys to help you?"

Preacher cut his eyes to the little boy. Eddie was gobbling down his sandwiches as fast as he could. It was evident to Preacher that the sick little boy had not had sufficient food in a long time.

Elam dropped his quirt on the table. "Mountain Man, you have had your way in this town for long enough. You been strutting about like a peacock. You need to learn a hard lesson, and I am just the man to teach you."

"Is that a fact?" Preacher hesitated for a moment, not wanting to bring any further grief to his parents. "Well, mayhaps you're right. I brung mountain ways to this town and expected folks hereabouts to accept 'em. I do apologize for that. But I don't apologize for standing up for the lad yonder. He's a mighty sick little boy. And he's got marks on his face that I just noticed under all that grime. Have you been beatin' on him, Parks?"

"The boy lacks discipline and motivation. Besides, he's bound to me and what I do is no concern of yours. But now that you have backed down from this issue, we'll call it even and forget it."

"Whoa!" Preacher said. "I ain't never backed down from no man. So don't you be puttin' the cart ahead of the horse." He looked at Eddie. "You want some pie or cake, boy?"

"Now, that's all!" Elam blurted. "I have had quite enough of this foolishness." He moved swift for a man his size. Elam slammed a heavy hand down on Eddie's shoulder and jerked him to his raggedy shoes. He flung the boy toward the door. Eddie struck the wall and cried out in pain.

Preacher took two steps forward and started his punch from down around his knees. The big hard right fist caught Elam on the side of the jaw and stretched the man out on the floor, blood leaking from his mouth.

"Oh, my God!" a local blurted. "Somebody run get Doctor Ellis."

Preacher knelt down beside Eddie. There was a bump on the boy's head and a slight cut oozing a tiny bit of blood. "Gimmie a wet cloth," Preacher said. When nobody moved, he added, "Now, damnit!"

One local ran out the door for the doctor while another handed Preacher a dampened cloth. Preacher gently bathed the frightened boy's face then picked him up and sat him in a chair. "You just take it easy 'til the doc gets here, boy."

"Mountain Man," a fancy dressed dude said, "you'd best haul your ashes out of here. Elam Parks is a big man in this state. You're prison bound when he wakes up."

Preacher ignored the warning. Obviously, Elam Parks had the whole damn town buffaloed. He looked up as his older brother rushed into the tavern.

The older man looked at the prostrate Parks and

blurted, "My God, Art! Have you taken leave of your senses? That's Elam Parks."

"No kiddin'? I'd a swore it was a brayin' jackass and nothin' more." He pointed to Eddie. "What's the story on this here boy, Brother?"

"He's a woods' colt. Elam bound him out of the orphanage to work for him. Nobody gives a hoot about that brat."

"Wrong, Brother. I give a hoot." The doctor ran in and started for the still unconscious Parks. Preacher grabbed his arm and halted him. "You check the boy first, Doc. Then you tell me about him."

Dr. Ellis hesitated, took a short look into Preacher's cold eyes, then shrugged his shoulders. He checked Eddie, put some antiseptic on the small cut and took Preacher's arm, leading him away from the boy.

"The boy is dying, Mister. Lung fever. It's a miracle he lived through the winter. The next winter will kill him for sure."

"All right. Now you can go check on stupid over yonder." He walked over to Eddie, past the out-of-town women who were vigorously fanning themselves, their faces flushed from all the excitement. "You got any belongin's, boy?"

"A few, sir."

"Go fetch them. You're shut of this town and its sorry people. You're comin' with me."

The boy's sad eyes brightened. "Really?"

"Really. Go on. Get back here as quick as you can." Preacher walked over to the bar and finished his beer. He watched through amused eyes as several men tried to get Parks up on his feet. "You best get you a hoist," he called. "It'll take it to get that moose up."

Parks finally managed to sit up on the floor, but his jaw was swollen and his eyes were glazed. Dr. Ellis bathed his face and the man's eyes began to focus. Pure hate was shining through, all of it directed at Preacher.

"Was I you, Parks," Preacher said, "I'd be real careful what come out of my mouth right about now. As upsot as you are, you just might let your butt overload it."

Preacher's brother rushed over to help Elam get to an upright position. He brushed at Elam's coat, all the while apologizing for Preacher's actions.

"That's right, Brother," Preacher drawled. "Suck up to him."

Elam shoved the men away from him. "Mountain Man, if you're in town an hour from now, have a gun in your hand."

"I'll prob'ly be in town. And if I am, I'll have a gun to hand, Parks. But you best remember this, Parks: I ain't no poor sick little boy. You level a pistol at me and the undertaker will be givin' you your last tidyin' up."

Parks snorted his reply and stalked out of the tavern just as Eddie was returning. He drew back his hand to strike the boy and Preacher said, "I'll break your arm, Parks."

Elam lowered his hand and stomped off. Preacher looked at the rags Eddie had stuffed into a sack and tossed them into a corner. "We'll get you some new duds, Eddie. But first we get you a bath and a haircut. Then we'll dust this town."

"Where are we going, Mister Preacher?"

"Where the air is pure and clean. Where them lungs of yours can heal. West, boy. To the mountains."

2

The barber was nervous as he cut Eddie's hair, but he managed to get the boy looking presentable without snipping off anything other than hair. Then it was into a hot tub with a bar of strong soap. While Eddie was washing off the grime, Preacher went to the general store and bought him new clothes, from underwear out.

Preacher checked his awesome four-barrel pistol and holstered it. He carried only the one pistol while in town; but even that made the local constable nervous. The county sheriff was half a day's ride away.

Preacher was under no illusions. He knew that Parks was no coward. If he said he'd come looking for Preacher, he'd come. Preacher returned to the barber shop and found a brand-new boy waiting for him. Good lookin' kid, too. Preacher looked at the wall clock. He had about twenty minutes left 'fore Parks would start on the prowl. He walked the boy down to the livery and bought him a pony. The horse was small, but strong limbed and Preacher guessed it had plenty of staying power. He bought a saddle and saddle bags.

"You know where Elm Street is, Eddie?"

"Yes, sir, Mister Preacher."

"I'm Preacher, boy. Not mister. You go over to Elm.

Second house on the right. Wait there for me. My ma and pa is there. You tell Ma I said to get that poke of food ready. I'll be along shortly."

"Mister Elam's a bad one. He's kilt men before, Preacher," Eddie warned.

"Not as many as I have. Go on."

Preacher made sure the boy was on his way, proudly riding his new pony, and then he stepped out into the street. The town lay silent under the cold sun. Preacher walked right up the center of the main street.

"You there!" the constable called to Preacher from under the awning of his office. "I order you in the name of the law to cease and desist."

"Go suck an egg," Preacher told him.

"I'm the law around here!" the man bellowed.

"Congratulations. Now go back into your office and drink coffee. Stay off the street."

"You can't talk to me like that!"

Preacher ignored him and kept on walking. A block ahead of him, Elam Parks stepped off the boardwalk and into the street, a pistol in each hand. The two men began closing the distance.

"This don't have to be, Elam!" Preacher called. "You abused the boy and got socked in the jaw for it. Now it's done and past. It ain't nothin' worth dyin' over."

But for Elam, time for talking was gone. He had been humiliated in his own town and had to redeem himself in the eyes of the citizens. He lifted a pistol and fired. The ball missed Preacher by several feet.

"You better make the next one count, Elam," Preacher called, his own pistol still holstered.

Elam fired his second pistol. Again he missed.

"Now it's over, Elam," Preacher called. "You took your shots and you missed. I ain't gonna fire. Go on home. You'll not see me nor the boy never again."

Elam was frantically reloading. "You son of a whore!" he yelled at Preacher.

Preacher's eyes hardened and he stopped in the street. "Insult me all you like. But don't never slur my mother's name. You hear me, Elam."

"You sorry, filthy trash!" Parks shouted. "Son of a whore!" He lifted a pistol and Preacher drew, cocked, and drilled him clean, the ball driving the third button of his shirt clear to his backbone. Parks stumbled and fell to the street, on his back.

The stores along the street and the houses behind them and on the side streets emptied of people, all gathering around the dead Elam Parks. Preacher reloaded the empty chamber and turned his back on the crowd. He walked to the house on Elm street. His parents had heard the shots and were waiting in the front yard, behind the picket fence.

Preacher's older brother came running up, all out of breath. He stood for a moment, panting, and then blurted, "My God, Mamma, Daddy. Art's done shot and killed Mister Elam Parks."

"He had it coming," the father said. "It's long overdue. I'm just sorry it had to be you who done it, Art."

"Had it coming!" the older brother said, horrified. "Daddy, how can you say things like that? Why, Mister Elam was a fine man. He . . ."

"Was a crook and a no-count," the father said. "Maybe with him dead and gone, now you can get that brown spot off your nose, boy."

Preacher laughed at the expression on his brother's face. The older brother turned toward him, his face red and his hands balled into fists.

"I'd think about it, brother of mine," Preacher said. "I'd give it real serious thought."

The brother stared at Preacher for a moment. "You're no brother of mine, Art. You've turned into a godless savage, just like the heathen Indians."

Preacher wanted real bad to hit him, but didn't want to do so in front of his mother. However, he figured his pa would probably enjoy seeing it. But he contained the urge to deck his brother and instead turned his back to him. The brother snorted and walked off. Preacher kissed his mother and held her close, both of them knowing this would be their last goodbye. He shook hands with his pa.

"You take care, son."

"I'll do 'er, Pa."

"God bless, son," his mother said. "I put a sack of food on your saddle."

"Y'all take care." Preacher walked to the small barn, Eddie keeping up with him. Two minutes later, they were riding out, heading west. Preacher did not look back. He would not have been able to see his ma and pa through the mist in his eyes.

"I thought we were going to head west, Preacher," Eddie remarked.

"We are, boy. But we'll head south for a time. Tell me about yourself."

"There ain't much to tell, Preacher. My ma and pa died with the fever when I was little. I don't even remember them. I was passed from pillar to post for a time, then the orphanage took me in. I was sick a lot, and no one wanted a boy who couldn't work. Mister Parks got me last year. I reckon I'd a died working for him."

"Prob'ly. But you gonna get well with me." Preacher paused. "At least some better. I think what you need most of all is good vittles, clean air, and rest."

Eddie tired easily and Preacher was in no hurry. He stopped often and made evening camp much earlier than he normally would. He avoided towns as often as possible. But he was under no illusions about what lay behind him. If Parks was the big-shot people thought him to be, there would surely be warrants out for him by now. But he wasn't worried too much about that, either. Worryin' caused a man to get lines in his face and gray in his hair.

Preacher skirted the town of Cincinnati and crossed the Ohio River by ferry and rode into Kentucky.

"That was some river, Preacher!" Eddie said, all excited.

"Wait 'til you see the Mississippi, boy. The Ohio runs into the Mississippi down in Southern Illinois."

"Will we see that?"

"We might. I was goin' to Saint Louie, but I think I'll skip that town this run. I'll take us down through Arkansas and then cut west from there."

"You're thinking that Mister Parks's friends might be after us, aren't you?"

The boy was very quick and very sharp. The lad didn't miss much at all. "Yeah," Preacher said. "That thought has crossed my mind a time or two."

"How old were you when you went west, Preacher?"

"Not much older than you, Eddie. My, but that was a time, back then. Back in the mountains. Why, you could go for months without seein' another white man. Now ever' time a body looks up, they's a damn cabin bein' built."

That was not exactly the truth, not even close to it. But people were moving west. It would be a few more years before the floodgates of humanity were thrown open and the real surge westward began. Many, if not most of the mountain men resented the pioneers' drive westward. They were, for the most part, solitary men—in some cases legitimately wanted by the law for various crimes—and they felt the vast West was theirs alone. But that was not to be. The mountain men were credited, however, with the carving out of much of the Far West. By 1840, the mountain man's way of life was very nearly a closed book, as beaver hats faded from vogue and the mountain men faded from view.

Many of the mountain men would drift back onto a civilized way of life, opening stores or turning to farming or ranching on a small scale. But many others either could not or would not change. They elected to stay in the mountains and eke out a living. Others, like Preacher, became scouts and wagon masters. And, like Preacher, living legends.

As the days on the trail drifted into weeks, and the weather warmed, moving silently into spring, Eddie began losing his cough and his face and forearms first blistered, then tanned under the sun and the wind. The boy began putting on weight and his face lost the sickly pallor and his eyes lost their feverish tint. Then, as Preacher and Eddie were making camp one afternoon in Arkansas, Preacher realized that the boy had not coughed up phlegm even one time that day.

All he needed was a chance, Preacher thought. Someone to take an interest in him and show him the right paths to take.

The mountain man and the kid drifted down to Little Rock. Preacher had been this way back in the twenties. He'd run up on them two kids, Jamie and Kate MacCallister. They'd been headin' for the Big Thicket country of East Texas, running from Kate's pa and a bunch of bounty hunters. Jamie and Kate, Preacher had heard, had gone on to have a passel of kids and Jamie later made quite a name for himself during the Texas fight for independence.

Preacher had heard that shortly after the fall of the Alamo, Jamie and Kate had pulled out for the Rockies in Colorado. Mayhaps he and Eddie would drift up that way and visit them.

Preacher provisioned up in Little Rock and didn't dally in doing it. Leaving Eddie with the horses, sitting in the shade and sucking on a piece of peppermint candy, Preacher stepped into a tavern for a drink and news. If there were warrants on his head, or bounty hunters after him and the boy, the tavern would be the place to hear it.

Preacher ordered whiskey and leaned against the plank bar, listening. It did not take long for him to learn the bad news.

"I'll not take up the trail of that mountain man," he heard a man say. "Not for five hundred dollars, not for five thousand dollars."

"I'd foller Ol' Nick hisself straight into the gates of hell for five thousand dollars," another said.

"Yeah, me too," another agreed. "Man, that's a lifetime's wages."

The first man said, "How you gonna spend it if'n you're dead? Man, this is Preacher we're talkin' about. He's nearabouts as famous as Carson and Bowie and Crockett and Boone."

"He's just one man traveling with a snot-nosed brat," the man who would traverse the gates of hell said.

Preacher was glad he had left the boy hidden in that little glen outside of town. He was suddenly conscious of eyes on him. He sipped his whiskey and then turned his head, meeting the direct gaze of the man who professed to have no fear of hell.

"Howdy, stranger," the man said. "Ain't seed you 'round here afore."

"Just passin' through," Preacher replied. "Come up from South Texas headin' north. Who you boys be talkin' 'bout that's so fearsome?"

"Some old mountain man called Preacher. He kilt an important gentleman back up in Ohio and taken a boy west with him. Big money on his head. Dead or alive."

Preacher nodded his head slowly. "I know a little something 'bout Preacher, boys. I trapped the High Lonesome for some years 'fore the fur price dropped. Preacher ain't old. I'd figure him for maybe thirty-five or so. And he's a ring-tailed tooter who was born with the bark on. I ain't never met him, but I know lots who has, and they'll all tell you the same thing . . . that you better let Preacher alone."

"See, I told you!" the first man said to his friends.

"He ain't but one man," the fellow with the desire to meet the devil persisted. "I'm supplyin' up and pullin' out in the mornin'. I am to get me a sack full of gold coins."

"Me, too," his two friends said in unison.

"Well, I wish you boys good luck," Preacher said, draining his cup. "Me, I'm headin' up toward Canada. Mighty pretty country up yonder."

Seated way in the back of the tavern, in the deep shadows, an old man wearing stained and worn buckskins sat, nursing a jug of Who Hit John. The old man smiled secretly and knowingly. He'd recognized Preacher the instant the mountain man had entered the saloon. Wolverine Pete had come to the high mountains back in the late 1790s, blazing a solitary trail and earning a reputation as being a man to ride the river with. He picked up his jug, corked it, and quietly slipped out the back of the tavern. He walked to the livery and saddled up, riding to the edge of town and reining up on a rise.

It was a good move on his part. About ten minutes later, Preacher came riding along, leading a packhorse. Pete rode down the trail and intercepted Preacher.

"Wagh!" Preacher said. "Wolverine in the flesh. I heard you got kilt up on the Cheyenne last year."

"I took me an arry in my back for a fact. I'm a-headin' for Saint Louie—in a roundabout way—to get 'er cut out. It's botherin' me fierce. They's big money on your butt, Preacher. That shore must have been some important uppity-up feller you kilt."

Preacher told him what happened.

Pete grunted. "Sounds to me like you give him ever' chance in the world to back off. But that don't mean you gonna get any slack cut you. I figure 'fore it's all said and done, they'll be forty or fifty men lookin' to collect that gold."

"They're welcome to try," Preacher replied.

"I wished I didn't hurt so bad, I'd go with you. Sounds like fun to me."

"I'll try to avoid 'em. I don't want the boy to get hurt."

"Sounds like you took a shine to this lad."

"He just needed a chance, and I aim to see that he gets it."

"You want me to lay up on a ridge and kill them fellers you was talkin' to in the bar?"

Preacher shook his head. "I'm obliged, but no. They didn't look like much to me. When they see how hard the trail is, I'm thinkin' they'll give it up."

"They might. You take care of yourself, ol' hoss."

"I'll do it, Pete."

Back at the shady glen, Preacher said, "We got man-hunters on our trail, boy. We got to shake them if we can. But we got to cross them damn plains 'fore we get to the mountains. Let's ride, son. We got hell nippin' at our heels."

3

"Were you the first mountain man, Preacher?" Eddie asked.

"Oh, no, boy. There was lots of men in the High Lonesome long 'fore I come along. I got there right in the middle of it all, though. We had some high ol' times, we did."

Eddie loved to get Preacher going on some of his exploits. The boy wasn't that sure that Preacher was telling him the truth all the time, but the tales were lively and entertaining and they helped pass the hours between supper and bedtime.

Preacher was teaching Eddie the ways of the wilderness as they crossed the Arkansas line and headed into the Territories. "Wild country from here on in, Eddie. And it gets wilder the farther west we go."

"Will we see heathen Indians, Preacher?"

"I'd just as soon we didn't, but we prob'ly will. I best start your learnin' about Injuns, Eddie."

"They attack and scalp people," the boy said.

"Well, some do and some don't. Personally, I don't think Injuns started that scalpin' business. I think they learned that from the white man some years back. Your Sioux and Cree Injuns, to name a few, place a lot of value on scalps, but other tribes place much more value on

countin' coup on an enemy or the stealin' of his horse.
And Injuns ain't bad folks, Eddie." He paused. "Well,
maybe with the exception of the Pawnee. I ain't *never*
been able to get along with them damn Pawnee. The
Injun just ain't like us, that's all. Their values is different.
You don't never want to show fear around an Injun.
Remember that always. Courage is something an Injun
respects more than anything else."

"Preacher?"

"Yeah, boy."

"You know there are men following us?"

"Oh, yeah. I been knowing that since yesterday afternoon. I wanted to see when you'd pick up on it. That's the
way it is, Eddie. People look at lots of things, but very few
actually *see* anything. I think it's them loud mouths I met
back yonder in Little Rock. I don't want to have to hurt
none of them, but I'll be damned if'n I'll let them hurt us."

Preacher had armed the boy and stopping often along
the way, had taught him how to shoot both rifle and
pistol. Preacher still carried his muskets, but back in
Ohio, he'd picked up a couple of 1836 breech loading
carbines, and one kiss 1833 Hall North breech loader
rifle. The breech loaders gave him a lot more firepower
because they took a lot less time to load.

"What are you going to do about those men back
there, Preacher?"

"I don't know, boy. Yet. But I got to discourage them
and that's a fact."

"Is there a reward posted for you?"

"Yep. I don't know how much, but I 'spect it's a princely
sum for the news of it to have traveled this far." Preacher
pointed to a meandering creek, lined on both sides by
cottonwoods. "We'll face them down over yonder."

Preacher took his time making camp, and making certain that Eddie was safe from any wandering bullets,
then squatted down by the tiny fire he'd thrown together
and boiled some coffee. He figured the men behind him

would show up in about half an hour. He checked his guns and waited.

He didn't miss the time mark by more than a few minutes. Three mounted men reined up when they spotted Preacher, sittin' big as brass by the fire, drinking coffee right out in the open, making no attempt to hide himself.

At that distance, Preacher couldn't be certain, but the men looked like those who'd been braggin' back in Little Rock. They rode toward the camp, muskets at the ready.

"Hallo the camp!" one hollered.

"Come on in," Preacher returned the shout. "If you're friendly, that is. If you're not, you best make your peace with God, 'cause if you start trouble with me, you'll damn well be planted here."

The trio hesitated, then rode on. "You!" the man who wanted to shake hands with the devil blurted, as the men reined up close to the camp.

"In the flesh," Preacher said, standing up, his hands close to the butts of his terrible pistols. "What are you three doin' doggin' my back trail?"

"We're a-lookin' for a wanted desperado called Preacher."

"You found him, hombre. Now what are you goin' to do about it?"

The men exchanged glances. Preacher had the advantage, and the men, although unskilled in man-hunting, were fully aware of that fact.

The man who held a kinship with the devil cleared his throat and said, "In the name of the law, I command you to surrender."

Preacher laughed at him. "The Injuns call me Ghost Walker, White Wolf, and Killing Ghost. Now, before you push me to show you why I'm called that, you boys best turn them ponies around and head back to Arkansas."

"Cain't do that," the second man said. "We done made our brags back to home that we'uns was gonna bring you in—dead or alive."

"You boys is makin' a bad mistake," Preacher warned them. "That shootin' back in O-hi-o was a fair one. I give that Parks feller more'un a fair shake. Now back off and let me be."

The man who warned to sit down with the devil got his wish. "I can feel that gold in my hands now," he said. Then jerked up his rifle and leveled it at Preacher.

Preacher snaked the big, heavy four-barreled monster from his leather holster and blew him out of the saddle. The double shot took him in the chest and face, making a mess out of the man's head.

The man's companions fought their spooked horses for a moment. One of them lost his musket in the process. When they got their horses calmed down, they sat staring at Preacher. The mountain man now stood with both hands filled with those terrible-looking pistols.

"You kilt Charlie Barnes!" one man said after finally finding his words.

"Shore looks that way," Preacher said. "Either that or he's mighty calm."

"Whut do we do now?" the remaining man asked.

"You boys dismount, careful like, and I'll tell you."

The two men carefully dismounted and stood before Preacher.

"Lay all your guns on the ground," Preacher ordered.

Guns on the ground, Preacher said, "Now bury your buddy."

"We ain't got any shovel!"

"Then use your hands and a stick! Move!"

While the men were struggling to gouge out a hole, Preacher stripped their horses of saddle and bridle. He kept their pack horse and supplies.

Charlie Barnes now planted in the earth, Preacher said, "Now strip down to the buff, boys."

"Do what?"

"Strip, boy! Are you deef?"

The men took one look at the eight barrels pointing

at them and quickly peeled down to bare skin. "This is plumb humiliatin'!" one said.

"Now get on your horses and ride," Preacher ordered.

"Bareback? Like this?" the other one shrieked.

"Like that. Or I'll shoot you both and leave you for the buzzards. What's it gonna be?"

"But they's highwaymen back yonder. We ain't got no means of protectin' ourselves."

"One look at you two, nekked as a jaybird, and any outlaws will laugh themselves silly at the sight. You got ten seconds to get clear 'fore I start shootin'. If I ever see either of you followin' me again, I'll lay up and ambush you. And that's a promise."

Ten seconds later, the two would-be man-hunters were gone, moaning and complaining about their discomfort.

Preacher chuckled and stoked up the fire. "Come on out, Eddie. Let's fix us something to eat and see what we got new in supplies."

"Those men are gonna sure be rubbed raw and sore time they get back to town," the boy said.

"I 'spect so. Break out the fryin' pan, boy. I'm hungry."

While Eddie cut slices of bacon, Preacher inspected the newly acquired supplies. The men had provisioned well. The added supplies would take Preacher and the kid a long ways. Preacher stripped the saddle and bridle from the dead man's horse. It was a fine animal; too fine to be turned loose. Preacher could trade the horse for something later on up the trail. The men had brought along enough powder and shot to stand off an army. One had brought along a fowling piece, a fine double barreled shotgun that just might come in handy along the way. There was nothing like a shotgun all loaded up with nuts and bolts and the like to take all the fight out of a troublemaker. Preacher had seen men cut literally in two with a shotgun.

"Those men might try to come back," Eddie said, laying strips of bacon in the pan.

"Yep. I 'spect they will, boy. Tonight I 'spect Charlie Barnes will have company come the dawnin'."

"We could move on."

"We could. But we ain't. Learn this, boy: You start takin' water from one man, pretty soon you gonna take it from another. Then runnin' away becomes a habit. Eddie, out here, a man's word is his bond and a man's character, or lack of it, stays with him forever. I tried to warn them three back in town. They didn't pay no heed to my words. Barnes paid the price. Them others will too, I reckon. We'll see."

The boy smiled shyly. "If I was set loose in the wilderness bare-butt nekked, I figure I'd try to get my clothes back too. Wouldn't you?"

Preacher returned the smile. "I 'spect."

Preacher lay in his blankets and listened to the two Arkansas men as they made their return to the camp by the creek. He had to suppress a chuckle as the barefoot men stepped on rocks and thorns and oohhed and ouched and groaned along, trying their best to be quiet, but losing the game something awful. He figured it was right around midnight.

Preacher slipped from his blankets and picked up the club he'd chosen hours before. He really did not want to kill these two, just discourage them mightily. He glanced over at Eddie. The boy was sleeping soundly, a habit that he would soon break if he wanted to survive out here.

Preacher slipped like a ghost out of camp and away from the dying eye of the fire. By now he had the men spotted. It wasn't all that hard to do. Their lily white skin was shinin' in the faint light like a turd on top of a white-icin' birthday cake. Preacher slipped around and camped up behind them, his moccasins making no sound as he moved from tree to tree. Preacher had to put a hand over his mouth to keep from laughing at the sight. The men had wrapped some sort of leafy vine around their waists. Looked to Preacher like it was poison ivy. The men must have tore the stuff down in the dark, not realizing what they were wrapping around their privates and over their buttocks.

They'd damn sure know come tomorrow, what with all the itchin' and scratchin' they'd be doin'.

Preacher whacked the one in the rear on the back of his noggin, and when the man in front turned around, Preacher laid the shillelagh across his forehead. Both men dropped like rocks.

Being careful to avoid the poison leaves, and it was poison ivy, Preacher tied them up, back to back, ankle and wrists, and left them on the ground. He returned to his blankets and went to sleep, a smile on his face.

The men probably realized it would only lead to more knots on their heads if they hollered during the night, so they remained silent until Preacher was up just before first light, coaxing some coals to fire and making coffee.

"Mister Preacher?" one called. "We is in some awful discomfort over here."

"I don't doubt it," Preacher called, setting the coffeepot on the rocks. "You got poison ivy wrapped all around you."

There was a long moment of silence. "Well, hell, Jonas!" the second man said. "No wonder I been itchin' all night."

"Mister Preacher?" Jonas called.

"What is it?"

"If'n you'd give us back our clothes and saddles, we'd git so far gone from here by noon we wouldn't even be a memory in your mind."

"You ain't gettin' your supplies back."

"You can have 'em, Mister Preacher. With our blessin's."

Preacher had already piled their clothes up and had them ready. He cut the men loose. "You boys head on down to the crick and pat mud all around your privates. It'll help take the itch out of that poison ivy."

"I know better than to wrap myself in poison ivy,"

Eddie said contemptuously, watching the men gingerly make their way to the creek. He looked at Preacher. "You could have killed them."

"Yeah. I could have. But they're followers, not leaders. That Charlie Barnes, he talked them into this. There's a time to kill and a time to talk, boy. I think it says something like that in the Good Book. I need to get me a Bible. It's right comfortin' to read them words. Had me a Bible. Lost it last year. I think I left it with Hammer."

"Hammer?"

"My old horse. Some scum kilt him. I tracked them and kilt them. Hammer was a good horse. I miss him. We rode a lot of trails together."

Jonas looked at his companion, both of them sitting in the creek, letting the water momentarily ease the itching and burning. He whispered, "That mountain man tracked down a bunch of men who kilt his horse and kilt them."

"I heard. I knowed we was makin' a mistake when we let that Charlie Barnes talk us into this. Jonas, you ain't never gonna say nothin' about this, is you?"

"No, not a word."

"You promise?"

"Cross my heart and hope to die."

"Let's spit on it."

The men spat and their secret was sealed.

Both Eddie and Preacher noticed the men were a mighty sorry lookin' pair as they climbed up the creek bank and joined them around the fire. They walked funny, too.

Preacher had cooked bacon and pan bread and he told the pair to sit and eat.

"We'll eat and be proud to do it," Jonas said. "But if you don't mind, we'll stand."

"I understand. You boys stop ever' now and then on your way back home and bathe the infected areas with mud if you can't find no goldenseal root to powder up and put on it. Apple cider vinegar is real good too."

"Much obliged, Mister Preacher."

"Think nothin' of it. But in the future, you boys best choose your company with a tad more care."

"You can bet on that," the younger of the two said. "Our days of man-huntin' just begun and ended with this trip."

"Wise decision, son," Preacher said drily.

4

Preacher and the kid were gone within the hour. As they rode, Preacher pondered what Jonas had told him just before the two would-be man-hunters—now officially retired—rode out for home, both of them sitting in their saddles very carefully.

"The way I heard it, Mister Preacher, they's forty or fifty men huntin' you. Maybe more than that. Prob'ly more than that. For they's big money on your head. Several thousand dollars as of a couple of weeks ago. That must have been a real important man you kilt back east."

"Them men behind us know I'll be headin' to the mountains, Eddie," Preacher told the boy after only a few minutes on the trail. "If any of 'em has any smarts, and I 'spect some of them do, they've headed straight west and will be tryin' to get ahead of us, for an ambush."

The boy looked at Preacher. "So if they think we're going straight to the mountains, we don't go."

Preacher smiled. "You catch on real quick, lad. That's right. We don't go . . . leastways not right off."

"Where are we going, then?"

"North. Straight north. We got staple supplies to last us a long time. I'll kill us a deer or two and show you how to make jerky. We'll keep the skins and make you some proper clothing, or I'll have some fitted buckskins tossed in when I trade that spare horse. We're gonna be skirtin' the edge of Pawnee country, and me and them damn Pawnees never has got on worth a damn. Once they know I'm in their territory, and they'll know, bet on that, we'll have us a fight on our hands. But I get along with the Sioux and the Crow and most others."

The mountain man and the boy turned their horses and rode toward the plains. When Eddie caught his first glimpse of the plains he was speechless. It seemed to stretch forever. Mile after mile of waving grass and an endless horizon that seemed impossible to ever reach.

Preacher smiled at the boy's expression. "Takes your breath away, don't it, lad?"

"Yes, sir."

"I've knowed people to go mad out here. Wind blows all the time. It's the vastness of it all. And the buffalo, boy, I can't describe 'em. I've seen thousands and thousands of them on the move. Maybe they was millions of them. The Good Lord alone knows. The earth beneath your feet trembles when they pass. The buffalo is life itself to the Plains Injuns. The buffalo and the horse. The Injun is a fine horseman. They worship the horse. Call him Spirit Dog, Holy Dog, Medicine Dog. The Injuns make their tipis from buffalo skins, they wrap up to keep warm in buffalo robes, they eat the buffalo, they use the soft skin of a buffalo calf to wrap newborn babies in, and the hide of a bull or cow will be used as a buryin' cloth. They use parts of the hide to make drums, moccasins, shirts, leggin's, and dresses for squaws. They use buffalo hair to make rope. The horns of a buffalo is used for drinkin' cups. The bones is used to make all sorts of Injun tools. The paunch of a buffalo is used as a cook pot. Without the buffalo, the Injun would prob'ly cease to be."

"You like the Indians, don't you, Preacher?"

"Most of 'em, yeah. I've lived with 'em and I've fought 'em. I've had me a squaw now and then. I been captured and tortured by 'em, and I've laughed and joked and ate with 'em." He reined up and swept a strong hand across the panorama that lay before himself and the boy. "Look at it, Eddie. The plains. Far as I know, they ain't another sight like it in the whole wide world. And there never will be again. For when the white man comes, and he's comin', they'll junk it all up and try to change it. They'll plow lines in the earth and change the flow of rivers and kill off all the buffalo herds. They'll kill off the wolves 'cause the settlers is ignorant of the ways of the wilderness. Each animal is dependent in some ways on other animals. The wolves kill off the old and the weak in a herd. Without them, the herds wouldn't be healthy. But the white man don't understand that. They *could* understand it, but they won't. I tell you, boy, there ain't nothin' prettier in the world than layin' in your blankets at night and listenin' to wolves sing and talk to one another."

"Won't they attack you?"

"Naw. Them's old wive's tales from scary people. There ain't never been no healthy, full growed wolf ever attacked no human person that I ever heard tell of. Hell, I've had 'em for pets. A body just has to understand the ways of the wolf and respect 'em, that's all. But they's do's and don't when it comes to wolves. Don't never corner one. You do that, you got big trouble on your hands. Don't never get between the he-wolf and his mate. They don't like that. A wolf pack is a real complicated type of society, Eddie. They have leaders and co-leaders. They real protective of their young. The male and the female take turns carin' for their pups." He smiled at the boy and lifted his reins. "Now you see why some Injuns call me White Wolf. I'm a brother to the wolf. I had one big ol' buffalo wolf stay with me for weeks one time. He must have weighed a hundred and fifty pounds. I'd toss him scraps of food and at night he'd sleep so close to me I could feel his breath. But I never touched him and he never touched me. But we was brothers. I knew it, and he knew it."

"What happened to him?"

"I don't know. One day he just veered off and was gone. He sat on a rise and watched me ride off. He threw back his head and talked to me until I couldn't hear him no more."

"That's sad."

"Yeah, it was. I ain't never forgot it, neither."

"I think I would have liked to have been a mountain man," Eddie said wistfully.

"You'd have made a good'un, boy. I saw right off you got what it takes."

Eddie smiled the rest of the day.

Just a few miles from where someday the town of Wichita would stand, men had gathered. And what a strange collection of men it was. Some were eloquently dressed in the most up-to-date sporting clothes on the market. Others wore homespun, and some were dressed in buckskins. A few carried the most modern hunting rifles, made especially for them, while others carried long flintlock rifles and shotguns. Some carried short-barreled muskets. But despite their difference in dress and speech and weaponry and levels of education—or lack of it—they shared one thing in common: they were bounty hunters. Most were here for the money, but a few were here solely for the enjoyment of the blood sport of man-hunting—the most skilled and elusive game on earth. The ultimate sport. At last count, taken that morning, there were sixty-five gun-totin' men gathered, twelve servants, four cooks, one hundred and five horses, and twenty pack mules. Oh, yes, and seven reporters.

There were two Englishmen, two Frenchmen, two Prussians, one Austrian, and one nobleman from Spain. The men had been communicating by letter, mapping out this expedition for two years. They had originally planned to travel Out West and shoot Indians. But after they had all gathered at a grand hotel in New York City, and heard of this Preacher person, why, this seemed like it would be so much more fun. One could always find a savage to kill. All the servants and cooks were in the employ of the "hoity-toity," fancy-dressed foreigners. They all beat it across the country just as fast as they could.

They called themselves professional adventurers, and to most men they were brave; they had traveled the world in their quest for the ultimate game animal. They had faced hardships and they were certainly not lacking in courage. Although it would be safe to say that they were all a tad shy on the commonsense side. They were arrogant, aloof, and looked down on anyone who wasn't nobility. They all had some fancy title stuck in front of their names like sir, count, duke, baron, or prince.

On the other side of the coin, so to speak, were the bulk of those about to take out after Preacher and the boy. Most of them were the hard ones. Professionals in in the art of man-hunting and tracking. There were about ten men who were along for the adventure of it all, or what they thought starting out would be adventure. They would all soon learn that trying to track down and kill Preacher was no grand adventure. Sixty-five men were riding deeper on to the Plains that next morning. By the time they reached the Rockies, only about forty would be left. Forty guns against Preacher and the kid. One of the trackers leading the bounty-hunters was a renegade Pawnee called Dark Hand, so named because of the strange, large birthmark that covered nearly his entire right hand. Dark Hand despised Preacher. Hated him with a wild fury that was almost blinding in its intensity. Preacher had killed Dark Hand's older brother and Dark Hand had fought Preacher twice over the long years that followed, and twice Preacher had bested him, the last time leaving him for dead. But Dark Hand lived . . . and hated.

At that moment, Preacher and Eddie were no more than seventy-five miles away, west and slightly north of the location of the bounty hunters, camped along the Walnut.

A tiny band of wandering Cherokee, fleeing from the Big Ticket country of Texas after the death of their chief, Diwali, approached the camp of Preacher and Eddie and made the sign of peace.

"Come on in," Preacher called, knowing the Cherokee probably spoke English better than he did. Preacher had just killed a deer and told Eddie to start slicing it up.

"Ghost Walker!" one of the older Cherokees said, as he dismounted. "I saw you some years ago, when I was with a scouting party north of Bent's Fort."

Preacher shook hands all around and invited the Cherokee to sit, rest, and eat.

While the venison was cooking, the leader of the band said, "There are many men gathering only a few days' ride from here, Ghost Walker."

Eddie and Preacher exchanged glances, Preacher knowing that the furtive exchange would be caught by the vigilant Cherokees.

"You know any of them?" Preacher asked.

"Bones Gibson."

Preacher grunted. Bones Gibson was a first class man-hunter. He was first class in everything, including his ruthlessness. Some say, and Preacher didn't doubt it, that Bones had killed more than a thousand Indians and more than a hundred white men during his long career as an Indian fighter and man-hunter. It was also said, and Preacher didn't doubt this either, that Bones had never lost a man once he got on his trail. But Bones had never been west of the Mississippi and had no experience with the Plains Indians.

Preacher looked at Eddie. "I won't lie to you, son. We're in for it."

The boy nodded his head, a solemn expression on his face. Even he had heard of Bones Gibson.

"The men have with them a Pawnee tracker called Dark Hand."

Preacher cussed under his breath. Again, he looked at Eddie. "Dark Hand hates my guts, Eddie. I killed his brother and whupped him twice. The last time I thought I killed him. I should have made certain. Goddamnit! Bones is gonna have half a dozen hardcases that have been with him for years. Andy Price, George Winters, Horace Haywood, Mack Cornay, Cal Johnson, and Van Eaton, I'm sure. Van Eaton is a bad one. Just as bad as Bones, and maybe a little worser."

"We are moving north to Canada," the spokesman for the Cherokee said. "Perhaps there we can find peace." He looked around and received nods of approval from the other men. "Why don't you and the boy ride with us? Your pursuers are looking for two sets of tracks, not many."

Preacher shook his head. "No. 'Cause when they find us, and they will, they'd kill you all for helpin' us. And don't think they wouldn't. But I do 'preciate the offer."

The Cherokee ate and socialized and then moved on, leaving Preacher and the boy alone by the small fire. "We got to move fast, Eddie. We got to reach the mountains. Once we's in the High Lonesome, them ol' boys will play hell takin' us. I know places there that even the Injuns don't know about." Preacher was thoughtful for a moment. "We can move a lot faster than that mob behind us. But we'll be riding right through Kiowa and then Southern Cheyenne country, after that it'll be mostly Utes. I get along all right with the Cheyenee. Kiowa and Utes can be right testy. You never can tell about them. Let's hit the blankets, boy. We ready steady tomorrow."

Bones Gibson sat on his horse off to one side of the gathering and watched with a sort of grim amusement on his hawklike face as the many men tried to get packed and mounted up. The sun was just beginning to peek over the horizon. Horses were pitching and bucking as their riders were getting the kinks out of them, mules were braying and snorting, and men were cussing and hollering. All in all it was a scene of chaos and confusion.

Bones's right-hand man, Van Eaton, a heavily muscled, sour-faced man who was little more than a brute, said, "I don't see why you let them igits come along."

"Preacher will kill probably twenty or twenty-five of them long before we finally corner him. We can use their supplies and mounts as ours give out."

"I don't like them reporters along."

"We couldn't refuse them. Freedom of the press, and all that. But if they can't keep up, that's going to be their hard luck."

Van Eaton curved his thick lips into something vaguely resembling a smile. "Yeah. I see what you mean. Accidents do happen along the trail."

"Exactly."

"Bones?"

"Yeah?"

"Preacher ain't no pilgrim. And we all best keep this in mind: When we get up into them mountains, all of Preacher's friends is gonna be lined up solid agin us."

"That's true. But from what I've been told, there are few real mountain men left at this date. Certainly not enough of them to cause us any real worry. And I got that from a very reliable source."

But Van Eaton was far from convinced. He shook his

head. "When we hit them mountains, we best double the guard and sleep with one eye open."

Bones glanced at his long-time friend and ally. "I don't remember you ever being this worried before."

"Ain't none of us ever been this far west, Bones. We been all over the Smokies and the Blue Ridge and the Adirondacks and the Greens and so forth, but never out here. I ain't never seen no country like this. It's . . . there . . . well, there ain't nothin' out here, Bones. It's . . . *empty*."

"Except for thousands of Indians," Bones reminded him. "But you and I have fought Indians hundreds of times."

"We also knew the country, Bones. And we ain't never fought no Plains Injuns. We're gonna lose men on this job. Lots of men. If it wasn't for all that money them silly foreigners offered to pay us, I'd say to hell with it."

"Van, those guns they's carrying is worth thousands of dollars, and they got thousands more in cash money with them. I seen some of it. The rings they's wearin' is worth a fortune. No, Van, them fancy pants, nose-up-in-the-air gentlemen ain't never gonna come out of the mountains alive. But we are. Rich enough to retire."

Van Eaton smiled. "You got it all worked out, don't you?"

"I always do, Van. I always do."

5

Knowing that their chances for survival were nil if they were caught out in the open plains by sixty-five or so men, Preacher and Eddie packed up, saddled up, and rode out before dawn that morning, heading straight west. Seventy-five or so miles away, the gang of man-hunters finally pulled out, about two hours after.

Indians from several tribes saw Preacher and the boy as they crossed the great expanse of rolling hills and waving grass, but they made no hostile moves toward them. They all knew Preacher and most felt he was as one with them. If the boy rode with Preacher, then he too was one with them.

The Indians also saw the huge group of heavily armed and mounted men coming up behind Preacher. They watched the trackers study the ground and knew the men were after White Wolf and his pup.

But this was not their fight. And it would not be their fight unless the large group of men attacked them. For the Indian to mount an attack against such a large and well-armed army of men would be foolhardy. Nothing could possibly be gained by it.

"Preacher will not run long," one Indian remarked.

"No," another said. "There will be blood on the moon when Ghost Walker has his belly full of running."

"I think he runs because of the boy," yet another said. "When he finds a place where the boy will be safe, he will turn and make his move."

"It would be interesting to watch," the first one said.

The others smiled. "But dangerous, and would not serve us in any way."

That was true, the Indians agreed, then wheeled their horses and rode back to their village.

Preacher finally found what he was looking for. The country had turned higher and drier, the grass shorter, and the landscape dotted with buttes, cliffs, and mesas. Preacher stowed Eddie and told him to stay put. He tied sacking over the hooves of Thunder and Eddie's pony, and walked the horses back to where he'd found a blind canyon. There, he removed the sacking and rode the horses deep into the canyon. Then he replaced the sacking and walked them back out, staying close to the wall and carefully removing all signs of his departure.

He picketed the horses and then ran back to fetch Eddie and the other horses. He found a small creek and led them back along it. By the time Bones and his men reached the creek, the water would have cleared and the hoof marks would be long gone.

"Now, Eddie," Preacher told him, "we got about a day and a half, maybe two days, 'fore those men reach us. I know that Bones and Van Eaton don't know this country. What I don't know is whether Dark Hand does. I'm bettin' that he don't know this is a blind canyon. I got to shorten the odds some. And this is how you and me is gonna do it . . ."

"Preacher rides into the canyons to try to lose us," Dark Hand said to Bones. "But it is a clumsy attempt. I find his tracks going in. Nothing coming out."

"Is there a way around it?" Van Eaton asked.

"There is a way around everything," the Pawnee said, making no attempt to hide his contempt for the white man. "But we would lose much time. But time is what we have. I do not like this canyon country. I say we go around."

"Be lots of twists and turns in there," said Mack Cornay, a thug from Maryland. "Preacher could do 'most anything. Head in any direction, or circle around and come in behind us."

Horace and Haywood and George Winters had dismounted and were studying the tracks that were plain before them. There was no doubt about it. Preacher and the kid and their pack horses had entered the pass and had not come out.

"I say we got no choice but to foller," George said. "If we don't, we run the risk of losin' them."

Bones looked up at the sun. Not yet noon. They had plenty of time. He made up his mind. "Let's go. We might trap him in there and end this show here and now."

High atop the mesa above the entrance to the blind canyon, Eddie and Preacher looked at each other and grinned.

"They took the bait," Preacher said. "I can't believe it, but they done it. All right, Eddie. You know what to do at my signal."

The boy nodded and then Preacher was gone.

The reporters from New York and Boston and Philadelphia did not like this canyon. It was hot and still and not one breath of breeze entered to fan them. John Miller, on assignment from a New York City paper, glanced at the Philadelphia journalist and saw that Raymond Simms was not happy about it either. William Bennett, writing for a magazine out of Boston was behind them, and one look at his face told Miller that he too was very unhappy about this present situation.

When their editors had handed them this assignment, all the men had been thrilled beyond words. They would be going into wild, savage, untamed, and unexplored country. They could all write books about their adventures, make a lot of money, and perhaps aid in bringing an outlaw to justice. But back in Missouri they had been told by a dozen well-placed gentlemen that Preacher was no outlaw. He had worked for the government and was a highly respected scout and trail-blazer. And they had finally realized that Bones Gibson and his men were nothing more than common murderers, thugs, and hooligans, under the dubious disguise of bounty-hunters.

But it was too late to turn back. The reporters were depending on the bounty-hunters to guide them back to civilization. In other words, the eastern reporters were all lost as a dim-witted goose.

Dark Hand had fallen back to the middle of the column. He did not like these twisting canyon trails and he felt in his belly that Preacher had set up some sort of trap.

"I say," Sir Elmore Jerrold-Taylor said, twisting in his saddle and looking around him, "isn't this grand fun?"

Baron Wilhelm Zaunbelcher agreed, adding, "But I am so disappointed that we have not been able to kill any savages. Let's hope our luck will change."

Duke Sullivan said, "But what magnificent country we've seen. The vastness of it boggles the mind."

His mind hadn't been boggled just yet. But it was about to be.

All of a sudden, the trail ended against a sheer rock wall. For a moment, Bones was stumped. That confusion abruptly ended when the man next to him, Bill Front, toppled from his saddle, shot through the head. Cal Johnson screamed as Front's brains splattered all over the front of his shirt.

Dark Hand had leaped from his horse before the echo of the shot began reverberating around the canyon and jumped for the protection of a rock overhang.

Boots Baldwin was the next to go down, the front of his

shirt suddenly stained with fresh blood. He fell dying against another man and took him to the ground with him.

Preacher and Eddie had worked for most of a day and a half rigging another surprise for Bones and his party. At Preacher's yell, Eddie slapped Thunder on the rump and the animal jumped, stretching the rope taut. "Haww!" Eddie yelled, and the animal strained and a wooden platform gave way, spilling hundreds of pounds of rocks of various sizes down into the narrowest part of the canyon trail. The rocks took other rocks with them as they tumbled down the incline, some of them huge boulders, and within a matter of seconds, the trail was blocked by a pile of boulders twenty feet high and fifty feet deep.

Preacher had both hands filled with those terrible pistols of his and was wreaking havoc on those trapped inside the narrow walls of the dark trail.

Preacher had gathered up bushes to dry and he lit them and began throwing them onto the canyon floor. Then he started throwing small bags of black powder into the flames. The results were even better than he had hoped for. The concussion of the explosions brought down more rocks, hopelessly blocking the trail in a half dozen more locations. Horses were bucking and jumping and screaming in fright, throwing riders all over the place. Dead, dying, and wounded men were lying on the sand, many of them calling out for help that no one was able to give.

A warrior's smile on his lips, Preacher ran around the lip of the blind canyon to where Eddie was, and together, they got the hell out of there.

None of the reporters had been hit by any of the rounds Preacher had fired, but they had experienced the sensation of having the crap scared out of them.

Bones squatted down after he realized that no more

shots were coming their way and assessed the situation.
It was terrible. It was going to take them a good day and
a half, maybe longer, to dig their way out of the huge
piles of rocks blocking the trail in half a dozen places.
And they'd lose another four or five days tending to the
wounded. Normally, Bones would have left the wounded
to fend for themselves. But with the reporters along, he
couldn't do that. They would write him up as a monster
or worse.

"Damn you, Preacher," he softly offered the oath.
"Damn your eyes."

Dark Hand squatted down beside him in the churned
and bloody sand. "I tried to warn you about Preacher.
Do not underestimate the man. Not ever."

Bones ignored that. "How many men down?"

"Eight dead. Nine others wounded. Two of them will
not live through the night."

"One man and a snot-nosed kid and they take out
nineteen men and we never even got a glimpse of them."

Sir Elmore Jerrold-Taylor turned to one of Bones's
regular gang and said, "Your Mister Preacher appears to
have no fair play in him, whatsoever."

Andy Price looked at the Englishman for a long
moment, then shook his head, which had a big knot in
it from a falling rock, muttered something under his
breath, and walked off to help move the tons of rock.

"Brutish lout!" Sir Elmore said.

"This here's Big Sandy Crick, boy," Preacher said, reining up and stepping down. "We'll make camp here."

They had been riding steady from before dawn to
nearly dark for several days. Preacher figured they were
at least a week ahead of the man-hunters and could
finally afford to relax and rest the horses.

"How far to the big mountains, Preacher?" Eddie
asked, as he gathered up dry wood for a smokeless fire

without having to be told. Preacher was as proud of the boy as if he were of his own blood.

"Five days easy ridin'."

"Preacher?" Eddie's tone was soft.

"Yeah, boy?"

"I know you been thinking I'm all better and such, but I know the truth. I ain't gonna make it, Preacher. There are too many scars on my lungs. And the sickness affected my heart, too. It's weak. Right now, with me all tanned and such, it's like the quiet before the storm. But I can't get no better."

"Boy . . ."

"No, Preacher." Eddie shook his head and smiled. "I know. Believe me, I do. But I'm not afraid of dying. Really, I'm not. I've been baptized. And I believe in heaven. So let's you and me just have a real good time for as long as it lasts, all right?"

Preacher looked long into the boy's eyes and saw the truth there. He sighed and said, "All right, Eddie. We'll have a high ol' time until who flung the chunk. I got cold mountain lakes for you to see and catch big trout out of. I got waterfalls and wild rushin' streams for you to witness. And meadows bustin' with flowers of all colors. We'll have us a summer of fun, you and me. But mayhaps you be wrong about yourself, boy."

But Eddie only smiled sadly.

Bones and company buried their dead and tended to their wounded and the reporters noted it all in their journals. They carefully coded their words in case Bones or some of his men who could read might get their hands on the journals, for they were not being kind to Bones or any of the other men with him. The reporters now realized, after listening to some of the men talk, that Preacher was no desperado, and the shooting back in Ohio had been a fair one. The thousands of dollars now on Preacher's head was not an officially sanctioned reward, but money put up by friends and family of Elam Parks. And the reporters now were having doubts that any of them would live to tell of this terrible travesty of justice. For, to a man, they believed Bones and his men intended to kill them, and the so-called noblemen who were on this blood sport.

The reporters began to make friends with one of the men who had come along for the adventure of it, a man from St. Louis who was having a lot of second thoughts about this trip. His name was Jim Slattery.

On the evening before they were to resume the hunt, Jim came to the reporters' fire and squatted down, pouring himself a cup of coffee. In a soft voice, he said, "I figure in about a week, we gonna be about sixty-seven miles north and some east of Bent's Fort. I'm fixin' to leave this den of thieves and murderers and head there. Y'all want to come with me?"

"I've heard of that place," the Boston reporter said. "We could perhaps hire an escort back east from there."

"I'm sure you could," Jim agreed. "They's supply wagons rollin' in and out all the time, so I was told. Boys, I got me a real bad feelin' about the company we're in. I think them foreigners are in for a rude surprise. If Bones and his bunch has their way, I don't believe none of them hoity-toity barons and dukes and counts and the like is gonna come out of this alive. But they're a nasty lot themselves, so I don't hold out a lot of sympathy for them."

"Nor do we," another reporter said.

"All right then. That's settled. When I'm ready to make the jump, I'll give you boys the high sign. Stay loose."

"Mr. Slattery, what do you think is going to happen to this Preacher person?"

Jim grinned. "Preacher is a war hoss, boys. That little deal back in the canyon should have warned off any reasonable-thinkin' man. Damn shore did me. What do I think is gonna happen? Well, I think these ol' boys is gonna chase Preacher and the sick little boy until they catch up with them. And when they do, they're gonna be the sorriest bunch of people east or west of the Mississippi River. That's what I think."

"We are all in agreement with that. Tell us, Mister Slattery, why we have not seen any savages."

"They've seen us. You can bet on that. We're too big a bunch for them to attack. Now, I ain't gonna lie to you, when we leave the main body, we're gonna be in considerable risk. We're gonna have to ride light, fast, and cautious. But if we have any kind of luck at all, we'll make it. We're all armed, and from what I've been told, it'll take a big bunch of savages to attack us. Dyin' young ain't real attractive to an Injun." He stood up. "Stay ready, boys. Night."

Across the way, Van Eaton had been watching the Missouri man and the reporters through very suspicious eyes. "I think them reporters is plannin' on pullin' out when they get a good chance," he said to Bones.

"Good," the leader of the group said. "I hope they do. They'll be fair game for any band of hostiles who spot them. None of those reporters can shoot worth a damn. The reason we haven't been attacked is because of our size. Wherever those nitwits are thinking of heading, odds are they'll never make it. With them gone, it'll be a whole lot easier for us to kill Preacher and the kid."

"Bent's Fort," Van Eaton said. "That's the only place they could be heading."

Bones was thoughtful for a moment. "Let them go. Even if they do make it through and tell their story to the Army, and the Army decides to do something about it, this hunt will be long over before patrols can find us. I say good riddance."

"That kid had something to do with that ambush back yonder," Van Eaton said, his eyes shining hard and cruel. "I want that little puke alive. I'll skin him and listen to him holler."

"You can sure have him. Might be fun listenin' to him squall. Say, cut me off a hunk of that venison, Van. Talk like that makes me hungry."

6

While Eddie and the horses rested, Preacher prowled around and found what was left of three wagons. He looked at the shaft and head of an arrow still embedded in the charred wood of a wagon bed. Kiowa. They had probably been on a raiding party and come up on these poor folks, he mused. But he could find neither graves nor bones. He rambled through the burned wreckage looking for anything that might be salvageable. He found a saw and laid it to one side. He had a use for that. He found a good sized piece of lead and a bullet mold, which he took. He also found a small Bible. He opened the cover and tried to make out the writing, but the weather had blotted the words. He saved the Bible; most of it was still readable and Preacher did find comfort in the words of the Good Book. Besides, he felt that Eddie might like to have it. The boy had said he liked to read the Bible.

That got Preacher to feelin' maudlin, and with an effort, he shook off the depression. When the boy's time came, it would just have to be. Eddie seemed resigned to it.

Back at the camp, he hauled out the shotgun and went to work cutting off most of the barrel. He cut it down and hefted it. Now it was one of the most dangerous weapons man ever devised. A sawed-off shotgun at close range could stop just about anything that moved.

Eddie carried two smaller caliber pistols hooked onto his saddle, with two or more in the saddlebags. Whether he would use them against a human being was something that Preacher did not know, but he had a hunch that Eddie would not hesitate to cock and fire if it came right down to the nut-cuttin'.

Preacher stowed the now short-barreled shotgun and gave Eddie the battered Bible he'd found. "Figured you might like to have this, boy. I found it in what was left of some wagons over yonder."

"I wonder who they were?"

"No way of knowin', boy. There ain't a sign of a grave nowheres." He shrugged his shoulders. "But that really don't mean nothin'. Even if they was buried, it was prob'ly in a shallow grave and the critters dug 'em up and et 'em then scattered the bones." He watched the boy shudder at that prospect and said in a softer tone, "That'll not happen to you, Eddie. I give you my word on that."

"That makes me feel better," the boy replied, a somber expression on his thin, tanned face. "Preacher? Are there any towns out here?"

Preacher chuckled, "No, boy. Nothin' like a town. Some south of us is Bent's Fort and it's sorta like a town. Further on west they's a big adobe buildin' with log walls around it where some mountain men live with Mexican and Injun wives. I understand they taken to farmin' now. Don't know how long that will last.* But towns?" He shook his head. "There ain't no towns 'til you hit the West Coast. And that's a far piece."

---

*Not long. Fremont visited there in 1842 and reported all was well. The next year when mountain men came through, the place was deserted. The town of Pueblo was started around 1860.

"I'd like to see the ocean," Eddie said, a wistful note to his words.

"Mayhaps you will, boy."

Eddie smiled. "No," he said softly. "I won't. But you have. Will you tell me about it?"

Preacher leaned back against a fallen log and stuffed and lit his pipe. He pondered that question. "The Pacific Ocean. First time I seen it I couldn't believe my eyes. The water was blue. And when it come crashin' up aginst the rocks along the shore it made a thunderous noise and spray and foam went to flyin' ever'where. Liked to have scared my horse to death, and my heart beat some faster too. I rode down there and took me a swaller of that water. Spit it out fast. Salty water. Ain't fit for man nor beast. I can't see how a fish could live in it, but they do. And they's monsters in the ocean that eat folks. Now, I ain't never seen none of them monsters, I won't lie about that, but I was told about 'em by some sea-farin' men. They tell me they's somethin' called an octo-pussy that's got about twelve arms that's twenty-five feet long each and the arms has got suckers on it; that's what holds you whilst the thing eats you." Preacher and Eddie both shuddered at that thought.

"It was a whale in the sea that ate Jonah," Eddie offered.

"Say! You're right, it was. Tell you what, why don't you read some aloud from the Bible whilst I rustle up some vittles?"

"Any passage you favor, Preacher?"

"Naw. I'll leave that up to you."

The boy turned to Psalms and read aloud the 23rd. Preacher soon realized that the boy had that one memorized, but said nothing about it. Must be plumb awful to be so young and knowin' that any day could be your last, Preacher thought. That there is a mighty brave little boy. He's got more courage in his big toe than a lot of men have in their entire body.

Eddie had stopped reading and Preacher saw that the boy had read himself to sleep. He covered Eddie with a blanket and set about making supper as quietly as he could. He thought to himself, "Another day of rest and then we head for the mountains. I got a lot to show the boy, and prob'ly not a lot of time to get it done."

Shortly after crossing into what would someday be Colorado, the reporters, led by Jim Slattery, slipped away from Bones and his men and simply vanished into history. Somewhere between the White Woman and Bent's Fort, the small party of men met their fate. But no one knows what that fate was. Not one trace of them, their horses, or their equipment has ever been found. Their newspapers and magazines hired scouts to try to find out what happened, but to no avail. It was doubtful they became lost, for historians have noted that Jim Slattery was an experienced woodsman and a fine warrior. Over the years that followed their disappearance, several hundred Indians from numerous tribes were asked about the party of men. If any of the Indians had any knowledge about the eight men, they went to their graves carrying the secret.

The West holds many such mysteries, and it yields its secrets reluctantly. Only one man is reported to have known what happened to the reporters and to Jim Slattery, and he did not solve the mystery until almost a quarter of a century after their disappearance. He died an old, old man, near the turn of the century. It is said that the old mountain man told only one person, the legendary gunfighter that he helped raise: Smoke Jensen.

But that is quite another story.

"Well?" Bones demanded impatiently.

Dark Hand and two other trackers stood up and shook

their heads. "Lost it," the Pawnee admitted. "These are not their hoof prints."

Bones threw his hat on the ground in frustration. Three weeks had passed since the ambush in the blind canyon and Preacher and the kid seemed to have vanished into the air.

Only the noblemen seemed unperturbed by the delay in finding their prey. It didn't make any difference to them if the hunt took five weeks, five months, or five years. They all had more money than they could spend in ten lifetimes. Besides, this was good fun. The air was clean and fresh and quite invigorating, the scenery magnificent, the food tasty. The company was lousy and the conversations lacking in grammatical correctness and substance, but one couldn't have everything.

"I say, old boy," Sir Elmore Jerrold-Taylor called to Van Eaton. "Do calm yourself and try some of this wonderful pâté, won't you?"

Van Eaton told the Englishman where to put his pâté, and stalked off. He walked to Bones and said, "Let's give this up and head on back, Bones. We ain't never gonna find them two in all this wilderness."

That idea was becoming more and more appealing to Bones. They were camped on the eastern side of the Rockies and Bones had to admit he had never even dreamed of country such as this. Mountains two miles high, in country that looked so rough it seemed incredible that any human being could possibly live there.

Bones was beginning to understand why that breed of men called mountain men were held in such awe and respect. He just thought he'd seen mountains and rough country in the Smokies.

"All right," Bones said. "Let's talk to the fancy-pants crowd and see what they say."

"Why, heaven's no!" Jon Louviere said. "The hunt must continue. We're paying you to guide us, so guide on."

Bones put it to his men.

"Arapaho and Cheyenne behind us, Ute in front of us and all around us," Dark Hand pointed out. "Is not good."

"I figure we been real lucky to get this far without havin' trouble with the savages," Jimmie Cook said. "I think we're pushin' our luck to go any deeper. But if them lords and the like want to go on payin' us . . . I'm for it."

"Exactly where the hell are we?" Sam Provost asked.

"Just east of Ute Pass," Dark Hand said. "None of you have seen rough country yet. The Rockies are just beginning here. Preacher does not know it, but I left my tribe and spent two years in these mountains. I do not know them as well as he does, but I am not lost."

"You really think we can find them?" Bones asked.

The Pawnee was honest in his reply. "We will be lucky if we do. Or unlucky," he added.

Bones nodded his agreement with both remarks. He did not know whether to go north, south, or west. But he did feel strongly that Preacher had not doubled back to the east. Bones had forty-eight men left, six of them still suffering from wounds that had left them just able to sit in a saddle and not much more.

"In your opinion, Dark Hand," Bones asked, "where do you feel in your heart Preacher went?"

"Deep in the mountains," the Pawnee answered quickly. "West and slightly north of here."

"You've been there?"

"One time only. It is wild country. And do not allow yourselves to be trapped in there when the winter comes. You will surely die."

"Do mountain men live up there in the winter?" Willy Steinwinder asked from the group of noblemen.

"Some of them. But they are used to hardships. It does not bother them."

"Bah!" the Austrian scoffed. "This is nothing compared to my Alps. Let us push on."

"Yes. Quite right," Burton Sullivan said. "And if we see

painted hostiles, we shall engage them. I feel the need for some blood-letting."

The Pawnee looked at the Englishman. "You are a fool!" he said bluntly. "The Ute, the Arapaho, and the Cheyenne have all been watching us since we approached the shadows of the mountains. You think that pack horse broke loose the other night? Bah! A warrior slipped into camp and took it. That is sport with my people. You all sleep like the dead. If you continue to sleep in such a manner you will all *be* dead." He walked off.

"The guard is doubled from here on," Bones said. "Dark Hand knows what he's talking about. We push on at first light."

As the crow flies, Preacher and Eddie were only about seventy miles from where Bones and his man-hunters were camped. But traveling through that country is not counted in miles, rather in days and even weeks. They were camped along a tiny rushing stream in a camp so cleverly disguised that Bones and party could ride to within twenty-five feet of it and not know it was there. The Utes knew it was there, but they did not bother Preacher and the boy. They knew some sort of deadly hunt was taking place, and they were curious about that. They were both amazed and appalled that such a large band of white men would want so desperately to kill so frail-looking a boy. The Utes shook their heads and again thought how silly white men were.

Preacher had been their enemy and he had been their friend, as he would be again. For that was the way of things. But for now, the Ute and Cheyenne chiefs passed the word: Leave Ghost Walker and the boy alone. And leave the stupid white men alone. Steal their horses if you like, but let them play out this game to its end.

"The Indians know we're here, don't they, Preacher?"

Eddie asked. He wasn't feeling well and Preacher had made him a soft bed of boughs and was letting him rest.

"Oh, yeah. I see sign of them near'bouts ever' day. They're curious and puzzled 'bout what's goin' on. Injuns is naturally curious folks. And the ways of the white man is real strange to them. It's puzzlin' to 'em why all them men is chasin' us. They can't figure out what harm we is to them." Preacher looked over at Eddie and saw the boy was asleep. He walked over to him and put a hand on Eddie's forehead. Hot. Real hot.

Preacher had found some catnip plants and he crushed some and made a tea. While he was letting it steep, Eddie moaned and opened his eyes. Preacher was at his side. "Ain't feelin' so good, right?"

"I'm hot, Preacher."

"I can fix that." He poured some of the vile smelling liquid in a cup. "It don't smell very good, but it's good for you. Sip it, Eddie. Trust me."

Eddie wrinkled his nose at the smell. "Smells like old dirty socks."

Preacher laughed. "Yeah, it do, don't it. Wait 'til you taste it. It tastes even worser. But it'll knock that fever right out. My mamma used to have us drink this ever' day, and we never was sick. I want you to drink three cups a day, Eddie. Ever' day. You start sippin'."

Preacher found some wild onions and Indian potatoes and started up a venison stew. The broth would be real good for Eddie. "A body don't have to starve in the wilderness, Eddie," Preacher talked as he worked. "But to survive in the wilderness, you got to work with nature, not aginst it. You drink your tea and sleep. Sleep is good for a body. When you wake up, this here stew will be ready to eat and it'll be larrepin' good. If you wake up and I ain't here, don't worry. I'll be prowlin' around."

Preacher sat the kettle to one side so it would simmer slow, and rifle in hand, he worked his way up the mountain until he found him a vantage spot. He took his spy-glass from his pouch and extended it, then slowly looked the country over. He saw a few plumes of smoke, but they had been there for several days, and he knew that it was a small camp of Utes about fifteen miles off. He saw no other signs of life.

He wondered for a moment if Bones had given up the hunt. But he shook that off. Bones wasn't known for givin' up. He had to take a prisoner from the group and find out what the hell was going on. The only problem was, he couldn't leave the boy alone.

Well, there was one thing he could do: He could take the boy down into the Ute camp and see if they'd take care of him. He'd rather go into a Cheyenne camp, for he'd always gotten along well with the Cheyenne—except for a few minor skirmishes over the years—and the Cheyenne revered children. But he didn't know of any Cheyenne village close by. So it was the Utes or nothing.

Preacher worried about that all the way down the mountain. But when he reached his camp, he stopped worrying about getting into and out of a Ute village alive.

About a dozen Ute warriors were waiting for him, and one of them had a hand on Eddie.

7

The man with a hand on Eddie lifted his other hand, palm out, in a gesture of peace. Preacher lifted his hand as recognition flooded him. The Ute was a tribal chief called Wind Chaser.

"Ghost Walker," Wind Chaser acknowledged. He patted Eddie's shoulder "Boy sick."

Preacher deliberately laid his rifle aside and walked away from it, a move that did not go unnoticed by the other Utes. "Yes, he is, Wind Chaser. But I'm gettin' him well."

"No get well running all over the mountains," Wind Chaser said.

"I was gonna bring him to your village and see if you'd take care of him whilst I checked my back trail."

That pleased the Ute. He solemnly bowed his head. "My woman take good care of him. How is he called?"

"Eddie."

"Ed-de," Wind Chaser repeated. "Means what?"

This was always difficult to explain to an Indian. Indian names meant something, or stood for an event or happening. "He's named after his father."

"Ummm. Confusing. But I have never understood the white man's ways. Why men chase you and boy?"

This, too, was chancy and Preacher chose his words carefully. "The boy was a slave. His master was cruel. You can see what condition he left the boy in. I took the boy and the man came after me with a gun. I kilt him. The man's friends put a bounty on my head."

"Ummm," Wind Chaser said. "Yes. This is true. My warriors have been close to their camp and heard them talk. But there is more."

"More?"

"Yes. But my warriors did not understand it, and I do not understand it. There are men of great importance among those who hunt you and Ed-de. Men who have slaves who see to their needs. Cook for them, wash their clothes, and saddle their horses. It is all very strange."

Damn sure was. Preacher sat down by the fire and poured a cup of strong coffee. He took a sip and passed the cup around. It was returned empty and he poured more until the pot was empty. He stirred the stew. He shook his head. "I don't understand it, Wind Chaser. It's confusing to me, too. But it's noble of you to offer to care for the boy whilst I scout the camp of my enemies."

Wind Chaser shook his head. "It is nothing. I remember a winter when Ghost Walker provided meat for my old father and my family while we were away at war. A debt is something that must be repaid."

Preacher had forgotten all about that. That had been a good fifteen years back. Preacher went and fetched the horse that Charlie Barnes had ridden. He handed the reins to Wind Chaser and spoke to the chief in his own tongue, using sign language when the Ute words did not come to him. "The boy is very sick and knows he is going to die." Wind Chaser's eyes widened at that. "Eddie wishes to have a set of buckskins like mine before he passes from this world to the next. Please accept this horse from me to you in exchange for the buckskins."

Wind Chaser rose and carefully inspected the horse, his eyes shining at the sight of the animal. "One small set of coverings is not enough for such a fine animal. I will have my woman make you a fine set of buckskins. Is that fair?"

"That's fair."

"Eddie is a brave boy," Wind Chaser said, kneeling down and stroking the boy's hair. He faces death like a Ute, without whimpering and whining. He will be warm and safe in my own lodge. When you return from your scouting, you will be welcomed in my village like my brother. We go!"

"See you, boy," Preacher said to Eddie with a wink. "I'll be back in a couple of weeks. You mind your manners, now, you hear?"

Eddie smiled and nodded his head. This was a grand adventure for the boy, and he showed no signs of fear.

Wind Chaser slashed down with a hand and a big brave picked up Eddie and gently carried him to Eddie's paint pony, already saddled. That told Preacher that the Utes had watched every move he and Eddie had made since coming into the mountains.

"I will not lead those men to your village, Wind Chaser," Preacher said.

Wind Chaser shook his head. "You come when and how you like, Ghost Walker. If those men hunting Ed-de come to my village, they will be fed a good meal and then we shall see how well they die. Do not worry yourself about Ed-de. He will be cared for."

The Utes left like wisps of smoke, flitting silently through the timber.

Preacher sat for a time, eating the stew and drinking coffee. The Utes would take care of Eddie and defend his life to the last man. If an Indian gave his word on something, chisel it in stone. Preacher rose and began construction of a crude corral for the pack horses and a cache for his supplies. The animals had access to water and forage and if food ran out, or a puma or bear threatened them, they could easily break out of the brush enclosure. Preacher erased all signs of the camp, packed a few things, saddled up Thunder, and was gone that afternoon.

Dark Hand looked nervously around the camp. He had just returned from his afternoon's prowling and did not like what he had seen, or rather, what he had *not* seen.

"What's wrong with you?" Van Eaton snarled at the Pawnee. "You're makin' me nervous."

"We are alone," Dark Hand said.

"What do you mean, alone?"

"No Ute. No Cheyenne. No Arapaho. We are alone."

"Why . . . you ninny! That's good."

"That's bad," Dark Hand contradicted. "That means the chiefs have met and agreed to stay out of the fight. That means that Preacher is on the hunt. For us. He is probably out there now, looking at us. Waiting. Watching."

"Now, just how did you come to that?"

"It is the only thing that makes any sense."

"Well, it don't make no sense to me," Van Eaton said sourly.

"Yes. That makes sense to me, too," Dark Hand said haughtily.

Van Eaton watched the Pawnee walk off. He figured he'd been insulted but he didn't quite know how. He looked all around him. Birds were singing and feeding, squirrels were hopping around, all having grown used to the presence of the large body of men. Van Eaton snorted. "Preacher out there," he muttered. "Hell, he ain't within fifteen minutes of his camp."

Preacher was about two hundred yards away, lying on his belly in some brush. Part of him was clearly visible to the naked eye, if anyone would just make a very careful visual inspection of their surroundings. But he knew none of the men would. What Preacher was doing was one of the oldest of Indian tricks—hide where your enemy would least suspect.

Preacher was puzzled by what he saw and the few words that he could hear. He couldn't figure out who those fancy-dressed men were, and what they were doing with the likes of Bones Gibson. Nothing about this made any sense to Preacher. Those duded up men had servants and cooks waitin' on them hand and foot. So why were a bunch of rich folks like them tied in with Bones, and why were they hunting him?

Preacher saw Dark Hand looking carefully all around him. He immediately averted his eyes so he would not be staring directly at the Pawnee. Dark Hand spoke with Van Eaton for a moment, and then walked away.

Preacher watched the Pawnee until he disappeared and then backed away from the scant cover and into the thicker brush and timber. He didn't think Dark Hand had spotted him, but he wasn't going to take any chances. He made a slow half circle of the camp until he found a good spot to lay under cover until dark and he could make his move, or until one of them in the camp came out alone to answer a call of nature.

A half a dozen came out to the area together and Preacher could do nothing except listen to them swear, grunt, and make other disgusting sounds. Then his ears perked up when he heard one say, "Them royal folks has upped the ante on Ol' Preacher and the kid."

"Yeah, I heared," another said. "But what they want is foolish to me. They want us to take Preacher alive, and then turn him a-loose unarmed and on foot so's they can hunt him down for sport."

Preacher blinked at that. *Sport?* What the hell kind of people were these fancy-pants men? Royal folks? What in the world did that mean?

"But Van Eaton wants the kid," a third voice was added. "What did the kid do to get on Van Eaton's bad side?"

"I don't know," yet another voice said. "But Van Eaton

ain't got but one side, and it's all bad. He's even worser than Bones, and that's sayin' a lot. He says he's gonna skin him alive slow-like just to listen to him holler."

Preacher felt a coldness wash over him with those words. A dark and deadly hand touched his heart. Any man that would torture a kid, of any color, was too low to let live. And if Preacher had his way, Van Eaton would not be counted among the living for very much longer.

Skin Eddie? What matter of men were these people? How low-life could man be? Preacher figured he was right close to just about the lowest of the low.

Preacher fought back with some effort an urge to rise up and blast these men into eternity. But doing that would only wound the tip of the snake's tail. He wanted Bones, Van Eaton, and those fancy-dressed men. And he wanted just one man from this bunch to question. And if he didn't want to talk to Preacher, Preacher knew a way to loosen his tongue—he'd just turn him over to the Utes.

Preacher lay under cover until dusk. Then he got his chance to grab one of Bones's men. A man he'd heard call John Pray wandered over to the area, alone, and started to drop his trousers. Preacher coshed him with a leather pouch filled with dirt and the man hit the ground unconscious. Preacher tossed the man over one shoulder and quickly took off.

When John Pray awoke he fully expected to get whacked on the head, like had happened three times already that night during the ride from camp. His head hurt something fierce. But no blow came. He tried to move his hands, but they were tied behind his back and his back was hard up against a tree. He looked across a hat-sized fire into the hard and cold eyes of a man dressed all in buckskins.

"You be Preacher?" John croaked out the question.

"I be Preacher."

"Are you gonna torture me?"

"If I have to. And believe me, John Pray, I will."

John believed him. Oh, how he believed him. "What do you want to know?"

"Everything. Front to bottom and side to side. You tell me ever'thing you know about this gang that's chasin' me and the boy, and I'll cut you loose. And that's a promise. You can either hook up again with Bones, or clear out. It's up to you. Start talkin', John Pray."

John Pray was a brigand and a scalawag, but he was no fool. He opened up and talked for a full ten minutes, nonstop. So complete was his confession, Preacher didn't have to ask him a thing.

When John Pray fell silent, Preacher hauled out his Bowie and cut him free. Preacher gestured toward the coffeepot. "Help yourself."

"Mighty nice of you," John said sarcastically. "Considerin' that you're sendin' me to my death."

"I ain't sendin' you nowheres, John Pray."

John sipped and smiled. "You know damn well I can't go back to Bones. They'd know I talked and kill me for sure. I ain't got no hoss and no guns. The savages will kill me 'fore I get ten miles from here."

Preacher picked up John Pray's brace of pistols, shot and powder, and knife. He tossed them to him. "I took the liberty of unloadin' them pistols. You got ample shot and powder. 'Bout ten miles from here, anglin' south, they's a crick. Follow it down to Ute Pass. Stay southeast 'til you come to another crick. That's Rock Crick. Follow that and you'll come to a settlement. Mex and Injun women and mountain men that's done takin' up plowin' and plantin'. You got money in your purse 'cause I seen it. They'll sell you a horse. Bent's Fort is due east of there. Keep ridin' and don't never come back to these mountains. If I ever see you again, I'll kill you, John Pray. Now, git gone!"

John Pray was gone in a heartbeat, not even looking back. Preacher immediately doused his fire and took up Thunder's reins and was gone in the other direction, putting miles between the man-hunter and himself before he settled down for the remainder of the night in a cold camp.

At dawn, Preacher gathered dry wood and built a tiny fire under the overhang of branches and boiled water for coffee. He was so angry he had to struggle to keep his emotions in check. A bunch of goddamn foreigners were planning to use him like some wild animal to hunt down . . . for sport. Preacher had a dirty opinion of people who hunted animals for sport and trophy and not for food. And Indians took an even sourer view of folks like that. Indians hunted animals for survival. They never killed what they couldn't use.

Preacher calmed down some and drank his coffee and chewed his jerky. He mulled over his situation. Counting the cooks and servants, he was outnumbered about fifty-some-odd to one. He knew that common sense told him to get Eddie and head deep into the mountains. Bones and them goddamn foreigners would never find them. Preacher knew that. But Preacher didn't much cotton to runnin' away. That cut against the grain. It wasn't that he hadn't run from trouble before, because he had. There was a time to fight and a time for a feller to haul his ashes. Said that plain in the Bible—sort of. But damned if Preacher was gonna run from the likes of Bones Gibson and a bunch of fancy-pants counts and barons and dukes and princes and so forth.

Now, about the boy. Eddie was safe in the Ute village. Bones would never attack an Indian village, even if he could get close enough without bein' seen, which he couldn't. Bones was arrogant, but he wasn't stupid.

Preacher drank the last of his coffee and made up his mind as the fire began dying down to coals. All around him lay the magnificence and majesty of the Rockies. Birds were singing and squirrels were playing and chattering.

He had done nothing to any of those men huntin' him. They wanted to do harm to him and Eddie. They wanted to use Preacher like some poor chased animal. But that would never happen. They wanted a war. Well, all right. That could happen. Preacher could damn sure give them a war. But this war would be on Preacher's terms—Preacher would lay down the rules of warfare. And they would be harsh. This would be a war like none they had ever seen. Count on that.

Preacher doused his fire and covered all signs of the camp. He saddled up Thunder and packed his few supplies and stepped into the saddle.

He rode for about fifteen miles before topping a rise and there, staying in the timber, he surveyed his surroundings. This was his country. The High Lonesome. The Big Empty.

And it was about to run red with blood.

8

Bones had shifted his camp.

It only took Preacher about one minute to determine which direction they'd gone. He did not immediately follow the tracks. Instead, Preacher threw together a small fire, made some coffee, and then sat for a time, ruminating.

Bones and Van Eaton had assumed rightly that John Pray would blab, telling Preacher everything that he knew. Dark Hand would point out that he'd been right all along in saying that Preacher was close-by, watching. So the smart move would be to shift locations. But this time it would be a much more secure camp, one that could be easily guarded and defended while the man-hunters made new plans.

The men had made no attempt to hide their tracks, so to Preacher's mind, that meant they wanted him to follow. "They think they gonna ambush you, Ol' Hoss," he muttered. "They got some boys layin' in wait for you to come amblin' along so's they can put a ball in your noggin. So you just sit right here and figure out where the main bunch is headin' and then circle around and do some dirty work of your own."

John Pray had told him that the Pawnee, Dark Hand,

had spent a couple or three years in this area. That was news to Preacher, but he didn't doubt the man's words. It made sense to him. Without someone who knew this country, Bones and his men would have been wanderin' about like a lost calf a-bellerin' for its mamma. So where would Dark Hand lead the men now that they knew Preacher was on the prowl?

That was a question that Preacher could not answer. Putting himself in Dark Hand's moccasins, he could come up with several dozen places where he'd go. But what he could do was pretty much determine the direction. Preacher carefully extinguished his fire and swung into the saddle.

"Let's go see what misery we can cause, Thunder. Then we'll go check on Eddie."

"We lost the mountain man!" Van Eaton said, an evil smile curving his lips.

"We will never lose Preacher," Dark Hand said sourly. "And he will not fall into your stupid and clumsy attempt to ambush him."

The men had taken a break and were watering their horses and resting after several hours of riding over rough country. Tatman, a Rogue out of Indiana, looked at the Pawnee, disgust in his eyes.

"'Pears to me, Injun, that you're 'bout half skirred of this Preacher."

Dark Hand smiled, sort of. "I fear no man. But I have much respect for many. Preacher has been in this country ever since he was a boy. He is respected, if not liked, by all. Songs are sung about him around the night fires, and stories are told and retold about his courage and cunning and fierceness in battle. Do not take your enemies lightly. To do so is to die. If you would but open your eyes and your brain, you would know that the Utes in this area have made a pact with Preacher. If you would have but looked at the signs back at our old camp, you would have seen one horse only. That means the boy is safe somewhere. Preacher would not have left him alone in the wilderness. This is grizzly and puma country. And this is also Wind Chaser country."

By now, the camp was silent, the men standing or sitting, all listening to the Pawnee speak.

"Wind Chaser is a war chief of the Utes. Very brave and very cunning in battle. I think the boy is in Wind Chaser's village. I know that we have been watched, and I think the watchers are warriors from Wind Chaser's village. For the time being, they are going to leave us alone. This fight is between us and Preacher. Any attempt to take the boy would mean instant death for us all." His eyes touched the eyes of every man in the camp. "Or a very long and slow and painful death by torture. Chances are slim that any of you will see one of Wind Chaser's warriors, but if by accident you do, do not shoot. Make no hostile moves toward any Indian you might glimpse. We must concentrate our efforts on finding and destroying Preacher. No one else."

Tatman snorted. "I still say you're skirred of Preacher."

Dark Hand cut his eyes. "You are a fool. I do not think you will die well."

"Injun," Tatman said. "You don't call me no fool!"

"He just did," Bones said. "And I would suggest we all pay heed to his words. Now mount up. Let's get out of here."

Bates and Hunter, the two men Bones had assigned to spring the ambush on Preacher, were growing restless. And more than a bit edgy. It was getting late in the afternoon. They both felt that Preacher should have been along hours before. And they both felt that Preacher had figured out Bones's plan and that the ambushers were now the hunted.

It was a feeling that neither of them liked.

Suddenly to their right and in the dark timber, came the unmistakable sounds of a mountain lion on the prowl. The cough and huff and angry snarl. Hunter and Bates both turned to face the chilling noise.

But they could see nothing. No movement of brush or low branches. The mountain wind died down to no more than a whisper and the men waited, their hearts thudding heavily in their chests. They were both uneducated men, neither able to read or write, and both very superstitious.

Preacher, crouched no more than fifteen feet away, suddenly split the high mountain air with the scream of a panther. Bates fired his rifle and hit nothing and Hunter peed his dirty underwear. Preacher screamed again and the horses of the men broke loose from their picket pins and went racing off, eyes wild with fear.

"Shoot your damn gun, Bates!" Hunter yelled, frantically reloading.

"At what?" Bates hollered.

Two young Ute braves, in their late teens, hiding and watching on the other side of the animal trail, had to shove their fingers in their mouths to keep from laughing at the antics of the two frightened white men. They knew it was Preacher on the other side of the trail, and not a panther. This was going to be a good story to tell around the night fires. They would entertain the whole village with its telling. They might even make up a dance, showing how frightened the silly white men were. Yes, they would definitely do that.

Hunter got his rifle charged and brought it to his shoulder just as Preacher picked up a rock and flung it. The fist-sized rock caught Hunter in the center of his forehead and knocked him down and goofy. His rifle went off and the ball missed Bates by about an inch, slamming into a tree. Bates yelled as blown-off bark bloodied one side of his face.

"You've shot me, you goose!" Bates hollered, dropping

his rifle and putting both hands to his bloody face. Bates suddenly stepped on a loose rock, lost his footing, and began flailing his arms in a futile attempt to maintain his balance. He lost and went rolling down the side of the rise, yelling and hollering for help. He banged his head on about a half dozen rocks on his way down and came to rest against a tree, totally addled.

The two young Utes were rolling on the ground, clutching their sides in silent hysterics at the sight unfolding before their eyes. This story and dance would be remembered and retold and danced for years to come. This was the funniest thing they had seen since Lame Wolf's fat and grumpy and ill-tempered wife, Slow Woman, sat down on a porcupine's tail while picking berries one day. Even Lame Wolf thought that was funny. Until she hit him in the head with a club and knocked him silly. Slow Woman never did have much of a sense of humor.

Preacher knew the young Utes were on the other side of the trail. They were good in the woods, but not as good as Preacher. And by now he could see them rolling on the ground in silent laughter. That was good. They would tell Wind Chaser and he would have them dance it out and the entire village would be amused.

Preacher stepped out of hiding and jerked the shot, powder, and pistols from the near-unconscious Hunter. He picked up both rifles and vanished into the timber. He caught up with their horses and led them off. Bates and Hunter were going to have some tall explaining to do when they caught up with Bones and party. If they caught up with Bones.

The two young Utes left in a run, back to their village. They could not wait to tell this story.

Wind Chaser was clutching his sides, his face contorted with laughter long before the young braves had finished telling their story. When they had finished, he wiped his eyes and said, "Our hunters have brought in much meat this day. We will feast and dance this evening. Ed-de will be entertained and be happy with this news." He pointed at the two young Utes. "You two go now and bathe and prepare your dance for this evening. You have both done well." He rose and entered his tipi to tell Eddie of the feasting and dancing and story-telling that evening. Good food, rest, and the attentions of the women had done the boy good. His fever was gone and he was able to walk about for short periods of time. Wind Chaser had talked it over with his wife and they had both agreed to ask Preacher if they could have the boy, for as long as Man Above allowed him time to live. If Preacher did not agree, well, that was the way it had to be. But Wind Chaser felt he could prevail upon the mountain man. He had known Preacher for a time, and known of Preacher for a longer time. And Preacher possessed uncommon good sense for a white man. Not as much sense as an Indian, of course, but one could not expect too much of a white man.

Preacher had found him a snug little hidey-hole for the evening. He had trapped a big, fat rabbit and it was on a spit. He was smiling about his day's work as he drank the strong black coffee and savored the good smells of food cooking.

Hunter and Bates had staggered into the camp of Bones and company just about dark. Both of them were footsore and weary, and both had knots on their heads.

Bones took one look at the pair and said, "I don't even want to hear about it." He turned and walked away.

Van Eaton took his plate of food and joined Bones, sitting down on the ground. "We got to talk, Bones."

"So talk."

"If Dark Hand is right, and I 'spect he is, and the Utes has taken a likin' to the kid, we can scratch him off the list. We won't be able to get within five miles of that Ute camp."

"Agreed."

"Preacher is playin' with us. He could have kilt both them men but didn't."

Bones nodded his head in sour agreement.

"I just don't like it, Bones. It's a black mood that's layin' on me. I get the feelin' that Preacher is tryin' to tell us that if we'll leave now, we can leave alive. But if we stay, he's gonna turn this game bloody."

"After seeing Hunter and Bates, I tend to agree with you. But them crazy foreigners has upped the ante, Van." He stated the amount and Van Eaton almost choked on his food. He swallowed hard and stared at Bones. Bones nodded his head. "You heard me right. We don't even have to think about robbing them. They're offering us enough money to retire on, Van. Think about it. With that much money we could both buy them farms and horse breeding stables and the like we've always talked about. We could live like gentry."

Van Eaton thought about that for a moment, his eyes shining with greed and cruelty and cunning. "Yeah. And oncest we got shut of the foreigners, we could kill ever'body 'ceptin' our own men and we'd have twicest the money."

"That's right. And them crazy lords and dukes and such has agreed to divvy up money right now if we'll stay. And they's this to think about: We might not even have to kill the men to get the money. You know damn well if we stay, Preacher is gonna kill fifteen or twenty, at least, 'fore we get him. Maybe more than that. Probably more than that. We could just take the money off their bodies and nobody would be the wiser."

"Is them lords and such carryin' that much money on them, Bones?"

"No. Of course not. But they are carrying bank drafts that's legitimate. All they got to do is fill them out and they're good. I know that for a fact. They're kill-crazy, Van. All of them. I ain't never heard tell of some of the things they claim to have killed. Rinossoruses and wild crazy-sounded animals all over the world."

Van Eaton blinked at that. "What kind of ossorusses? What the hell kind of animal is that?"

Bones shook his head. "I don't know. I never heard nothing like it. They may be tellin' great big whackers for all I know. What do you say, Van? Do we take the deal?"

Van Eaton slowly nodded his head. "Yeah, Bones. We take the deal."

"I got a plan," Bones said. "And it's a good one. The way I got it figured, it shouldn't take no more than a week to push Preacher into a pocket and let them fancy-pants foreigners kill him."

"And then we can get gone from this damn wilderness." Van Eaton looked around him at the night. The mountains were shrouded in darkness and it was cold for this time of the year. "I really hate this damn place, Bones. You can't get warm at night. Can you imagine what it's like out here in the *winter?*"

"No. And I don't want to find out, neither. I just can't imagine anybody in their right mind who would want to live in this godforsaken place."

At the Ute village, Eddie was having the time of his life watching the two young Indians act out what they had witnessed earlier that day. The boy was laughing and clapping his hands, his belly full of meat from the feast. Wind Chaser gently put his arm around the boy's shoulders and patted him.

Deep in the wilderness, Preacher snuggled deeper into his blankets and slept to the sound of wolves talking back and forth to each other. It was a comforting sound to the mountain man, for many people, both Indian and white, believed him to be a brother to the wolf. Some even went so far as to say Preacher was part wolf himself.

They were not that far from the truth.

9

Preacher rose from his blankets and squatted for a moment in the grayness of pre-dawn. In the brush and timber surrounding the little pocket of clearing where Preacher had made his camp, he could see gray and black shapes moving silently about, slowly circling him but making no attempt to enter the clearing.

"My brothers," Preacher said softly, his eyes on the big ever-moving wolves "You've come to warn me."

Low snarls greeted his softly-spoken words.

"So today it really starts," Preacher whispered. "They're really gonna come after me."

As one, their mission accomplished the wolves vanished, running deeper into the timber.

Kit Carson once said that Preacher was the "gawd-damnest feller" he'd ever seen. He had a way with animals like no man he'd ever known. Ol' Bill Williams said Preacher was spooky. He felt that Preacher could actually talk to animals, most especially with wolves. Jim Beckwouth once told a writer that of all the mountain men he'd ever known, the man called Preacher was the most fascinating. John Fremont confided in his friends that the mountan man Preacher was almost mystical in his dealings with animals. He swore that he actually witnessed a pack of wolves playing with Preacher one day, in a small meadow deep in the Rockies. He said that when they all tired of playing, they fell down on the grass and flowers and rested in a bunch, Preacher right in the middle of the huge wolves. Jim Bridger said that Preacher could be as rough as a cob, mean as a grizzly bear, and as gentle and compassionate as a mother with a baby.

Smoke Jensen, the West's most talked about, written about and feared gunfighter, whom Preacher took under his wing as a boy to raise after Smoke's pa died, wrote later in the biography, that the man called Preacher was a highly complex man, who lived under only one set of rules, his own. He said that Preacher was an inordinately fair man, but once his mind was made up, and his moccasins set on the path of his choosing, would brook no interference, from any man.

If those who made up the party who were now hunting Preacher for sport had known anything at all about the inner workings of the man, they would have immediately packed up and left the mountains as quickly as possible.

But they did not really know the matter or manner of the man they sought. And by the time they finally found out, it would be too late for most of them. It wasn't just that Preacher was a mountain man. For there were mountain men, albeit not many of them, who were as skittish as an old maid in a men's bath house. It was the individual himself that should have been studied closely. Bones had never had any experience with Preacher, or with men like him. His reputation as a successful man-hunter had come about by chasing down escaped convicts, weakened by physical abuse, poor food, and brutally hard work. He had chased down embezzlers who by the very nature of their work were not physically imposing people. Bones had chased down and captured—or shot dead—men who had killed their wives and wives who had killed their husbands. He had killed or captured ignorant farm boys who broke jail after some minor infraction. True, Bones had tackled some mean and vicious men and emerged victorious. But he had never taken on anyone who came even close to being in Preacher's league.

As for the royalty who were members of this party of man-hunters, to them this escapade in the wilderness was still nothing more than good sport and fun. Quite entertaining, really, don't you know? It was irritating to them that Bones had forbidden them to kill a savage or two, but perhaps when this Preacher matter was concluded, then they could hunt some Indians. They'd never taken a scalp, and that would be quite a novel thing to take back to show their friends. They were all looking forward to scalping some savages.

It just never entered their minds that they might be the ones to get killed and scalped.

Preacher struck first, three days after he'd waylaid Hunter and Bates. He still had it in his mind that he could maybe harass them into leaving the mountains. There was no way he could have known that the blood-hungry royalty had upped the ante on his head. He had checked on Eddie and found the boy was happier than he had ever seen him.

Wind Chaser was uncommonly blunt with Preacher. "My woman and I wish to keep Ed-de as our own, Preacher."

Preacher nodded his head. "And what does Eddie think about that?"

"He is a child. He does not know what is best for him. As adults, we do."

Preacher had to hide his smile. The Indian and the white man were so much alike, in so many ways, and yet, so far apart that their two cultures could probably never co-exist side by side.

"Well, when the time comes, I'll talk to Eddie. If it's all

right with him, it's all right with me, Wind Chaser." He smiled and to soften his words added, "And I'm purty sure it'll be just fine with Eddie."

Wind Chaser smiled. "The boy will want to stay with us. You will see."

"I 'spect you're right. I've cached supplies all over these mountains, Wind Chaser. So I'm gonna leave my horses with you and go this on foot."

Wind Chaser had noticed the huge pack and had suspected as much. He nodded his head. "This is no longer a game, White Wolf. Why don't you take some of the warriors and end this foolishness once and for all?"

Preacher shook his head. "This is personal, Wind Chaser. I talked to the wolves the other mornin'. They told me."

Wind Chaser felt the hair on the back of his neck hackle and he resisted the temptation to step back, away from Preacher. He had heard about Preacher and his relationship with the great gray wolves that roamed the countryside. It was just that sort of thing that made many people, Indian and white alike, believe the story that Preacher had been found as a baby and raised by wolves, suckled on their milk. Preacher had, of course, heard the story, and, naturally, being Preacher, he had never done anything to dispel the myth. Indeed, whenever he got the chance, he added a few words to strengthen the myth. The more Indians were spooked by him, the safer he was.

"Your brothers, the wolves, they were close to you?" Wind Chaser asked.

"'Bout as clost as me and you is right now."

"Ummm!" Wind Chaser said softly.

Smiling, knowing Wind Chaser would repeat the story and the legends about him would grow all over the Indian nation, Preacher walked out of the Ute village and made his way toward the timber. His pack would have bowed the back of a normal man. Preacher walked like he was carrying a pack full of feathers.

"Not a sign of him," the teams of men reported back to Bones after an all day search in an ever-widening circle around the base camp of the man-hunters.

"We seen savages," Mack Cornay said. "Plenty of them. But all they done was look at us. They didn't make no move, no gesture, nothin'."

"No tracks of that big rump-spotted horse he rides?" Van Eaton asked.

"No. Nothin'."

"He is on foot," Dark Hand spoke from where he sat on the ground. "He has hidden supplies all around and is now living with some wolf pack."

"Aw, hell!" George Winters said. "No human man lives with wolves. They'd tear him to pieces. All that talk is nothin' but poppycock and balderdash."

Dark Hand shrugged his shoulders in total indifference to what these foolish white men believed. Dark Hand and Preacher were about the same age, and Dark Hand had heard many things about the mountain man called Preacher over the years. Much of what was said about him was indeed nonsense. But some of the talk was true. Dark Hand knew that Preacher was not unique in his ability to get along with wolves. He knew of Indians who possessed the same talent. He also knew that Preacher did not sit with the spirits for guidance. Preacher was just a very highly skilled woodsman—as good as any Indian—and he had honed those skills to a knife blade sharpness.

Dark Hand also knew that Preacher had not killed the man called John Pray. He had scouted for miles the day after Pray had vanished and found where Preacher had taken him, tied him, questioned him, and then turned him loose.

And most importantly, he knew he would be much better off if he would leave the company of these foolish white men and strike out on his own. But the white men fascinated him. They were so ignorant about so many things. Dark Hand never tired of listening to the babble. They prattled on and on about the most unimportant subjects.

Tatman said sarcastically, "All right, Injun. You seem to think you more'un the rest of us. So what is Preacher gonna do now?"

"Start killing you," the Pawnee said matter-of-factly.

"Oh, yeah?" a big, ugly unwashed lout called Vic said, standing up. "I reckon you think this here Preacher is just gonna walk right in this camp and start blastin' away, huh?"

Dark Hand smiled knowingly. None of the white men had taken note that when he sat, he sat with his back to a boulder, or log, or tree. No one seemed to notice that Dark Hand utilized every available bit of cover even when in camp. How these men had lived this long was amazing to Dark Hand.

"No," the Pawnee said. "He will not come into camp firing his guns."

"Well, then," Vic said, his voice dripping with ugly sarcasm, "I reckon you think he'll call down lightnin' or something to strike us all dead? You seem to think this feller is some sort of god."

Dark Hand sighed. An instant later, Vic cried out and looked down at the arrow that was embedded deeply in his belly. Vic screamed as the pain hit him hard. His legs seemed to lose strength and he stumbled and sat down heavily on the ground. "Oh, mother!" he hollered, "Oh, my dear sweet mother!"

Dark Hand had bellied down on the ground before the first yell had passed Vic's lips, presenting no target at all for Preacher, and he was certain it was Preacher lurking in the dark brush and timber around the camp.

The men started shooting wildly, hitting nothing and accomplishing only the wasting of lead and powder. Dark Hand suspected that Preacher had turned and slipped away as soon as he saw the arrow strike its mark. That was what he would have done, and Preacher could be as much Indian as he was white when he had to be.

When no more arrows came silently and deadly out of the brush, the men slowly began crawling to their knees and reloading. The cooks and servants of the gentry remained where they were, belly down on the ground, eyes wide with fear.

"Halp me!" Vic bellered. "Oh, sweet baby Jesus, halp me."

There was nothing anyone could do for the man. The arrow had torn through his stomach and when they laid Vic out on the ground and cut away the back of his jacket and shirt, they could see that the point was very nearly all the way through his back.

"Go ahead and shoot him," Jimmie Cook said. "I don't want to have to listen to all that hollerin' for days and nights."

Sir Elmore Jerrold-Taylor waved to one of his men. "Franklin here has received some medical training. See what you can do for this unfortunate wretch, Franklin."

Franklin knelt down and inspected the puncture wound. "I will have to push the arrow out the back, remove the barbed point, and then pull the arrow out from the front. But I fear the lining of the stomach has been penetrated front and back so all that would accomplish is a great deal of agony for the man. He will die no matter what I do."

"Oh, very well," Elmore said. "Wilson," he called to one of the cooks. "Be a good fellow and fix some tea, will you? I feel the need for something warm and soothing. Something to calm the nerves, don't you know?"

Preacher's big rifle boomed and Elmore's plumed hat

went sailing about twenty feet away. His Lordship yelped and unceremoniously hit the ground, belly down in the mud.

The Frenchmen, Louviere and Tassin, jumped behind a fallen log and landed right on top of the Prussian, Rudi Kuhlmann, knocking the wind out of him. Preacher's rifle boomed again and the Austrian, Willy Steinwinder, got a faceful of bark splinters as the heavy ball smacked into the tree he was trying to hide behind. One of Bones's men, Cal Johnson, sprinted for cover just as Preacher fired one of his pistols. Cal turned a flip in the air as the ball slammed into his right leg and sent him sprawling and hollering. Preacher fired again and the ball whined off the big iron cook pot and went ricocheting wildly and wickedly around the camp. One of the servants ran into a tree and knocked himself silly. Van Eaton jumped for cover and landed squarely in a big pile of horse crap. He was so afraid to move that he lay in the dung and suffered the indignity, cussing Preacher loud and quite emotionally. Bones had jumped behind a boulder as the rest of the camp sought cover wherever they could find it. Dark Hand lay safe behind a fallen tree and took silent satisfaction in watching the panic of the white men.

Just before Preacher took off for safer territory, figuring he had done enough damage for one day, he turned and unloaded his pistols into the panicked camp. The sound was enormous and the double-shotted barrels spewed lead in all directions.

Baron Wilhelm Zaunbelcher was just getting to his fancy, hand-made boots when Preacher cut loose and Horace Haywood jumped into the slight ground depression and landed right on top of the Baron. The Baron did not appreciate that at all and began roaring in German. Horace figured rightly that Wilhelm was giving him a sound cussing and rared back and slugged the Baron right on the royal snoot. Horace and Wilhelm, ignoring the whining lead balls, began rolling around on the ground, cussing and punching and kicking and biting and gouging, the blood and the mud and the snot flying in all directions.

Bones rose to his knees and looked at the fist-swinging, bleeding, cussing men, rolling around in the dirt. He shook his head in disbelief.

Horace tried to knee Wilhelm in the groin and then gouge him in the eye with a thumb.

"Oh, I say now!" Burton Sullivan called. "That's a foul. Unfair. Unfair. Fisticuffs is one thing, but ungentlemanly behavior simply won't be tolerated here. I must protest this. Why . . ."

Jack Cornell busted the duke in the chops and Burton went down, his mouth bloody. He jumped to his boots and assumed what was then considered a proper stance for bare-knuckle fighting—the left arm stretched out, left fist knuckles to the ground; the right fist held close to the face. "I'll thrash you proper!" Burton said.

"That'll be the damn day!" Jack replied and bored in. Much to his surprise, Burton Sullivan knocked him flat on his butt.

Dark Hand lay behind cover and smiled at the antics of the white men. With danger all around them, the fools were making war against each other. To Dark Hand's way of thinking, it had to be some sort of a miracle from Man Above that the white race had survived this long.

"Break them up!" Bones yelled to his men. "Right now. We can't afford this. Preacher might be back at any moment. Do it, damnit!"

The cussing and fighting men were hauled apart and led off, to be widely separated from each other until they cooled down. Cal Johnson's leg was bathed and bandaged by Franklin; but Cal was going to be out of action for a time.

Vic was moaning and carrying on something awful. Van Eaton walked over to the man. He stood looking down at him for a moment, then cocked and lifted his pistol.

Vic yelled, "No, Van! Don't do it, man. Please, no. For God's sake!"

Van Eaton coldly shot him in the head, abruptly silencing the moans. "Gettin' on my nerves," Van Eaton said, recharging his pistol.

The camp was silent for a moment. "Oh, well. What the hell? He wouldn't have lasted the night noway," Mack Cornay said. "I'll get a shovel."

"No!" Bones called. "We don't have the time. Just roll him over the side of that ravine yonder and let the buzzards have him. We're breaking camp."

"Where to this time?" Van Eaton asked.

"The scouts found a much better place. It'll be harder for Preacher to slip up on us." He looked around him. "I sure don't want a repeat of this day."

10

By the time the man-hunters ended the confusion in their camp and stopped fighting among themselves, Preacher was long gone. When Bones asked Dark Hand if he was going to attempt to pick up Preacher's trail, the Pawnee looked at the man as if he had taken leave of his senses.

"That's what Ghost Walker would like some of us to do," he told Bones. "I tell you, those who pursue Preacher now will not return."

"By God, I'll pursue him!" Tatman said, picking up his rifle and moving toward his horse. "That Injun's yeller. I knowed it all along."

Dark Hand shrugged that off and turned his back to the ignorant loudmouth.

"Take Brown with you," Van Eaton told him.

"I shall accompany the men," the Frenchman, Jon Louviere said.

"Suit yourself," Bones told him.

"I'll go with them," Burton Sullivan said. "I just don't believe this man is the will 'o' the wisp you people claim him to be."

"Good show, Burton!" Sir Elmore shouted.

"Hip, hip, hooray!" Robert Tassin yelled.

Dark Hand grimaced at the very premature congratulatory shouts and poured himself a cup of coffee. The Pawnee watched the four men ride out and thought: Some of you will not return.

"Hell, he's a-foot!" Tatman said, reining up about a thousand yards out of camp, leaning out of the saddle and studying the ground. "We got him now, boys. He's ourn for shore."

"Splendid!" Louviere said.

"Do push on," Burton urged.

About a mile from camp, a rattlesnake, as thick as a man's forearm and made as a hornet, came sailing out of the brush and struck Brown's shoulder and landed stretched out from saddle horn to Brown's thigh. Brown, terrified out of his wits, let out a wild whoop and left the saddle just as the snake bit him on the leg. The snake left the saddle with the frightened and yelling man, biting him several more times before Brown hit the rocky ground. Preacher screamed like a panther and the horses went into a panic and began pitching and bucking, doing their best to throw off their riders.

Burton Sullivan's butt left the saddle and he went rolling and squalling down the steep grade to the left of the trail. Jon Louviere dropped his rifle and grabbed onto the saddle horn as his horse became more panicked and started bucking more fiercely. His rifle discharged when it struck the ground and the ball struck Tatman in the shoulder, knocking him out of the saddle. He hit the ground, screaming and cussing the Frenchman. Brown was dying beside the trail, the rattler having bitten him a dozen or more times, the last few times on the neck and face. The bounty-hunter was already beginning to swell grotesquely.

Tatman landed about two feet from the horrible scene and clawed at his pistol. The snake shifted its attention from the dying man to Tatman and opened its mouth to strike. Tatman finally pulled the gun from behind his belt and shot the rattlesnake, blowing its head off.

Preacher picked up a rock and flung it, the heavy stone impacting against the side of Louviere's jaw and slamming him from the saddle. The Frenchman, out cold, landed on top of Tatman, knocking the wind from Tatman, and bringing a scream of pain from the frightened and wounded man.

Burton Sullivan, several hundred feet below, had no idea what was taking place above him. He was frantically attempting to claw his way up the rocky incline. He had lost his fancy rifle and one of his pistols and was thoroughly disgusted. He had busted his head on a rock and it was bleeding. His safari clothing was ripped and torn and he had lost one boot. All things taken into consideration, this day was not going well at all.

And it was about to get worse.

By the trail, Preacher had taken all the guns and powder and shot from the dead and wounded men. He was waiting for Burton Sullivan when the man finally, panting and grunting, hauled himself over the side.

"You lookin' for me, Fancy-Britches?" Preacher asked.

Burton gazed upward and into the coldest eyes the Englishman had ever seen.

"I say now, my good fellow," Burton gasped. "Can't we discuss this like civilized men?"

"Nope," Preacher said, and busted the man on the side of his jaw with one big fist.

The nobleman's feet, minus one boot, left the incline and down he went, rolling butt over elbows. He went back down the grade a lot quicker than he came up. He rolled over rocks, smashed into small sturdy trees, and uprooted bushes in a frantic attempt to halt his descent. He finally came to rest all tangled up in a pile of thorny bushes. He was so addled he thought he was a child back in England.

"Oh mummy," he muttered. "I'm afraid I've poo-pooed in my nightie."

"I'll kill you for this," Tatman told Preacher, pushing the words past the pain in his shoulder.

"I doubt it," Preacher told him, settling one moccasin against Tatman's big butt. Preacher shoved and Tatman began his journey down to join Burton Sullivan at the bottom of the incline.

After two trips, Burton had pretty much cleared the way, so Tatman didn't really encounter much in the way of obstacles on his way down. He must have been covering about fifty feet a second when he slammed into Burton Sullivan, who was just getting to his shaky boots, his back to the incline. Burton, his butt filled with thorns from the bramble bush, and his mind foggy, was staring dreamily down at a lovely little creek about twenty feet below when Tatman slammed into him. Both of them sailed over the edge and landed in the creek.

Preacher looked down at the pair and laughed at them, wallowin' around in the creek. Preacher knew that creek was snow-fed year round and that the water was icy cold. Them two down yonder was liable to come down with pneumonia.

Preacher hoped they did.

Van Eaton recovered the money the noblemen had paid to Brown, stuck it in his pocket, and then shoved the body over the side for the buzzards to eat. Van Eaton didn't give a damn about Brown, or anybody else for that matter, but this meant that Preacher was slowly whittling away at their strength. And the man was still playing with them. He just didn't seem to be taking this hunt seriously. It seemed to Van Eaton that to Preacher, this manhunt was . . . well *fun!*

At that thought, the hired killer looked nervously around him. Van Eaton didn't like these Rocky Mountains.

He didn't like them at all. He quickly walked over to his horse, swung into the saddle and took off.

I should have killed him, Preacher thought, on his belly about two hundred yards from where he'd waylaid the four men. That Van Eaton is one cold hombre. He sure wouldn't give a second thought to killin' me.

But Preacher still clung to the rapidly fading hope that the men would give up this foolishness and let him be. Deep within him, however, he knew they would not. That sooner or later, he was going to have to start killing them on sight. The problem was, he didn't want to kill these men. Well . . . maybe Bones and Van Eaton. The world wouldn't miss them at all. These noblemen, now, that was something else. Preacher figured them to be nothin' more than just spoiled rich boys who'd suddenly got all growed up without the maturity that came with bein' an adult man. And he hadn't meant to hit that man with the rattlesnake. Problem was, when you start flingin' rattlesnakes about, you got to be careful, 'cause they can whip that head around and give you a fearsome bite. That knowledge sort of threw Preacher's aim off some. It wasn't that he was feelin' bad about Brown, 'cause he wasn't. After all, the man had been out lookin' to kill him.

Preacher looked carefully around him, then rose up and began trailing Van Eaton. Which wasn't a big deal. Any ten-year-old Injun boy could have done that with one eye closed. Van Eaton did not know this country and that would have been evident to anyone with any knowledge of the land. From all the smoke from cook fires he'd seen plumin' up into the air, Preacher had a pretty good idea where Bones had chosen to camp. He'd try one more time to warn these men off, to stop this foolishness. If they didn't heed his warnings, then Preacher reckoned, he'd just have to get nasty about this thing.

* * *

Jon Louviere's jaw was swollen up something frightful. He could just barely speak. Which came as a great relief to most of Bones's gang. Burton Sullivan sat gingerly on a pillow in front of a roaring fire, a blanket wrapped around him. The long and numerous thorns had been plucked from Sullivan's butt, his skin had lost its blue color from the icy waters, and he had stopped shaking. Both Louviere and Sullivan had been thoroughly humiliated by what had taken place. But their eyes shone wildly and silently spoke volumes of revenge.

Tatman was not badly injured, the ball punching a hole in the fleshy part of his left shoulder and passing through without doing any major damage, except to his pride. All during the cleaning out of the wound, he had cussed and spoke of dire consequences should he and Preacher ever meet again. Bones sat with his back to a large rock and listened to it all with a disgusted look on his face. It wasn't that any of the men lacked courage, for he knew that those who'd stuck with him thus far had more than their share of that. He was just sick of Preacher making fools of them all. Playing with them like this was some sort of kid's game.

Problem was, Bones didn't have a clue as to how to bring the hunt to a conclusion. He was going to use the boy, somehow get him away from Preacher and use the brat as leverage. But with the boy in the protective hands of the Utes, that was out. No one in their right mind would attack an entire Ute village; not with as few men as Bones had, anyway.

And to make matters even worse, Dark Hand had told the gang, with no small amount of satisfaction in his voice and smugness on his face, that the Indians were watching it all, spying on them. Ute and Cheyenne for sure, and probably Arapaho, too, and were making up dances and telling stories about how foolishly this large band of white men were behaving. Now Preacher was out-foxing them all and making them look stupid. That really rankled both Bones and Van Eaton. A bunch of filthy ignorant savages making light of them all.

Bones watched as Van Eaton rode back in and stripped the saddle off his horse and rubbed the animal down. No matter how evil the men were, they knew to take good care of their horses. Horses were life in this country.

"Any sign of Preacher?" Bones asked, after Van Eaton had poured coffee and walked over to squat beside him.

"No. But I shore felt his eyes on me. I 'spect he followed me here."

"Well, if that's the case, we best get ready for more fun and games from him. Make sure the guard is doubled and changed ever' two hours so's they'll stay fresh."

"Will do."

"Did you get the money from Brown?"

"Shore did. I stashed it in my gear."

"What'd he look like?"

"Turrible sight. All swole up like nothin' I ever seen afore." He shuddered. "I seen that big rattler, too. Damned if I'd pick that big ugly thing up alive and fling it at anybody. Personal, I think Preacher's 'bout half crazy. I was tole a lot of these mountain men is off the bean somewhat."

"I can believe it. This country would drive a body loony. What are you grinnin' about?"

"Thinkin' 'bout his majesty over yonder rollin' butt over boots down that hill and landin' in them briars. I'd a give a pretty penny to seen that."

He and Bones started snickering at the thought and had to cover their mouths so the others would not hear. Van Eaton sobered after a moment and said, "I'll tell you the truth, Bones. I ain't lookin' forward to the night."

"Neither am I," Bones whispered. "But just maybe Preacher feels he done enough for one day."

"I hope so. I ain't had a good nights' sleep in I cain't 'member when."

He wasn't going to get much sleep that night, either, for Preacher had found the camp and was planning his mischief with a grin on his face.

11

"Eight guards," Preacher muttered under his breath. "I got them scared, for a fact."

He had slowly circled the camp, then made himself comfortable and waited for the guards to change. Every two hours, he noted. These folks are learnin'. Man stays on guard more'un two hours, he tends to get careless.

Preacher waited until the shift changed at midnight, and then waited for another thirty minutes or so before he made his move. With all the supplies he'd taken from Bones's men, Preacher had gunpowder to burn . . . in a manner of speaking. Preacher slipped around to where the horses were picketed and went to work for a few minutes. Then, having to really struggle to keep from giggling, he took aim and chucked a bag of powder into what was left of a dying campfire. Coals aplenty to do the job. Preacher had already found a good spot to watch the show, and he almost made it. He had tossed a second bag of powder into another fire but he thought he'd missed the dying coals. Obviously he hadn't. The big bag of powder blew and the quiet camp turned into a scene of mass confusion.

The horses pulled their pins and jerked free of the picket line and stampeded right through the camp. Ever seen what fifty or so wild-eyed horses and twenty odd big runnin' mules can do to a camp? Preacher jumped behind a rock when the action started and the outcome went way beyond his wildest expectations. The explosions blew hot coals all over the place and set a dozen or so blankets on fire and that only added to the chaos. The horses ran right over the fancy tents of the gentry and Preacher had never seen such a sight as that. In the light from the fires, the gentlemen were exposed in their nightshirts. Several of them had what looked to Preacher like little bitty fish nets tied around their heads. Damnest sight he'd ever seen, for sure.

Sir Elmore Jerrold-Taylor got in the way of a big Missouri and that mule knocked him about twenty feet from point of impact. Sir Elmore landed right smack dab on his butt on that rocky ground and commenced to squallin'.

Bones got himself run down by a spooked horse and before the dust and smoke got so bad that Preacher couldn't see, Bones was on all fours, scurryin' away like a big ugly bug. Van Eaton had climbed a tree, so Preacher just hauled out one of his pistols and let 'er bang.

But the smoke and dust threw his aim off and the ball took a chunk of meat out of Van Eaton's butt. Van Eaton started screamin' and turned loose of the branch he was holding onto and fell about fifteen feet, landin' hard on the ground.

Preacher took aim at a running man and squeezed off another shot; the fall flew true and the man stumbled and fell, pitching face-first onto the ground.

Preacher changed locations, flitting soundlessly through the timber, staying low, working his way around the scene of wild confusion. The only one in the camp he was really worried about was Dark Hand, but his worry was needless. Dark Hand had left his blankets before the echo of the first explosion had faded and jumped into the narrow space between two boulders.

And there he sat. Dark Hand would choose his own time and place to confront Ghost Walker. And this night definitely was not the time nor the place. All the advantage was Preacher's.

Mack Cornay jumped onto the back of a galloping horse and grabbed a double handful of mane, trying to halt the frightened animal. But the animal was not to be stopped. The horse raced into the timber and Mack was knocked from the horse when his face impacted with a low limb. Mack hit the ground, his nose busted and his front teeth missing.

A man-hunter known only as Spanish made the mistake of taking to the timber after Preacher. Not a wise thing to do. Preacher noticed the movement behind him and to his left and waited, crouched in the brush. When Spanish drew up even with Preacher, he caught the butt of Preacher's rifle in his gut and doubled over, all his breath gone. Spanish lay on the cold ground, gasping for breath and unable to move. Just to be on the safe side, Preacher quickly tied the man's hands behind his back with a length of rawhide. Preacher tossed the man's weapons into the night and took off.

Preacher continued his circling of the camp, which by now was beginning to settle down somewhat. But the dust and smoke were still thick.

"He shot me in the butt!" Van Eaton hollered. "Feels like it's on fire!"

"My buttocks are on fire!" Willy Steinwinder yelled, frantically slapping at his rear end. A running horse had knocked him into some burning blankets and ignited his nightgown. Prince Rudi Kuhlmann tossed a bucket of water on him.

Preacher underwent a mental wrestling match for a moment, and better judgment won. He left the camp and headed for his hidey hole and safety. He needed a few hours sleep. He figured the bounty-hunters would spend the rest of the night trying to round up their horses and mules, picking up their scattered supplies, and seeing to the needs of the wounded. They'd be after him with vengeance come daylight, but by then, Preacher would have once more shifted locations.

At daylight, the man-hunters began assessing the damage done to their camp, and it was extensive. The tents of the royalty had been burned beyond repair. A lot of their supplies were either missing or destroyed. Two men were wounded and a half a dozen more were injured.

"Indians watched this," Dark Hand announced, returning from a scouting of the timber around the camp. "I don't know what tribe, but several were in the woods. They left heading north. That might mean nothing, or it might mean they were Arapaho."

"Preacher?" Bones asked.

"I lost his trail. He was heading east when I could no longer track him. He took to the rocks."

Dark Hand went to the fire for coffee, leaving Bones again doing some fancy cussing.

Van Eaton and Willy Steinwinder were laying on their bellies, Van Eaton due to the bullet from Preacher's pistol, Willy because of burned buttocks. Van Eaton's rear end was bandaged and Willy's spread all over with lard. Neither man was terribly pleased with their present situation but Willy did express his discomfort much more eloquently than Van Eaton.

Preacher was up at dawn and took a quick wash in a little creek . . . a very quick wash, for the water was ice cold. He boiled coffee, ate some berries for breakfast, and then packed up and moved out.

About a mile from his old camp, Preacher ran into some Arapaho. They grinned at him and the leader said, "You gave us much enjoyment last night, White Wolf.

The behavior of the white men was funny. We will have a fine time retelling the story. We thank you. Go in peace."

The Arapaho rode off without another word.

"I ought to start chargin' admission," Preacher muttered, then shouldered his pack and moved on.

"How far back to Bent's Fort?" Bones asked wearily, his eyes sweeping the devastated camp.

"As the crow flies, 'bout two hundred or so miles, I figure," Andy Price said.

"Soon as we get the mules rounded up, take ten men and head there. We got to have supplies. His Lordship, Sir Jerrold-Taylor done made up a list and he'll give you the money. You ought to be safe with that many men. You 'member that valley we rode through southeast of here? We'll be there. We'll do nothin' 'til you boys get back. Last night's affair done scattered and ruint near'bouts ever'thing we got. Head on out."

"You want me to see about pickin' up some more men?"

"Yeah. If you can. But don't tell nobody who it is we're chasin'. Preacher is bound to have friends there." Bones gave the man some gold coins. "Just tell them we're after a murderer and they's big money in it. This here gold ought to get their attention."

The men were gone by midday. It was to be a long, hard trip, and no one in the camp expected their return in under a month. Three weeks at best.

"Pack it up," Bones ordered. "This time, by God, we'll secure our camp and do it right."

Preacher watched the men through his spy glass. He knew immediately they'd sent a party back for supplies. And he saw right off he'd have little chance of slipping into this new camp. The men were working steadily, clearing away brush, cutting down and hauling in logs, and laying out fields of fire. This was going to be a regular little fort.

"Somebody down yonder's had some military experience," Preacher said, collapsing his spy glass and standing up. "They're buildin' a stockade. This is a good time for me to check on Eddie."

Eddie was all decked out in a brand-new set of fancy buckskins. He grinned when Preacher walked into the village. But the boy was not well, and there was sadness in Wind Chaser's eyes.

"He dies slowly before our eyes," the Ute said. "And there is nothing that anyone can do."

"Except make him happy," Preacher spoke in low tones.

"That we are doing. My woman, and the whole village. Come, Ghost Walker. Sit, eat. Let us talk about ridding ourselves of these silly white men who hunt you . . ." He smiled. "Or try to hunt you."

Over a thick, rich stew, Preacher said, "It's time for you and your people to be moving to the hunt, Wind Chaser. Past time, actually."

Wind Chaser smiled. "You are wrong if you think we stay because of Ed-de. We stay because the buffalo are late in coming this year. We are leaving soon, though. Ed-de wants to go with us."

Preacher nodded his head. "It'll be an adventure for him. Prob'ly his last one."

Wind Chaser's face tightened at that, but he said nothing. Privately, he agreed with Preacher's assessment. Neither man had any idea that it would be the last adventure for most of Wind Chaser's band.

The sounds of a horse ridden hard reached the men and they stood up. The young brave jumped off at Wind Chaser's lodge. "Crooked Arm says the buffalo are moving."

Wind Chaser gripped Preacher's shoulder. "You should

come with us, Ghost Walker. The hunt will be fun and we shall all feast until our bellies swell."

"I got business to tend to, Wind Chaser. I'll speak to the boy and then be gone. I know you got packin' up to do."

Preacher kept his goodbye brief. He didn't want to get all emotional, besides, Eddie was all flustered with excitement and rarin' to get gone huntin' buffalo. The boy was trembling with anticipation. Preacher suddenly had a bad feeling about this trip. But seeing that the boy was all set up to go, Preacher kept his feelings to himself.

"You mind your manners, now, boy," Preacher said, placing a hand on Eddie's frail shoulder.

"Yes, sir, Preacher. I will."

"I know you will, Eddie. You're a good boy. Might be a while 'til you and me hook up again. But we will. That's a promise. So you take 'er easy, you hear? You mind what Wind Chaser says, too. You hear?"

Eddie laughed. "I hear. I'll see you, Preacher."

Wind Chaser's band was not a large one to begin with, and many of the men had gone on ahead to scout for the buffalo. What was left was mainly women and kids and a few warriors. Preacher stood and watched them break camp and head out. He waved his farewells and then saddled up and rode out, in the opposite direction.

He made camp early that afternoon, high up and protected by huge boulders. That night, he woke up with a stir and listened. Seemed to him like he could hear the faint sounds of gunshots. But they faded away or were lost in the sighing winds and Preacher snuggled warm into his blankets and drifted back off to sleep.

Over bacon and pan bread and coffee, something in the far distance caught Preacher's eyes. He dug out his spy glass and extended it. He could just make out the circling of buzzards. A lot of buzzards, and they were already making their slow glide down to the ground to feast on the dead . . . whatever it might be, human or animal, and Preacher had a hunch it was human.

Preacher suddenly lost his appetite as a feeling of terrible dread settled over him, hanging on his shoulders like a stinking shroud. He knew that many buzzards didn't congregate over a lone dead animal. It would have to be a whole herd dead, and that just wasn't likely.

With an effort, Preacher forced himself to eat what he had cooked, 'cause in the wilderness, it was good practice to eat when you can, drink when you can, and rest when you can, 'cause you never knew when the chance might come again.

He drank his pot of coffee and then rinsed the pot and scrubbed out his frying pan and cached it with the bulk of his supplies. He made sure his stock had plenty of grass and water, and then slowly saddled Thunder.

"I know what's down there, Thunder. I know in my heart and it makes me sick to think about it. I don't wanna go down yonder, but I gotta. I gotta," he repeated, and then swung into the saddle and started for the valley far below and to the north.

He could smell the scene long before he reached it. The buzzards had torn open the bodies, exposing the innards to the air.

The first thing he came up on was Eddie's little paint pony, lyin' dead. The sorry man-hunting trash had cut its throat and let it bleed to death. Preacher looked at the pony for a moment.

"You was a good horse to a good boy when he needed some good in his life, pony. I won't let the buzzards have you."

He rode on, reading the signs as he went. They were easy. Wind Chaser and his band had made camp along the banks of a stream. That night, when they were settled in, Bones and his bunch had hit them, and hit them hard. He knew it was Bones's bunch 'cause the lone white man he found dead he'd seen several times before.

"I'll not bury you, you sorry son!" Preacher said, considerable heat in his voice.

He found Wind Chaser beside his woman. The chief had died protecting his woman and their children. It didn't take an experienced eye to see that the women had been raped, and used badly. Preacher felt a chill run over him when he saw that Bones and his men had even raped the little girls.

"Sorry white-trash," he muttered.

But he couldn't find Eddie. He didn't want to fire a shot and bring Bones and his people back, so he rode amongst the dead, using a Ute lance to knock the buzzards away. He really didn't have anything against the carrion-eatin' critters; they were just doing what God had put them on the earth to do, but damned if they were gonna do it in front of him. Least not with people he had known and liked.

Preacher rode around the circle of death twice, looking for the boy. He had steeled himself for the worst. But it was worse than even he had thought.

He found Eddie and almost lost his breakfast.

12

The boy had been dragged to death.

The boy's new buckskins were bloody and torn. Preacher just could not bear to look at him any longer. He dismounted and gently laid a blanket over what was left of Eddie. Preacher squatted down for a moment and tried to piece together what had happened.

He figured that Wind Chaser and his small band had been spotted by scouts from Bones's camp. John Pray had told him that the foreigners had expressed a desire to kill some Indians. Bones and his party had waited until the Ute camp had settled down and then had slipped up on them under cover of darkness. This was Ute country and Wind Chaser had felt no great need for a lot of security. How Bones and his men had managed to pull this off was a mystery to Preacher, and probably always would be. The important thing was that they had done it. And Eddie was dead.

With a sigh, Preacher stood up and began the task of burying the dead. And he had to do this right, for more than one reason. If Wind Chaser's scouts returned and found this massacre, the entire Ute nation would go on the warpath, and no white man would be safe for months or even years to come. Preacher couldn't allow that to happen.

Preacher built him a travois and began toting the bodies to a dry off-shoot of the creek. He placed Wind Chaser and his family together and carefully caved in part of the bank over them. He did that with all the Utes, choosing his spots with care. Then he took bushes and small saplings and transplanted them in the soil that covered the Indians. It took him most of the morning to get it done, stopping often to look around him for trouble and every fifteen minutes or so taking up his club to knock buzzards away from the remaining bodies.

He searched the area, gathering up everything that had belonged to the tribe and scattered it throughout the timber: clothing, utensils, tipi poles; everything he could find. Then he carefully cut squares of sod out of the earth, worked throughout the afternoon greatly enlarging the hold, dragged and sometimes having to muscle the pony into the hole, and then burying Eddie beside his little paint pony. Preacher carefully replaced the squares of sod and toted water from the creek to dampen the disturbed earth, making certain the grass would stay fertile and grow, ensuring Eddie a proper grave.

As the sun was setting, Preacher stood over the grave of the boy and took off his hat. It was rare for Preacher to be at a loss for words, but for a long time late that afternoon, words failed him.

"This here was a good boy, Lord," he finally said, the waning rays of the sun casting shadows about him. "He never done a harm to nobody. I reckon he was about ten years old and in all them ten years, he never knew much comfort. Shore didn't know no love and affection 'til he come to the Utes. They give him a home, and it was a good one."

Suddenly, Preacher realized he was crying, tears streaming from his eyes and rolling down his tanned cheeks. He remembered the last time he shed a tear it was over Hammer's body. He sure had liked this little boy.

He waited for a few moments, wiped his face, and said, "Eddie liked this little paint pony, Lord. So I'd consider it a debt owed if You'd let this here horse into heaven with him. I think You'll find they'll serve You well.

"Now them Utes I buried this day, well, they didn't have no fancy church buildin' like them so-called civilized Christians back East. But what they did have was a belief in Man Above, and that's You, and their church was the whole wide country around them. I think that's a fittin' thing, since it was You who created it all. Includin' the Utes.

"I reckon Eddie and his pony is standin' beside You now. Or maybe beside Jesus, or one of them appissles, or somebody up yonder. Leastwises I shore hope so. I'd hate to think I done all this for nothin'."

Preacher held up the Bible he'd given to Eddie after finding it amongst the ruins of the burned out wagons back on the Big Sandy. "This here is the Good Book, which I'm shore You can plainly see. I ruminated some about plantin' this with Eddie and his little pony. Then I decided I'd keep it and read it from time to time. I ain't no Christian man, but I do find the words to be right comfortin'. I'm a-fixin' to read it now, 'cause what I'm gonna read is one of Eddie's favorite verses. I ain't no real good reader, so You excuse my stumblin' around on any big words I might run acrost."

Preacher read the 23rd Psalm, then closed the Bible and tucked it away in his parfleche. "I reckon that about does it, Lord. I don't know what else there is to say. I'm gonna miss this boy. I liked him. That's all. Good evenin'."

Preacher turned to go, hesitated, then once more stood over the grave. "Well, there is somethin' else. Them no-count, trashy heathens over yonder behind them log walls in that valley done a terrible thing last night. They's rich men over yonder that's had a fancy education and all the trimmin's that most of us don't get. They knew better. As a matter of fact, all them men over yonder knew better. Now, Lord, there ain't no law out here in the wilderness. But they is justice, and I aim to see it done." He patted the buckskin parfleche containing the Bible. "I know that somewheres in the Good Book it says that vengeance is mine, sayeth the Lord. Well, I'm a-fixin' to relieve You of that burden for a time. Now, if You don't cotton to me doin' that, You best fling down a mighty lightnin' bolt to strike me dead. 'Cause that's the only thing that's gonna stop me." Preacher closed his eyes tightly and braced himself for a bolt from Heaven. When none came, he expelled air and said, "Thank You kindly. Now if You'll excuse my language, Lord, I'm a-fixin' to go kill me some sorry sons of bitches."

13

Bones had figured Preacher would come after him, and he had prepared for the visit. The fort in the middle of the pretty little valley had been reinforced with rocks and logs and dug up earth. Every bush had been pulled up, every tree cut down for hundreds of yards all around the stockade. Grass for several hundred yards all around the little fort had been repeatedly trampled down by horses and mules.

"You think you're smart, don't you?" Preacher muttered. "Well, you are, Bones. But you ain't near'bouts as mean as me. So that means I got it all over you."

After burying Eddie and the others, Preacher rode up into the high country to think things over and to clear his head. He knew better than to wage war when angry. Man has to be cold when he fights. Anger causes mistakes, and when outnumbered the way he was, Preacher knew he couldn't afford to make any mistakes.

Preacher sat his horse up on a ridge, in the timber, and ruminated for a time. Then he smiled and headed out. Maybe he couldn't get in that stockade, but he figured he sure knew a way to get them inside out. Might take him a couple of days to get it done, but he'd do it.

Willy Steinwinder limped down to the creek to get some water for coffee. He stood for a moment, looking rather confused. He closed his eyes, shook his head, and opened his eyes again. Same thing. He walked back to the stockade and up to Bones.

"There is no water in the creek."

"What?" Bones asked, looking up.

"The creek is dry."

"I don't believe it. That's impossible!"

"Go look for yourself."

"Well, I sure will!"

Everybody walked out to look. The creek had dried up to no more than a tiny trickle in the center. Dark Hand sat on the bank and chuckled.

"You find this funny, Injun?" Jack Cornell asked.

"Yes. Most amusing. Preacher has dammed up the creek. Now what are you going to do?"

Jack Cornell wasn't going to do anything. Not ever again. Preacher didn't think he could make the shot, but he did. He had Jon Louviere's fancy hunting rifle and it was about the best rifle Preacher had ever had his hands on. It was handmade for Jon, that was evident. The workmanship was flawless. So Preacher loaded 'er up, sighted in, and let 'er bang.

He held high because of the distance and dead centered Jack Cornell in the chest. Cornell was stone dead before he hit the ground, his spinal cord severed. The others scattered for the protection of the stockade or hit the ground.

But no more shots came. Preacher worked his way out of the valley by following a ravine when he could and bellying the rest of the way. He figured he had at least three weeks before the others came back from Bent's Fort, and since he was sure they'd bring back some more ornery ol' boys with them, Preacher had decided to whittle down those that stayed behind.

He figured he had a right good start this morning. He was aimin' to whittle down one or two more come this evenin'.

Bones sat behind the earth and long walls and cussed Preacher. Van Eaton sat on a pillow and joined in. Willy Steinwinder had a few choice words to say about the mountain man, but he soon recognized the futility of that and fell silent. The men knew they had to move; without water they could not last long.

"We could go upstream and tear down that dam," Jimmie Cook suggested.

"You want to volunteer to do that?" Bones stopped cussing long enough to ask.

"I reckon not," Jimmie replied.

"That's what I figured." Bones stood up. "Come daylight we're splittin' up into five man teams and takin' out after Preacher. I ain't havin' no more of this."

"Oh, good show!" Sir Elmore said, clapping his hands. "Good show."

Bones almost shot the man right then and there. But he had found out that the gentry might be a tad foolish, but they weren't stupid. The bearer bonds, or bank notes, or whatever in the hell they were, weren't worth a damn unless the signature matched up with the one on record back in St. Louis. And since Bones could just barely write his own name, there wasn't a chance in hell he could copy any of the gentry's handwriting, and he knew it. Torture was out, for the royalty would guess they would be killed anyway and just scrawl their name, making the certificates worthless. So they had to be kept alive and escorted all the way back to St. Louis. And that really irritated Bones.

"We managed to bring enough water up to water the stock and have some for ourselves," George Winters said.

"Will we come back here for the evenin' tomorrow?" Bones was asked.

He shook his head. "No. We'll meet up over yonder in the timber west of here. This place is worthless to us now." He walked to a gun slit and looked out. The sun was going down.

"You reckon Preacher will be back and try to Injun up on us tonight?" Spanish asked.

"He will return this night," Dark Hand said. He had not gone with the men on their raid against Wind Chaser and his band. Wind Chaser had befriended him one time, and he could not bring himself to do harm to one who had been his friend in a time of need. He wished desperately to convey that fact to Preacher.

And Dark Hand had already, several times, prayed to the Man Above that the group he was with did not run into any Utes. He had watched from a distance as Preacher very cleverly hid the evidence after the night raid. But he knew, as Preacher surely did, that it would not fool a determined search.

Dark Hand stood peering through a gun slit in the logs. He could sense Preacher's presence, ever more strongly as the last rays of the sun began to fade.

"You think he's out there, don't you, Dark Hand?" Robert Tassin asked.

"Yes."

"Well, he's a fool then!" a man called Cobb snapped. "What does he think he's gonna do? Attack this stockade? That would be stupid."

Dark Hand smiled as he turned to face the man. "It is dark now, Cobb. Do you wish to be the first to leave these walls to relieve yourself?" Cobb said nothing. "No?" Dark Hand said. "I thought not."

Preacher was working closer as the night fell softly all around him. He stopped his stealthy advance at the far side of the creek bank. He took his bow, strung it, and selected an arrow from the quiver. He waited, watching the stockade. Those inside had lit candles or lamps and they had a fire going. Stupid, Preacher thought. The gun slits were lit up like a chandelier: rectangular pockets of light in the darkness. Every so often the shape of a head would appear briefly, then pull back.

Preacher calculated the distance. Easy shot. He waited with the patience of a stalking panther.

Davidson walked to a slit and peered out. Everyone inside the walls heard the wet smack and turned. Davidson stood on his boots for a few seconds, the shaft of the arrow protruding from his forehead. Then he toppled over and fell on his back. When he hit the ground the pistol in his hand discharged and the ball just missed Bones's head by a few inches. Bones stretched out on the cool earth.

"Douse them candles and lamps!" Bones yelled, cold sweat covered his body. "Put out them fires."

"Drag Davidson's body out of here and heave it over the walls," Van Eaton ordered. He had watched Davidson put the money given him by the gentry into his pack. He'd get it before they pulled out in the morning. Easy money.

There would be nine teams and then some pullin' out, Van Eaton thought. That meant the odds of Preacher trailin' any particular team was one in nine. Not the best odds in the world but better than nothin'.

Van Eaton knew what Bones was planning. With nine teams working the area, there was a good chance they could box Preacher in and end this man-hunt. But they would all have to be very careful. Preacher was like a ghost in the woods.

Percy lit the stub of a cigar and another arrow came whizzing through a gunslit, this time on the other side of the stockade. The arrow thudded into a log, just missing Spanish, and the man yelped and flattened out on the ground.

"Good God!" Bones yelled. "Don't fire up no more matches."

"Isn't this exciting?" Sir Elmore whispered to his friend, Prince Juan Zapata.

Zapata's eyes were shining with anticipation of the upcoming hunt. "I cannot wait until the morning," the Spaniard replied. "The mountain man is indeed a worthwhile adversary."

"We'll have to do this again sometime," Rudi Kuhlmann said. "It is fraught with danger but very exhilarating."

"Oh, quite," Burton Sullivan agreed.

"Igits!" Van Eaton thought, listening to the royalty whisper amongst themselves. "I ain't never in all my borned days seen such a goofy bunch all gathered up in one spot."

Preacher had worked closer, passing through the horses in a crude corral. He calmed them with touches and whispers and made his way to the log walls of the stockade. Bones had placed no guards outside the stockade. Not very smart of him, Preacher thought. Then he stopped cold.

No way! No way that Bones would not put guards outside the log and rock and earthen walls. He wouldn't leave the horses unguarded. He wasn't that stupid. "Damn!" Preacher thought. "I been boxed. Unless I was awful lucky."

Preacher did not move, remaining as still as a rock. Only his eyes shifted, searching the darkness. And when his eyes touched a shape he almost jumped out of his moccasins. The man was no more than ten feet away. Preacher could make out the shape of the man's head, and the long barrel of his rifle. Fortunately for Preacher, the guard had his back to him. The night had turned cloudy, and there would be no moon. Already a few large drops of cold rain had fallen. If the dark building clouds held true, in a very few minutes this night was gonna produce a rain that would be a real toad-strangler.

Preacher pulled out his razor-sharp, long-bladed knife and held it close to one leg, so no stray glimmer of light would reflect off the blade.

"You see anything, Cleave?" the whisper came from a gun slit about a foot from where Preacher stood.

"Nothin'," the guard replied. "But the wind is freshenin' and it's gonna pour down any minute. That's when Preacher will make his move. Bet on it."

"I just spoke to MacNary on the other side. He ain't seen or heard nothin' neither. I'm bettin' Preacher has done his deed and got gone back to his camp 'fore the rain comes."

"I just want to kill that Preacher and get back to civilization," Cleave said. "I don't like these mountains."

"Knock off the talk!" Bones called. "You'll give away your position."

Cleave muttered something about Bones under his breath and leaned up against the logs, still with his back to Preacher.

Preacher cut his throat and lowered the body to the ground. He began working his way around to the other side of the stockade, moving very slowly. John Pray had told him about MacNary, and MacNary was a bad one. A thug and a brigand through and through, a man who would do anything to anybody, man, woman, or child, if the price was right. Preacher had come into the cleared area to stampede the horses, but Bones had used a length of chain to fasten the crude corral gate, and Preacher had to nix that plan.

Thunder began to rumble in the distance and that covered any slight sound that Preacher might make. The clouds began dumping a very light rain and Preacher decided he'd pushed his luck enough for one night. When the shape of MacNary came into view, Preacher shot him and then jammed the muzzles of those terrible pistols into a gun slit and began firing as fast as he could.

Inside the log walls, the wound and fury was enormous. The lead balls were slamming into the logs, whining off of cook pots, and terrorizing those who had thought themselves to be safe and secure. A thug called Dutch screamed as a ball took him in the side. An Arkansas man known only as Wilbur began choking on his own blood as a ball took him in the throat and put him down. The flashes from Preacher's multi-barreled pistols blinded those inside the logs and before their eyes could once more adjust to the darkness, Preacher was gone, running through the night.

The men rushed outside of the stockade. But the darkness of the night and the now heavy-driving rain obscured the fast fading form of Preacher.

About two hundred yards from camp, knowing he could not be seen, Preacher stopped and turned around. "I am Preacher!" he shouted. "The Indians call me Ghost Walker. White Wolf. Man Who Kills Silently. None of you will ever leave the mountains. You will all die. I have given you all the chances you will ever get. Make your peace with God. Some of you will die tomorrow."

"I was under the impression the man was a near cretin. Illiterate," Sir Elmore said. "That was a very eloquent little speech."

"Now how does he propose to carry out that rather ominous threat?" Rudi Kuhlmann asked, stuffing snuff up his nose. He sneezed explosively several times in a row and the bounty hunters standing close to him, their nerves stretched as tight as a guitar string, almost shot him.

Dark Hand was the only one who had not rushed outside. The Pawnee squatted near the gate to the stockade. "Preacher means what he says," Dark Hand said. "It is my suggestion that we all leave these mountains at first light and do not look back."

"Yeller," Tatman said, his arm in a sling, easing the pressure on his wounded shoulder. "I knowed you was yeller all the time."

Dark Hand did not reply. He had moved back from the door and was packing up a few belongings. He had made up his mind. He was going to look up Preacher and make his peace with the man. If Preacher would accept it, the two would never again make war against the other.

The Pawnee was very swift in packing. He was through before the others even thought about reentering the stockade. Dark Hand was not missed the next morning.

14

Preacher saw Dark Hand coming from a long way off. He got out his spy glass and scanned the country behind the Pawnee. No one else in sight. Then he noticed that Dark Hand was riding with his rifle in a boot and his pistols nowhere in sight. His bow was in his quiver, and not strung. He was riding with his big knife sheathed and hung by a cord around his neck.

"Wants to palaver," Preacher muttered. "That's odd."

Preacher stepped out from his camp into a clearing on the slope and waved his arms. He watched Dark Hand straighten on the horse's back, and then angle toward him. About fifteen minutes later, Dark Hand was reined up in front of him.

"Light and set, Pawnee," Preacher said. "I got coffee and bacon and bread if you feel like partakin' of my grub."

"You would feed me?"

"Sure."

"I accept. But watch closely my backtrail. There are a few in that bunch of blood-hungry fools who have the ability to track well."

"You left 'em?"

"Forever and ever." He dismounted and led his horse into Preacher's camp, picketing the animal with Preacher's stock. He squatted down by the fire and took the plate of food and the cup of coffee Preacher handed him. "It is one thing to make war against men. But not women and babies. I took no part in that."

"I didn't see your moccasin tracks nowheres about there. I knew that Wind Chaser had befriended you a time or two. Eat. We'll talk when you're done."

When the Pawnee had finished, Preacher poured them both more coffee and they smoked. Dark Hand said, "It is one thing to hate when there is a reason for it. But my hatred for you had become unreasonable. My brother attacked you. You did not attack him. I attacked him. I attacked you, twice. You did not attack me. My hatred was stupid." He abruptly stuck out his hand and Preacher smiled and shook it. Dark Hand said, "From this day forward, we do not make war against the other. Is that agreeable with you?"

"Sure is."

"Good. Now I will tell you something. I was scouting the other day . . . two days ago . . . and came up on two Cheyenne. They were young men, and I have seen enough blood. I made peace and they did the same. We ate and smoked and talked. They had spoken with some Kiowa a few days before who had spoken with some Delaware who had just left the trading post on the river. A very large group of white men was there. They had just come in from the East. Far to the east. The Delaware told the Kiowa and the Kiowa told the Cheyenne and the Cheyenne told me that the men were buying huge amounts of supplies and they were all well armed. They also were a loud talking bunch and smelled bad. They did not bathe and the odor from their bodies was awful, the Cheyenne told me what the Delaware had told the Kiowa who told the Cheyenne. I believe these men will join Andy Price who should be at the fort by this time buying supplies for Bones and his people and the arrogant men with them.

"Preacher, my heart is very sad about the little sick boy who was killed. I saw where you buried him with his horse. That was a good thing you did. He will need his pony to cross to the other side of life. But his grave will not fool the Utes when they return to find out what happened to Wind Chaser. And they will return, Preacher. After the hunt. Listen, I have what I think is a fine idea. Why don't you ride to the strong Ute camp and tell them what happened? They will see to the fates of those who did that terrible thing."

"No," Preacher said with a shake of his head. "I can't have Utes killin' ever' white man who comes along. We're not all bad, Dark Hand."

Dark Hand grunted at that and Preacher understood and had to smile. The white man had not given the Indians many reasons to trust them. But the Indians hadn't exactly welcomed the white man with open arms, either. Preacher understood that there was right and wrong on both sides. There always is when two strong cultures clash. What was considered barbarism and savagery to the white man was an accepted way of life to the Indian.

"Well, if Bones has more men comin' out to join him, I reckon I best get on with whittlin' down the odds."

"I would say that you have made a fine start toward that," Dark Hand said, a distinct dryness in his tone.

The eyes of the Indian and the white man met, and both of them chuckled. Most whites felt the Indian did not have a sense of humor. They were wrong. The Indian had a fine sense of humor. They just didn't show it very often around whites.

Dark Hand finished his coffee and stood up. "I go now, White Wolf. You will not see me again while this silly war is going on. Months from now, should we meet again, remember that you will always be welcome in my camp."

"And you in mine, Dark Hand," Preacher said, extending his hand.

Dark Hand shook the hand and walked to his horse. He was gone seconds later.

Preacher stood for a moment. "First Pawnee I ever really made friends with," he muttered. "Damned if he didn't turn out to be a right nice feller."

"Tracks lead off yonder," Van Eaton pointed, reporting back to Bones. "I betcha that Injun went straight to Preacher."

"No matter," Bones said. "I'm glad to be shut of him. I never did really trust him."

The teams of men were packed up and ready to mount. The royalty had been separated at Bones's orders. He wanted to keep as many alive as possible. He wanted his money, and the gentry were no good to him dead.

"Let's go," Bones said, swinging up into the saddle. "We'll meet an hour before sunset."

One team was to head straight for the new camp and get it ready. The other teams were to concentrate on tracking and finding Preacher. They didn't know that Preacher was, at that very moment, making the search very easy for them.

"Got him!" Spanish called out. "He ain't near'bouts as smart as he thinks he is. Look here."

The team members, including Robert Tassin, gathered around. The tracks were plain as could be. They didn't know that Preacher had been laying down sign all morning, trying to get them to see the tracks. For this sign, Preacher had jumped up and down in one place, broke off a branch, and built a small fire. He figured if this didn't work he'd have to find him a white rag and stand out in the open and wave it at the men.

"We've got him!" the French aristocrat said excitedly.

"Let's press on, men." He spurred his horse and entered the timber.

"No, you don't," Spanish muttered. "Preacher is mine." He jumped ahead of Tassin and unknowingly and certainly unwillingly, saved the Frenchman's life.

Preacher's rifle boomed and Spanish went down, leaving the saddle like a sack of potatoes as the big heavy caliber ball blew a hole in his chest and shattered his heart.

"Merde!" Tassin said, jumping from the saddle and taking cover behind a tree. He looked all around him, but could see nothing. He looked over at Spanish. The man lay motionless on the ground, his shirt front bloody.

Tassin lifted his rifle, looking at where he'd seen a faint puff of smoke. If the Frenchman had been the man-hunter he thought he was, he should have guessed that as soon as Preacher fired, the mountain man would shift locations. The only thing that saved Tassin's life was the turning of his head as one of the team, a large, big-bellied, rather obnoxious fellow called Percy, stepped on a branch and it popped. Preacher's rifle crashed and the ball blew bits of bark into the side of Tassin's face, stinging and bringing blood. Had he not turned at the sound of the branch breaking, the ball would have blown a huge hole in his head.

Badly frightened, Tassin bellied down on the ground, presenting as small a target as possible. This was just not turning out well at all.

"You boys made a bad mistake," Preacher called from the brush. "You best say your prayers."

"Hell with you, Preacher," a thug called Hubert yelled. "We got you now."

"Then come get me," Preacher challenged. A second later he changed position, moving several yards to his left. Rifles boomed, the balls whizzing harmlessly to the position where Preacher had been.

"Oohhh!" Preacher moaned, trying to keep from laughing. "You got me, boys. Oohh, it hurts somethin' turrible.

Damn your eyes, you've kilt me. Tell my poor ol' ma good-bye for me, boys." He managed to suppress a giggle.

Hubert gave out a loud shout of triumph and lurched to his feet.

"Get down, you fool!" Percy hollered.

Hubert suddenly realized he had made a perfectly horrible error in judgment. He froze in wild-eyed and openmouthed fear and panic. Preacher dusted him, shooting him from side to side, the ball making a huge bloody hole as it exited. Hubert fell dead to the ground.

"Get out of here!" Percy yelled. "Work your way back. He's got us cold in this brush."

Paul Guy made a jump for his horse and Preacher's rifle boomed again. Paul's leg buckled under him and collapsed to the ground, crying out in pain.

Preacher slipped quietly away. He'd dealt this bunch enough misery. He figured rightly that all the shooting would bring the others at a gallop. Preacher was a brave man, but no fool. He'd fight this group of man-hunters on his own terms, not on theirs. He slipped over the crest of the rise and jumped into the saddle. He had him a brand new little hidey-hole all picked out.

Bones took one look at the sign that Spanish had found and snorted in disgust. He looked at what was left of this team of men. "He suckered you all."

"Whatever in the world do you mean by that remark?" Jon Tassin shouted, holding a bloody handkerchief to his face. "I demand an answer!"

"Tricked you, that's what I mean. Preacher deliberately left this sign, hopin' you'd be dumb enough to follow it. And Spanish was dumb enough." He savagely kicked the dead Spanish in the side. "Stupid, igit!"

"Let's proceed with the hunt!" Willy Steinwinder shouted. "After him, men!"

"Just hold on, hold on!" Van Eaton said. "That's what

Preacher wants you to do. He's layin' up in the brush or behind some rocks just over that hill yonder. Now just settle down."

"Van Eaton's right," Bones said. "We got to sit down in a safe place and plan this out, carefully."

"I'm for that," Percy said. "I've helped hunt down a lot of men. But I ain't never seen no human bein' like this here Preacher person."

"Yeah," Paul Guy said through clenched teeth, as he wrapped a dirty rag around the wound in his leg. Preacher is more like a wild animal that somehow got as smart as us."

A huge ignorant lout called Doyle said, "Preacher said last night that some of us would die this day." He looked nervously around him. "He was shore right."

Bones sensed the moment was getting spooky to some of the men. Down on the flats, he could see the rest of his party riding toward the ridges. He already had too many of the royalty gathered here. "Evans, you take Doyle and head off those other men. Preacher would love to catch us all bunched up near the timber."

Doyle and Evans didn't need a second invitation to leave this scene of blood and death.

Bones took off his hat and scratched his licy head. "We got to start actin' like an army and thinkin' like generals."

"I am a general!" Rudi Kuhlmann said.

"I thought you was a prince?" a man called Falcon said.

"I am. I'm a general too."

"Me, too," Wilhelm Zaunbelcher said. "And so is he." He pointed to Juan Zapata. "Well, why don't you start generalin', then?" a man called Flores asked.

Sir Elmore Jerrold-Taylor smiled. "We thought you would never ask. Catching this Preacher person is easy. We'll show you how."

"Oh, yeah!" Bones said beligerently.

"Oh, yes," Tassin said. "Just watch and learn."

15

"That's odd," Preacher muttered, watching the man-hunters through his spy-glass. They were all packed up and riding away. He watched the riders until they were no more than tiny dark dots in the distance. He collapsed his glass and tucked it away, then squatted down and gave this some thought.

"Them ol' boys want me to think they're pullin' out, when I know damn well they ain't doin' no such thing. Now, why would they want me to think that? Ummm." After a moment, he smiled and said, "So's I'd follow them and ride right into an ambush, that's why. Well, I ain't a-gonna do that."

Preacher thought a while longer and then began to break camp. He figured they would take the same route back that they took comin' in, so he'd just make a wide circle and see if he could get a few miles ahead of them. He'd be right there to greet them.

"This ain't a-gonna work," Flores grumbled. "We ain't seen hide nor hair of Preacher."

Bones and party, now led by the royalty, were on their third day of travel, and the thought was creeping into the minds of many of the man-hunters that

Preacher had not taken the bait and was not going to fall into the trap.

By late afternoon of the third day, the man-hunters had traveled about sixty miles from their last contact with Preacher. They had not seen one living human being. They did not know that most of the Indians were far to the north, hunting buffalo.

"Yeah," Bobby Allen said. "I'm a-gettin' hongry. I hope Mack finds us a good spot to camp pretty damn quick."

"Right purty," Mack Cornay said, looking at the coolness provided by the shady trees that lined both banks of the little creek. "This'll do just fine."

The man-hunters were in a long and narrow flat, running north to south between the snow-covered peaks of the Rockies. Cornay waited until the main body was in sight, and then began waving his hat. Rudi Kuhlmann, riding point, spotted the signal and angled the column off toward Mack and the creek.

Rudi could not understand why one minute he could see Mack, and the next instant he could not. He did not know the terrain ahead of him; did not know it was very deceptive, with ravines and gullies and wallows on the east side of the creek. And Mack Cornay was in no condition to be aware of anything. Preacher had thrown a fist-sized rock at the man, the stone slamming into the back of Mack's head and knocking him from the saddle. Mack lay on the ground, unconscious. Preacher had taken the man's weapons, his powder horn, and his shot, and vanished into the bog across the creek.

A knowledgeable man can traverse a bog, but he'd better know where to put each step, for there was mud there that could take a man down to his waist, or beyond. The bog ran for about fifteen hundred yards one way and was about half a mile across. Indians avoided the place, knowing it could be a death trap for both man and horse. Venomous snakes lay above the shallow water on clumps of grass, sunning themselves.

Rudi rode up to the creek and sat his saddle for a moment, looking down at Mack, thinking the man certainly chose a strange time and place to take a nap. Preacher's rifle barked and Rudi was slammed from the saddle, the ball tearing through his shoulder and almost blinding him with white-hot pain. He hit the ground on his belly, knocking the wind from him.

Bones and Van Eaton and a few of the others immediately left the saddle and bellied down in the knee-high grass. A few of the less-experienced, including all the royalty, raced their horses toward the wounded Rudi.

Preacher fired again from the bog and a man called Scott did a back-flip out of the saddle, dead before it impacted with the earth.

Wilhelm Zaunbelcher, shouting oaths in a guttural tongue, threw caution to the wind and galloped his horse through the creek. But the horse had more sense than the Baron. He refused to enter the bog, stopping quite abruptly. Zaunbelcher went flying out of the saddle and landed in the mud at the edge of the bog. He sank about six inches. Zaunbelcher thought he was in quicksand— he wasn't, but there was quicksand in the bog—and immediately panicked. He began screaming in fright, kicking his feet and waving his arms and flinging mud in all directions.

Sir Elmore Jerrold-Taylor drew a short saber from a saddle scabbard and shouted, "Charge, men!"

"Charge?" Bones said.

"I think that's what he said," Van Eaton replied.

This was the day of horse-sense. Elmore's horse refused to step into the bog, putting on the brakes and sliding to a halt. Like Baron Zaunbelcher, Sir Jerrold-Taylor left the saddle and went flying through the air, slowly turning as he flew. A Red-breasted Nuthatch flew past the Englishman and gave the huge creature a very strange look.

"Yna, Yna, Yna," the Nuthatch chirped, and flew on to

tell his mate there was something very weird going on in the bog.

"My word!" Sir Elmore said. He landed right next to the Baron and when he impacted with the mud, the point of his saber jabbed Zaunbelcher in the ass and the Prussian came roaring up out of the bog, looking and sounding very much like some terrible monster from a swamp.

Benny Atkins realized he had made a bad mistake by following the nutty foreigners up to the creek and had jumped from the saddle, heading for the trees. Preacher's rifle sang its deadly song and Benny took a ball in his hip, turning him around in a haze of pain before he collapsed to the ground. He tumbled into the creek.

Preacher let himself sink into the mud until only the top of his head and his nose remained above the surface. He was behind a clump of grass and could not be seen. His one rather fervent wish was that there was not a big rattler sunning on the clump. The sun would be cycling soon, shadowing the valley in darkness. Preacher would mud swim out of the bog under cover of night. He rather hoped that some of the men would step into the bog, but he knew that was not very likely.

Sir Elmore reached up and jerked Zaunbelcher back into the mud and safe from rifle shot and they lay quite still for several long moments before they began cautiously working their way back to solid ground.

"Oh, drat! I lost my saber," Sir Elmore said.

"Excellent," Zaunbelcher said. "I hope you never find the damn thing."

The rest of the man-hunters waited until shadows began casting long pockets of darkness before they moved. And even then, they did so very cautiously. None of them had been able to spot Preacher and they did not know whether he was still out there in the bog.

"Creep out of that swamp or whatever it is careful-like," Bones called to Elmore and Wilhelm. "Stay low leadin' your horses back here. We got to get gone." To

Van Eaton he said, "Have the boys start draggin' the wounded out."

"Right."

"What about Scott?" a man called.

"Leave him," Bones said, cutting his eyes to Van Eaton.

"You boys get gone," Van Eaton said. "I'll see to Scott."

Preacher heard the calling back and forth and let the men leave, noting which direction they took. Just in case they were trying to set up a trap—something he doubted—Preacher remained in the bog for an hour after they'd left. Then, at full dark he carefully worked his way out of the bog and back to his camp, about three miles away. He washed himself at a tiny run-off and brushed the now dried mud off his buckskins. Something was nagging at his mind but he could not bring it to full light. He shook his head and gave it up. It would come to him.

He cooked his supper and boiled his coffee over a tiny fire. As he ate and drank, he tried to figure out what was nagging at him. He knew it was something he'd seen, and seen that day, but whatever it had been remained elusive to him. He laid out his blankets and with rifle and pistols fully charged and close to hand, Preacher sighed and went to sleep.

He awakened with a grunt of anger about an hour later. Scalps. That's what he'd seen. There had been scalps tied to the manes of the horses of them silly foreigners.

And one of them had been Eddie's.

16

"So much for the generals leadin' us anywhere," Van Eaton groused that evening. "I told you it was a bad idea."

Van Eaton shrugged that off. He already knew it was a bad idea. He glanced around at his shot-up men. They were a pitiful-looking bunch and a lot of the enthusiasm for the hunt had been knocked out of them by Preacher. Bones had never before encountered such a man as Preacher. What Bones didn't know about any number of things would fill volumes, but just about any experienced mountain man would have behaved pretty much the same as Preacher as far as fighting ability went. Most mountain men would have been content to just run Bones and his so-called man-hunters out of the mountains, and then they would have gone on about their business. But there were a few who would have done just exactly what Preacher was doing.

"We got to find us a hidey-hole and stay low 'til Andy gets back," Bones said. "The men just ain't in any shape to go much farther and they damn shore ain't in any shape to mix it up with Preacher."

"You mighty right about that," Van Eaton said.

Up until almost that very moment, if Bones and his

bunch had really wanted to give up the hunt, Preacher just might have let them go. But not after seeing Eddie's scalp tied onto the mane of that horse. That snapped it with Preacher.

Preacher lay for a long time in his blankets after the nagging thought had awakened him in all its horror. Bones and them knew that was a white boy they dragged and scalped . . . or scalped and then dragged, the dread thought came to him.

The dirty scum! He didn't give a damn if those that went for supplies came back with a hundred extra men. Anybody who joined up with Bones Gibson, Van Eaton, and them silly and savage foreigners was dead meat.

The longer he thought about that previous afternoon, the more scalps he could identify. Wind Chaser had a streak of gray right down the center of his hair. Preacher had seen that one tied to the mane of Van Eaton's horse. Wind Chaser's woman's hair had a sort of auburn tint to it, since she was the daughter of a mountain man. Bones had been displaying that one. And their kids had taken after their mother, with lighter hair than the others in the tribe. Preacher had seen their scalps, too.

Preacher looked up at the starry heavens. This high up, the stars seemed so close he could almost reach out and touch them. But Preacher was in no mood to appreciate the beauty of the night. He had something else on his mind.

Killing.

Preacher picked up their trail about mid-morning. And for a moment, it confused him. The trail led south and east. Dismounting, he studied the tracks. There was still the very faint outline of older tracks, and he recognized those as being the men who had left for supplies and returning from Bent's Fort. Horses and mules. Then he realized what Bones was doing. His bunch was pretty well shot up and hurtin'. So he was tryin' to link up with his other party, hopin' they was bringin' reinforcements. Preacher figured that when they joined up, they'd hole up for a time, and then come after him with a vengeance.

"Suits me," Preacher muttered. "Just fine. The more the merrier, Bones. Bones. Somebody shore named you right. 'Cause your bones is gonna bleach white as snow in these mountains, you kid-killer. I swear it."

Preacher didn't follow Bones and the others. He turned around and headed back north. He wanted time to kill a couple of deer, make some pemmican, smoke and jerk some meat, and just lounge around and eat some venison steaks. He'd found him some wild peas and prairie turnips and wild taters. Mix all that up with some pieces of venison and toss in some rose hips and sage and a body had him a lip-smackin' good stew. Preacher got all hungry around the mouth just thinkin' 'bout it.

The weary and bloodied bunch linked up with Andy Price and the gang of men he was bringing back from Bent's Fort. Bones eyeballed the bunch and figured about half of them would turn back once they took a good look at the Rockies. Fifteen or twenty more would pull out after the first sneak attack by Preacher. Those that stayed would be lean and mean and hard and tough.

"They's another bunch comin' up behind me," Andy told him. "I tole 'em to head on back. This ain't no game. But they're still comin' on. They're city toughs. Some of them come all the way from New York and Philly and Boston and them places. I don't understand how they've made it this far. They don't appear to know north from south. And you never in your borned days seen so many different kinds of guns. One of 'em's got two pistols. Each has a cylinder that holds six rounds and revolves. He called them revolvers. Strange lookin' things."

"They're what?" Van Eaton asked.

"Revolvers," Andy repeated.*

"Damned if I know," Andy said. "But I don't think they'll ever catch on."

"How do they work?" George Winters asked.

"Did you hear anything about the hunt back at the fort?" Bones asked.

"Oh, yeah. That's about all that folks talk about. And that's strange, too."

"How so?" Van Eaton asked.

"Well, they was a goodly number of mountain men there, but none of them seemed to be a bit concerned about Preacher. Near'bouts all of them said the joke was gonna be on us. One big mountain man told a bully boy from New York—let's see, how did he put it? Oh, yeah. "'Ye'll nar leave them mountains if'n ye go yonder with a blood lust for Preacher. Ye been warned by us who knows White Wolf. Heed our words.'"

"How about Jim Slattery and them writers who left us?"

"They never showed up, Bones. Nobody there has seen hide nor hair of them."

"Injuns got them," Van Eaton opined.

Bones was thoughtful for a moment. "That mob comin' up behind us just might be what we need. Preacher will be so busy tryin' to figure out what to do, mayhaps some of us can slip off durin' the confusion and kill him."

*A Nichols and Childs belt model revolver. About .34 caliber. Only a very few were made. Manufactured about 1838 or '39. The cylinder revolved using a mechanical device called a pawl that was attached to the hammer.

Sir Elmore had walked up. He said, "Say now. That is an excellent thought. By jove, I believe you've quite probably stumbled upon the solution to our problem." He patted Bones on the shoulder. "A very admirable bit of ruminative prowess, my good man." He smiled and walked off to share the good news with his fellow adventurers.

Andy shook his head. "I was hopin' them fellers would learn to talk right whilst I was gone."

"No such luck," Van Eaton said. "They's even worser than before."

Preacher spent his time relocating his caches of supplies, jerking a goodly amount of meat, resting and eating and getting ready for war. He was completely unaware of the second band of men hunting him. While Bones was waiting for the wounds of his men to heal, and Preacher was preparing himself mentally to dispose of the entire worthless, no-count, disagreeable lot of them, summer came to the mountains in full bloom. The valleys were pockets of color in all hues.

Utes had returned from a very successful hunt and were puzzled by the disappearance of Wind Chaser and his small band. Warriors from Wind Chaser's village were frantically and desperately searching for their families. But so far they failed to search the little valley where Eddie and Wind Chaser and his band had met their deaths. But they would. The wilderness was vast, and it was impossible to look everywhere. The warriors from Wind Chaser's village mistakenly headed north and west in their search, and the little valley, now covered with summer's blossoms, remained untouched, for the time being.

Had they run into Dark Hand, he could have and would have told them what had happened, but Dark Hand had traveled north and east, to rejoin his own people, who were camped over in the unorganized territory that lay just south of the Missouri River.

Sir Elmore had found his saber but wisely kept it sheathed and out of sight because Baron Zaunbelcher had threatened to break it if Elmore ever drew it again.

Most of Bones's men were healed up enough to ride, and those that weren't properly healed could either suffer the discomfort and ride, or stay and be left behind. All chose to ride.

The second band of man-hunters was just about the most disreputable looking bunch of ne'er-do-wells that Bones had ever seen. And when the likes of Bones Gibson thought somebody was trash, they couldn't get much lower if they crawled under a snake's belly.

Bones had ridden back to eyeball the second bunch, to see if there might be any men in there that he could use. He found a few possibilities, but for the moment, would stay with what he had. He was back up to strength, just over forty men.

This bunch, he thought sourly, would not last a week in the mountains, not if just one of them made a hostile move against Preacher. Preacher would turn on them like a wild animal and run them all back to the Mississippi. If they made it that far. Bones wisely decided to distance himself from this mangy looking pack of so-called man-hunters.

"You there!" the gruff shout stopped Bones as he was just riding off.

Bones turned to stare at the burly lout who was striding toward him. "What do you want?"

"Where's this here murderer called Preacher?"

Bones laughed at him. "You want him, you find him."

"I'm Lige Watson." The man acted as though that was supposed to mean something.

"So?"

"I'm the toughest man in all of Pennsylvania."

Bones laughed at him. "Then you best head on back to Pennsylvania, Watson. 'Cause out here, you're nothin'."

"We'll see about that."

"Not for very long, you won't." Bones left it at that and rode away.

"Holy jumpin' elephants!" Preacher said, peering through his spy-glass. He took a second look just to make certain his eyes weren't deceiving him. They weren't.

It looked to him like about forty or so in the first bunch, and that would be Bones's men, for he could pick out Bones in the lead. Another forty or so in the second bunch, layin' back about a mile behind Bones.

"I shore ain't gettin' to be a right popular feller," Preacher muttered, putting away his glass. "Damned if that ain't a regular army down yonder. Forty in one bunch and forty in the other. They gonna be fallin' all over one another 'fore this is through." He smiled a wicked curving of his lips. "I'm gonna have me some fun come the night."

What was fun to Preacher could be downright unsettling to others . . . and sometimes lethal.

The floor of the long narrow valley was dotted with campfires, with a dark space about a mile in length between the two camps of man-hunters. Lige Watson, the self-appointed leader of the second bunch, walked through the camp, inspecting "his men," as he liked to call them.

To Lige, they looked like a very formidable army. In reality, they were about as sloppy a rag-tag bunch of losers as had ever gathered anywhere. The group was made up of those types of people who are constantly out for an easy dollar, who expect the world to give them a handout, who always blame others for their problems, who could never keep a job because the boss "picked on them." Among the second group were strong-arm boys, thieves, hustlers, pimps, forgers, murderers, rapists, and every other kind of no-good anybody would care to name.

Really, the social and moral difference between Bones's group and Lige's bunch was minuscule. There wasn't a man in either group worth the gunpowder it would take to blow his brains out.

"Lookin' rale good," Lige said to his friend, Fred Lasalle, after completing his walk-through of the camp. "I'd put these boys up aginst just about any group twicest our size."

"Did you git to talk to any of them royal highnesses?" Fred asked.

"Well, sort of. I spoke to one and he tole me that in all his years he had never stood so clost to such an odorous cretinous moronic specimen of foul humanity."

Fred blinked. "Well, you done good, then, din you?"

"I don't rightly know. I reckon so."

"What do all them words mean, Lige?" Derby Peel asked.

"Means we all right, I guess."

"Thought so."

With the exception of the rendezvous of the mountain men, which had now ceased to be, never had such a large gathering of white men occurred in the Rockies. The stench of unwashed bodies could be smelled for hundreds of yards. No self-respecting Indian would get within an arrow's range of such a group. The smell alone probably contributed to saving their lives from Indians looking for a scalp.

"Whew!" Preacher muttered, as he drew closer to the encampment. His nose wrinkled at the stench of unwashed bodies. A buzzard would have a tough time competing with this bunch, he thought.

Preacher lay on his belly in the tall grass less than fifty

yards from Lige's camp and looked over the scene that unfolded before him. It was only slightly less than incredible. The fools had fires blazin' that were big enough to roast a whole buffalo. The big ugly bully-lookin' man someone had called Lige was probably the leader of this skunk-pack, Preacher reckoned. He looked like a man who had a real high opinion of himself the way he strutted around. Preacher took an immediate dislike to him. He'd seen men like Lige before, men who'd come to the mountains and tried to fit in with other trappers. They had not lasted long. Mountain men were hard to impress.

"Well, boys," Lige said to his friends who'd come west with him. "Tomorrow we start huntin' down this Preacher person. I don't figure on it takin' no more than a week. Prob'ly less than that."

Preacher smiled and moved closer until he reached a pocket of darkness. Then he stood up and slipped into the camp. Many of the men were dressed in buckskins so no one paid any attention to Preacher as he walked through the camp and straight up to Lige.

"Howdy," Preacher said. "I got a message from Bones if you be Lige."

"I'm Lige. What's on your mind?"

"Well, Mister Lige, don't get mad at me, I'm just deliverin' the message. Bones said for your men to bring your cups and come on over. They's whiskey a-plenty and food for all. Says both our bunches had best get to know one another. But he said for me to tell you to keep your butt out of his camp. Says if you show up he'll stomp your gizzard out."

"He said *what?*" Lige hollered.

"Oh, he said a lot, Bones did. But I dasn't repeat most of it. It was right insultin' and personal."

"You tell me, mister!" Lige growled the words, as a large crowd gathered around.

"Well, now, don't get mad at me," Preacher said.

"I'm not gonna get mad at you. You just tell me what Bones said."

"Well, he said you smelled worser than a skunk and prob'ly had about as much sense as a jackass. And he called your mamma some real turrible names, he did. I just won't repeat them slurs aginst a good woman. I just won't do it. God might strike me dead."

Lige was so mad he was hopping up and down.

"If you don't mind," Preacher said. "I'd like to leave that bunch of name-callers over yonder and join up with you, Mister Lige. I think Bones is settin' up an ambush for your boys. That's what it looks like to me. Besides that, I just cain't abide a man who'll call another man he don't even know a low-down, no-good, buzzard-puke-breath, dirty son of a bitch like Bones said you was."

Lige's eyes bugged out and his face turned red. His ears wriggled and his adam's apple bobbed up and down. "You stay here," he said to Preacher, finally finding his voice. "I think you a good man. Let's ride, boys. We got a nest of snakes to clean out."

Within seconds, the camp was deserted. Preacher grinned and began wandering through the camp, picking up what supplies he felt he might need. "Gonna be real interestin' over at Bones's camp in about five minutes. Real interestin'." Chuckling, Preacher faded into the night.

17

"Riders comin', Bones," a guard called. "Looks like that new bunch."

"Now, what you reckon that pack of ninnies wants?" Van Eaton asked.

"They certainly are coming in quite a rush," Baron Zaunbelcher remarked.

Lige and his group rode right through the camp, knocking over pots and scattering bedrolls and sending men scrambling to get out of the way.

"What the hell do you think you're doin', you half-wit?" Bones yelled to Lige.

Lige and his men jumped off their horses. "I got your message, you big mouth no-count!" Lige yelled, marching up to Bones. "And this is my reply." Lige rared back and flattened Bones with a right to the mouth.

Lige's men jumped at Bones's men and the fight was on.

Preacher could hear the shouts and yelling and cussing more than a mile away. Carrying several huge sacks filled with powder horns, food, weapons, candles, matches, and what-have-you, Preacher walked away toward the high-up country. He would have taken several blankets, but they all had fleas hopping around on them.

Bones jumped up and popped Lige right on his big snoot. The blood and the snot flew and Lige's boots flew out from under him and he landed on his butt.

Bob Jones had tied up with Mack Cornay and the two men were flailing away at one another. Derby Peel had squared off against Van Eaton and the men were exchanging blows, each blow bringing a grunt of pain and the splattering of blood. Fred Lasalle looked around for somebody to hit and his eyes touched on Sir Elmore Jerrold-Taylor, standing beside a fancy wall tent. Fred walked over to the clean shaven and neatly dressed Englishman and without a word being said, slugged him right on the nose. Elmore hollered and grabbed at his busted beak. He drew his hands away and looked at the blood. "I've been wounded!" he yelled.

Jon Louviere jumped on Fred's back and rode him to the earth while Stan Law busted Baron Wilhelm Zaunbelcher in the mouth. With a roar, the Prussian drew back one big fist and sent Stan rolling through the dirt, then turned and kicked Fred Lasalle hard in the belly with a polished boot. That put Fred out for the duration.

Will Herdman jumped on Andy Price and went to pokin' and gougin' and kickin' and bitin' until Andy threw him off and began stomping on him. That went on until Cantry, a good friend of Will's, ran over and hit Andy on the head with a club. Andy's eyes rolled back, he hit the ground, and he didn't wake up for an hour. Will, battered and bloody, said to hell with it all and stretched out beside Andy.

The men in the camp, with the exception of the nobility, who quickly retired to their tents and tied the flaps closed, fought until they were exhausted. Almost to the man, they fell down to the ground and lay there, chests heaving.

Finally, Bones, lying flat on his back in the grass, managed to gasp out to Lige, "What in the hell brought on all this, you igit?"

"Don't you be callin' me no igit, you low-life," said Lige, who was also stretched out on the cool grass. "And you know what brung it on."

"I don't neither!"

"Do too!"

"Don't!"

"Does!"

"I do not!"

"You think about it. You know!"

"I don't know! Why the hell do you think I'm askin'?"

Even though he wasn't a very smart man, that managed to get through to Lige. He thought about it for a moment. "You sent a feller over to our camp to see me and he said you said a lot of bad things about me."

"I never sent no feller over to see you! And I ain't said no bad things about you. I *thought* a bunch of bad things, but I never said 'em aloud."

Lige ruminated on that for another moment. He raised his bloody head and looked around. "Say, where is that feller anyways?"

"Back yonder at our camp, I reckon," Sutton said, holding a rag to his bloody mouth.

A tiny spark of suspicion entered Bones's head. He raised up on one elbow, the eye that wasn't blackening and closing because of a right cross from Lige's fist narrowed. "What did this here feller look like, Lige?"

"Wal, he were dressed in buckskins. Sorta tall and you could tell he was muscled up right good. He were clean shaven 'ceptin' for a moustache. And he moved real quiet like. Come to think of it, and I just thought of it, he had the coldest, meanest eyes I ever did see."

Bones flopped back on the ground. "You igit! That there was *Preacher!*"

"*Preacher?*" Lige hollered. "You mean the man we're a-huntin' come a-struttin' and a-sashshaying bold as brass right up into the big fat middle of our camp and tole me them lies?"

"Yeah." Bones heaved himself up to a sitting position. "Now you might git some idea of the type of man we're huntin'."

"Nervy ol' boy, ain't he?" Lige muttered around a swollen mouth.

"You could say that," Bones replied.

When Lige and company returned to camp, Lige found a note written on a scrap of paper and stuck on a tree limb. He laboriously read the missive.

"What do it say, Lige?" Fred Lasalle asked, peering over Lige's shoulder.

"It says, 'Git out of these mountins. I won't warn you agin. This here is yore only warnin'. Preacher?"

"The man must think he owns these here mountains!" Hugh Fuller said.

"Yeah!" a man called Billy said. "To hell with him."

A huge hulking monster of a man whose hands extended past his knees, giving him a distinct apelike appearance, said, "I don't like this feller Preacher. I'm a-gonna tear his arms out when I find him and beat him to death with 'em."

"Way to go, Lucas," a much smaller man, only about five feet tall yelled. "That'll be fun to watch."

Lucas grinned at the man. What teeth had not rotted out were green and his breath could cause a buzzard to faint. "You and me, Willie. We'll catch this Preacher and be rich."

"All right, boys," Lige hollered. "Gather round. Come on, come on. I got things to say." When the camp had quieted down and the men gathered in a circle, Lige said, "At first light we start huntin' this murderin' no-count. And we'uns is gonna be workin' side by side with them ol' boys over yonder in the other camp. I think . . ."

"Hey!" a man hollered. "My powder horn's gone. Jeff, didn't you lay out a side of bacon to slice?"

"Yeah. Why?"

"Well, it's gone too."

The men all ran to their bedrolls and blankets and

tents. Soon, many of the men were cussing and stomping around.

"Preacher stole all the stuff," Bob Jones said. "He took enough powder to blow up half these mountains."

Preacher wasn't at all interested in blowing up the mountains. He had others things in mind.

The Cheyenne war chief called Bear Killer sat on his horse and looked down at the huge body of men in the valley below. He, along with representatives from the Ute, Arapaho, Kiowa-Apache, and the Southern Comanches were all traveling east, to make peace with each other. The location was about seventy-five miles east of Bent's Fort. The gathering of various tribes and the making of peace between them had been the idea of High Backed Wolf, a Cheyenne chief, a very famous warrior, and a man known for his diplomatic skills. He felt it was foolish to fight amongst themselves. After the historic meeting, which history only skims over very lightly, those tribes never again made war against the other.

Bear Killer looked down at the white men and shook his head. "Preacher cannot fight so many men and win. Perhaps we should wait until darkness comes and slip into the camp of the white men and help Preacher," he said to one of his warriors.

But the warrior shook his head. "No. Standing Bull said that Tall Man of the Arapaho told him that Preacher wants no help. This is a personal matter."

"Ummm. Yes. I remember. Preacher is indeed a brave warrior. I hope we never have to fight him again."

"Little Eagle told Stands Alone that the white men down there smell terrible. They do not wash their bodies and are very loud and vulgar. They kill animals and birds and leave them to rot on the ground. They do not dig proper places to dispose of their waste. They are not good people. They are wasteful and ignorant."

"I hope Preacher kills them all. If there are any left upon our return, we shall give Preacher some help in ridding our land of these worthless men. Without his knowledge, of course."

The Indians waited until the whites had passed and then rode on to their historical meeting on the Arkansas.

Several miles away, watching from near the timber line, Preacher could just make out the long double line of riders as they headed north. Preacher mounted up and headed south, staying in the timber far above the valley floor, no more than a shadow as he worked his way along.

He saw Bear Killer and his warriors and they saw him. The men passed within a few hundred yards of each other, lifted right hands, palms out, and rode on without speaking. Preacher picketed Thunder near water and began working his way toward the sprawling camp of the man-hunters. Using his spy glass, Preacher studied the camp. It was just about like he'd figured. Bones had left no guards behind. Only the cooks and servants were there, and Preacher wanted them gone. So far they had taken no part in the man-hunt, and Preacher held no animosity toward them. He spent the better part of an hour working his way up to the camp.

Preacher almost scared one of the servants out of his shoes when he suddenly rose up out of the grass about a yard from the man and said, "Howdy!"

The man dropped a load of tin plates he'd just washed and clutched at his chest, his mouth open and his eyes wide with fear. The others stood still and stared at Preacher. None of them made any move toward the rifles that had been placed around the camp in case of hostiles attacking.

"Relax," Preacher told the cooks and servants. "I ain't here to do none of you no harm. Y'all dish me up a plate of that good-smelling grub and a cup of coffee and we'll talk." Preacher sat down on the ground while a cook quickly served up a heaping plate of food.

Preacher thanked the man and said, "You boys reckon you could find your way out of these mountains?"

"Certainly," a man-servant replied. "I served in the British Army before gaining employment with the Duke. My experience with rugged terrain is vast."

"Is that a fact? Well, was I you boys, I'd busy myself packin' up and then I'd get the hell gone from here. Y'all ain't tooken no part in huntin' me, and I'm obliged to you for that. Your bosses is miles north of here, lookin' for me in all the wrong places, as usual. Now boys, when they do catch up with me, it's gonna get right nasty. Start packin'."

The servants and cooks exchanged glances. One said, "What about the savages?"

"They ain't gonna bother you none. They got themselves a big pow-wow down on the Arkansas. The four main tribes is gonna make peace with each other. 'Sides, they's enough of you and y'all's well armed. It would take a powerful big bunch of Injuns to attack you. When you get down to Bent's Fort, you ask around and hook up with supply wagons headin' back east and tag along with them for extree safety."

Several of the men turned and began packing. The others soon followed suit. One said, "The horses do not belong to us. There will be warrants issued for our arrest."

Preacher smiled. "There ain't nobody gonna be alive to issue no warrants, boys. There ain't none of that bunch gonna leave these mountains. Or damn few of them. So y'all take whatever you feel like takin'. Now, y'all seem like right nice fellers. So I'm gonna give you some advice. Y'all are all foreigners. You don't know nothin' about the West, and the men who has spent their lives out here. Look at me."

The cooks and servants stopped packing and looked.

Preacher patted the stock of his rifle. "This is the law out here, boys. No fancy robed judges or high-falutin' lawyers or badge-totin' lawmen. This is all there is. Now y'all hooked up with some mighty bad company. Maybe you didn't know what you was gettin' yourselves in for. I'll think that. 'Cause if you give me reason to think otherwise, I'd not look kindly upon you."

"We were told it was a hunting expedition," one said. "We had no reason to think it was anything else. We did not learn the truth until we were far from civilization back in Missouri—if civilization is the right word—and were in the middle of all that vastness."

"Pack and git!"

When the men had left, Preacher began gathering up all the blankets, tents, food, clothing, and medical supplies. He piled everything up and then went to the other camp and did the same. Then he set fire to the mess and began running across the valley floor to the slopes. When Bones and the gentry spotted the smoke, they'd come gallopin'. Preacher smiled as he ran effortlessly across the meadow. There was gonna be some mighty irritated folks when they saw what he'd done. Mighty irritated.

BOOK TWO

I can be pushed just so far.

—HARRY LEON WILSON

18

"The dirty, rotten, no good . . ." Bones went on a rampage, cussing and jumping up and down and throwing himself about like a spoiled child in the throes of a temper tantrum.

The men had managed to save quite a number of articles from the fires. But their tents were gone as were many of the blankets and spare clothing.

To heap insult upon injury, Preacher had left another note reading:

I WARNED YOU

A dozen men from Lige's bunch exchanged glances and without saying a word, mounted up and rode out. If they had any luck at all, they could catch up with the cooks and servants and ride back east with them. They wanted no more of Preacher.

Bones and Van Eaton and the royalty watched the men leave without comment. They were glad to be rid of them. Lige cussed the deserters and shook his fist at them and shouted dire threats until he was hoarse, but that was all he did.

Unbeknownst to Lige's people, at the orders of the

royalty, Bones, Van Eaton, and men had buried a great deal of supplies that were carefully wrapped in oilcloth and canvas.

"That was good thinkin'," Bones said to Sir Elmore after he had calmed down.

"Naturally," the Englishman replied.

No man among them had any way of knowing that a small group of settlers and a few missionaries had already left Bent's Fort, heading for the Rockies to establish a settlement and a church. The problem was, they were being guided by a man who was so inept he would have trouble finding the altar in a church.

"I am thrilled beyond words," Patience Comstock said to her sister, Prudence, as they bounced along in a wagon. "This is such a grand adventure. We'll be doing the work of the Lord by bringing God to the savages."

"Yes," Prudence agreed, tying her bonnet strap under her chin. "And won't Father and Mother be surprised to learn about that Preacher man they told us about back at the fort? Just think, Sister, a man of the Cloth so well-known and so devout, so . . . so, strong in his faith and loved by all that even the savages call him Preacher."

"Yes, sister. But I wonder why the Methodist Board of Missions didn't tell us about this man?"

"Well, he might be of another faith, dear."

"Of course. I'm sure that's it. No matter. We're all doing God's work." Patience tucked a few strands of auburn hair back under her bonnet. "I'm sure he's a fine gentleman."

"That dirty son!" Bones muttered, looking at the scorched boots he'd managed to pull from the smoldering mess. "I paid good money for these back in St. Louis." He tossed the ruined boots aside. "Preacher.

Preacher? How did a man like that ever get the name of Preacher?" he questioned with a snarl.

As it turns out, early on Preacher was captured by Indians and while they were mulling over whether to kill him outright or torture him to see how brave he was, the young man started preaching the gospel—sort of—to them. He preached for hours and hours and hours until the Indians finally reached the conclusion that he was crazy and turned him loose. Once the story got around, and that didn't take long, he was known as Preacher.

Preacher did nothing for several days except watch. He had been sure that once he burned the supplies of the man-hunters, they'd all give up and go home. He'd told the cooks and servants that he was going to kill all those after him just to get them moving. The truth was, Preacher's deep grief and hot anger over the death of Eddie and Wind Chaser had tempered somewhat. He could kill ten times the number of those men after him and that wouldn't bring the dead back to life.

He just wanted this over and to live his life in peace.

"Damn," Preacher said, lowering the spy glass. "What's it gonna take to discourage them fools down yonder?"

Some of the men were real woodsmen and frontiersmen. They'd been smoking fish and meat and making jerky and really eatin' pretty high on the hog. And Preacher had seen where a whole passel of supplies had been dug up. He had stung the man-hunters some, but that was about it.

Preacher didn't know it, but his troubles were only just beginning.

"Oh, sister," Patience said to her twin, Prudence. "Aren't they magnificent?"

"Breathtaking, sister."

They were gazing at the Rockies.

One of the settlers, a good solid, sturdy young man of German stock, named Otto Steiner, walked up to the twins' wagon. "Quite a sight, ja, ladies?"

"Oh, Mister Steiner, they are just beautiful!" Patience cooed.

"Ja, ja. All of that. Well, I just want to see those lovely rich valleys and lakes in those mountains where a man and his wife can raise kids and vegetables and have cows and fish and hunt. We go on now." He waved at the scout, who was now sober, having exhausted his supply of whiskey. "We go, man. Take us through the mountains."

The scout, known only as Wells, nodded his head and picked up the reins. "I ain't gar-enteein' nothin'. But we'll give it a shot."

"What do you mean, sir?" Patience demanded. "We were told back in Missouri that you knew this country."

"Wal, they lied. I ain't never been this far a-fore. And to tell you the truth, I ain't real thrilled about goin' no further, neither. So I don't think I will."

"What does that mean?" Otto asked.

"Means I quit." Without another word, he rode away, heading east. He did not look back.

The four wagons and eight people suddenly looked awfully tiny with the majestic mountains looming in front of them.

"Well now," Frank Collins said, walking up with his wife of only a few months with him. "This sort of leaves us in a pickle, doesn't it?"

"The Lord will see us through," Jane Collins said, smiling up at her husband.

Hanna Steiner joined the group, as did Paul and Sally Marks. "I didn't like that Wells person anyway," Hanna said bluntly. "He was a very untidy man who did not bathe enough and he cussed. I cannot abide a man who swears."

"Ja, Hanna," Otto said. "You are right about that, you surely are."

"Well!" Patience said, flouncing on the wagon seat. "We must press on." She picked up the reins. "The Lord is with us and surely He will hear our prayers this evening and send His man of faith in the wilderness, Preacher, to guide us through. I am certain of that. Onward, people. We'll lift our voices in Christian song as we travel through the wilderness." She popped the big rear mules on the butt with the reins and off they went, creaking and lurching and singing across the Plains, only a few miles from the Rockies. The faint sounds of song could be heard as the young pioneers headed bravely into the unknown.

The fare in the camp of Bones had decidedly gone downhill with their cooks leaving and much of their supplies destroyed. It was now mostly venison and beans. And not one sign of Preacher had been found by the daily patrols. It had been two weeks since the cooks and servants left and Preacher had burned their camp.

"I think the man has fled," Robert Tassin said.

"I concur," his countryman, Jon Louviere agreed.

Bones and Van Eaton, sitting on the ground a few yards away, listened but said nothing. It really made no difference to either man. The longer they stayed out, the more money they made. The rules and rates of the "game" had changed. With the exception of Bones and Van Eaton, each man was being paid five dollars a day, a very princely sum for the time. Bones and Van Eaton were receiving substantially more. In addition, when, or if, Preacher was found, and the aristocracy killed him, each man in the group would receive a cash bonus. The entire group could have the reward money posted on Preacher's head. Literally. For the reward money could only be claimed by bringing Preacher's head back as proof. A carefully packed glass jug and pickling solution had been brought by the second group.

Up near the timber line, Preacher was getting bored. His hopes that the hunting party would go away and leave him alone had been dashed. On this clear and crisp mid-summer morning, just as dawn was lighting the horizon, Preacher reckoned it was time to open this ball and he was going to lead the band. He picked up two rifles and headed out.

Patience and Prudence and party had broken camp and were on the move. They were about eight miles away at dawn.

The camp of the man-hunters had shifted, the unwashed multitudes crawling out of their blankets, shaking out the fleas and various other bugs and headed for the creek for coffee water.

Bones was squatting by the fire, warming his hands and waiting for the water to boil. He was always surly in the mornings and this morning he was surlier than usual. Even Van Eaton did not dare to speak to him. The gentry were gathered together, as usual. They preferred their own company to that of the unwashed.

Bones reached for the coffeepot just as a rifle ball banged against the big iron kettle and ripped off, the flattened and ragged ricochet striking a man-hunter in the center of the forehead and dropping him dead on the ground. Bones kissed the earth, flattening out on his belly.

One of Bones's original group, Joey York, was a tad slow in reacting and Preacher's second shot ended his man-hunting days forever. The ball from the fancy hunting rifle punched a hole in Joey's chest and knocked him into a cookfire, setting his clothing and greasy hair ablaze. The ensuing smell was not exactly conducive to a good appetite.

"Did anybody spot the smoke?" Van Eaton yelled, from his position behind a tree near the creek.

"Do we ever?" Tom Evans called.

"Somebody pull Joey out the fire," Bones said. "The smell is makin' me ill."

One of the second party, a man called Stanley, jumped up and made it halfway to the smoldering body of Joey before Preacher nailed him, dusting the man from side to side. Stanley stumbled and fell dead without making a sound.

"He's got to be in that little stand of trees over yonder," Cal Johnson yelled, sticking his head up and peering over the log he was hiding behind. "But that's a good three hundred yards off. Man, he can *shoot!*"

Preacher's rifle boomed and Cal lost part of an ear. He fell back behind the log, squalling in pain as the blood poured. "Oh, God, he's kilt me!" Cal screamed.

Falcon glanced at him. "Naw. You'll live. But you gonna be wearin' yore hat funny from now on."

"Jesus!" Stan Law yelled. "Joey's stinkin' something fierce. Cain't nobody haul him outta there?"

"You want him out, you haul him out," Horace Haywood called. "I ain't movin'."

A man called Hoppy, because of the way he walked—one leg was shorter than the other—jumped up and hip-hopped toward the fire. Preacher fired again and now Hoppy's left leg was equal to his right. The ball took off about half of his left foot. Hoppy flopped on the ground, screaming to high heaven.

"Charge, men!" Sir Elmore ordered. "Into the fray!"

"Charge yoresalf!" Derby Peel told him.

"By God I will!" Sir Elmore said. "Where's my saber?"

Baron Zaunbelcher quickly scurried away from Elmore.

"Stay down!" Bones yelled. "Don't be a fool. Preacher's got us cold."

"He's movin'!" Jimmie Cook yelled. "Headin' off to the south. If he makes the crick, he's gone for sure."

Sir Elmore jumped up, waving his saber. Baron

Zaunbelcher was keeping a good eye on the Englishman. "Now's our chance. Charge, men!" Elmore ran toward the creek, waving his saber. Burton Sullivan and Willy Steinwinder right behind him.

"Oh, Lord!" Bones said, crawling to his boots. "Come on, boys. We can't let nothing happen to them silly people."

En masse, the entire camp—those who were able— came to their feet, all running after Preacher, waving rifles and pistols and yelling and cussing. But Preacher had left the creek and was hiding among the trees that lined the bank. He caught sight of the sun flashing off of Elmore's blade and sighted in. The ball clanged against the polished steel and Elmore's entire body experienced the sensation of a railroad spike being hit with a sledge hammer. For a moment, before Burton hauled him down, Elmore looked like a man with a bad case of the twitches.

Using his second rifle, Preacher took aim and put a ball into a man's belly and the man tumbled to his knees and then slowly fell into the creek, face first. Two minutes later he had drowned. Preacher watched the entire running human wave hit the ground and he took off running, zigging and zagging through the grass and brush, heading for the ridges. Very quickly Preacher was out of rifle range and gone. He reached his horse and headed south.

Back at the camp of the man-hunters, they were busy patching up the wounded and seeing to the disposal of the dead. Elmore's right hand had stopped its twitching. He was looking sorrowfully at his slightly bent saber.

"Throw it away," Zaunbelcher urged.

"Indeed not! It's only bent a little. My father carried this sword during the War of 1812."

Baron Zaunbelcher almost said he now knew the reason the British lost, but thought better of it at the last second.

Preacher had put several miles behind him and the now scared, shook-up, and bloody band of man-hunters. He wasn't worried about them following him; not this soon anyway. He threaded his way through the timber, topped a ridge, and looked down into one of the prettiest valleys in this part of the country. He stared hard at the scene before him. He blinked. But the scene remained unchanged.

Four wagons, a half a dozen cows, one of which was probably a bull, and riding horses.

Four wagons? Here? Now?

Preacher rode down the grade and across the meadow just as the pilgrims were climbing down to the lush grass and flowers of the valley floor. Preacher had not had a bath in several days and it had been a couple of weeks since he'd shaved. His buckskins were stained and his hat had damn sure seen better days. He knew he looked rougher than a cob and meaner than a bear, but at the moment, he didn't much care. He rode right up to the wagons and got himself a jolt. Two of the finest-lookin' women he'd put eyes on in awhile stood side by side. Twins, with no difference he could spot in them at all.

"Howdy, folks!" Preacher called. "Y'all ain't got no drinkin' whiskey with you, now has you? I feel the need for a little Who Hit John."

"Sir!" one of the twins piped right up. "I'll have you know we are on a mission for God. We do not sanction with the partaking of strong drink."

"Do tell. Well, I'll be damned."

"And we do not hold with swearing, either!" Hanna said, standing with hands on hips. She was a trifle ample across the beam for Preacher's liking, but still a handsome woman.

"You don't say? Well . . . dip me in buffalo crap and call me stinky."

One of the twins stepped closer and stared at him. "Sir? Are you a mountain man?"

"I reckon. I been in these mountains ever since I was knee-high to a frog. What are you folks doin' out here all by your lonesome?"

Everybody started talking at once in a babble of voices.

Preacher dismounted and stood silently before them until they settled down. When quiet prevailed, Preacher said, "I was just kiddin' y'all 'bout that whiskey. I got me a couple of jugs stashed up in the brush that I stole from some guys."

"You . . . *stole* some whiskey?" Prudence asked.

"Yeah."

"Why?"

"So's I could drink it."

"There are other people close-by?" Otto asked.

"Oh, yeah. I'd guess near'bouts seventy or so about five miles yonder way." He pointed.

"*Seventy?*" Patience blurted.

"Yeah."

"What are they doing?"

"Doin' their best to kill me, ma'am."

"Kill you!" Sally shrieked. "Why?"

"'Cause I been killin' as many of them as I could, that's why."

The men and women all wore stunned looks on their faces. "You have been . . . killing them?" Frank Collins asked.

"Oh, yeah. I reckon up to the moment I've kilt . . . well, oh, fifteen or twenty, I reckon. But it's all right, 'cause they started it."

"You have personally killed fifteen or twenty men in your life?" Prudence asked, her face pale.

"Oh, no, ma'am. That's just in the last few weeks. I lost count on how many men I've kilt over the years. White men, that is."

"What . . . what is your name?" Patience asked.

"Preacher."

Patience paled.

"How many other men out here are called Preacher?" she asked in a tiny voice.

"Just me."

Patience fainted.

19

Otto caught the woman before she hit the ground and gently placed her in the shade of the wagon.

"What's the matter with her?" Preacher asked. "She comin' down with the vapors?"

Prudence glared up at him. "You . . . you . . . brute!"

"What did I do?" Preacher questioned, looking at the men and women.

Frank Collins said, "Really, nothing, sir. We all were under the impression that you were a man of God, that's why Patience fainted."

Preacher was clearly puzzled. Something was all out of whack here and he couldn't figure out what it was. "A man of God? I been called a lot of things over the years, but damned if I've ever been called that."

"Sir," Hanna said, looming menacingly before him. "I must insist that you refrain from swearing."

Preacher sighed. Before he could tell Hanna what was foremost on his mind, and after doing that would probably have to shoot her husband, Patience moaned and sat up.

"I had the most terrible dream," she said, her face flushed. "I dreamt that we were confronted by a horrible man who drank whiskey and ran around killing people."

Her eyes began to focus and they focused on Preacher. "Oh, my word! It wasn't a nightmare."

"Now, I have been called that a time or two," Preacher admitted. "Y'all splash some water on that female's face and get her up. I got to talk to y'all. This just ain't no place for pilgrims to be at any time, most especially right now." He looked at Hanna. "You make some coffee and put on some grub. I got a case of the hongries flung on me. I'm goin' over yonder to that crick and take me a wash and a shave. I'll be back."

"Well!" Hanna flounced about as Preacher turned his back to her and swung into the saddle.

"Do it," Otto told her. "I think that, if I understand correctly his quaint way of speaking, we are in trouble here. I want to hear what he has to say."

Prudence helped Patience to her feet and got her unflustered. Fifteen minutes later, Preacher reappeared. His buckskins were still stained, but he had taken a short bath and shaved the heavy growth of beard from his face.

"He really is a very handsome man," the women all silently concurred.

"He really is a very dangerous man," the men all silently concurred.

Preacher poured a cup of coffee and squatted down. The coffee was weak for his tastes, but he made no mention of that. "Now listen up, pilgrims. I got to tell you what's goin' on. Then you make up your own minds 'bout what kind of man I am. Not that your opinion means a damn to me. But I don't like to be judged wrongly."

While the bacon and fried potatoes were cooking, Preacher took it from the top, beginning with him and Eddie leaving civilization back east and the reasons why. When he finished telling about burying Eddie and his little paint pony, the only dry eye in the bunch was his. A couple of minutes later, he said, "Well, that's it, folks."

"I wonder why we heard nothing about the bounty on you?" Frank Collins asked.

"Prob'ly 'cause y'all don't frequent taverns and saloons and the like," Preacher told him. "Nor do you associate with them that does." He smiled. "Them mountain men back at the fort who told you I was a preacher of the gospel . . . you 'member any names?"

"Well," Hanna said. "There was this huge fellow called Horsehide Jack."

Preacher started grinning.

"Yes," Patience said. "And there was another gentleman with the unsightly name of Pistol Pete."

Preacher's grin spread.

"And one great bear of a man they called Papa Griz."

Preacher laughed. "Them ol' boys was havin' a high ol' time puttin' you folks on, was what they was doin'. Don't feel hard toward 'em. They didn't mean no harm. They was just funnin'. Humor gets sorta dark out here in the wilderness. 'Cause a lot of the time, they ain't a whole hel . . . heck of a lot to laugh about."

"I fear that because of my insistence that we press on," Patience said, "I have placed us all in great danger."

Preacher thought about that. "Maybe," he finally said. "But not if y'all will play along with a lie I'm dreamin' up right now."

"Whatever in the world do you mean, sir?" Prudence asked.

Preacher grinned and told her.

Preacher had carefully stashed the pilgrims and their livestock and wagons in a little canyon on the east side of the valley and told them not to light fires nor venture past the tree and brush lined entrance of the canyon. Then Preacher set out to find some man-hunters. Only this time he didn't have killing on his mind. Well, not much anyway.

"Look!" Van Eaton cried out, pointing.

The small group of men looked at the man with a white handkerchief tied to the barrel of his rifle.

"By the Lord!" breathed Sir Elmore. "That's our quarry."

"He wants to talk," Bones said. "He's comin' under a white flag. We'll honor it."

The gentry with him looked at Bones as if he had gone mad. "You can't be serious, sir!" Robert Tassin said.

"I'm serious. A white flag is a white flag. We'll honor it."

Preacher rode slowly toward the six man team, stopping about ten yards from them. Bones and Elmore rode out to meet him. "You boys got another problem facin' you," Preacher said. "Not near 'bouts as dangerous as me, but a problem nonetheless."

"And what might that be, sir?" Elmore asked.

"The Methodist Church sent out a flock of missionaries to bring the gospel to the heathens. They're holed up over yonder in a valley. I run into them some time back and told them what was goin' on here, 'tween us. The scouts that brung them in has gone back with a message to the church board and the President of the United States. They tooken all your names back on paper to give to important folks back east. Anything happens to them missionaries, and you'll all have federal warrants out on you. The war 'tween us is still on, but them Bible-shoutin' folks had best be left alone."

Sir Elmore Jerrold-Taylor's back straightened. "Sir, no harm shall come to those missionaries. I am a Christian myself and believe strongly in the Lord."

Preacher had no immediate comment on that, but his thoughts were grim. If this fool really believed himself a Christian person, then Preacher could pass for a duck. "Fine." He looked at Bones. "How about you boys?"

"They'll stay clear."

"Them missionaries, over my objections, has volunteered to set up a make-shift hospital and take care of the wounded. That all right with you?"

"Fine with me."

"That's wonderful," Sir Elmore said. "That's very gracious of them. But you destroyed all our medical supplies," he added with a pout. "That wasn't very sporting of you."

"Well, shame on me," Preacher said sarcastically. "My goodness! You just can't depend on nobody nowadays to be a good sport, can you?"

"Oh, quite true. Quite true."

Preacher shook his head at the Englishman's words. He couldn't figure out if the man was serious or just a teetotal damned fool. He backed Thunder up some twenty feet or so. "Now you boys do the same," he told the men. When they were about fifty feet apart, Preacher said, "Next time we see each other, you best start shootin'. 'Cause this is the last time I aim to be cordial with you."

"We'll do that, Preacher."

"Head on out," Preacher ordered.

"Don't you trust us?" Sir Elmore asked.

"Hell, no." He leveled his rifle. Bones and Elmore turned their horses, rejoined the group, and they all got gone.

"Do you trust these bounty hunters to keep their word, Preacher?" Otto asked.

Dark in the missionary's camp. The women had cooked up a fine meal and Preacher was laying back against his saddle, drinking coffee and smoking his pipe. "'Bout as far as I can pick up a grizzly bear and throw it."

"You said one of the nobility was called Zaunbelcher, is that correct?"

"Yeah. He's a baron. Whatever the hel . . . heck that means."

"It's a fine old family," Otto said. "But starting about

a century back, they began marrying very closely. I'm afraid insanity is running in their blood now."

"I don't doubt that a bit. But you don't have to worry about that no more."

"Oh? Why?"

"'Cause I'm a-fixin' to stop his clock, that's why."

Paul Marks stared at Preacher across the fire. "You are going to fight seventy-odd men all by yourself?"

"They was close to a hundred or better when I started. And they'll be about ten less this time tomorrow."

"You say those deadly words so . . . casually." Patience said. "Doesn't human life mean anything to you?"

"Them folks huntin' me ain't human, Missy. You think about that."

A coyote pack started up, lifting their voices to the sky. The women shivered at the sound.

Preacher smiled. "The Injuns call them Song Dogs, ladies. They're sacred to some tribes. Coyote won't hurt you. Neither will a wolf if you leave the poor beast alone."

"Song Dogs?" Prudence questioned.

"Shore. Just listen to 'em. They's makin' pretty music. Just listen and enjoy it."

"You ever been married, Preacher?" Frank asked.

"The Injun way, yeah. I got kids. Y'all prob'ly frown on that, but that's the way it's done out here. And don't think Injuns take marriage lightly, 'cause they don't. Injuns is human people. Their ways is just different from ours, that's all. I don't agree with a lot of what they do, but then, I do agree with a lot they believe in and practice. When this little trouble of mine is all cleared up, I'll sit you down and try to convince you to head on back east. The Injuns don't want your religion, and they don't need it."

"Whatever in the world do you mean by that?" Patience cried. "They're poor unsaved heathens."

"They ain't no such of a damn thing, Missy. They worship the same God you do . . . in a way, that is. Their

God has many names, but they all amount to the same thing. Man Above, Wakan Tanka, Grandfather Spirit, Great Mystery Power, Heammawihio—The Wise One Above. The God of the Pawnees is Tirawa, and they sacrifice a human to that God. And it's a terrible sacrifice, too. Now, I don't hold with that a-tall." Preacher picked up a handful of dirt and let it slowly dribble to the ground. "This is Grandmother Earth. The earth is life. The Injun respects the land and the critters on it.

"No, folks, the Injun has their own religion. When an Injun dies, his soul, tasoom, in Cheyenne, travels up the Hanging Road." Preacher smiled again. "That's the Milky Way to us. The Injun believes that after death everything is good; there is no reason to fear death. And that only those who take their own lives won't never rest in a peaceful village in the Land Beyond. Now as far as I'm concerned, that pretty much goes along with what's in the Good Book."

"But they must be baptized in the blood to be saved!" Patience said.

"I don't believe that, Missy. And I don't believe a person's got to congregate, neither. I think if a body accepts that there is a higher power over us all, and tries to live right, that person ain't gonna be denied entrance to the Land Beyond. You think there ain't gonna be no horses and dogs and cats and coyotes and wolves in Land Beyond? If that's the case, I don't want to go."

"You don't mean that, sir!" Hanna almost shouted the words.

"That's blasphemy!" Sally said.

"I just figure it's the truth," Preacher replied. "Be a mighty sorry damn place without critters to make friends with." He stood up and stretched. "Y'all sleep sound. I'll be around. But I'll be pullin' out 'fore dawn. Y'all might not see me for a few days." He walked off, quickly lost in the darkness.

"The man is either a simpleton and a fool, or a highly complex person," Frank Collins remarked.

"He's no fool," his wife said softly.

"He certainly is a very confident man," Paul Marks said.

"I . . . don't believe I have ever met a man quite like him," Patience admitted. "He is . . . delightful."

He was also gone when the pilgrims awakened the next morning. While they slept soundly, Preacher had built up the fire, made coffee for them, and left them a rather ominous note.

YOU FOLKS BEST TAKE TO SLEPIN LIGHT.
OR YOU GOIN TO WAKE UP
SOME MORNIN AND BE DAID.

While Hanna, the self-appointed cook for the group, was slicing bacon, the sound of a single shot came faintly to the gathering of young men and women.

"Oh, dear," Patience said. "I hope nothing has happened to Mister Preacher."

Hanna looked at her and smiled.

Prudence looked at her and frowned.

The men glanced at one another and winked.

Their wives said to their husbands, "Now, you stop that!"

About three miles away, Bones squatted down in the brush and looked at the dead man. He was one of Lige's group who had gone into the woods to take care of his morning's business and instead got him a bullet in the head.

Bones was extra cautious this day as he crouched behind a tree, presenting no target at all. There had been something in Preacher's voice yesterday that told him game time was all over. The mountain man was through playing; from now on, it was going to be a deadly business.

"Is the wretch dead?" Duke Burton Sullivan yelled.

"Yeah."

"Oh, drat!"

Bones inched his way back to the edge of the camp he would have sworn was as secure as a fort. He knew damn well that Preacher, as soon as he fired, had changed position. He was probably on the other side of the camp now. Waiting as silently and as menacingly as a big puma. Watching through those cold hard eyes. It was not a real comfortable feeling.

"Everyone turn around," Bones said. "Until we're in a circle. Preacher'll have no choice but to stand and fight and die, or leave. Now move out."

But Preacher had already left the area. He had slipped in a ravine a few hundred yards from the enemy camp and snaked over the lip a hundred yards later. He'd had him a hunch that sooner or later Bones would wise up and do something smart for a change. It was about time for him to start using his noggin.

"Preacher!" a man shouted from the camp. "I know you ain't gonna answer me, but just listen. Me and two others want out. We're through. We quit."

"You yeller skunks!" Lige yelled.

"Call us whut you will, Lige. We're quitting this here hunt. Preacher! We're ridin' out. We're done. Don't shoot for God's sake."

God, Preacher thought. How come when the goin' gits tough, sorry low-lifes like them yonder start callin' on God when they never give Him a thought 'fore now? Preacher remained still and silent and waited.

The men took a chance that Preacher wouldn't shoot and quickly packed up, saddled up, and rode out.

Cuts it down some, Preacher thought, watching the three men until they were out of sight.

The men in the camp began their fanning out in an ever broadening circle and Preacher pulled out. He figured they'd be looking for him all morning, and he had some things he wanted to do. He began leaving a very faint trail, knowing that some of those in Bones and Lige's camp were real woodsmen and wouldn't fall for too obvious a trail. He laid the trail winding out of the valley and up into the mountains. He left a broken branch here, a scar on bare ground there, as he left the valley and headed for the high up. He'd already done all the work for the surprise he had in mind. Now if Bones and them would just come to the party.

20

"He's gettin' tired," Van Eaton said. "I tole you we'd wear him down after a time."

"I do believe you're right, old boy," Burton Sullivan said. "Come, come. Let's press on."

Not using his spy-glass for fear the sun would reflect off the lenses, Preacher squatted up near the tree line and watched the tiny, antlike figures pause for a time, and then move on, following his faint trail. "That's right, boys. Just like the spider, I'm a-waitin'. So come on."

Preacher moved over to his already picked out and readied position and waited. Those below had sense enough to know they'd kill a horse trying to ride up, so they dismounted and were spread out, coming up in a single stretched-out line, about a thousand feet wide.

Preacher made himself comfortable and settled down for a time. He knew it would take the men below him thirty minutes or so to get where he wanted them.

"He slipped and cut himself here!" Tige shouted. "He's hurt and headin' for the high up, jist like a damn animal."

Bones and Van Eaton inspected the blood. And it was blood. Preacher had found where a big puma had killed a deer and hid the carcass after eating. He carefully looked around him, for the deer was still warm, and then put the heart and liver in a piece of the animal's hide and got the hell away from that place. He didn't want to have to fight no mountain lion . . . not just yet anyways.

"You mighty right about that," Bones admitted. "He's hurt bad, too. Look at all that blood. Come on, boys. We got him."

"Superb!" Jon Louviere said.

"The blood trail goes right up this grade," Falcon said. "I don't know how bad he's hurt, but he's leakin' some."

High above them, Preacher put his back against the rock wall behind him and both feet against a huge boulder. Once he got that rock rollin', it would pick up hundreds of other rocks and give Bones and them some grief . . . a lot of grief, Preacher hoped. While all the dust was fillin' the air, Preacher would shift over to another spot he'd inspected and rigged up, and supplied with a few goodies.

The men grew closer and Preacher smiled. "Bye, bye, boys," he whispered, and laid into the boulder.

There was no place to run. This high up, only a few scrub trees grew in their weird twisted shapes. They offered no protection against the tons of rocks coming down the grade at avalanche speeds.

One thing could be said about the nobility. They were all excellent mountain climbers and all had a healthy respect for the mountains. All were uneasy about this high-up, long, and ragged, rocky grade. They'd seen terrible accidents in the Alps, and this smelled like a tragedy about to happen. They lagged back and to one side.

Willy Steinwinder heard it first, and experienced the ground begin to tremble under his expensive hand-made boots. "Slide!" he yelled, and started running for safety, the others in his party right along with him.

The other men looked up, horror and fear in their eyes, their dirty and unshaven faces paling at the furious sight tumbling toward them.

A man from Tennessee glanced over at his friend, Webber, just as a melon sized rock, traveling at great speed, slammed into Webber's face and took his head off. The blood spurted a good three feet into the air. The Tennessee man had about two seconds to scream before the rock slide buried him.

Bones ran soundlessly to one side, Van Eaton right beside him. They got clear of the major slide, but both were pelted with fist-sized rocks and both were bloodied and bruised.

Lige Watson lost his footing as a rock slammed into his head and sent him sprawling . . . but knocked him safely out of the major portion of the slide.

Jimmie Cook was flattened by a huge boulder and bloody bits and pieces of him were scattered all the way down to the valley floor.

Four men from Lige's group were pinned down and could do nothing except scream in fright and stare in horror and wait for death to clamp its cold hand around them, which it did, leaving no trace of the men behind.

The men were running for their lives, knowing it was hopeless; for many this was to be their last race. Behind them, shattered and bloody arms and legs were sticking grotesquely out of the dirt and rocks.

Preacher had shifted positions as soon as the dust began to rise from the tons of rocks tumbling down the grade, and was belly down, watching the massive slide snuff the life from the bounty-hunters.

It was over in less than a minute. But the dust was so thick it restricted visibility for several minutes. A man from Maryland known only as Teddy staggered out onto the now barren slope and stood dumbly for a moment. Preacher's rifle barked and Teddy began rolling down the grade, a big hole right in the center of his back.

"The dirty son!" George Winters cussed Preacher. "He ain't even givin' us time to tend to the dead and wounded."

Bones gave the man a disgusted look and said nothing.

Van Eaton looked at George. But like Bones, he kept his mouth shut.

Lige's bunch were the ones who had taken the real beating as far as loss of men. They had been so eager to trap and kill Preacher, they had forged ahead of the others and taken the brunt of the rock slide. Counting himself, Lige had about twenty men left. At least that's what he figured. Lige wasn't a very good counter.

High above them, Preacher's rifle cracked and Lige had about nineteen men left. A Delaware man dropped like a stone and began rolling down the grade. Several dozen horrified eyes watched the body slowly gain speed and finally land with a thud on the valley floor.

Bones, Van Eaton and his men, and the dusty and the now grime-faced nobility, knew better than to try to move. They all had witnessed Preacher's precision with a gun and knew that as long as it remained daylight, to move was to die.

"Stay down!" Rudi Kuhlmann yelled.

"I cain't take no more of this!" a man from Illinois screamed. "Spencer was kin of mine. I seen them rocks knock his brains out. Damn you, Preacher!" he shouted, standing up. "I'll kill you, Preacher. I'll . . ."

Die. Preacher's rifle sang its deadly song and the Illinois man slumped to the rocky grade, on his knees, a large stain appearing on the front of his shirt. The man had a very puzzled expression on his face. "No," he spoke for the last time. He finally fell over on his back, head pointed downward. He slid for a few yards, stopped, and was still.

"This is the way it's gonna be, boys," Preacher's faint shout reached the men. "You better face facts, you bird-brains. I know these mountains, you don't. I know ever' stream, cver' crick, ever' valley, ever' box canyon, and ever' cave. I could have kilt all of you a hundred times over, but I was hopin' you'd come to your senses and clear on out and leave me be. Now what's it gonna be?"

"I'm through, Preacher!" a man yelled. "You let me go and I'll never come back."

"Go on, then."

"Nelson," Van Eaton said.

"Let him go," Bones said. "More for us when the end comes."

"If we're alive when the end comes," Van Eaton replied.

"You and me got no choice in the matter. This is personal with Preacher, now."

"This ain't worth no five dollars a day," another man yelled. "I'm headin' out with Nelson."

"Fine," Preacher said.

"Sal," Van Eaton said.

"I've had it!" one of Lige's men shouted. "You hear me, Preacher? I'm haulin' my ashes back to New York State."

"Git gone, then."

"I'll see you in hell, Preacher!" another of Lige's men shouted. "But I don't want no more of this."

"Tell your mommy hello and stay close by her side," Preacher yelled. "I 'spect she'll be glad to see her wanderin' boy come home."

"You mighty right 'bout that."

"Anyone else?" Preacher questioned.

No one else chose to leave. Preacher knew that these staying behind were the hardcases. There would be no give in them and no quittin'. They were in this until the end.

Lige slowly counted his men. Near as he could figure it, counting himself, out of the original bunch, sixteen were all that was left. He shook his head. "I wouldn't have believed it possible," he muttered.

"Did you say something?" Wiley Steinwinder questioned the man.

"It just ain't reasonable that one man could do this much damage," Lige whispered.

"I will admit it is somewhat incredible," Sir Elmore

joined the conversation. "But this just makes it all the more exciting. Gads, what a formidable foe we face."

"Idiot," Van Eaton muttered. "I wish to God I'd never got mixed up with this pack of ninnies."

"You want to quit, Van?" Bones whispered.

"We cain't, Bones. Dark Hand is shore to have tole Preacher that you and me was in the bunch that tortured that kid. We got to see this thing through or elsest we'll be lookin' over our shoulders 'til the end of time."

That was the feeling among those of Bones's group who stayed. They had to finish this. For, to a man, they felt that Preacher would spend his life tracking them down. They were wrong. They could have left and Preacher would have gone on his way.

After a moment of silence, Preacher told them that. "Go on home, boys. If you say it's over, it's over. I mean that. They's been too much killin'. Let's stop it right now."

"He's lyin'," Bones told his people, having to shout across the barren slope, over the rocks and dirt that would forever cover many of his men.

"I ain't neither!" Preacher yelled. "I ain't never knowin'ly broke my word. Leave and don't come back and we'll call this even. You got my word on that."

"The hospital of the missionaries is safe ground for us all!" Bones yelled. "Any there is safe. You agree?"

"Does that include me?" Preacher hollered.

"Tell him yes and when he makes his appearance, we'll kill him," Sir Elmore urged.

"I agree to that," Tassin said.

But Bones shook his head. "No. Think about it. Maybe one of us will get wounded and have to go there for patchin' up. We'd be fair game."

"Unfortunately, he's right," Baron Zaunbelcher reluctantly said. "The camp of the missionaries must be declared neutral ground."

"All right, Preacher!" Bones yelled. "You got a deal."

"Let me hear the gentry say that. I want their word.

They claim their word is damn near holy, so let me see if they got the class to keep it."

That made the nobility angry. One by one they shouted their agreement to Preacher's terms.

"Pick up your wounded and tote 'em out of here," Preacher yelled. "Long as you don't make no funny moves, I'll hold my fire."

"Give us your word on that!" Juan Zapata shouted.

"You got my word on it."

The man-hunters cautiously left their hiding places and began seeing to the wounded. Preacher held his fire, content to watch. It took most of the afternoon to carry the bone-shattered men down the slope to the valley and get them in the saddle or on quickly made travois.

What they did not know was that Preacher had left the scene about fifteen minutes into the gathering and hauling off of the wounded. He packed up the supplies that he had cached and went over the top of the mountain.

Several miles from the slide area, Preacher stopped at a spring and washed the sweat and grime from his body and hair. Before the first wounded were on their long and painful way to the "hospital," Preacher rode into the neat little camp of the missionaries. They had rigged up several lean-tos as shelter for the wounded.

"Them rickety-lookin' things ain't near 'bout gonna be enough," Preacher told them, walking over to the fire and pouring a cup of coffee. "But I don't care if you lay 'em out on the ground for the varmints to chew on. Just 'member, y'all agreed to this scheme."

"We are sworn to serve our fellow man," Hanna said. "We follow the teachings of the Bible. Sometimes it is with an effort, and sometimes we fail, for we are mere mortals and therefore shall never attain perfection, but it is our duty."

"Mighty noble of y'all," Preacher said, sitting down with a sigh and relaxing. "Does my heart good to know they's people like y'all in the world. But if it's all right, I'll jist lay right here and watch y'all do all this good work."

"You are coming close to blasphemy, sir," Patience told him.

"I ain't neither. I'm tellin' the truth, that's all. Beats a lie, don't it?"

Patience flounced away, but not before stealing a flirtatious glance at Preacher.

Preacher ignored it.

He was dozing when Otto's frantic yell brought him awake and reaching for his rifle. He relaxed when he saw it was the wounded men from the slide.

Patience, Prudence, and the others in the group stared at Preacher in disbelief. "You . . . one man . . . did all *that*?" Frank Collins asked.

"And a heap more that's comin' up behind this first sorry-lookin' bunch," Preacher said, pouring himself a cup of coffee and stretching out. "And they's a goodly number of others all dead and buried under tons of rock and dirt. I done a purty neat job of it if you ask me."

"Incredible," Hanna said. "You behave as if you are proud of all the pain and suffering you have inflicted upon your fellow human beings."

"Oh, I am!"

"Disgusting!" Prudence said.

The first batch of wounded rode in and reined up. They stared at Preacher in wonderment and ill-disguised hate and hostility.

"Howdy, boys!" Preacher called cheerfully. "Looks like y'all run into some trouble, My goodness, what happened to y'all? Did you tangle with a whole passel of grizzly bar or get in the way of a buffalo stampede?"

"Very funny," Van Eaton said, painfully dismounting and limping back to the travois behind his horse.

"What's the matter with your head, Van Eaton?"

Preacher asked. "How'd you git all them bumps on your noggin?"

Van Eaton lost his temper and reached for the pistol in his belt. A hard hand clamped down on his wrist and squeezed. Van Eaton thought for a second his wrist was going to be crushed. He looked into the broad peasant face of Otto Steiner.

"This is neutral ground, friend," Otto said. "But don't cause me to lose my temper. Back before I found Christ, four men came out of the darkness one night to rob me. I broke the back of one, the neck of another, and smashed the brains out of the other two. And I do not joke. I do not have much of a sense of humor."

"Neutral ground," Van Eaton hissed through clenched teeth, reeling from the pain in his wrist. "I give you my word. And I'll shoot any man who violates it."

Otto released his wrist and Preacher called out, "Have some coffee, Van Eaton. Supper'll be on in a few minutes. You best partake. It might be your last one."

21

Preacher had to hand it to the men and women who had wandered west to serve their God. They did a bang up job when it came to fixing up the wounded.

"We've all had medical training," Hanna told him.

Later, when Bones and Lige and most of their people had left, Preacher sat by the fire drinking coffee. He became conscious of eyes on him and looked up. Patience was staring at him.

"You think I enjoy all this killin', don't you?"

"Frankly, yes. I do."

"Well, you're wrong, Missy. 'Cause I shore don't. I've done given them ol' boys out yonder a dozen chances to back off and let me be. They could ride out of here tonight and I'd not give them another thought. Hell, Missy. I give them all another chance to leave this day, up on the slide."

"He ain't lyin' 'bout that, ma'am," a man with two busted legs spoke up. "He done it."

"More'un oncest," another wounded man said. "And I shore wish I'd a took his invite."

"And he's let some go," a third man offered up. "I tell you this, Preacher. When I can ride, you've seen the last of me."

Most of the bruised, banged-up, and broken men in the camp agreed, except for one loudmouth brute.

"Not me. I aim to kill you, mountain man. I'm gonna track you down and skin you alive. Then I'm gonna cut off your head, pickle it, and tote it back east to claim my reward."

"Why?" Patience asked him, a horrified look on her face.

Preacher smiled into his coffee cup and said, "That's Ed Crowe, ma'am. He's a murderer, a rapist, and a brigand through and through. But he claims to have repented his evil ways. Now he's a bonney-e-fied man-hunter workin' with Bones and Van Eaton. Two of the sorriest men on the face of the earth."

Ed cussed Preacher until Otto showed up and said, "If you do not stop that filthy language, I will gag you. If that doesn't stop your vulgar mouth, I just might rip out your tongue with my bare hands."

"Otto!" Hanna cried. "Please. Do remember who we are and what we represent."

"Be still," he told her. "There is a time and place for all things. Including violence."

Ed Crowe must have believed the big man, for he shut his mouth and after that, as long as he was in the camp of the missionaries, when he spoke, it was free of profanity.

"I . . . guess I've misjudged you, Preacher," Patience said. "I apologize for that."

Preacher waved it off. "I just wanted you to know that I ain't no heartless savage, Missy. And that I really didn't want all this killin' and did try to stop it." He stood up. "I best be goin'. Bones and Lige and the gentry and the rest of that pack of no-counts will be gunnin' for me at first light. I don't want no shootin' around this camp."

Before she could form a reply, Preacher had vanished into the night.

* * *

Bones and his bunch had pulled themselves into a tight little camp right next to a fast runnin', spring-fed stream. And there they stayed. They posted guards that stayed alert and were changed often. Each day, under a white flag, an unarmed man would ride to the camp of the missionaries to check on the wounded, and then ride back. Other than that, they did not leave camp. Preacher had no way of knowing what they were planning, only that it would probably be better than any previous plan. So far, everything they'd tried had failed miserably. For now, all he could do was wait and watch and see.

Preacher was determined that he would not start the next round of gunfire. He had given some thought to just picking up and moving on. But he knew the man-hunters would just come after him . . . after they did, God only knew what they would do to the missionaries, and Preacher had him a pretty good idea what they'd do to the women.

The mountain man felt that he was in between that much talked about "rock and a hard place."

He had not been back to the missionary's camp and make-shift hospital. He felt that would be just too dangerous for those good folks.

On the fifth day of inaction, Preacher got lucky. Just as dusk was spreading its first shadows all over the valley floor, Preacher sat in the brush on a slope viewing the scene below him through his spy glass. About a quarter of a mile from the camp of the man-hunters, a covey of birds suddenly shot up into the air.

"Now what's all that about?" Preacher muttered, shifting the glass and studying the area in question. But he could see nothing. Then he spotted a very slight movement in the tall grass. After studying the area for a moment, he collapsed the pirate's glass and smiled.

"Very good, Bones," he muttered. "Yes, indeed. You got more sense than I gave you credit for havin'." He picked up his rifle and moved out. Preacher thought it was a good thing he'd taken a long nap that afternoon, for it looked like it was shapin' up to be a long night.

The night was black and the air was heavy with moisture. A bad storm was building, and if a body has never been in the high-up country when a thunderstorm hit, you just can't imagine the sound and fury. The pounding of the thunder is unbelievable and the lightning so fierce it'll stand you hair up on end.

Preacher studied the sky and figured he had about an hour before the full brunt of the storm struck. He also figured he could do a lot of damage in an hour.

Mack Cornay froze like a rock when he felt the cold edge of a Bowie knife touch his throat. He started sweating in the coolness of the night air when Preacher said, "You just never learn, do you, boy?"

Mack was so scared he was afraid to reply. He remained stone-still as Preacher shucked his pistols out of his belt and laid them to one side.

"Are you gonna kill me?" Mack whispered, his voice a tremble in the darkness.

"I shore ought to. You would if you was in my moccasins, wouldn't you?"

"I reckon. Can we deal?"

"What do you have that I want?"

"Information."

"Talk."

"Me and Frenchy is on this slope. Cobb is about a quarter mile to the south. Pyle is acrost the valley with Hunter. Flores is closin' the box north and Percy is comin' out later this night to put the lid on to the south."

"That's right interestin' news. What is your name, boy?"

"Mack Cornay. Please don't kill me, Preacher. I'll git gone ifn you'll let me. I swear that on my mother's head."

Preacher thought about that. "How you figure on gettin' your horse away from the camp without bein' seen?"

Sweat was running down Mack's face. He thought hard for a moment. "I cain't. But I can slip into the missionary camp and take one of the wounded feller's horse. And I'll do it, too. You bet I will. For God's sake, Preacher. I'm beggin' for my life, man."

Preacher removed the razor sharp knife from Mack's throat and the man was so relieved he slumped face-down on the cool earth. "Thank you, Jesus," Mack whispered. "I'm comin' home to see you, Mamma."

"Get gone, Mack," Preacher told him. "And you know what I'll do if I ever see you again."

"You'll kill me." Mack didn't put it as a question. He knew the answer.

"You got that right. Move! And be damn quiet in leavin'. You hear me?"

"Yes, sir, Mister Preacher. I'll be like a ghost."

"I ever see you again, you gonna be a ghost. Now get the hell gone from here."

Mack Cornay turned and looked at Preacher. "Thank you, Preacher."

"Take your rifle and pistols and clear out," Preacher told him.

Mack slipped quietly into the night. The odor of his fear-sweat lingered sourly for a few seconds and then the wind carried it away.

Preacher moved out. He would save Frenchy for last, for the man from Louisiana was known to be a bad one to tangle with. Preacher began working his way south. He'd heard some about Cobb, but nothing that impressed him.

Preacher laid a sturdy stick up 'side the head of Cobb and the man dropped like a stone into a well. Preacher trussed him up and waited for the man to come out of his addle.

"Oh, my dear sweet God!" Cobb said when he came to and his eyes began to focus.

"How come people like you always call on God or Jesus when you get in a tight?" Preacher questioned. "You damn shore don't pay no heed to His words 'til you do."

"I be good from now on," Cobb whispered, like he never heard Preacher's question. "Dear sweet Mamma, pray for me."

"Disgustin'," Preacher said. He popped Cobb across the face with a big hard hand. That got Cobb's attention. "Didn't your mamma whup you none whilst you was growin' up?"

"She beat me some."

"'Pears to me she didn't beat you enough. What am I gonna do with you, Cobb?"

"Turn me a-loose, I hope!"

"So's you can run tell Bones and them silly uppity folks what I'm doin' this night? Not likely."

"I wouldn't do that!"

"I think I'll just truss you up real good and let the bears eat you."

"Oh, Lord, Lord, please save me from this heathen!" Cobb cast his supplication to the heavens.

"Heathen? You call *me* a heathen?"

"I didn't mean it, Mister Preacher. I swear I didn't. You got me so bumfuzzled I ain't thinkin' straight."

"I tell you what I'm gonna do, Cobb. I'm gonna test you right good. I'm gonna see if you're a man of your word."

"I'm an honorable man, Preacher. You just ax anybody. They'll tell you."

"I bet they will," Preacher said drily. "I'd bet at least a penny on it. Cobb, I want you gone from these mountains. And I mean gone and stayed gone. I'm tired of all this fuss and bother. You know that ravine that cuts 'crost this valley?"

"Oh, yes, sir. I do for a fact. Runs all the way 'crost it. Comes within a few hun'red yards of the missionary camp. I know it real well. I bet I could . . ."

"Shut up an' listen. You beginnin' to babble. I want you to work your way down this slope and git in that ravine and over to the missionary camp. Then I want you to take one of them spare horses over yonder and git gone. I unloaded your weapons. So don't even think about pointin' any of 'em at me."

"I wouldn't. I swear it."

"Cobb, listen to me. I don't never want to see you again. You hear me?"

"Yes, sir. I do. I really do. And you ain't never gonna see me again."

"I better not ever see you again," Preacher said menacingly. "'Cause if I do, I'm gonna strip you buck-ass nekked and stake you out over an ant hill. Then I'm gonna pour honey all over your neck and head and sit back and watch whilst the ants gather and eat your eyes."

Cobb shuddered and crapped in his pants.

"Whew!" Preacher grimaced and fanned the air with a hand. "Git outta here!"

Preacher smiled as Cobb scurried away. Maybe he had missed his calling; he should have been an actor. He was sure convincing this night.

But he wasn't quite that lucky with Frenchy. Frenchy turned around when Preacher was about five feet away from him. Lightning flashed and Frenchy's eyes widened and his mouth dropped open. It took him about one second to recover and grab at the pistol behind his belt.

One second was the time Preacher needed. Preacher closed the gap and slugged Frenchy just as his hand closed around the butt of his pistol. Lightning flashed again and a cold rain began falling, slicking over the already treacherous footing on the rocky slope. Preacher lost his balance and fell down, dragging Frenchy with him. The two men hit the ground hard, with Preacher landing on top of Frenchy, knocking the wind from him. Preacher slammed a fist against the side of Frenchy's head, causing his hands to loosen their grip on Preacher's shirt. Preacher hit him again just as hard as he could and Frenchy's fingers lost their grip altogether, and his hands fell to the ground.

Preacher caught his breath and then quickly trussed

the man up. Already the Louisiana man was moaning and twitching. Preacher had just set the man up, his back to a rock, when Frenchy came to and opened his mouth to yell. Preacher jammed a handful of dirt into the man's mouth.

"You yell and I'll cut your throat," Preacher warned. "You understand?"

Frenchy believed him, for his eyes widened at the thought of that prospect and he nodded his head. Frenchy spat out the dirt and said, "What do you want, Preacher?"

"To give you a chance to get gone, Louisiana Man."

"You gittin' soft in your old age, Preacher?"

Preacher chuckled as the cold rain pelted them both. "You think I am, Frenchy?"

"No," Frenchy was quick to reply. "But you won't kill me while I'm tied like this."

Preacher hesitated. That was a fact and somehow Frenchy either knew it or had sensed it about the mountain man. "That's right, Frenchy. But what I can do is knock you silly, tote you up the mountain, strip you down to the buff, wedge you up under a run-off, and then let the weather do the rest. And I'll do that, boy—don't you doubt it for a second. I'm used to the high country. This cold rain don't bother me none. But you now, well, pneumonia'll kill you shore. Think about that."

Frenchy's eyes told Preacher he didn't doubt that at all. When he spoke, Preacher sensed he had won. Maybe. "All right, Preacher. You cut me a-loose and I'm gone."

Preacher freed the man's wrists and stepped back. "Frenchy, don't even think about makin' no funny moves or goin' back on your word. This will be the last chance you get. I mean that, boy. When I get done with this night's work, I aim to hallo Bones's camp in the mornin'. If they ain't packed up and pulled out by noon, the killin' starts."

Frenchy nodded his head. "You put Mack and Cobb on the run, didn't you?"

"Yeah, I did."

Frenchy shook his head.

"They was both weak sisters. I didn't figure they'd last this long. You won't put no more on the run, Preacher. You best know that now."

Preacher sensed then that he hadn't won this one. Frenchy was going to make his try. "Then they're fools, Frenchy. Don't you be one."

"Oh, I ain't no fool, Preacher. I just don't like you."

"That's your option, boy. But it ain't worth dyin' for. You best take heed to them words. I'm givin' you a chance to go on back to Louisiana. Take it, Frenchy. I been there. The women is pretty, the wine is sweet, and the food is the best there is. Hell, Frenchy, you don't even know me. I'm offerin' you your life. Think about it."

"What you say is true."

Frenchy stood up slowly, a strange smile on his lips. He faced Preacher. He didn't say a word as his hand flashed for his knife.

Preacher's right hand clamped around Frenchy's wrist just as the blade came free of the scabbard. Preacher twisted and shoved the big-bladed knife to the hilt in Frenchy's belly, just under his rib cage. Frenchy gasped in pain and staggered back. He stopped just as lightning flashed and looked down at the handle of his knife. He raised his head and looked into Preacher's eyes.

"No man has ever bested me with a blade. No man ever done that."

"They's always someone better, Frenchy. You should have had enough sense to know that."

Frenchy sank to his knees. He screamed just as thunder rolled and pealed and echoed around the mountains. His mouth filled with blood and he toppled over.

Preacher gathered up his weapons, powder, and shot. He looked down at the dead man and thought about his night's work so far. "Well, I reckon two out of three ain't all that bad."

22

Preacher took Frenchy's words to heart about there being no more who would quit and called it a night. He began carefully making his way back to his camp—a hidden cavelike overhang that nature had concealed so well Preacher doubted that any living being had ever before set a foot in the place. The storm was full-blown now, a real rip-snorter. Preacher built a small fire for coffee and food. He saw to Thunder and then stripped down to the buff and dried off, changing into another set of buckskins. He sat by the fire, deep in thought.

After tomorrow, when Preacher would tell those remaining man-hunters that if they didn't give up this foolishness and ride on out, it would be shoot-on-sight, he knew he would have to back up his threat with action. Problem was, he just didn't want to do that.

"What else can I do?" he muttered, as the bacon sizzled in the pan and the water started to boil for coffee.

The flames danced silently, offering him no answer to his question.

"Just do it, I reckon," Preacher said.

* * *

When the missionaries awakened, Preacher was sitting under the canvas over the cooking area, drinking coffee. It gave them only a slight start, since by now they had accepted that Preacher could move like a ghost.

"I hope y'all brought a whole bunch of medical supplies," Preacher said without looking up. "This here war is fixin' to get real nasty."

"How did you know we had awakened, sir?" Otto asked.

"I heard you open your eyes."

"That is ridiculous!" Prudence said.

Preacher shrugged.

"I believe him," one of the wounded men said.

"I suppose you left this lovely valley littered with dead and dying men last night," Hanna said.

"Just one. And I give him a chance to ride out 'fore I done the deed. Just like I'm a fixin' to give the rest of that pack of hyenas out yonder ample warnin'."

"And if they don't heed your warning?" Paul Marks asked.

Preacher turned his head and stared at the man. The look in the mountain man's eyes made Paul queasy in the stomach. Without realizing he had done so, he backed up a couple of steps.

"I'm tired of foolin' around with these people. I'm tired of bein' hunted. I'm just by God tired of it. And I ain't gonna put up with it no more. I can't just leave. I do that, you folks will be in for a real bad time of it. And I think you women know what I mean. And it ain't y'all's fault. You just happened to come along at a real bad time." He shook his head and poured more coffee. "I just don't see no other way out of this mess."

"There ain't no other way out, Mister Preacher," the man with broken legs spoke up. "I'd make a bet that you convinced Cobb and Mack to leave last night. If so, that's all that's leavin'. The rest will stay to the last man."

"You done some good guessin'," Preacher said. "I met

up with three last night. Frenchy decided to play his hand. His cards run out."

Ed Crowe opened his mouth. "I don't believe you kilt Frenchy, mountain man. I say you're lyin'."

Preacher glanced at the mouthy man. "When you get on you feet, Crowe, you and me is gonna go 'round and 'round. So you got that to look forward to."

"You don't scare me none!" Ed sneered.

"I'm real glad to hear that. Now shut up. Your whiny voice is gratin' on me."

Ed wanted to say something else. He wanted to pop off real bad. But the look in Preacher's eyes warned him silent. Ed dropped his gaze from Preacher's cold stare and shut up.

Patience and Prudence set about making breakfast— pan bread and bacon—and Preacher ate in silence until one of the wounded men called his name. He looked over at the man.

"You know them fancy gents is all 'bout half tiched in the head, don't you?"

"I figured it."

"Crazy as ever seen," another wounded man said. "And I've seen some crazies in my time."

"And both Bones and Lige has some real crazy folks ridin' with them," the first man continued. "Lucas and his buddy, Willie, they're 'bout two boards shy of a straight picket fence, if you know what I mean. But they're dangerous."

"They like to kill, you mean." Preacher did not put it as a question.

"Yeah. I believe so."

Preacher nodded his head. "'Preciate it." He rinsed out his plate and placed it on a table. "I'll see you folks later on. You best get some bandages ready. You gonna be needin' 'em."

He mounted up on one of the horses of the wounded men and rode out. Otto had told him about Cobb and

Cornay. The two men had staggered into the camp late the night before, both of them frightened out of their wits. They hadn't even paused for coffee. Just went straight to the picket line, saddled up, and rode out. They headed south. Said they were leaving the mountains and it would be a cold day in hell before they ever returned.

Otto had volunteered to ride over to the man-hunters' camp and tell them that Preacher wanted to speak to the men, all of the men. Preacher told him where to have the men meet him.

Preacher was sitting on a ledge overlooking the valley when the men rode up. En masse. He was taking a chance that one of them might take a shot at him, but it was a risk he was willing to take to put an end to this foolishness.

"All right, boys," Preacher called from the rock ledge. "Gather in close and perk your ears up good. By now you prob'ly found Frenchy and you know that Cobb and Cornay is gone. Here's the deal. Listen up, 'cause I ain't gonna say this but one time. You boys has wooled me around long enough. I'm done playin'. You can ride on out of here right now, and live to tell your grandkids about this stupid hunt. Or you can stay and die. If you ain't packed up and gone from here by mid-afternoon, I'm gonna start killin' you wherever and whenever I find you. No more deals after this one. That's all I got to say. Git the hell out of these mountains." Preacher turned and vanished from the sight of those below him.

The group of men sat their horses for a moment. No one spoke.

Tom Evans broke the silence. "You think he means all that, Bones?"

Bones thought for a moment and then nodded his head. "Yeah, I do, Tom. I think this hunt just took a bloody turn."

The royalty twisted in their saddles and looked the

men over. Sir Elmore called out, "Any of you men want to leave?"

Slowly, the men began shaking their heads. They were all making more money on this hunt than they could possibly make back where they came from. And they all stood a chance of making a small fortune. They weren't about to give that up.

"Preacher'll be on the prowl come the night," Van Eaton opined. "We best get back and get ready for him."

But Preacher had changed his tactics. He wasn't about to enter that valley after the man-hunters. They were going to have to come to him. He'd taken his pirate glass and studied the man-hunters' camp late that same afternoon. "Fools," he muttered. "Plain damn fools. You was warned, boys. Now you gonna learn these mountains is *mine!*"

A man named Jeff, from Lige's bunch, found that out the hard way the following afternoon. He decided he'd go kill him a deer, for they were all tired of smoked fish and jerky. He hadn't gotten five hundred feet off the valley floor when Preacher's rifle boomed. Jeff tumbled out of the saddle and hit the ground hard. When he opened his eyes, he was in a world of pain and looking up into the cold eyes of Preacher.

Those back at the camp had heard the single shot and exchanged wary glances. They all knew what it meant, and it didn't mean that Jeff would be bringing in any venison.

"Don't . . . leave me here to die alone!" Jeff gasped.

"Why not?" Preacher asked, a hard edge to his voice. "You come a-huntin' me, not the other way 'round."

"I got . . . information."

"Then you better talk fast, boy. 'Cause you ain't got long."

"Them down yonder is . . . gonna take you alive and . . . torture you. Then when they's had their fun . . . they's gonna turn you a-loose nekked and hunt you down."

Preacher shook his head in disgust. "How did you ever agree to go along with something like that?"

"It was my idee!"

Preacher could but stare at the man for a moment. "Anything else?" He asked wearily.

"Yeah. Them good-lookin' wimmin is gonna get used hard. After . . . we . . . them . . . is done with you. Pass 'em around 'til we git tarred of 'em. Kill the men slow to make 'em holler."

"Them fancy-pants foreigners go along with that plan?"

"Oh . . . yeah. They lookin' forward . . . to it." Jeff closed his eyes and died.

Preacher went through the man's pockets and found a handful of gold coins. He kicked a few rocks and leaves over the body and took Jeff's horse. He rode straight to the missionary camp. First thing he noticed was that Ed Crowe was gone. There were six men still out of action due to broken bones. Preacher gathered the men and women around him, within earshot of the wounded men, and laid it on the line for them. He was blunt and left nothing that Jeff said out.

"No, by God, they won't!" a man spoke up, his voice angry. "We would have died if it hadn'ta-been for these good folks here. I done a lot of mean things in my life, but I ain't never put a hand on no good woman nor gentleman like these men is. We got our guns and ample powder and shot and patches. You go on and don't worry none about these folks. Bones and them will have to kill us to get to them. Right, boys?"

The three other men were very vocal in their defending the missionaries. Preacher eyeballed each of them, finally concluding that they meant it. It takes a sorry type of man to molest a woman, and these men were several cuts above that. No angels, mind you. But not gutter-slime, either.

"You boys'll do," Preacher told them.

"You'll stay for food?" Patience asked Preacher.

The mountain man shook his head. "Too risky for y'all. By now, Ed Crowe's done told Bones and the others about these boys here talkin' hard aginst this hunt and their decision about not comin' back to their camp." Preacher held up a finger and thought for a moment. "But I tell you what I'll do to tip the balance some. I'll just wing me four or five tomorrow and then they can't do nothin' to y'all if some of their own men is here bein' taken care of by us. How's that sound to you?"

Patience stared up at him. Finally she found her voice. "Well, that certainly is an idea that none of us would have ever thought of."

"Good. Tomorrow I'll go bust some arms and legs and such and they'll have to bring them here. You make damn sure you get their guns from them and hide them good, you hear?"

"Whatever you say, Preacher."

"Y'all get ready for some new patients 'bout noon tomorrow." Preacher turned and left the camp.

That night, Preacher crept up close to the camp of the man-hunters and began taunting them. He cussed them loud and long and then he shifted locations, slowly circling the camp. He traced the ancestors of the nobility back to apes swinging from vines in the jungle and got them so mad they had to be physically restrained inside the camp.

"All of you is lower than a snake's belly!" Preacher shouted out of the darkness. "You couldn't whup a bunch of old women—none of you. I never seen such a bunch of yeller-livered cowards in all my borned days. Man-hunters, my butt! Ain't none of you ever fought a man 'til you come up on me. And you're all so skirred of me you can't sleep at night. I've bested ever' one of you so many times I'm feelin' plumb ashamed of it. I'm gonna go cut me a switch to use on you when I catch you. All of you act like a bunch of foolish children."

"Tomorrow you die!" Baron Zaunbelcher screamed out into the night.

"Stick it up your nose," Preacher told him. "You better leave these mountains, buzzard-breath. You best tuck your tail 'tween your legs and run on back to mommy and daddy in the castle and hide under the bed. That is, if you have enough sense to find the bed."

Zaunbelcher was so furious he was jumping up and down and screaming oaths.

Preacher then started in on the other gentry until the blue-bloods were livid.

Then Preacher started in on Lucas and his friend Willie, comparing them to an ape and a monkey. And that was the nice thing he said about the pair. Willie grabbed up weapons and fired blindly into the night while Lucas, trembling with rage, beat on the ground with his huge fists and roared out curses and threats until he was hoarse.

Preacher laughed and taunted the men until he had nearly the entire camp of man-hunters in an uproar of anger. Then he faded into the night. He had a hunch that come the morning, they'd be out looking for him.

"Damnit, it's a trick!" Bones said to the royalty. "Can't you see that? Preacher was tossin' insults at us to make us mad. He knows if we get mad we'll do somethin' stupid. And we can't afford to do nothin' stupid."

But his friend Van Eaton sided with the others. Preacher had been especially hard on Van Eaton, calling the man some terrible names.

"That mountain man dies tomorrow," Van Eaton said, pushing the words through clenched teeth. "That's it, Bones. He dies tomorrow."

But a lot of people had spoken words along the same lines. Preacher had buried them. If he felt like burying them, that is.

23

The man-hunters left ten guards at the camp, chosen by drawing lots, and the rest pulled out just after dawn. They were all angry to the core but most had tempered their wild anger down to a hot bed of coals. Bones had prevailed upon them to cool down: don't go after Preacher unless they had a clear head.

Preacher had laid down sign, albeit not too obvious, for he knew there were some real woodsmen in the bunch, and was waiting. He figured they'd come up on him sometime about mid-morning. He had chosen his spot with caution, taking pains to ensure himself several ways out. And he had made up his mind that if he got even the smallest opportunity, he was going to put a ball or two into some of those blue-blooded snooty-nosed gentry. Right in the butt, if he could. 'Cause that's what they'd become to Preacher: a royal pain in the butt.

Preacher was under no illusions. He knew he was in terrible danger. He knew that the slightest miscalculation on his part, and he'd be dead. Or worse, taken alive for torture. If anyone were watching, it would seem that he was taking this manhunt much like a game. They would be very wrong in that assumption. Preacher worked out in his mind every move in advance. He was confident, but only because he'd lived and survived by his wits and skill ever since he was a young boy.

Preacher waited.

Bones had spread his group out into teams, a good tracker with each team. He alone felt in his gut that Preacher was up to something. But he'd asked the trackers if the sign was too obvious and to a man they had agreed it was not.

"He ain't doin' this a-purpose," one had said.

"It's just that he ain't as good as he thinks he is," another one had opined.

But Bones still had his doubts. By now he had reached the conclusion that Preacher really wasn't as good as people said he was—he was *better!*

"I'm going over there to scout!" Prince Juan Zapata shouted, pointing toward a rise just at the edge of the valley, before the earth began to swell into mountains.

Before Bones could yell for him not to leave the group, the rich, spoiled Spaniard had spurred his mount and was gone at a gallop.

"Fool!" Bones muttered.

Juan topped the rise and dismounted to stretch his legs. He looked all around, and then bent over to pick a flower to place in his hat. Preacher's rifle boomed and the Prince took a heavy caliber ball right in one fleshy cheek of his royal butt.

Zapata jumped about three feet into the air and commenced to squalling loud enough to wake the dead.

Preacher had not been sure he could even make the shot because of the long distance, but he held high and was right on target. It surprised the hell out of the mountain man. Because of the distance, the ball had lost much of its power when it impacted with Zapata's regal ass, but it still had enough zip to imbed deeply in his rear end.

Preacher never in his life saw so many people leave so many saddles in that short a time.

"Sure a bunch of skittish folks," he muttered, reloading the fancy hand-made rifle that had once belonged to one of the Frenchmen. He tried not to remember which one it was. "Fine shootin' rifle. Be a damn shame to shoot a feller with his own rifle," he said with a grin.

He watched as the men began moving through the grass to the aid of the still-squalling Prince. Preacher took a chance that he might hit something and sighted it just ahead and above the head of a growing snakelike path in the tall valley grass. He gently squeezed off a round.

A man jumped up and grabbed at one leg. Preacher grinned. Looked like another one of those fancy-pants folks.

"My leg!" Duke Burton Sullivan screamed. "He shot me in the leg!" he yelled as he fell down to the ground.

"Smart, Preacher," Bones muttered, his face pressed against the coolness of earth. "Now I know why you done what you did last night. Fill up the hospital and we have to keep the missionaries alive to treat the wounded. You no-good, miserable . . ." He cussed for a moment, then added, "For an ignorant mountain man as I was told you was, you sure have a headful of smarts."

For reasons known only to him, Bates foolishly jumped up and made a run for the wounded Prince and Duke. He came close to making it.

"We'll sure give it a try," Preacher muttered, pulling his rifle to his shoulder.

The fancy hunting rifle banged and Bates had a leg knocked out from under him. He did a flip and hit the ground, hollering to the high heavens.

"Now that was a lucky shot," Bones muttered.

"You got lucky on that one, boy," Preacher muttered. "Let's get gone from here."

After five minutes or so had passed, Bones crawled to his knees. He sensed, more than knew, that Preacher had done his work and was gone. "All right, people. Let's gather up the wounded and get them to the gospel-shouters."

Bones looked over at Zapata, lying on his belly. "He can't ride, so some of you rig up a travois."

"This sorta knocks our plans in the head, don't it, Bones?" Van Eaton spoke softly.

"Yeah."

"And I was lookin' forward to dallyin' some with them women over yonder. I like 'em with some meat on their bones. That there Hanna hottens up my blood something fierce."

"Go find a cold crick and jump in it," Bones suggested.

"Hell, I took a bath last month!"

When the dejected and bloodied bunch of man-hunters reached the site of the make-shift hospital in the middle of the wilderness, they were quick to note that not only were the missionary men armed, and armed well, so were the wounded. Even the women had shot-guns strategically placed. Took Bones about one second to understand that if they made a try for the women, a lot of men were going to die, for several of the wounded were more than fit to travel. That meant they were staying behind deliberately to act as guards.

Bones cut his eyes to Van Eaton. His right hand man had picked up on it, too. He nodded his head slightly.

"I must have medical treatment!" Prince Zapata yelled. "I demand it."

"Put him over there," Otto said, pointing and trying to hide his smile. "I'll see to his wound."

"I demand you stop that smiling at me!" Zapata shouted. "I am seriously wounded."

"You don't demand anything from me," Otto bluntly told him. "And I never heard of anyone who died from being shot in der butt."

Bones, Van Eaton, and those who helped bring the wounded to the make-shift hospital took their leave and being careful to stay in the center of the long valley, made their way back to camp. It was a weary and dejected bunch of man-hunters. Even the shoulders of the nobility slumped a bit as they rode. Nothing had turned out the way they planned. But the thought of calling off the hunt was nowhere in their minds.

For the others, over coffee and hot food, the talk was, surprisingly, not of quitting, but of what to do next.

"Corner him and burn him out," Pyle suggested.

"Corner him?" Flores looked at the man. "How? Most of the time we don't even *see* him."

"I wish we had some cannons," Falcon wished aloud. "We could blow him out of the mountains."

No one chose to respond to that. But a few of the men did smile at the ridiculousness of the remark.

"I got an idea," Sam Provost said. "Let's do to him like he done to us. Let's insult him and make him mad. Then he'll lose his temper and do something stupid."

"He'd see through that charade," Jon Louviere said. "Whoever told you Preacher was a stupid man was very badly misinformed. He is very intelligent and cunning. Which makes this game all the more exciting."

Van Eaton looked at the man. "Game? This is a game to you?"

"But of course."

"Man," Van Eaton said, shaking his head, "I can't figure none of you all. We got people dead all over these mountains. That Preacher has put lead in near'bouts all of us at one time or the other. He's destroyed our camps, burned our supplies, stampeded our horses, ambushed us, caused rockslides, thrown snakes at us, made fools of us, and he ain't even got nicked one time. And you think it's a game?"

Bones poured more coffee and sat back down. "It's done got personal to me now. The money aside, it's a matter of honor. If we don't corner Preacher and bring his head back in that there jug, we're all done as bounty-hunters. We'll never be able to get another job. News of this will get out. You can just bet that them that quit and headed back east has done told the story to anyone who'll listen. Folks is laughin' at us all over the place. I can't have that. I won't tolerate it. I ain't leavin' these mountains 'til Preacher is dead and we got his head. I'll die first."

Bones had finally expressed what had been in the minds of the rest of the men; the constant thought that silently nagged and dug at their pride. One man was making fools of them all. That just wouldn't do. To a man, they couldn't allow it. The hunt had to go on. The men didn't have a choice, or so they thought.

"We got to leave the valley and take to the mountains," Tatman spoke up, raw hatred for Preacher burning in his eyes. "We got to stop thinkin' like this was back east and start thinkin' like a mountain man."

"By jove!" Sir Elmore piped up. "I think you've got it!"

"Maybe so," Bones said. "Maybe so. It's worth a try. We'll leave ten men behind to guard the horses and the camp, and we'll strike out on foot. We'll each take supplies for three days and fan out in the mountains." He looked at Tatman. "Good thinkin', Tatman. Real good thinkin'."

"What are them igits doin' now?" Preacher muttered, peering at the men through his pirate glass. "Looks like a bunch of ants scurryin' about down there." He studied the activity for a moment longer, then put away his glass and shook his head. "They're comin' after me on foot. They done lost what little sense they had left. They're comin' right at me, in my country, on foot. Lord have mercy!"

With a smile that would have caused a savage alarm,

Preacher picked up his rifle and moved out. Now he'd show them how this game was really played. "Ants to a honey trap," Preacher muttered.

Tom Evans was the first to discover how far out of his class he was. Something smashed against the back of his head, dropping him into darkness. When he came slowly swimming out of unconsciousness, he thought for sure he was dead. He might as well have been. Preacher, and he was certain it was Preacher who'd hit him with something, had taken his shot bag and his powder. He'd busted Tom's rifle and pistols and snapped the blade off his fine knife. He had peeled him right down to the buff, and had even taken his boots. "Halp!" Tom hollered. "Somebody come halp me."

About a half a mile away, Homer Moore was waking up. He had a fearsome headache and a big lump on the side of his head that hurt like the devil when he gingerly fingered it. And he didn't have a stitch on. He looked wildly around him. His weapons were gone, as were his clothes. He was as defenseless as the day he'd been born. "Oh, Lord!" Homer said.

Cliff Wright heard a noise behind him and turned. He caught a rifle butt under his chin that knocked him cold. When he came around, he was hanging upside down from a tree limb by his bare ankles. Like the others, he had been left bare-butt nekked and could see where his weapons had been rendered useless by somebody. Preacher, he was sure. Cliff started hollering for help. He didn't know how he was gonna live this down. Come to think of it, he didn't know how he was going to *get* down. "Halp! Halp!" he yelled.

Tatman came charging through the brush and Preacher busted the man's right knee with the butt of Homer's rifle. He smashed the knee to pieces and Tatman was out of the game for a long time. The big man passed out from the pain. When he awakened, his weapons were gone.

He began crawling for safety, moaning and cussing and dragging his knee-broken leg.

Derby Peel turned around about three times and got himself lost as a goose in the dense forest and underbrush. He panicked and began running and yelling. He fell into a ravine, landed on his rifle, busted the stock of his rifle and broke several of his own ribs in the process. He passed out from the pain in his side and chest.

The men were so widely separated, and the country so rough and heavily timbered and thick with brush, the cries of the totally embarrassed men could not be heard. It was only by accident that Derby Peel was found, lifted out of the ravine, and toted off to the missionary's hospital.

"The ignorant fool fell into the ravine and landed on his rifle," Lige remarked. "How damn clumsy can you get?" He turned around just as Preacher hurled a fist-sized rock that caught the big man in the center of his forehead and knocked him sprawling to the ground.

Jeremy King, one of Lige's bunch, whirled around, lifting his rifle. Preacher blew a hole in his chest and Jeremy landed on his back, dead eyes open and staring at nothing.

The woods erupted in wild gunfire, but Preacher had dropped to the ground an instant after he fired and the balls hit nothing except air, leaves, branches, and thudded harmlessly into the timber.

Tom Evans and Homer Moore, who had been wandering about trying to find their clothes, chose that time to blunder into the clearing . . . bare butt shining.

"My God!" Fred Lasalle blurted. "Them boys ain't got no clothes on."

"I always did wonder 'bout them two," Bob Jones said.

"What's all the shootin' about?" Tom asked.

"Git down, you fools!" Stan Law hollered. "It's Preacher up yonder."

"Don't get over here next to me," Bob warned.

Their worries were needless, for Preacher was a good

quarter of a mile away, running through the timber. He spotted movement ahead and stopped, bellying down on the ground. He smiled when he recognized Van Eaton as one of the men.

Van Eaton moved just as Preacher squeezed off a shot. The ball slammed into a tree and Van Eaton got a face full of splinters that bloodied him and scared him. He dropped to the ground, sure that he'd been mortally wounded.

Preacher quickly reloaded and wriggled into a better spot. Sam Provost raised his head up and took the last look of his life. Preacher shot him between the eyes.

That was enough for Van Eaton. Leaving Sam's body behind, he and the other man with him, Horace Haywood, ran from the area. They'd gone about two thousand yards when they came up on Cliff Wright, dangling butt bare and all from a tree limb. One side of his face was bloody and scratched something awful. The men stood and stared in disbelief for a moment.

"Y'all want to stop that bug-eyed gawkin' and cut me down and find me something to wear!" Cliff hollered.

While Horace was cutting him down, Van Eaton asked, "What happened to your face? Did Preacher do that?"

"No!" Cliff snapped the word. "A big bear did. He come by about an hour ago and reared up two-three times a-sniffin' at me. Like to have scared me half outta my wits, let me tell you. Then he rared up on his back legs, reached up and slapped the pee outta me and just wandered off. I hate these mountains, Van Eaton. I mean, I really, *really* hate these mountains. I hate these mountains nearly 'bout as much as I hate that mountain man. And I *do* hate Preacher."

"All your guns is ruint," Horace told him. "And I can't find your clothes nowhere." He took off his jacket and handed it to Cliff. "Wrap that around you."

Van Eaton held up a hand. "Wait. Let's go back and

peel the clothes offen Sam. He shore ain't got no more need for them. And his boots'll fit you too, Cliff."

"Suits me. I'll get his guns, too."

But Preacher had smashed Sam's guns, leaving them useless, and taken his powder and shot.

"Crap!" Van Eaton said, as Cliff removed the dead man's clothing. "Now I see what he's doing. If this keeps up we'll be throwin' rocks at him."

Lige and his dwindling bunch came cussing through the timber, dragging a moaning Derby Peel on a hastily made travois. Lige's head was bloody and there was a huge knot in the center of his forehead.

"What happened to you?" Van Eaton asked.

"Preacher," Lige said, a surly note to his voice. "He flung a rock at me."

Van Eaton sighed and muttered, "Now he's throwin' rocks at us. Good Lord Amighty." He pointed to Peel. "All right, all right. What about him?"

"He either fell into a ravine or Preacher throwed him into it. He's stove up pretty bad. Busted some ribs, I reckon," Homer said, red-faced. He was wearing Jeremy's jacket which wasn't quite long enough to cover his essentials, and Tom was wearing the dead man's pants.

"Where's your guns?"

"Busted up. Gone. I don't know. Preacher took all our powder and shot, too."

"Halp!" The shout came faintly to them. "Somebody come halp me. Over here."

"That's Tatman."

Van Eaton rubbed a hand over his unshaven face. "I hope to hell he's wearin' his britches. I done seen enough men's bare butts this day to last me a lifetime!"

24

The missionaries were amazed and somewhat amused that one man could inflict so much damage on so many. And to a person, they all realized something else about this legendary mountain man called Preacher. He could have easily killed all these men who now were straining their meager medical facilities and knowledge. But despite his tough talk and dire threats, he had elected to injure most and not kill.

If the missionaries were secretly amused, the manhunters certainly were not. The nobility were livid with rage, and Bones and Van Eaton and Lige were so mad they could scarcely speak.

No plan they had conceived thus far had worked, and Preacher had made fools of them—again—toying with them as if they were little children.

"This is mighty fine venison you cooked up, ma'am," Tom Evans said to Patience. "One of your men shot this today, did he?"

"You might say that," she replied.

"Huh?" Tom said.

"Preacher brought it in about an hour before you gentlemen arrived," Prudence told him.

Tom's face turned beet-red and he almost choked on his food. He suddenly lost his appetite.

Duke Burton Sullivan was tempted to hurl his plate into the fire, but thought better of it. That would be very bad manners on his part. Prince Juan Zapata muttered some curses in his native tongue and laid his plate to one side. Derby Peel shook his bruised head and wished he had never left home. Tatman, his knee set and immobilized, was the first to admit—to himself—that the whole bunch of them were outclassed. None of the newly wounded men had any idea that Preacher was less than a hundred yards away, watching the scene through very amused eyes. After a time, Preacher picked up his rifle and slipped away. Bones and his men would not be expecting an attack on their main camp this soon after their fiasco in the mountains. Preacher thought he'd just go stir things up a bit.

Back at their own camp, Bones and Van Eaton sat to one side and looked over what was left of their group. It sure was a pitiful sight. Beat-up, bloodied, bruised, and embarrassed, the men were silent and sullen this late afternoon. But incredibly, almost to a man, there was no thought of giving up.

Joe Moss, one of Lige's group, got up from the ground to pour a cup of coffee. On his way to the fire, he paused to speak to Alan James, a man from his home state. Joe turned and Preacher's rifle boomed from the dusk and the shadows, the ball shattering Joe's left knee and knocking him screaming and thrashing about on the ground. Alan leaped for his rifle and brought it to bear. But there was no target. Only the darkness presented itself.

"Oh, Sweet Baby Jesus!" Moss hollered, jerking in pain. "I'm ruint for life."

Before the echo of the shot had faded, every man in camp had bellied down on the ground. Every man except Alan. He stood crouched, rifle at the ready. Preacher's rifle boomed again, and Alan was spun around like a top, the big ball breaking his hip bone. He fell across Joe's shattered knee and Joe screamed and dropped into unconsciousness. All over the camp, men were cussing and casting about dire threats. But nobody got up to carry any of them out.

Preacher slipped across the valley and headed for his own camp. Somebody would be transporting the newly wounded over to the missionaries, and true to his word, Preacher would not ambush anyone doing that. He knew the man-hunters would not honor that if he was the one wounded, but that was their rock to mentally tote around. Preacher's conscience was clear and he planned on sleeping well that night.

The next morning, Sir Elmore, Baron Zaunbelcher, Willy Steinwinder, Bones, Van Eaton, and Lige rode over to the camp to see about their friends. They almost went into apoplexy when they saw Preacher, lounging comfortably and drinking coffee.

"Howdy, boys!" the mountain man called cheerfully. "Did y'all get a good night's sleep?"

"Just remember, this is a neutral zone," Frank Collins reminded the men.

"We'll honor it," Bones said. He looked at Preacher. "You got more than your share of nerve, Mountain Man."

"I reckon." He pointed to the several bouquets of wild flowers that now brightened the camp. "But I wanted to show the ladies how much I 'preciated them bein' here. So I picked them a bunch of flowers. Purty, ain't they?"

Willy Steinwinder's face became ugly and mottled with rage. When he got his anger under control, he said, "You . . . picked those flowers?"

"Well, they shore didn't leap out of the ground and into my hand. I think y'all ain't bein' very gentlemanly 'bout this here situation."

"What do you mean, sir?" Baron Zaunbelcher demanded.

"Y'all didn't bring nothin' for the ladies, did you?"

Steinwinder turned his back to Preacher and looked up at the blue of the sky. He muttered darkly under his breath.

Preacher wouldn't let up. With a straight face, he said, "Here I am, havin' to hunt game so's the very men who was doin' their dead level best tryin' to kill me will have somethin' to eat. Now, that don't seem real fair to me. Seems like y'all would see fit to contribute somethin'."

The men stared at Preacher. A thousand thoughts were running through their heads but they were speechless. Stunned into silence. All of them.

Tatman hollered, "Kill him for me! Just hammer back and kill that smart-aleck for me!"

Bones found his voice. He looked at Preacher. "Took their guns, did you?"

"It seemed a smart move at the time, yeah."

Bones had also noticed that Preacher had a sawed-off shotgun lying across his lap. Bones knew what a sawed-off shotgun could do. He'd seen men cut in two with them. So he was very careful to keep his hands as far away as he could from his pistols. "So what now, Preacher?"

"Y'all can pull out and I'll forget all about this."

Van Eaton said, "You know can't none of us do that, Preacher. And you know why."

"Pride's a terrible thing sometimes, Van Eaton. You really figure it's worth dyin' for?"

"When you're in our line of work, yeah, I do."

"Maybe so. But y'all could change your line of work, you know?"

"My good man," Sir Elmore piped up. "I have a sporting proposition for you."

"I just bet you do. What is it?"

"Your mummy and daddy still living?"

"Yeah. My mum . . . mother and father is alive."

"Could they use ten thousand dollars?"

"Who couldn't?"

"Well . . . there are some of us who . . . never mind. My proposition is this: As soon as Juan and Burton are up to it, we shall put up bank notes worth ten thousand dollars. We'll, ah, let the good missionaries hold the notes. Then the eight of us hunt you. In an area that can be worked out. If we kill you, your parents are richer by ten thousand dollars. I mean, face facts man, we're going to kill you eventually. Why not make your parents' lives a bit easier?"

Preacher blinked, then blinked again. This fool really believed what he just spouted. Preacher chuckled softly. "No, mister high falutin' mucky muck. I think I'll pass. But I will take this time to try to get somethin' through your heads. I've tried before, but perhaps this time I can get through to you. You boys ain't gonna kill me. I may get bit by a rattler or a hydrophobia skunk; my horse might step in a hole and toss me and break my neck. I may get mauled by a puma or kilt by a grizzly. Some Injun might get lucky and do me in. All sorts of things can happen to a man out here in the Lonesome. But I'll tell you all what ain't gonna happen: you boys ain't gonna kill me. You best understand that."

"Oh, that's piffle!" Elmore said with a wave of his hand.

"No, it ain't neither piffle," Preacher said. "Whatever that means. It's pure fact. Now, boys, I mean what I say. This ain't fun and games. Whilst you're in this camp, you're safe. But out yonder," he pointed to the valley and beyond, "you're fair game to me."

Sir Elmore looked down his aristocratic nose at Preacher. "I must say, sir, that there is little distance between you and a fool."

Preacher smiled. "You mighty right about that. I figure five feet at best."

* * *

Before he left the missionary's camp, Preacher had asked if they had any kind of opiate to knock Tatman and a couple of others out. Otto assured him they did, and they most certainly would do just that.

Preacher left the camp feeling better. Otto was not a real trusting man when in the company of brigands and thugs. And the man was ox-strong. Had arms on him 'bout the size of Preacher's thighs. If Otto ever got his hands on a body, it would be all over 'ceptin for the buryin'. And Hanna wasn't no delicate bloomin' flower herself.

Preacher awakened in the wee hours of the morning. No sense of danger awoke him. It was the workings of his mind. For years Preacher had prowled the mountains and ridden the country in relative peace. He had run-ins with Indian and whites alike, all mountain men did. Indians who resented the coming of the white man and trashy whites who raided trap-lines and the like. Preacher had never been known as a trouble-hunter. And he tried to shy away from those who did want trouble. But the past two or three years had been rough on him. As his reputation grew, so did the people who came looking for him to make a name. Seemed to him the immigration of eastern folks heading for a new life out west had brought him nothing but headaches.

Preacher sighed and reached out to feel the coffee-pot. The coffee was still warm enough to taste good. Without getting out of his blankets, he reached for the cup and poured it about half full. The coffee was just right. Black as sin and strong enough to bend nails. Good.

Preacher lay back, his saddle for a pillow, and tried to figure out the best thing he could do. If not for the missionaries, he thought he'd just pull out and hole up 'til winter.

But he couldn't do that with the gospel-shouters in the valley. Bones and his men would have their way with the women and the men. Preacher did not want to go through life with that on his conscience.

So, he concluded, he had to see this fight to the end whether he liked it or not. So all right. But he thought he knew a way to do it without any more killing . . . or at least keeping it to a minimum.

With that issue settled in his mind, he went back to sleep.

25

The man fetched water from the creek, returned to the camp, and squatted down in the dim light of pre-dawn. He laid twigs on the coals, then added heavier sticks when the kindling burst into flames. He lifted the coffeepot and his right hand and arm went numb when a heavy caliber rifle ball punctured the pot and tore it from his hand. The early riser leaped for the safety of darkness and away from the campfire. The entire camp of man-hunters was awake and belly down on the cold ground. They watched through startled eyes as a fire arrow arched its fiery way through the air and landed on a pile of dirty, flea-infested blankets just vacated by Lige Watson. The blankets burst into flames and tall shadows lept around the murk of the camp. Another fire arrow landed inside the crude corral and the horses were spooked. They smashed through the flimsy barricade and spilled out into the valley, running wild.

Sutton leaped to his bare feet and Preacher cut him down with a ball in his leg.

Preacher had carried four rifles and his bow with him that morning, determined to put as many men out of action as possible, hopefully without killing any of them. If he could get enough of them wounded and unable to

ride, he would take the missionaries and lead them away
from this place and then maybe he could go on with his
life and live in peace.

"Anybody see where he is?" Bones tossed out the
question.

"No," Van Eaton replied from a few yards away. "It
wouldn't make no difference no how. He moves as soon
as he fires."

With the light increasing, Preacher ruined another
big coffeepot, the big ball sending the pot flying.

"Two pots left," Tom Evans said sorrowfully. "And
them horses are still runnin'."

"It'll take us the better part of two days to round them
all up," Fred Lasalle said.

"You uncouth savage!" Jon Louviere yelled. "Stand up
and fight like a man."

Bones shook his head and muttered, "I swear them
people get dumber and dumber with each passin' day."

"I challenge you to a duel!" Sir Elmore screamed.
"Meet me in honorable combat!"

"Sure he will," Van Eaton mumbled.

Another fire arrow soared gracefully through the air
and landed in the grass behind the camp and flames
began licking their way higher and higher. Bones had
ordered the camp built inside a lazy half circle of the
creek, so the flames had but one way to go—straight into
the camp.

"We gotta put out that fire!" Bones yelled. "It'll burn
ever'thing we got if we don't."

Hugh Fuller jumped up and grabbed a bucket of
water. Preacher broke his arm with a ball. George
Winters ran for his saddle and his sleeping blankets and
Preacher cut his leg from under him. Preacher fired at
another running man and missed him clean. Using his
last loaded rifle, he shot Ray Wood in the side. Preacher
gathered up all his empty rifles and began working his

way around to the rear of the camp. The flames were leaping into the air and the smoke was thick.

"Stay on your belly and toss water or beat blankets on the ground in front of you!" Bones yelled. "Beat it out with your hands if you have to."

"Get shovels or use your blades to dig a break!" Van Eaton added, panic in his voice.

The smoke was so thick none of the man-hunters could see the single, odd-shaped arrow arch through the air and land in the middle of the flames. But they could all damn sure hear and feel the explosion as the bag of powder attached to the arrow blew, sending fire and sparks flying all over the place.

The concussion knocked one man down and stunned several others closest to the explosion. Another arrow landed and a second explosion rocked the smoky camp. Sir Elmore was only a few feet away from the second explosion and the explosion rendered him sillier than a happy lunatic for a few moments. He was wandering about the fire and smoke humming and playing patty-cake until Baron Zaunbelcher tackled him and brought him down.

Preacher figured he'd done a fair amount of damage and caused enough confusion for one morning. He ripped the hammers off three of the rifles, put them in his pocket and tossed the rifles aside. He took off at a run, circling the camp and heading in the direction of the running horses. He figured he'd have a good hour before any of the men came after him.

He managed to calm down and get hands on four of the trembling horses. He led them off into the mountains and turned them loose. They might return to the camp, and they might not. He left them on rich, belly high grass near water.

Several hours later, he watched from a distance as the wounded were taken to the already overburdened, make-shift hospital. Near as he could figure, both groups

combined had about thirty men still able to ride and
fight. That was still too many for Preacher's liking.

He suddenly smiled. The deal was no shootin' or
ambushin' whilst the wounded was taken to the hospital.
There wasn't nothin' said about what might happen on
the return trip.

"Now, that's sneaky, Preacher," he whispered. His smile
widened. "Damn shore is!" he said aloud. "I'm proud I
thought of it, too."

He counted the mounted men. Fifteen of them. They'd
only managed to round up about a third of the horses.

He worked his way to the valley floor and made himself comfortable beside the creek bank. An hour later,
common sense told him to abandon his plan. Bones had
sent riders far ahead of the main group's return, riding
on both sides of the creek bank with rifles at the ready.
Preacher forded the creek, bellied down in the grass,
and snaked his way clear. He smiled as he spotted the
returning group. Bones was wising up. He'd split the
group into two parties. One on the far side of the long
valley and the other near the creek.

"You're learnin', boy," Preacher muttered. "But not
fast enough to do you no good."

Preacher counted the men in the returning groups.
He knew he'd wounded three, maybe four. He counted
them again. One was missing. "Gettin' sneaky, aren't
you, Bones?" Preacher whispered.

He stayed right where he was. Preacher could be more
Indian than an Indian if he had to, and he figured this was
a good time to do just that. He moved only his eyes. Birds
soon became accustomed to the motionless presence and
paid him no heed. It was a few minutes before dusk when
Preacher sensed, more than heard, the man. Whoever he
was, he was damn good. But Preacher knew there was no
way the man could know where he was. What he had done
was take a guess and it had proved out to be a good one.

The man, and it turned out to be a man Preacher had

heard called Bobby, came within twenty feet of Preacher. And Bobby was good. Real good. He moved as quiet as a mouse through a church. He moved so good that Preacher lost him. He couldn't see him, he couldn't hear him.

Preacher knew he was in trouble.

All right, Hoss, he thought. You played it smart and got yourself in trouble. Now what?

Bobby made the mistake of emitting a slight grunt when he jumped and that was the only thing that saved Preacher's life. He rolled to one side, leaving his rifle behind, and Bobby's tomahawk got buried in the dirt. Preacher kicked out, his foot catching Bobby on the knee and staggering him just long enough for Preacher to jump to his moccasins. Bobby immediately jerked a pistol out of this belt and Preacher's left hand shot out and clamped down on the man's wrist, preventing him from leveling the pistol. Locked together, the two men fought with fists. Preacher with his right, Bobby was his left.

Preacher slammed a big right fist again and again into Bobby's face, smashing his nose and pulping his lips. Bobby smashed a fist into Preacher's face and the blood from both men mingled in this death struggle. Bobby tried to back-heel Preacher but the mountain man had expected that and was ready.

Preacher heard the gun cock and finally managed to grab hold of his knife. He drove the blade into Bobby's side and twisted. The man-hunter screamed and pulled the trigger. Preacher felt a tremendous blow in his side and knew he'd been hit. How hard, he didn't know. But he knew it was bad. He jerked out the knife and cut Bobby from belly to backbone, then released the man.

Bobby fell to the ground. "At least I got lead in you," he gasped.

"You ain't gonna live long enough to enjoy it, though," Preacher spoke through gritted teeth against the throbbing pain in his side.

"I 'spect you be right about that, mountain man." That was the last thing Bobby said. He shuddered once, then closed his eyes and died.

Knowing the shot would bring man-hunters at a gallop, Preacher got gone from there.

"All right," Bones said, staring at the two distinct blood signs. He had inspected Bobby's pistol. "We lost Bobby, but he got lead into Preacher, and judgin' from the blood, it's a bad wound. And this time it's real."

"Let's proceed at once!" Sir Elmore said.

"No!" Bones snapped with adamance. "Not in the dark. Think about it. Preacher gonna be holed up like a hurt panther, lickin' his wounds. A wounded animal is the most dangerous. We go blunderin' out there now, some of us ain't gonna be returnin'."

"At least with Preacher hurt, we can all get a decent night's sleep," Van Eaton allowed.

Preacher was weak when he arrived at his mountain camp. Before leaving the valley floor he'd grabbed up enough makin's for several poultices and now he set about boiling water. He took off his shirt and inspected as best he could the wounds. And there were two, one in front, and the exit hole. Preacher had several bullet scars on his hide, and knew if the wound had been a killing one, he'd a been dead by now. But the bullet holes needed tendin', and the sooner the better. And he was already weak from the loss of blood. He made a broth from part of a venison haunch he'd hung up high and while that was simmerin' he cleaned out the wounds and applied the hot poultices. He added salt to the broth, for when you lose blood you crave salt. Then he drank two cups of the broth and felt a bit better. He put water on for coffee and lay back on his blankets to rest.

Preacher was a realist, and he knew he was in real trouble. He was weak and in no shape for a fight. He'd heal quick—he always did. But he had to stay quiet for several days. As he lay warm by the fire, he reviewed his back trail. He'd left plenty of sign leavin' the scene of the death struggle, but he soon began erasin' his tracks. It wouldn't fool no Indian, but it might fool those with Bones. He had to have several days of rest. Preacher knew that wounds healed much quicker in the high up country . . . he didn't know why, but thought it probably had something to do with the cold, clean air.

He finally went to sleep just as the small fire was dying down to coals.

The trackers lost Preacher's sign less than two miles from the death scene in the valley. They started working in ever widening circles, but it didn't prove out. The mountain man had vanished without leaving a clue.

"They's got to be a drop of blood," Van Eaton insisted. "A broken twig, a bent leaf—something!"

"Look for yourself," Titus, the Kentucky man, said matter-of-factly. "Wounded he may be, but it didn't slacken none his ability to hide a trail."

At that moment, Preacher was less than a half mile from the man-hunters. But people who are unfamiliar with the mountains fail to realize that there are literally hundreds of places to hide without detection. Preacher had left his horses at the missionary camp and on foot, left practically no sign.

And in hiding, Preacher never disturbed the natural look of the landscape, using nature at its purest for concealment. Preacher rested while Bones and the nobility stomped all over the place and accomplished nothing except for the raising of blisters on their feet.

Finally, Bones called a halt to the search for Preacher and pulled everybody back to the main camp in the valley. There just wasn't any point in continuing. To the man-hunters, it seemed as though the mountain man had simply dropped off the face of the earth.

"Don't y'all be frettin' none about Preacher," Dirk, one of the newly converted men at the missionary camp told the women. "Hurt he may be, but that man is tough. And he knows ways to use what nature has provided to get hisself healed up."

"That's right," Will, another ex-man-hunter added. "That ol' boy is part wolf, part cougar, part bear, and all around mean when it comes to who flung the chunk. His kind is hard to kill. I seen a man up in the Blue Ridge one time take six balls in him and he still kept on comin'. He kilt them that was shootin' him and the last I heard, he was still alive and doin' right well, he was. There ain't no harder man in the world to stop than a feller who knows he's in the right and just keeps gettin' up and keeps on comin' at you."

Otto rode in and dismounted. "They've moved their camp," he told the group. "Over to the next valley west of here. This time they chose well. Preacher would be wise not to attempt any attack on this camp."

"If he's alive," Patience said, a gloomy note to her voice.

Otto smiled. "Oh, he's alive. I spoke with him not more than two hours ago."

Everyone started talking at once and Otto waited until the hubbub of voices had died down.

"He's still not a hundred percent, but very close to it. He's used Indian potions and poultices. We must learn those, people. Their healing powers are nothing short of miraculous. Preacher is fine."

Dirk gave Patience a friendly wink. "Told you," he said with a smile.

26

"We're just about out of everything," Van Eaton announced. "If we stretch coffee and beans and flour, we might last another ten days. No more."

"Them gospel-shouters has a-plenty," Dutch said. "I say we go take it and have our way with them women."

Three weeks had passed without any of the man-hunters so much as glimpsing a track of Preacher. Preacher had moved very little. He had stayed alive by trapping rabbits, snaring mountain trout in fish-traps, and eating berries and tubers. After each rabbit, he would move the trap to a different location, sometimes no more than a few yards away. He was healed up and if anything, he was tougher and stronger than before. He was definitely leaner and meaner. He had killed a deer with bow and arrow and had passed the time by making himself a new pair of moccasins.

Now it was time to move.

Preacher had given up trying to understand the inner workings of the minds of those chasing him. He knew only that he was going to put an end to this hunt. He also knew that many of the men he had wounded would have by now left the missionary camp and rejoined

Bones and his bunch. So much for trying to limit the killing.

So, on a fine morning in late summer, Preacher made his way to a place the Indians called Echo Point, the summit rearing up just over fourteen thousand feet in the thin air. It was a place where a shout could be heard for miles in all directions.

"I am Preacher!" the mountain man shouted, the words bouncing from valley to valley. "I am called Ghost Walker. White Wolf. Killing Ghost."

His words reached every human ear within miles. The Indians smiled and looked at one another in satisfaction, and the white stiffened in shock.

"That's cocky! . . ." Bones hissed.

"Magnificent!" Otto said.

"To those who hunt me, your time has come. You will not leave these mountains. Your flesh will rot and your bones will bleach under the sun and be scattered by the critters. You've hunted me and shot me and done your best to kill me. But I live. I live! Now I hunt. Now you will know the fear of the hunted. I will stalk you during the day and cut your throats while you sleep at night. You . . . all . . . will . . . die!" Preacher thundered.

"Big blowhard!" Tatman said, hobbling about the camp on a crutch. His knee was far from healed, but it was just about as healed as it was going to get with the time he had left to him. He hobbled over to where Joe Moss sat on a log, his own busted knee wrapped securely and stuck out in front of him, and carefully sat down. "We owe that mountain man, don't we, Moss."

"In spades," the man said bitterly. He pulled out a knife and began sharpening the blade on a stone. "I want to skin him alive; keep him screamin' for a long time."

"Yeah, yeah! That's a good idee, for shore."

Derby Peel walked over, favoring his healing ribs, and agreed with what Moss had to say. "Just let me be there when you do it, boys. I owe him too."

"Least you can walk," Tatman said. "Me and Moss is crippled for life. It just ain't right what he done to us. It just ain't right. Cripplin' a man ain't no fair way to fight. It just by God ain't."

"Shore ain't," Moss agreed. "That man has condemned me to be a cripple for the rest of my days. There just ain't no justice in his world, that's for shore."

Bones and Van Eaton had heard the words and exchanged glances. "I ain't quittin'," Bones spoke softly. "I can't quit."

"I know," his friend replied. "I didn't say nothin' about quittin'. Just that we're soon gonna be out of supplies. Well," Van Eaton said with a sigh, "least we'll be together when the deed is done."

Bones gave him a sharp glance. "What the hell do you mean by that?"

"Aw, come on, Bones," Van Eaton whispered. "Look around you. Men all shot up an' limpin' an' crippled an' moanin' an' groanin'. One man done all that. One man, Bones. We ain't gonna beat that mountain man, Bones. And you know it well as me."

Bones made no reply. Just sat with his head down staring at his filthy hands.

Van Eaton stood up and put a hand on Bones's shoulder. "We been friends for nigh on thirty years, Bones. And we've made a right considerable sum of money chasin' wanted men. But I got me a feelin' in my guts that this here is our last run. Bones? We could always head west and change our names."

"No," Bones said firmly. "That mountain man ain't gonna make me turn tail like a whipped dog. Van Eaton?"

"Yeah?"

"You see me buried proper, all right?"

"All right. You do the same for me if I go first."

"You know I will."

On the other side of the camp, the nobility had listened to Preacher's words and promptly dismissed them as mere prattle. They had already discussed the matter of supplies and had decided that they'd give this hunt about ten more days and then head out of the mountains before winter. But they would return the next spring to resume the hunt. This had been the most exhilarating time of their spoiled, pampered lives.

Juan's butt had healed up well. Rudi's shoulder was a bit stiff but functioning. Burton's leg had healed up nicely as well.

They were ready for the hunt to resume.

Preacher strolled into the missionary's camp nonchalantly, as if he'd been gone for no more than an hour instead of three weeks. "Howdy, folks! Y'all got any vittles to eat?"

Everyone crowded around, inspecting him. Preacher looked to be better than he was the last time they'd seen him. Patience said so, speaking for all in the camp.

"It's the pure mountain air that done it. That and good clean Christian livin', of course," Preacher replied with a straight face. He looked around him. The area where they had housed the prisoners was empty. "What happened to all your patients?"

"Some died," John said. "They're buried in the meadow yonder. Most recovered and went back with Bones." He pointed to four clean-shaven and bathed men. "These four, Dirk, Simpson, Will, and Jim, have accepted Christ into their lives and are going to stay with us."

"Well, by golly, I think that's grand, boys." Preacher shook each newly converted hand and the former rogues and man-hunters grinned at him.

Dirk said, "You don't have to fret none about anything

happenin' to these folks, Preacher. Me and the boys would give our lives for these fine people."

Preacher stared hard at the man, and silently agreed that Dirk meant it. "I believe you. You're a good man."

His plate of food was ready and Preacher sat down and dug in. He ate that and then ate another full plate before he was full. He leaned back with his pipe and a cup of coffee and sighed. "Y'all got any medicines left?"

"Some," Prudence said. "But not a large amount. Why?"

"Y'all better get ready for some more patients. 'Cause after I finish this coffee and smoke, I'm fixin' to go huntin' me some no-counts."

Otto said, "We offered them salvation. They refused. Some even openly scoffed at us. Since that time we have posted guards out at night and none of us ever go without our weapons. The women have all had firearms training."

"That's good. 'Cause if y'all plan on stayin' out here, sooner or later you women will have to pick up a gun and kill you an Indian or a brigand. I just hope that when the time comes, you won't hesitate none in the pullin' of that trigger." He paused to puff on his pipe. "When I get done with my business, I want to set you folks down and talk to you 'bout your plans on settlin' in this country. It ain't the wisest choice you could have made. But that'll wait 'til another day."

"Our mission remains clear and our course is unalterable," Patience told him.

"Uh-huh," Preacher said. "We'll see."

"Preacher," Otto said, quickly changing the subject, "I've seen the man-hunters' new camp. It's a good one for defense. The best they've chosen."

Preacher smiled. "I've seen it too. And they couldn't have picked no worser place. I'm headin' over there now. I'll see you folks tomorrow or the next day. Bye."

* * *

Preacher lay in the rocks above the camp and studied it more closely through his glass. Bones couldn't have picked a worse spot if they'd all got together and held a stupid contest.

The camp had good water and there was graze for the horses, but the whole place was surrounded by timber. And Bones had built permanent watch shelters for the lookouts. Preacher memorized their locations and then stretched out for a nap. He planned on a busy evening.

Twice he'd lined up Tatman in his sights and twice Preacher had let the man live. He just couldn't pull the trigger. He just could not bring himself to shoot a man he'd made a cripple for the rest of his life. Preacher knew that if the conditions were reversed, Tatman would shoot him without blinking. . . . but maybe, he thought, that's one of the main things that separates us.

It would have seemed incredible to others, but for a moment, Preacher felt a twinge of pity for the group of man-hunters. He'd never seen a more beat-up and raggedy-lookin' bunch of men in all his days. They looked plumb pitiful. And he knew from the meager rations they were dishin' up that the bunch was nearly out of supplies.

From his position in the timber, Preacher counted the men. He shook his head. Way too many of them. The missionaries wouldn't stand a chance of beating them off if the man-hunters attacked in force. And if they ran out of supplies, they would attack and take what food the gospel-shouters had, and Preacher knew they had plenty.

Preacher experienced that old feeling of being "between a rock and a hard place" land on him again. Whatever he decided to do, he had to keep the safety of the missionaries foremost in his mind.

Damn! he thought.

He thought a lot worse than that when one of the men

stepped out of the campfire lit clearing and into the woods and came within a few feet of peeing on him.

I do get myself into some predicaments, Preacher thought sourly. The man finally closed up his britches and walked back into the clearing.

Preacher slowly backed away from the clearing, carefully avoiding the wet spot left by the man-hunter. He could have killed several of those chasing him—and he knew he probably should have—but for the time being, he left them live. He also felt he would probably regret that decision later on.

But Preacher wasn't going to leave the vicinity of the camp without first raising a little hell, letting the man-hunters know that he could move unseen among them any time he liked. He paused and gave that some thought. No, he concluded. No, he wouldn't do that. As much as he wanted to, he finally realized that wasn't such a good idea.

Preacher was torn with indecision. He just didn't know what to do. He knew what he *should* do, but he couldn't bring himself to do it. For the hundredth time, he wished these people would just go away and leave him be.

Preacher had the same feeling now as when years back, his older brother had told him there wasn't no such thing as Santy Claus.

For two days, Preacher watched the man-hunter camp and waited for them to do something. But all they did was eat and sleep and lounge about and act like they didn't have a care in the world. But Preacher had some cares. He knew he had to get those missionaries out of there before the snows came. People who had never experienced a winter in the high country had no idea just how fearsome a thing it was. The temperature could fall to way below zero faster than anybody would believe possible. And the passes would be clogged with snow. A man who knew the country and was on a good horse could make it. A wagon? No way.

The next morning, early, Preacher was in the missionary camp. "Pack up," he told them bluntly.

"I beg your pardon, sir?" Prudence questioned.

"Are you hard of hearin', woman? I said pack up and harness up. I'm gettin' you people out of here."

"You don't understand, sir," Hanna said. "We . . ."

Preacher waved her silent. " I understand more than you do, lady. I know it's damn near autumn. And I know I can't allow you people to be trapped up here when the snow comes. All the signs—if you know how to read them, and I do—point to a fierce winter. Y'all just don't know what winter is like in the mountains. Folks, we're high up. Higher than you realize. You just can't imagine what it's like up here in a blizzard. I can't get it through your heads that once the snow comes, you're stuck. You can't get them wagons out. Personally, I don't see how you ever got 'em *in.* You think you've seen winters back in New York or Maryland or wherever the hell it is you come from? You ain't seen nothin' 'til you seen snows piled tree-top high and winds fifty mile an hour and temperatures thirty below and water froze so solid you can walk a horse acrost it. You'll die, people. And the ground will be froze so deep down, blastin' powder wouldn't even dent it and I'd have to wait 'til spring to dig your graves. Am I gettin' through to you? Good. Now pack up. We're leavin' and to hell with them foolish bountyhunters. With any kind of luck we'll be gone two-three days 'fore they realize it. Now . . . move!"

27

"Gone!" Bob Jones yelled, jumping from his horse. "They're gone!"

"Who's gone?" Lige said, standing up.

"Them missionaries, that's who."

Everyone in the camp gathered around him. Bones grabbed him by the arm. "Are you sure?"

Bob gave him a dirty look. "Sure? Hell, yes, I'm sure. I just come from there. And the campfire ashes was so old and cold they didn't hold nary a spark."

"The ground around the ashes?" Van Eaton asked.

"Cold."

"Two days at least," Ed Crowe said. "How about tracks?"

"Plenty of them. Headin' south. I figure that's why ain't none of us heard nothin' from Preacher. He's leadin' them gospel-shouters out."

Bones was thoughtful for a moment standing amid the cussing and loud-talking group. The four men who had left his group to stay with the missionaries were seasoned fighters with no back-up in any of them. Otto Steiner, Frank Collins, and Paul Marks all looked to be capable and tough. And Bones had no doubts about the women being able to fight right alongside their men. Add Preacher to that list and it made for a group who would stand tough and fight to the bitter end. True, Bones and company had them out-numbered about five to one, but sometimes numbers made little difference when the other men were fighting for their families and for God.

Sir Elmore Jerrold-Taylor had found his slightly bent sword and was waving it around. Zaunbelcher had moved quickly to the other side of the clearing. "Break camp, men!" Elmore shouted. "We follow and attack. To your steeds, men. Hurry."

No one paid the slightest bit of attention to him. By now the man-hunters had all come to the conclusion this his Lordsip was crazy as a bessie bug, and those with him weren't that far behind. Sir Elmore finally realized that no one was listening to him and walked off to pout.

"Well, we'll follow, for sure," Bones said. "But before we attack, I want to look this situation over."

"You mighty right about that," Van Eaton agreed. "Dirk and them others is no pilgrims. And them gospel-shouter men didn't look like no pushovers to me."

"I wonder where that damn Preacher is taking them?" Ligue Watson pondered about.

Preacher was taking the missionaries just as far away from the valley of the man-hunters as he could, driving them hard.

In two and a half days, Preacher had pushed the wagons over thirty miles. A phenomenal feat considering the country in which they were traveling. But there was just no way to hide the trail the wagons left in their wake.

Preacher wasn't too worried about any Indian attack, for the Indians would see he was taking the whites out of their territory, and that basically was what they wanted. But he was moving them out of Ute and Arapaho country and onto the edge of Cheyenne territory. Although

Preacher had always gotten along fairly well with the Cheyenne, a body just never knew when a band of young bucks might happen along and take that moment to attack.

"Notional," Preacher told Otto as they rode side by side. "Injuns is notional people. I reckon I understand 'em 'bout as well as any white man, and I'll be the first to tell you even after all the years I spent out here I don't really know all that much. A man can ride into near'bouts any Indian village and get fed and put up for the night and treated right well. It's when you try to leave that it gets right testy. Don't ask me why they do that, 'cause I just don't know."

"Because they are savages," Otto said. "Uneducated, Godless savages."

"They're uneducated accordin' to the white man's point of view, yeah. Smart as a body can get in their own right. I done told y'all they ain't Godless."

Dirk rode up. The women were handling the reins to the teams, while the men ranged front and back and to the sides of the tiny train. Dirk had been lagging back about five miles. "No sign of Bones yet, Preacher."

"They'll be along. But I think I can get us down to the hot springs for a soak 'fore they catch up to us. The ladies is gonna enjoy these springs."

They sure did, and it was only with the greatest of effort that the men didn't try to sneak a peek at the ladies as they bathed and soaked and squealed and giggled in their birthday suits, splashing and playing in the hot water.

Dirk stuffed rags in his ears and wandered off to read the Bible. Simpson and Jim volunteered to stand watch about a mile from the springs, and Will rode off to see about shooting some game. When the ladies were done the men took turns washing off days of grime and soaking out the kinks and stiffness in weary muscles and joints. Upon their return from the hot waters, Prudence got to battin' her eyes something fierce at Dirk—who was a fine-lookin' man—and swishin' her bottom and sashshayin' about. Dirk got so flustered he walked into a tree and damn near knocked himself goofy. Preacher figured if he could get Dirk and Prudence together and toss a bucket of cold water on them, he'd have enough steam to run one of them big ugly and terrible soundin' locomotives he'd seen back east.

Preacher finally had to take off into the hills to get away from Patience. There was nothing he liked better than a good roll in the blankets with a fine-lookin' filly. But this was neither the time nor the place for a romantic tussle. However, he had learned a few years back that missionary women wasn't no different from other women when the candle got snuffed out and they got cozy. Loud, too. Preacher couldn't hear out the one ear for two days after a night with one particularly fine-lookin' gospel-shouter lady, a few hundred miles west and north of where they was right at the moment.

Preacher moved the pilgrims out the next morning. He'd heard tell of a tradin' post about four days from the springs and though he'd never been there, he decided to make a try for it. The missionaries were sorely in need of supplies. By this time, there were over a hundred and fifty trading posts scattered through the West. In two years trading posts had sprung up all over the place as more and more people were leaving their homes east of the Mississippi and heading west.

"Don't expect no fancy place like y'all seen in St. Louis," Preacher warned the ladies. "And the men there will likely ogle you gals from toes to nose. White women is scarce out here."

It was the most disreputable looking place the missionaries had ever seen. But it was a right busy post, doin' business with Indian and white alike. Preacher spoke with a couple of trappers he'd met over the years and knew slightly, then went inside to get a drink of whiskey.

Damned if the first person he spotted when he stepped up to the rough bar was a man who'd swore on his mother's eyes he'd someday kill Preacher.

Mean Pete Smith almost swallowed his chewing tobacco when he looked up and saw Preacher. His mouth dropped open and his eyes bugged out.

"Shut your mouth, Pete," Preacher told him. "Flies is uncommonly bad this year."

"You!" Mean Pete hollered.

"In the flesh."

Mean Pete stood up.

"Take your rough stuff outside," the owner of the post said. "I'll brook no trouble in here."

"Shut up," Mean Pete told him. "Me and this rooster here got things to settle 'tween us."

"Whiskey," Preacher told the man behind the planks, doing his best to ignore Mean Pete. "And don't gimmie none with no snake-heads in it."

The man looked hurt. "I serve only the finest of whiskey, sir."

"Right," Preacher said drily. "Aged a full two days at least. Put a jug out here."

The bar was separated from the mercantile part of the post by a log wall. A brightly colored blanket served as a door.

"You better enjoy that drink, Preacher," Mean Pete said. "'Cause it's gonna be the last'un you'll have."

Preacher poured and sipped and grimaced. "I was wrong. This here stuff was aged 'bout one day."

"Did you hear me?" Mean Pete roared.

"Oh, shut up, Pete," Preacher told him. "You said the same thing last time we hooked up and I left you on the floor. Now sit down and be quiet."

Mean Pete wasn't about to sit down and shut up. He had taken an immediate dislike to Preacher years back and challenged him to a fight. Preacher whipped him. For the last twenty or so years, every two or three years

Mean Pete would come up on Preacher, challenge him to fight, and Preacher would tear his meat house down.

After gettin' his butt bounced off the floor six or eight times, Preacher figured Mean Pete was about the hardheadedest man he'd ever met. Now here he was again. Only now it seemed like he wanted gunplay. Preacher was tired of gunplay. Weary of it. And he didn't want to kill Mean Pete. He turned to face Pete.

Preacher asked, "Pete, where in the world did you ever get the name of Mean Pete?"

"Haw?"

"Your name. Who was the first to call you Mean Pete?"

"I disremember. What's that got to do with anything?"

"I was just curious. 'Cause I ain't never heard of no kick and gouge you ever won. And when them Kiowa come at us down on the Canadian that time all I 'member seeing from you was your big butt runnin' off. So how in the world can you be called Mean Pete?"

"Preacher," Mean Pete took a step closer, his hands balled into fists, "I just ain't a-gonna stand here and let you insult me. I'm a-fixin' to stomp your ugly face. And then I'm a-gonna shoot you."

"In that order?"

Mean Pete flushed and took another step. He was a couple of inches taller than Preacher, and maybe twenty five pounds heavier. Neither Preacher nor Mean Pete noticed when the blanket was drawn back and the missionaries all crowded into the opening, staring at the scene before them.

Mean Pete gave a whoop and a holler and jumped at Preacher. Preacher drew back and busted him smack in the face with the full jug of whiskey and Mean Pete hit the boards. Pete didn't even moan. He was cold out.

Preacher turned to the man behind the bar. "If the whiskey had been worth a damn, I wouldn't a-done that. And if you want pay for that snake-head poison, get the money from him." He pointed to Mean Pete. "Now give me a good jug 'fore you make me mad."

Patience fanned herself vigorously. "My word!" she whispered to Prudence. "He is such a *forceful* man."

Patience and Prudence were awakened that night by Preacher's somewhat drunken singing. It was a ditty he'd learned from a boatman in St. Louis one time and it was about a Scottish lassie named Lou Ann MacGreagor and her red sweater. Seems she filled it out rather well. The ditty seemed harmless enough until Preacher got to the second half of the song. Those verses concerned themselves with Lou Ann's undies . . . or as it turned out in the next verse, her lack of them. Just as Preacher got all tuned up to sing a few more verses, each one raunchier than the other, Patience and Prudence immediately began singing hymns, loudly. As Preacher's singing became lustier, the other missionaries quickly joined in Christian voice.

By all accounts, it was a rather odd mixing of tunes. Somehow, between Preacher's bellering and the sweet harmonies of Patience and Prudence and the others, Lou Ann MacGreagor got to the promised land and got all mixed up with the prophets and everybody was girding their loins and dancing naked on the rock of ages with the angels and the meek.

A drunken Arapaho staggered out of the barn, where he'd been imbibing with some friends and joined in, singing in his own tongue about a lost love . . . which in this case was his horse.

Preacher woke up the next morning rather confused. He just could not remember ever hearing that ditty sung in quite that manner.

He finally put it off to bad whiskey. But he couldn't understand why Patience and Prudence and Hanna and Jane and Sally were all giving him such dirty looks.

* * *

By noon it appeared that Preacher had been forgiven for his night of drunkenness and people were once more speaking to him, not that it mattered one whit to Preacher whether they spoke or not. His head hurt anyway.

"That loutish fellow back there," Otto said, riding up beside Preacher. "Mean Pete. Will he be coming after you?"

"Naw," Preacher said. "He was drunk. He never does remember our fights . . . might be 'cause they're so short. The one thing he does remember is that he don't like me."

"Why?"

"I don't know. He took one look at me years back and decided he didn't like me. We been havin' these head-buttin's ever since. Mean Pete is kind of a strange feller."

"I'm sure he must have his good points."

"If he does, he sure keeps 'em hid right well."

"Where are you taking us, Preacher?"

"Bent's Fort."

"But, sir . . ."

Preacher shook his head. "Otto, you and the others is fine people. Good people, and you mean well. But ain't none of you needs to be out here in the wilderness. Come back in ten years. You want to save souls, practice on whites first, 'cause the Injuns don't want you. I told you the Injuns got their own religion and they're happy with it. You've told me time and again that you want to farm. Fine. Go to Arkansas or Louisiana or East Texas and farm. You and Hanna have kids and be happy. You can find heathens to convert anywhere. This whole country's gonna bust loose in a few years. The Injuns claim all this country as their own. They pretty much put up with us trappers 'cause I reckon we're all more Injun than white after all this time out here and we don't meddle in their affairs."

"But, sir . . ."

"Hush up an' listen to me. When we get to the fort, y'all hook up with wagons headin' back east and go. Now, damnit, Otto, you know in your heart and your brain that I'm right."

The man sat in his saddle in silence for a time. He slowly nodded his head. "Yes, you're right, Preacher." He smiled. "But it has been a grand adventure."

"Tell your grandkids about it. Write a book about it. And think kind thoughts of me."

"Patience will be disappointed. She, ah, likes you, Preacher."

"She'll get over it. She'll find her some fine Christian man and get hitched up and I'll be just a fadin' memory in her mind. Now go tell the others what we're doin', Otto."

Patience and Prudence both let out a howl at the news, but they soon settled down as Otto convinced them that they could better serve their church in a more civilized area. Now all Preacher had to worry about was getting the pilgrims to safety. He knew a place about two days away where mountain men tended to gather for a ride to Bent's Fort. If he could reach them before Bones and his bunch caught up with them, the missionaries would be safe, for Bones and his man-hunters would never attack a dozen or so mountain men. If they were foolish enough to do that, it would be the last time they ever attacked anyone.

Preacher's luck held and two days later, a few hours before dusk, he led the wagons into the encampment of mountain men.

"Wagh!" a huge bear of a man shouted, rising from the ground upon spotting Preacher. "It's Preacher, boys. With a whole passel of pilgrims."

"That's the man who told us you were a man of the cloth, Preacher," Otto said.

"Horsehide!" Preacher hollered. "You big ugly moose! Ho, Papa Griz. I brung you boys salvation. God knows you heathens need some."

"We was ridin' for the mountains to lend you a hand, Preacher," a man called.

"Hell, I don't need no help. But I'd like to prevail upon you boys to help these fine folks I got with me."

The mountain men took one look at Patience and Prudence and Preacher knew his worries were over. The missionaries would be safe. Preacher would resupply from his friends and then head back to confront and once and for all close the book on Bones and his manhunters. Preacher wasn't lookin' forward to it, but it was something that had to be done. He sat down by the fire and stretched his legs out with a contented sigh. Most of the wild and woolly and uncurried mountain men were gathered around the missionaries, unhookin' the teams, helping the ladies down from the seats and ogling Patience and Prudence, hopin' to catch a glimpse of a nicely shaped ankle. These men were as wild as the wind and just about as hard to handle, but they could be as protective as a mamma bear with her cubs.

Preacher took the cup of coffee handed him. "Word from the Injuns we've talked to is you've raised unholy hell with them ol' boys a-huntin' you, Preacher," a man known as De Quille said.

"Yeah? Well, I'm a-fixed to raise me some more hell with them."

"You want a couple of us to ride along with you?"

Preacher shook his head. "Naw. There ain't but about thirty or forty of 'em."

De Quille smiled. "Seems to me there was two bunches of about forty each started out after you, Preacher."

"I been whittlin' 'em down some."

"Do tell? I got news, Preacher. Them warrants on you

has been lifted. There ain't no charges against you. It's all personal or both sidesnow, ain't it?"

Preacher looked at him and his eyes told the whole story. De Quille nodded his head. "That's what I figured," he said.

28

The next morning, Patience and Prudence held a short service before they pulled out. It was a strange, yet wonderful and moving scene. The rough and wild-looking mountain men standing with heads uncovered and bowed while the ladies sang sweetly and Otto said a short prayer. Fifteen minutes later, after the goodbyes, the wagons were rolling eastward.

Preacher sat by the fire, deep in thought, and finished the pot of coffee. He was trying to figure out a way to tell the men with Bones and those silly foreigners that all warrants against him had been lifted and if they killed him now, it would be murder. Then he wondered if that news would make any difference. Probably not, but he was going to try. Providing he could do so without getting his head shot off. One way or the other, he was going to end this man-hunt. If he could do it without spilling another drop that would be wonderful. But he had strong doubts. Like De Quille had said, and no matter how many excuses Preacher made, this was personal now.

Preacher made certain the fire was out, then he packed up and swung into the saddle. Might as well get this over with.

* * *

Bones and party had no knowledge of any trading post any closer than Bent's Fort, so they were riding straight south while Preacher was heading straight north. All of them heading straight toward canyon country. The only difference was, Bones and his bunch got lost in the maze of twists and turns and blind canyons. Preacher did not.

Preacher looped around the tortured maze of canyons, thinking even Bones would have more sense than to get all tangled up in there. He had stopped north of the canyons to rest and water his horse when the smell of death touched his nostrils . . . that sickly stench that he knew so well.

Preacher made no immediate move. Whatever it was out there was dead, and hurryin' wouldn't bring it—or them—back to life. And Preacher had him a hunch it was dead human bodies. Or what was left of them after the buzzards had feasted.

Preacher led Thunder, following the stink of death until he came to the scene. He ran around the scattered and torn-apart bodies, knockin' buzzards away until they finally got it into their pea-brains they were not welcome. It was something they were accustomed to, so they waddled off and waited with the patience of millions of years bred into them.

Preacher steeled himself and began trying to put body parts to the right body. What the buzzards hadn't worked on during the day, the critters had dined on at night. It was not a pretty sight; but one the mountain man had seen many times before. Buzzards will usually go for the belly, pullin' all the guts and soft organs out, the kidneys, and the eyes and mouth—diggin' for the tongue—first. Then they attack the rest of the body.

After a time, during which Preacher had to finally puke and get it over with, he finally concluded it had been a party of ten to twelve men, maybe as many as fifteen. And from the tracks, they'd each had them a pack horse or two. There was no sign of arrow or tomahawk, the men had not been scalped, so Preacher ruled out Indians. This was white man's work, and he had him a pretty good idea who'd done it. Bones and the scum with him. The men had been trappers, judging from what was left of their clothing. Their weapons and powder had been taken, along with their horses and all the supplies.

Preacher picketed Thunder and went prowling on foot until he found some sign. He recognized some of the hoofprints as horses being rode by Bones' bunch. He smiled. The fools was headin' straight into the maze. Odds were good they'd get lost, finally figure things out, and head right back this way. He would be waiting.

The bodies were, best as he could figure, 'bout two or three days old. He dragged the bodies and body parts into a natural ditch and worked the rest of the day covering them with rocks. Then he found a pointy rock and scratched into a huge boulder:

A PARTY OF ABOUT TWELVE MEN.
AMBUSSHED AND KILT BYBONES GIBSON
AND THE CRAP AND CRUD
THAT RODE WITH HIM. 1840. I THINK.

Preacher mounted up and rode for a couple of miles, then picketed Thunder on grass and took himself a long bath in a cold creek, usin' some soap that Hanna had given him. The soap was so strong it stung like the devil when he got it in his eyes, but it washed away the stink of the dead and got rid of a few fleas too, he was sure.

Dressed out in clothes that Frank and Paul had given him—he was airin' out his buckskins—Preacher put water on to boil and then tried to relax. He just didn't have an appetite at all for food—not yet anyways. The longer he sat and drank the hot, black, strong coffee and thought and brooded about the men he'd pieced together and then buried, the madder he got. He'd make a bet that he'd known some of those fellers. But the bodies had been so tore up there had been no way to tell. Those men had been ambushed, murdered, and then robbed of everything they had, right down to their britches and boots and jackets. They even took rings and amulets and such. Several of the men were missing fingers that had been hacked off.

Then, all of a sudden, it got real personal for Preacher. That body back yonder with no thumb on his left hand. Preacher had been with him when a Pawnee tomahawk had taken it off. Jon LeDoux was his name. And Jon had saved Preacher's bacon one time, too. Preacher's face tightened. Yeah. Up on Crow Crick, it had been. If it hadn't been for Jon, Preacher's bones would be rottin' under the ground. And Jon was never far from Ol' Burley Movant. Yeah. Bodies began to take shape now as Preacher could put missing fingers and scars and hair to faces. One of them back yonder had been Bill Swain, he was sure of it. And Bobby Gaudet had been a friend of Bill Swain. They'd all been down to the post to resupply and were headin' back into the Lonesome for the autumn season. Sure. That's why the wooden castoreum bottles had been left behind. Them ambushin' filth hadn't known what it was. Probably one of them uncorked a jug and seen how bad it smelled and left it. The grisly picture was beginning to take shape in Preacher's mind, and it was not a pretty one.

Now Preacher could, with almost dead accuracy, name every one of the men who'd been ambushed. He dug out a scrap of paper and a pencil and began writing down the names. Most of the men back yonder had kin, and they'd have to be notified. John Day had an Injun for a wife, but Preacher didn't have any idea where they'd chose to cabin in for the winter. Sam Curtis, on the other hand, didn't have anybody. He'd been an orphan when he ran off from the home and come west. Same with Onie. Preacher didn't even know Onie's last name or even if he had one. The others in the ambushed party would just have to lie in peace unknown, for Preacher couldn't put names to them.

But he could avenge them. And to hell with giving them murderin' ambushers any more chances.

"I found a way out," Jackson said, stepping down from the saddle and gratefully taking the offered canteen and drinking deeply. He wiped his mouth with the back of his hand. "But when we leave, stay bunched up; don't wander off. It's a twisted mess."

Actually, it wasn't that bad. It was just that these eastern men had never seen anything like the tortured and rocky canyons and it panicked them.

"Good work, Jackson," Bones said. "Get some rest. We'll pull out at first light."

"Preacher?" Van Eaton asked.

"God only knows where he is and what he's doing."

Preacher was waiting and watching about five miles inside the entrance to the canyons. He could see Jackson winding his way through the maze, lost as a goose and had been amused by the man's uncertain actions. Preacher had always found his part of the country rather pleasing; but it could be a mite hard on a man if he didn't know his way around.

While Bones and his party were resting that late afternoon, Preacher dislodged a few good-sized boulders and blocked the trail that Jackson had so carefully marked out with loads of rocks and dirt. He returned to his camp and fixed his supper, working with a cold and savage smile on his lips. Tomorrow should turn out to be right interesting, Preacher thought to himself.

"I thought you said this way was clear?" Lige asked Jackson, a surly expression on his unshaven face.

"It was, yesterday," Jackson replied. "Rock slides happen."

"Now what?" Bones asked.

"We either dig through all that piled up crap or take that other way through I told you about," Jackson said.

Those were the last words he ever spoke. Preacher's rifle boomed and the ball struck Jackson squarely in the center of his chest. He toppled off his horse and landed heavily on the sand.

Panic erupted on the canyon floor. Dozens of hooves churned up so much dust it blanketed the area like a thick, dirty fog. None of the man-hunters gave even a second thought to Jackson; not pausing long enough to see if he was dead or wounded. They just spurred their horses and ran for cover.

Preacher knew a dozen other ways out of the canyons, easier ways, for the area in which Bones thought he was trapped was really not that large. It just seemed that way to a man who was lost.

Preacher knew he was safe on the rim of the canyon. The sides were high and straight up. From where he sat, several hundred feet up, he could see two ways to leave this particular series of canyons. But he doubted those below would ever find them in time. He waited until the dust settled and the canyons were as silent as Jackson, sprawled on the sands.

"Bones," Preacher called. "I found them trappers you and your scum killed back yonder." He waited for denial. None came. "Some of them boys was friends of mine. And the worst one of them was worth more than the whole bunch of you. I been fightin' with my mind for days, tryin' to figure out if I should just go on and lose you crappy bunch of fools. Them you ambushed back yonder made up my mind. I can't let you people get back to civilization and kill more decent folks. I can't have nothin' like that on my conscience for the rest of my life. So y'all know what that means."

Preacher didn't expect any reply, and none came. "I just thought I'd let you know where you all stood," he called, then he began shifting locations, working his way around the edge of the rim, coming up, he hoped, behind Bones and his bunch.

"I warned you all repeatedly that we should have given those men a proper burial," Steinwinder chided all within the sound of his voice.

"Aw, shut up!" Sutton told him. "I'm tared of you and that flappin' mouth of yourn. Hell's far, boy. You was the one who wanted to scalp some of 'em."

He never got to say another word. Preacher's rifle boomed and Sutton took the ball through his head. He slumped against the now blood splattered, gray wall of the canyon.

"What a disgusting sight!" Steinwinder said, as he quickly moved to a more secure position, away from Sutton.

Preacher fired his second rifle and the big ball just missed Steinwinder's head, throwing sand in the man's eyes, and blinding him momentarily.

"I've been gravely wounded!" the Austrian hollered, stumbling to his feet. "Help me. I've been blinded."

Jon Louviere jerked him down and bathed his eyes with water.

Preacher was moving quickly, again angling for a better position. But the men had moved into the shadows of the canyon walls, and they were very difficult to spot. Preacher was all through playing games with the man-hunters. He wasn't interested in shots that only wounded. He wanted an end to this. And he hadn't been joking with Bones this time. Preacher was mad to the bone.

"We're trapped in here, Bones," Evans said. "Preacher'll just lay up yonder and pick us off one at a time."

"Maybe not. Jackson told me he'd found two ways out and marked both of them. Horace, you snake outta here and find that other pass."

"I'm gone," the man said, and began crawling out, staying in the shadows.

Up on the rim, Preacher passed up several shots that would have broken a leg or ankle or arm. He looked up at the sun. Nine o'clock, he guessed accurately. He had plenty of time.

Horace Haywood found the other exit, but it was narrow and dark and twisting and he didn't like the looks of it. But he liked it better than facing Preacher's shooting. He edged his way back to Bones.

"It's there, all right. But it ain't gonna be easy."

"Nothing has been on this trip," Bones said wearily. "Water the horses several times today. All that we can spare. Keep them fresh and in that pocket back yonder. Strip the saddles from them and rub them down good. Then tie down anything that'll rattle or make any kind of noise. That'll keep the boys busy for a time. And stay in the shadows and out of sight. Come full dark, we'll slip outta here."

Some of them wouldn't.

Flores mistook a round rock for Preacher's head. He slipped out of the shadows and lifted his rifle to his shoulder. Preacher's rifle sang its hot, smoky song and Flores was slammed back against the side of the canyon wall. "Mother of God," he whispered. "I am truly going to die in this horrible place."

"One place is as good as another," Prince Juan Zapata

said, the Spanish penchant for fatalism surfacing at last in the man. "You are Catholic?"

"*Sí.*"

"I will pray for you."

"Gracias, amigo."

Zapata's dark, cold, and cruel eyes looked at the man. "Amigo?" He chuckled at the familiar usage from a man far beneath his royal class. "Well, why not? You know, Flores, up there on that rim is a better man than all of us."

"I know," Flores whispered, both hands holding his bloody stomach. "But we found out too late. *Que hombre.*"

"Yes, he is. What a grand adventure this was going to be. Some adventure, right, Flores?"

Flores couldn't answer. He was dead. Zapata gently closed the man's eyes and lowered him full length to the sand.

"What were you discussing with that peasant, Juan?" Sir Elmore asked.

Zapata smiled. "You would never understand, Elmore. Not in a million years. I'm not sure I do."

29

Preacher had spotted the second way out of this series of canyons and left the rim above the man-hunters just after high noon. He'd seen Haywood crawling away and guessed correctly he was looking for another way out. Preacher had watched him return. From his vantage point, high above the group, Preacher would also see where the horses were being held and shortly after the man's return, had spotted unusual activity there. He figured accurately that Haywood had found the way out and the trapped men would try to slip away just after dark. That would be just fine and dandy. He could be waiting.

Preacher fired no more shots the remainder of that day. Just as the day began to cool and shadows were covering the entire canyon floor, Preacher heard several horses whining. Rifles loaded, he waited.

As the pass widened near where Preacher waited, the escaping men would be outlined faintly. Preacher would choose his targets with care, for he did not want to kill a horse. He also knew that if he got two this time, he would be lucky, for at the sound of the first shot, the man-hunters would put the spurs to their horses and leave the pass at a full gallop.

When the lead rider was faintly outlined, Preacher

sighted in and squeezed the trigger. The man tumbled from the saddle. Just as he'd predicted, the men behind the fallen man-hunter shouted and spurred their horses. Preacher grabbed up his second rifle and snapped off a shot. He saw the man jerk as the ball hit him, but the rider managed to stay in the saddle. Then the canyon was filled with dust and Preacher could see nothing. He reloaded his rifles and listened to the pound of hooves gradually fade into the early night. He wasn't worried; that many men would leave a trail anybody could follow. He'd pick it up come the morning. He made his way down to the canyon floor and stripped the saddle and bridle from the horse, turning the animal loose.

Preacher had been lucky, for the second man had been leading a packhorse. When the ball struck him, he lost the lead rope. Preacher smashed the weapons, rendering them useless, left the dead man where he was and took the packhorse back to his camp. The man probably had gold on him, but Preacher didn't want it. He relieved the animal of his burden and sat down to fix supper. He'd go through the newly found supplies at first light.

Over coffee, Preacher tried to put himself in the boots of the man-hunters. Where would they go? They were all eastern men, and most would want to get back to familiar territory. They did not know this country, and would probably elect to go back the same way they came. That was only a guess on Preacher's part, but he felt it was a good one.

Or was it? By now, the news of all those warrants against him being lifted would be common knowledge at Bent's Fort. Bones might not want to take the chance of running into any of Preacher's friends at the fort and risk gunplay. So the group might decide to head north and then cut east. Well, he'd know come the morning.

* * *

It was a silent bunch of men who finally reined in their weary horses and made camp. They had escaped the canyon but they all knew they had not escaped Preacher. The mountain man would be after them likes fleas to a dog.

They'd lost one packhorse, but still had supplies a-plenty to get them back to civilization. And to a man, that's where they wanted to go. They all agreed they wanted no more of the mountains and the mountain man called Preacher. Even the gentry agreed with that, albeit reluctantly.

"Preacher's gonna follow us if it takes him to hell," Van Eaton spoke softly to Bones. "We ain't never gonna be rid of that mountain man."

"I know," Bones said, weariness in his voice. Like the others, Bones was dirty and could smell the rancid stink from his body. His clothing was stiff with dirt and days-old sweat. "But I'm out of ideas."

"I got one," Van Eaton said. "We run like the devil his-self is after us."

"He is," Bones whispered. "He is."

Preacher had inspected the supplies, took what he needed, and turned the packhorse loose. Then he was on the trail of the man-hunters. He followed their tracks and found their now deserted camp. A dead man lay stiffening on the ground. Preacher figured it was the man he'd shot coming out of the canyon. Some of those with Bones had taken everything of value from the man, even taking his pants, jacket, and boots.

"You shore teamed up with a pack of lousy no-counts," Preacher said to the dead man. "But I reckon you wasn't no better than them so I ain't gonna waste my time plantin' you." He left the dead man and headed out, following the easy to see trail.

Bones was leading the men straight north. "You won't go north long, Bones," Preacher said. "You'll have to cut east in about three or four days. And I know where that'll be." He knew that Bones had some sort of a crude map, for one of the men who chose to remain with the missionaries had told him so.

"So I 'spect you'll be cuttin' some east today. Just about noon. I'll be a-waiting' for you, Bones. I'm gonna drive you back into the mountains, ol' son. You ain't gettin' out on the Plains. Not if I can help it. And I can help it." He lifted the reins. "Come on, Thunder. We got some hard travelin' to do."

"This ain't like Preacher," Bones said. "I don't believe for a second he's given up. So where is he?"

The nobility had been strangely silent for the past two days. They had finally begun to grasp the seriousness of it all. They had finally got it through their aristrocratic noggins that there was a very good chance they were going to die. Juan Zapata had sensed it first, back in the canyon. Robert Tassin had been next in line to understand the gravity of it all, and that feeling of doom had quickly spread to the others. They understood now that out here in the wilderness, their wealth and station in life meant nothing. They were in a situation where their money could not buy them out of it. And that knowledge was beginning to show on them. For the past two nights they had huddled together, speaking in low tones.

Bones knew the gentry was up to something. What, he didn't know. And he didn't care. He personally hoped they would break off and go it alone.

And that's exactly what they did.

The group had been traveling through a rough and dense part of the country, with each man having to concentrate on his own business. No one seemed to notice as the nobility began lagging behind . . . along with several other men. When Bones halted the group for food and rest at about noon, the gentry were gone, along with Dutch, Percy, Falcon, Hunter, and Bates.

"Hell with them," Van Eaton said. "I'm glad to be shut of the whole bunch."

"Yeah," Haywood said. "We got our money so who cares. Maybe Preacher will spend his time chasin' after them and leave us alone."

"But they took two of the mules and a lot of supplies," Lige pointed out.

Bones shrugged his shoulders. "I'm just glad they're gone. Good riddance."

Preacher studied the ground carefully. The bunch had separated here. Bones and his people were still headin' for the Plains, and twelve or thirteen others had continued on to the north. "Interestin'," Preacher muttered.

He had miscalculated where Bones would cut due east, and lost time in backtracking. But Bones had made a bad choice and had to travel through mighty rough country. Preacher figured he was only hours behind Bones. So he'd come up behind them. That was fine. He knew a short cut around this bushy tangle that Bones knew nothing about. And that might put him ahead of Bones. But it would be close. Real close.

"You seem to be the most capable among us, Mister, ah, Dutch," Sir Elmore Jerrold-Taylor said to the burly man. "So we have voted and you shall lead."

"Fine. First thing we got to do is get hid from Preacher. And I mean, hid good. When we get done restin' here, we'll take to that crick over yonder and stay in it long as we can. We'll leave it several times, but always come back to it. That'll cause Preacher to waste a lot of time huntin' for our tracks. We'll find us a place to hole up. Bet on it."

"Excellent thinking!" the duke exclaimed. "You get us through, and you shall receive a bonus."

Dutch nodded his head. "I want me a shot at Preacher. I owe that no-good. I really do."

"Perhaps you might think up a fine plan for an ambush, Dutch?" Baron Wilhelm Zaunbelcher suggested.

"I been thinkin' on one. I surely have."

Preacher beat Bones and his bunch by only a few minutes. But it was time enough for him to load up all his rifles and get into position. He would be shooting downhill, but the grade was a gentle one. And they had to come through, or try to come through, this pass, or else go miles out of their way. But Preacher wasn't going to allow them through . . . if he could help it.

Preacher let the first few riders enter the pass and then he emptied a saddle. Will Herdman was slammed out of his saddle, dead before he bounced on the rocky trail. Preacher grabbed up another rifle, but he was too late. Bones and crew were learning fast. Those who had entered the pass had left their horses and taken cover behind the huge boulders that littered the gap. Preacher reloaded and settled down for a long wait.

"Preacher!" Bones shouted from the mouth of the pass. "Listen to me, Preacher. The gentry is gone. They left us. We ain't got no more quarrel with you. This was a job of work, Preacher. That's all. You takin' this personal."

"You mighty right, I am," Preacher muttered. "You kilt Eddie, Wind Chaser, and his whole family and band. Then you kilt a dozen friends of mine. It's personal, all right."

"Preacher!" Bones shouted. "We're just a bunch of ol' boys tryin' to make a livin', that's all. And we didn't have nothing to do with killin' that boy or them trappers. That was all the work of the gentry."

"Sure," Preacher whispered. "Wonder how come it was that the supplies I took the other day still had a few traps amongst the other gear?"

"Look here, Preacher," Van Eaton shouted. "We made a mistake in comin' after you. But we're big enough men to admit it. Let's just call it quits and call it even. No hard feelin's, all right?"

Preacher had an idea. "I'll think on that for a minute," he shouted. He found a stick and put his battered old hat on one end. "All right, Bones. I'm comin' down and you and me, we can talk some. How 'bout it?"

"Get set to blow his head off," Bones told Van Eaton. "That's a good deal, Preacher," he shouted. "Ain't no reason at all why you and me can't be pards, now, is there?"

"Right," Preacher shouted back.

Preacher crawled on his belly for a few yards, and then slowly lifted the hat until the brim was even with the top of a large rock. A rifle cracked and the hat flew off. Preacher screamed as if in terrible pain and then fell silent. He quickly crawled back to his loaded rifles and waited. "You sorry . . ." He bit back the oath.

Preacher kicked at a rotting log and the log broke free and rolled a few yards, thudding against a rock. It sounded, he hoped, like a body falling.

"I believe we got him!" Lige shouted.

"I think we did," Van Eaton said, his words carrying up to Preacher.

"Good shootin', Van Eaton!" Evans said. "You finished the man for good this time."

"There's one I owe you, Van Eaton," Preacher muttered, sliding around into a better shooting position. "And you can bet I'll pay that debt."

Stan Law jumped up from his cover, a large knife in one hand. "I get to cut off his head!" he shouted. "Somebody bring the picklin' jar."

"No! I get to cut off his head!" Cantry shouted.

"We'll race to see who gets the head!" a thug called Billy yelled.

Preacher let them come, all of them, including Bones and Van Eaton, running up the grade, knives in hand, laughing and yelling and shouting and joking and racing to see who would get to cut off Preacher's head.

"Sorry, boys," Preacher said, then stood up. Holding two rifles like pistols, he fired, dropped those rifles, picked up two more, and emptied those. Then he grabbed for his pistols and really began uncorking the lead.

Billy went down, shot through the head. Cantry took a ball in the center of his chest and stopped abruptly, falling back against Bones and knocking him down, unknowingly saving the bounty-hunter's life. Stan Law took a ball through his stomach. The heavy ball, fired at such close range, tore out his back. Bob Jones stopped his running for a moment, and stared in horror at the growing carnage before him. He only had a moment to look before Preacher grabbed up his pistols. Bob took a double-shotted charge in the face and would have been unrecognizable even to his mother. Jose screamed in panic and turned around just as Preacher fired. The ball passed through his neck, just below the base of his skull. Paul Guy's bladder relaxed in fear and the last thing he would ever remember was that he had peed his pants.

Then the gang was running and rolling and falling and sliding down the grade, some of them losing rifles and knives and pistols in their haste to get away. When they reached the bottom, they didn't look back, just headed for their horses and galloped away.

Preacher glanced at the dead and dying sprawled grotesquely below him and without changing expression, began reloading.

"You a devil!" Stan gasped at him.

"I reckon I might have shoot hands with him a time or two," Preacher acknowledged. "The difference between us is, I know when to turn loose."

30

The man-hunters ran their horses over rough country, straight west, for several miles before the exhausted animals could go no farther. Reason finally overcame fear and Bones halted the wild retreat before he and his men killed their horses.

Slumped on the ground, trembling from fear, exhaustion, and shame, Bones looked at what was left of his party of bounty-hunters. He'd come west with just over forty men. He was down to fifteen, counting himself. He looked over at Lige, sitting with what was left of his bunch. Counting himself, Lige had been reduced to six men.

Bones Gibson shook himself like a big dog and stood up, amazed that his legs would support him. He was ashamed of himself for running away like a scared cat from a pack of dogs. He looked at the discouraged and thoroughly filthy bunch of men. "All right, people, listen up. Look at me, damnit, you dirty pack of cowards!" That got their attention. They stared at him, some of them through fear-glazed eyes.

Bones said, "We're through runnin'. I mean it. This is the end of runnin' from that mountain man. We're gonna get out of this fix, in an orderly retreat. We're gonna operate like an army from now on. With captains and lieutenants and sergeants and the like. And I'm the captain of this company. Anybody don't like it, leave and do it right now."

No one moved. But new interest now took the place of hopelessness in many eyes.

"I'm fixin' to give you my first order. Here 'tis: We take shifts guardin' while the others take a bath in that creek over there. And I mean bathe. With soap. Then we shave close and give each other haircuts. And we wash our clothes and air out our blankets. When that's done, and we all look like human bein's again, instead of like a bunch of people who just crawled out of a cave, then we make our plans. Now move. Move!"

It was almost dark when Preacher hunkered down and watched the last one die. He rolled them all into a pile and tossed brush and limbs over them. He smashed their weapons and threw them aside. Then he went back to Thunder, saddled up, and rode out. He knew of a little spot that was ideal for a camp. He'd pick up the trail of the man-hunters come the morning. Right now, he wanted some hot food and a good night's sleep.

Miles to the north, Dutch had halted the men and made a very tight and secure camp. Dutch was under no illusions. He'd come to realize they were up against a first-class fighting man who possessed all the skills needed to not only survive in this godforsaken country, but to prosper in it. Dutch was going to call on all of his eastern woodsman skills to avoid Preacher. He did not want a fight with the man until the odds were all on his side. And he felt sure that would come, sooner or later. But for now, they had to stay alive.

The royalty had stopped their foolish antics, all of them finally realizing this was not a game, not a sporting event. This was a life or death struggle against a very skilled and very determined fighter. And to a man, they had silently admitted they were out-classed by Preacher. And they had suddenly turned into the hunted.

It was not a feeling that any of them savored. Just the thought of it left their mouths experiencing the copper-like taste of fear.

Sound carries in the high country, and they had all heard the very faint sounds of gunfire to the south of them. They all wondered now many more men Preacher had killed.

"Canada," Sir Elmore said aloud.

"Beg pardon?" Dutch lifted his head and looked at the man.

"Canada," Elmore repeated. "We'll try for Canada. We'll be safe there."

"That's hundreds of miles away," Falcon said. "Up through the unknown. Winter's gonna be on us in a few weeks. We got to get out of these mountains."

"I concur," Zaunbelcher said. "I do not think any of us would live through a winter trapped in here."

Rudi Kuhlmann looked at the six men who had chosen to accompany the royalty. "Get us out of this alive, gentlemen, and none of you will ever have to worry about money again. And that is a promise."

"You got a deal," Dutch told him.

"We'll cut north in the morning," Bones told his group. "Head straight for Canada."

"Canada!" Lige blurted.

The men at least looked more or less human now that they had bathed and shaved and trimmed their hair. But their thoughts were still dark and savage when it came to Preacher. They had panicked back at the pass, and were ashamed of it. And each had silently promised nothing like that would ever happen again.

"That ain't a bad idea," Evans said. "I got some friends up there and they're doin' all right. They been up there for 'bout three years now. Huntin', fishin', trappin'. They're gettin' by, so's I hear."

"All right," Van Eaton said. "Canada it is. We'll pull out at first light."

"Now this is mighty interestin'," Preacher muttered, squatting down and studying the tracks. He had been following the tracks of Bones's bunch for two days. They had passed right by an easy way out of the Rockies and kept right on heading north. "Canada," Preacher whispered. "Canada? Now why did I think of that?" He didn't know, but the thought would not leave him. "Well, I ain't runnin' them ol' boys clear to Canada." He swung back into the saddle, curious now, and once more began his following the trail. He took his time, trying to figure out what in the world Bones had in mind this time.

Unbeknownst to either of the two groups, they were only about ten miles apart, and since Bones and his bunch were traveling faster, almost parallel to one another.

Preacher shared his supper with an old Indian and his wife who had stumbled onto his camp, and after eating, the men smoked and talked. The old man and his wife were of the Northern Ute, and both were not well. They were going back south to where they had first met, long ago, to build a lodge and die together.

The old Ute told him that there were two parties of white men, about eight or ten miles apart, both of them traveling north. He said he sensed evil in these men, and he and his woman had hidden both times. He said the men were not happy people; sullen and grim-faced. And they used bad language . . . at least it sounded bad to him.

The old man had heard of Ghost Walker, and was honored to be in the presence of such a fine and brave warrior. When Preacher awakened the next morning, he knew the old man and woman would be gone, and they were. Lying next to Preacher's blankets was a gift from the old Indian, one of the finest-made tomahawks Preacher had ever laid eyes on. Preacher hefted it and knew it was made to throw, and that was something he was a pretty fair hand at. He stowed it behind his sash.

As he rode, he smiled at the old Indian's news. So the gentry and the trash with them were only a few miles to the west of Bones's pack of hyenas. That was interesting.

"I believe we've shook him off," Fred Lasalle said, on the evening of the third day after the ambush in the pass.

"Maybe," Bones replied.

"I think we've lost Preacher," Percy said, at approximately the same time and sitting about six miles away from Bones's bunch.

"Maybe," Dutch said.

At that moment, Preacher was about four miles behind of both groups. He had cooked and eaten his supper, boiled his coffee, and then let his small fire burn down to only coals, just enough to keep his coffee hot. He sat with a blanket over his shoulders, drinking coffee and mentally fighting with himself.

He figured he'd more than avenged Eddie, Wind Chaser, and the trappers the man-hunters had killed and robbed. He ought to just give up this hunt and go on about his business.

Preacher had been fighting this mental battle for several days, and was no closer to a decision now than when he began. Even if there were some sort of law out here, he couldn't prove that Bones and his party had done anything. It would be his word against theirs. And if it came to that, Preacher might well be the one who ended up on the wrong end of the rope. Patience and Prudence and the others hadn't actually seen any of the man-hunters break any laws—and since everything had happened in so-called "disputed territories," he wasn't sure what country's laws applied where. Or even if there were any laws out here, was more like it. Preacher, like so many mountain men, was pretty much in contempt of the so-called laws of so-called "civilized people." Preacher felt that most of them were downright stupid.

Just before Preacher snuggled deeper into his blankets, for the nights were turning colder, he made up his mind to make no further contact with the man-hunters, other than continuing to push and follow them north. Well . . . he might accidentally hassle them a little bit. If the man-hunters started trouble, then he'd fight. But they would have to start it. He'd let Canada handle the man-hunters.

The weather grew colder, the days shorter, and the nights longer the farther north the men rode. Even though the two groups were only a few miles apart, neither group was aware of the other. But both knew that Preacher was still behind them, staying well back, but coming on.

Preacher had begun trailing one group for a day or so, and then swinging over and trailing the other. Both groups were aware of him. And the hunt became a game with the Indians. Word was passed from tribe to tribe and the Indians were amused by it all. If so many men were running away from just one man—even if that man was Ghost Walker—the fleeing men must surely be cowards and therefore not worth bothering with. They would not be brave under torture.

* * *

"What the hell is he doing?" Van Eaton threw out the question to anybody who might have an answer, although he knew no one in the group did.

"Following us," Bones said. "Driving us north. He's got something up his sleeve, for sure. And I think I know what it is."

"What?" Titus asked.

"I ain't got it all worked out yet in my mind. But I figure I'm close."

"Well, I'm gettin' right jumpy about him bein' back there," Tatman said. "It's gettin' hard to sleep at night, worryin' 'bout him slippin' into camp and cuttin' a throat or two. I say we ambush him."

"Maybe," Bones said. "Yeah, I been givin' that some thought, too."

Van Eaton said, "You don't reckon he's somehow got in touch with the Canadians and they're waitin' for us at the border?"

Bones smiled. "You always could read my mind, Van Eaton. Yeah. That's what I think he's done."

"How?" George Winters asked.

Bones shook his head. "I don't know."

"Preacher had the missionaries inform the Canadian authorities about us," Sir Elmore said, about the same time Bones's group was discussing what Preacher was doing.

What neither group knew was that there were no Canadian authorities within five hundred miles of where they planned on crossing the still ill-defined border. And what neither group knew was that they had crossed out of Ute country and were now in the territory of the Northern Cheyenne and Arapaho. Furthermore, neither the man-hunters nor Preacher was aware that they were all being carefully trailed by a band of Ute, who had some ideas of their own. For the moment, a rare event was happening: representatives of the Utes had met with chiefs of the Northern Cheyenne and Arapaho and agreed to a temporary peace. The Cheyenne and the Arapaho could fully sympathize with and understand what the Utes wanted, and they agreed to it, for the time being.

"I say we ambush Preacher," Zaunbelcher said. "If we plan it carefully, we can succeed. I am certain of that."

"Maybe," Dutch said. "And that's a big maybe. Preacher is a wily ol' curly wolf. The problem is, we don't never know just where he is. He disappears for days at a time."

"Wonder where Bones and them got off to?" Percy pondered.

"Who cares?" Dutch replied.

Preacher had felt eyes on him for the past two days. But it wasn't the kind of eyes that made the hair on the back of his neck stand up. It was more a curious feeling he felt. He circled and back-tracked, but he could not spot a soul.

It was Indians, he was sure, and probably Cheyenne or Arapaho, tribes that he got along well with. He was known to them, so why were they spying on him and not coming near his camp?

Preacher rode Thunder down into a creek, stayed with it for about a mile, and then exited on gravel. He tore up an old shirt and covered Thunder's hooves and walked him for about a mile. He picketed Thunder, climbed up on a bluff, and with his pirate glass in hand, bellied down, extended the glass, and began scanning the territory all around him.

It took a while, but his patience finally paid off. He smiled and put the glass away. "Well, I'll be damned," Preacher muttered. He knew the Ute riding in the lead. He was one of the big chiefs, Black Hawk. Then Preacher remembered something that caused his throat to tighten. He slowly shook his head. "You boys would have been far better off if you'd let me kill you back down south."

Then he noticed two Indians not five hundred yards away, below him. They were riding slow, studying the ground, trying to pick up Preacher's trail, and they looked frustrated because they had lost the trail and could not find it again.

Preacher watched them until they were out of sight. He made his way back to Thunder and then decided he'd just make his camp right where he was. There was water close-by, and plenty of dry wood. Besides, things were going to get real exciting in a very short time. Preacher decided he'd just stay out of sight.

After all, deep down, he was a peaceful sort of person.

31

"White Wolf has discovered us," Black Hawk was informed the next morning. "My scouts have found where he hid his trail and then watched through the long glass as we followed the two groups of men."

Black Hawk nodded his head solemnly. "And Ghost Walker did what?"

"Nothing. Returned to his camp, prepared his evening meal, and went to sleep."

Black Hawk smiled. "By doing so he has told us that whatever else happens to the evil men is in our hands. He will do nothing to interfere."

"How do you know that?" the man dared to ask.

Black Hawk shifted his obsidian eyes to the man, but did not take offense. "How I know is but one of the reasons I am chief of this tribe and you are not."

The man wisely nodded his head and backed away, knowing he had come dangerously close to overstepping that invisible line.

One of Black Hawk's closest friends and advisors chuckled in the misty morning air. "Good reply."

Black Hawk waggled one hand from side to side. "Not too bad for so early in the morning."

The two men laughed softly.

Black Hawk said, "We have gone far enough north. Today we begin taking a life for a life."

"Look!" Tom Evans cried, jumping to his feet and pointing to the east.

About a quarter of a mile away, on the crest of a hill, Preacher sat his horse and was staring at the camp of the man-hunters.

"What's he doing?" Derby Peel asked.

"He ain't doin' nothin'," Van Eaton said. "He's just starin' at us."

"There's a reason for it," Bones said, looking at Preacher. "Preacher don't do nothin' without thinkin' it through. But damned if I can figure out what it is."

The man-hunters turned at the sound of a thud. For a moment they were frozen where they stood, staring at the sight. Benny Atkins swayed on his feet, his eyes looking in horror at the arrow protruding from his belly. Then he screamed as the first waves of pain hit him. He sat down heavily on the ground, both hands holding onto the shaft of the arrow.

Clift Wright jumped for his rifle. He managed to bring the weapon to his shoulder just as an arrow entered the right side of his neck, the arrowhead ripping out the left side. His eyes widened in horror as blood filled his mouth.

Joe Moss, using a stick for a crutch, hobbled for his guns. He didn't make it. Two arrows tore their way into his flesh, one in his back and the other in his chest.

Preacher sat his horse and watched the scene without expression.

Ray Wood began yelling as mounted Indians charged the camp, seeming to come out of nowhere. Ray's yelling stopped abruptly as an Ute lance ran him through, pinning his flopping body on the cold ground.

Bones, Van Eaton, Lige Watson, and several more who

had already saddled their horses, left their supplies behind and fled the scene, riding hard. The other men were slaughtered. Some were taken alive . . . they were the less fortunate ones. Utes could be quite inventive with torture.

Ed Crowe died cursing Preacher. One of the attacking Ute, who spoke English, would wonder at that for the rest of his life. White men certainly did many strange things.

Alan James, Derby Peel, Fred Lasalle, Evans, Haywood, and Winters died in the camp. Tatman, Price, and Titus were taken alive.

With the blood lust running hot and high, one of the younger Utes galloped his horse toward Preacher, his lance-point level with Preacher's chest. A sharp shout from Black Hawk brought the brave to a halt just a few yards from Preacher. The young Ute stared hard at Preacher, then his eyes touched upon that terrible-looking pistol in Preacher's right hand.

"Back off," Preacher said in the Ute's own tongue. "I am not your enemy."

The young Ute lowered his lance and turned his pony's head. He rode back to the camp and jumped down, a scalping knife in his hand.

Preacher holstered his pistol and rode away.

Willie and Lucas, Lige Watson, Pierre, Homer, Calhoun, Van Eaton, and Bones made it out alive. The only supplies they had were what they had carried in their saddle bags.

"I can't believe no white man would just sit back and watch whilst red savages attacked other white men," Lige panted the words.

"What tribe was that?" Calhoun asked.

"Who knows?" Bones said. "They all look alike to me."

Homer fell to his knees and vomited up his fear, while

Willie and the giant, Lucas, clung to each other, both of them trembling in fright.

"Now we know why Preacher was layin' back," Pierre said. "He fixed it up with them savages to do us in. Damn his eyes!"

"Take anything we got and wrap them horses' hooves," Van Eaton said. "We got to hide our trail and find a place to hole up. It's the only chance we got. I'll make a wager them Injuns was from the same tribe as them we kilt in that valley. They ain't never gonna give up looking for us."

He turned and grunted as an arrow tore into his chest and penetrated his heart. Van Eaton had hunted his last man.

Lige Watson lost control of his senses and ran screaming from the shady glen. He ran right into the Ute lance. The Ute left him pinned to the ground. Lige would be a long time dying.

Pierre died on his knees, praying.

Homer was taken alive.

Calhoun ran blindly in panic, fighting the slashing branches and stumbling through the thick underbrush. He could not believe his eyes when he saw Preacher, sitting his horse about a hundred yards away.

"Help me!" Calhoun screamed, hearing the Utes coming up fast behind him.

"Man who needs help hadn't oughtta left home in the first place," Preacher told him.

"You'll burn in hell for this!" Calhoun screamed at the mountain man.

"I might," Preacher acknowledged. "But you'll be there afore me." He lifted the reins and rode away just as the avenging Utes reached the man.

Bones, Willie, and Lucas had lept into their saddles and whipped their near-exhausted horses into a run.

They didn't get far.

Bones and Lucas were taken alive, the Utes having known for days that Bones was the leader. His death would be most unpleasant. The Utes looked at the tiny Willie, trying to figure out exactly what sort of man he was. They'd never seen a dwarf. They finally decided it would be bad medicine to harm such a thing. They turned him loose.

Ignoring the screams, Black Hawk rode over to Preacher.

"Howdy," Preacher said.

Black Hawk studied the mountain man for a moment. "You know why we do this?"

"I know. All who are with you are family members of Wind Chaser's bunch."

In the Ute society, such offenses as stealing, adultery, and murder were private matters, the punishment left up to the family members.

"It ought to be that way in my society, too," Preacher added, knowing his words would please the chief.

"I have severely chastised the warrior who threatened you, Ghost Walker. But in battle the blood runs hot."

"I understand."

"Tell me about the other band of evil men."

Preacher hesitated, then said, "They are better mannered in the white man's way than the ones you just killed, but they are much worse in here." He pointed to his heart.

Black Hawk nodded his head at that. He understood perfectly. He turned his horse and rode back to the blood-spattered camp. Willie rode his horse over to Preacher. The little man was so scared he stank of it.

"What am I gonna do?" he asked.

"Stay just as far away from me as you can, Shorty. 'Cause I might take me a notion to kill you yet."

"You've got to help me. I can't survive alone out here!"

"That's your problem. You come a-huntin' me, to kill me. Now you want me to help you. No way. You'll survive. You know the way back. I got no sympathy for you a-tall. Now get movin'. Get clear out of my sight and do it fast. Git!"

Willie got.

Dutch was jumpy. He was all knotted up inside and couldn't keep his food down. Something was wrong. He had chosen this place to hide with great care, and felt they would be safe. But he hadn't heard a bird sing or a squirrel chatter all morning. The woods were as still as a graveyard.

"Something's awfully wrong around here, Dutch," Percy said, lumbering up, his big gut leading the way.

"Yeah. I feel it, too."

"I heard screamin' last night."

"You, too?"

"Yeah. It was faint, but I heard it. Like to have made me puke."

"I been told that Preacher is hell in any kind of fight—and we shore known that for a pure-dee fact now—but he don't go in for torture."

"Somebody was shore dyin' hard last night."

"Anybody else hear it?"

"Not that I know of. I was on guard. Give me goose bumps all over."

"Yeah. Me, too."

Percy looked toward the clearing and his eyes widened as if he'd seen a ghost. About four hundred yards away, there sat Preacher, just sitting in his saddle as big as you please, looking right at the camp. "Dutch!" Percy gasped. "I ain't a-believin' my eyes."

"What are you talkin' 'bout?"

"Preacher!"

"Preacher? Where?"

"Right there!" he pointed.

Dutch turned and as he did, his belly exploded in pain. He looked down at the shaft of the arrow that protruded from his gut. "Oh . . ." was all he managed to say before another arrow split his spinal cord and he dropped to the ground.

Percy shouted out the warning but it was too late, far too late. He took one step and went down with several arrows in his body.

The Utes were all over the camp a few silent seconds later and the fight was brutal and brief. The braves knew who to kill quickly, and who to take alive. They had been following the group for days, and after studying the men, Black Hawk had pointed out the gentry.

The royalty who had come to America to kill men for sport were no longer the haughty, sneering, arrogant bunch of several months back. They stood in a group, their hands bound cruelly behind them. They knew they were facing death, and they were not facing it well. They stank of fear and relaxed bladders and bowels. The sweat dripped from their faces and their legs shook so hard several had to be helped to stand as the stony-faced Utes stared at them, the contempt they felt for such fear showing only in their eyes. Preacher still sat on his horse out in the clearing, Black Hawk sitting on his horse beside Preacher.

"For the love of God, man!" Sir Elmore Jerrold-Taylor screamed at him. "Help us."

"For the love of God?" Preacher muttered. "For the love of *God?*"

"The white man calls upon his God to help him?" Black Hawk asked.

"Yes."

"Will this God of yours help them?"

"Well, now, I can't speak for God, but if I had to take a guess, I'd say no."

"Good. I would not like to fight a God."

Preacher held out a hand and the Ute solemnly took the offering and shook it. "I'll be goin' now, Black Hawk. You're welcome in my camp any time."

"And you in mine, Brother To The Wolf."

Preacher swung his horse and rode away. He wanted to put some distance between the Utes, their prisoners, and himself. He knew this bunch was going to die slow, long, and hard. And he knew why.

Black Hawk rode his horse into the center of the camp, his pony gingerly stepping around a sprawled out body.

"We have gold!" Burton Sullivan shouted at the chief. "We have money and jewels and all sorts of things we can give you."

"I will have them soon," Black Hawk said. "You have no more use for them."

"Filthy savage!" Baron Zaunbelcher screamed at the chief.

"Savage?" Black Hawk questioned. "You call me a savage? You are a very amusing person."

"Why?" Robert Tassin screamed at Black Hawk. "Why are you doing this to us?"

"I have done nothing to you. Yet. But I will."

"Why, damn you? Why?" Sir Elmore shouted.

Black Hawk smiled sadly. "Because Wind Chaser was my younger brother. I helped in his upbringing after our mother died. That's why."

EPILOGUE

Days later, Preacher holed up in a cabin he'd built some years back. He'd cleaned out the place, for pack rats and birds had been busy there, and then began cutting firewood for the winter ahead. He found his old scythe where he'd left it, sharpened it up with a stone, and worked for a solid week, from can see to can't see, cutting forage for his horses. He worked himself hard so he would not have time to think about what happened to the royalty, even though he knew perfectly well there was nothing he could have done to prevent it.

The entire Indian nation had put a death sentence on the heads of the man-hunters as soon as they learned of the massacre of Wind Chaser and his band. There was no way any of them would have been able to leave the mountains. And Preacher doubted that any of the men he'd sent packing had made it very far out. He didn't have a guilty conscience about what had happened, he just didn't want to think about it.

When his domestic chores were done, Preacher went hunting and started jerking and smoking the meat. He set out fish traps and began smoking his catch. He picked berries to make pemmican and dug up tubers and wild onions for the cellar. When he had done all he could do in preparation for winter, he relaxed. He hoped he wouldn't see a single solitary soul 'til spring. The past summer had given him a bellyful of people, both good and bad, but mostly bad. He occasionally thought of Patience and Prudence and those folks with them and wondered how they were. He knew they'd made it out of the wilderness safely, for a trapper friend of his told him that.

Preacher knew that the area west of the Mississippi was going to run red with blood very soon. As pioneer families began moving onto the land, the Indians were going to fight to preserve their way of life. It was going to be a terrible time for many years to come. But Preacher didn't know how he could do anything to prevent the blood from being spilled.

One fall afternoon Preacher sat on the porch, smoking his pipe and watching the sun go down. A family of wolves who were denned not far away had begun coming around and Preacher recognized both the male and his mate from a year or so back. They came around this evening to check on him.

"Howdy," he said to them, and then was amused in watching the young in their rough and tumble play. "Life's pretty good, ain't it?"

The wolves sat in front of the porch, cocked their heads to one side and looked at him.

"Yeah," Preacher said. "Life is pretty darned good. If a man just knows how to live it and rolls with the flow."

THE FIRST MOUNTAIN MAN:
BLACKFOOT MESSIAH

1

Preacher had to go east to travel west, he discovered, when he decided to accept an assignment from the U.S. Army. Times had been lean for a while. Trapping was a thing of the past. Only a handful of men clung to the old ways, trapped and traded pelts to a market with little demand. Not so the legend called Preacher. Wisely he had salted away ample gold and silver coin, even invested some, most recently in what sounded to many like a fool's venture; Mr. Fulton's steamboat works.

As the smoke-belching paddle wheelers proliferated, so did Preacher's profits. Although ten years of only investment income had severely drained his reserve, he could no more leave the High Lonesome than many of the mountain men. Which meant he had to take whatever he could get to stay in supplies and keep afloat. Thus it was that he grudgingly considered accepting a commission from the War Department to act as trail guide and scout for a regiment of Dragoons. Preacher read again the letter that had accompanied the commissioning papers that had yet to see his signature.

Word has come out of the Northern Rocky Mountains of the Unorganized Territory that the Blackfoot are

> *gathering in great numbers. The savages are being*
> *agitated by some holy man, who claims to have the way*
> *to bring back the White Buffalo and drive the white men*
> *out of the plains forever.*
>
> *It is vital in these unsettled times to secure our north-*
> *ern flank. A conflict with Mexico seems imminent and*
> *our nation could ill afford an Indian uprising when our*
> *attention shall be directed southward. To which purpose,*
> *it is the decision of the Secretary to dispatch a battalion of*
> *Dragoons to the area of the Bighorn Mountains in the*
> *northeast part of the Territory to serve as a presence in*
> *the area.*
>
> *The battalion is to depart Jefferson Barracks in*
> *Missouri, and proceed up the Missouri to the North Platte*
> *River, and from there into the high country of Wyoming*
> *where they will establish a fort. The purpose of this post*
> *will be to oversee the Blackfoot from a discreet distance,*
> *and to show the flag to the Cheyenne and Sioux.*

What a stupid idea, Preacher thought. Then, as was
the habit of many men who lived alone in the stunning
quiet of the High Lonesome, he spoke his ruminations
aloud.

"That'll only cause trouble where there's none now.
What's got in ol' Quincy's head?" Preacher was referring
to Quincy Vickers, an old friend. "He lived out here, and
trapped, and knows the Injuns. Maybe it ain't this idee
at all. Might be he needs his irons hauled out of the fire."

Knowing the striped-pants crowd from past experience, Preacher was well aware of their propensity for
overreaction and . . . for stupidity. He was to sign the
papers and take them to Bent's Fort, where two copies
would be sent by fast messenger to Jefferson Barracks
and Washington City. There he would pick up the first
installment of the fee offered him. After a heavy sigh and
an idle scratch of his thick, yellow-brown hair, Preacher

picked up a quill pen and dipped it in his ink pot. With meticulous care, he formed the letters of his name.

Preacher shut and latched the door to his wintering place, careful to poke the latch string back inside. He'd be busy all summer, most like. He curled a dally of the lead rope of his packhorse around the overlarge horn of the Mexican saddle and swung atop his most recent acquisition, a crossbreed Morgan stallion which had a sturdy mountain mustang for a dam. Preacher had named him Tarnation. He shook the reins and drummed heels into stout sides.

"Well, Tarnation, we'd best be eatin' miles. I reckon I can find some companionable fellers down Bent's Fort way to accompany me on this commission as they called it."

In his letter, Quincy Vickers had told Preacher that he was authorized to hire on up to four men, at a rate of three dollars a day. Leave it to the government, Preacher mused, to offer enough money for some men to kill over it.

Big Nose Harper and his sidekick, Algernon Bloore, had gotten roaring, stumbling, falling-down, crap-in-their-drawers drunk the previous night. Now, some seven hours later, they didn't fare much better. Still too soaked in alcohol to suffer hangovers, they nevertheless sought some "hair of the dog." Their source, no matter how ill-advised, was William "Nifty" Bates, who had recently opened a trading post and road ranch saloon at the summit of Trout Creek Pass. Nifty was frankly afraid of Big Nose.

Big Nose Harper was a bear of a man, with a barrel chest, long, thick arms, tree-trunk legs, and his most memorable feature which gave him his nickname, an overlarge nose that had been smeared over his face. He held in contempt all "shopkeepers," to which subspecies he considered Nifty Bates belonged, and he went out of his way to make their lives miserable. Nursing his alcohol fog, Big Nose now went about tormenting Nifty.

"This whisky tastes like frog pee. You waterin' it down again, you cheat?"

"N-n-no, not at all, Mr. Harper," the barkeep stammered. Bates would soon sell out, inspired in part by the events of that afternoon.

Harper slammed his pewter mug on the pine-plank bar hard enough to make dust rise. "I say yer waterin' it. An' m'name's Big Nose."

"No I'm not, Mr. . . . er . . . Big Nose."

Harper's mean, close-set eyes narrowed. "Are you makin' fun of my honker?"

"Oh, no. You—you told me to call you Big Nose."

Big Nose looked offended. "I never said no such thing. Any man calls me that's lookin' for a killin'. A pantywaist like you's good for a knuckle-drubbin'."

A shadow fell across the toes of the boots worn by Big Nose, cast by a figure that filled the doorway. "Why don't you pick on someone nearer your size, Big Nose? Or should I call you blubber ass?"

Harper spun to face his detractor. "Who in hell are you?"

"They call me Preacher."

"Folks say he's a mean one, Big Nose," sniggered Algernon Bloore, who was more than a few biscuits shy of a plateful.

"Shut up, Algie," Harper snarled. He sized up Preacher and found him wanting. Whisky had so clouded his reasoning that he failed to see the hard, deadly glint in the gray eyes of the raw-boned man in the doorway. "Now, if you'll oblige me by gettin' the hell outta here, I'll have another drink. Barkeep, make it snappy."

Emboldened by the presence of Preacher, Nifty Bates

took a stand. "No, sir. You've had too much. The bar is closed to you."

Harper cut his eyes to Algie. Surprise registered on both their faces. No man ever spoke to Big Nose Harper that way. Growling, Big Nose reached across the plank bar and balled the front of Bates' shirt in both hands. With a yank that looked effortless, and was, he hauled the proprietor off his feet and across the bar.

Taking quick, mincing steps, which caused his long, greasy black locks to churn in protest, Big Nose Harper crossed the room and threw Nifty Bates out into the dusty dooryard. He then dusted hamlike palms together and snarled a reply to Bates.

"I say who drinks an' who doesn't around here."

Preacher took exception to that. "Like hell you do."

Glee brightened the pig eyes of Big Nose. "Mr. Preacher, prepare to meet yer maker."

With that, he came at the living legend of the mountains, arms widespread for his favorite bear hug. It had crushed the life from seven men before this. Big Nose saw no problem in making it eight. Which proved to be a terrible mistake.

Preacher crouched and duck-waddled out of the grasp of those powerful arms. When Big Nose blundered past, Preacher popped up and slammed an open palm into the side of the brawler's head, cupping it over the ear. If not for the thick ropes of greasy hair, the blow would have burst the ear drum of Big Nose. All it did, though, was set up a furious ringing and made him even angrier.

Big Nose whirled and swung at Preacher's chin. Preacher pulled his head back a few inches and let the big knuckles swish past. Then he went to work on the exposed ribs of Big Nose. Soft thuds sounded clearly enough to be heard by Nifty Bates. Dull-witted Algie Bloore decided to get in some licks on Preacher to win favor from his companion. He got a solid kick in the stomach for his efforts, flew backward with a hefty grunt and smashed into the bar. At once he began to spew up the liquor he had consumed.

By then, Big Nose had rallied and again grappled to encase Preacher in a bear hug. Preacher would have none of that. He backpedaled and swung a short, hard right to the face of Harper. Big Nose's most prominent feature got a little bigger when Preacher connected with the much-broken bridge. Preacher followed with a left hook that snapped Harper's jaw shut with a loud click. A second later, arms and legs twined around Preacher from behind.

Always a sneak, though not bright enough to profit by it, a somewhat recovered Algie Bloore had maneuvered to where he could leap on Preacher's back. "I got him, Big Nose, I got him!" he yelled gleefully.

Instead of struggling, Preacher simply flexed his knees and rammed himself backward into a six-by-six upright that supported part of the roof. Algie's shout of triumph turned to a squeal of pain.

"B'god, b'god, I think my back's broke."

"You'll git over it," Harper growled. Then he came for Preacher.

Always obliging, Preacher stepped away from the post and let Algie fall limply to the floor. He met the onrush of his opponent with a series of fast lefts and rights. A small grunt came from Harper with each impact. Half a dozen and he staggered sideways, his vision blurred. Fresh rage welled up inside him and he reached for a knife.

A shaft of sunlight through the open doorway made the keen edge a streak of fire. Harper advanced on Preacher, who produced his Greenriver and took a couple of swipes through the air. When Harper lunged Preacher cut him across the back of the hand. The knife fell from pain-filled fingers. Preacher kicked it aside.

"Yeaaaaah!"

Preacher whirled to find a revived Algie Bloore hurtling

at him, a knife extended in one hand. Preacher parried and sidestepped. He kicked Bloore's feet out from under the slightly built, ferret-faced man and Bloore went sprawling on the plank floor. His face was gouged by the rough boards; his knife skidded across the room. Preacher paused to take stock.

Both men looked fairly well whipped. Big Nose Harper stood, slope-shouldered, his breath harsh and irregular, head bowed. He tried, clumsily, to wrap a bandanna around his wounded hand. Preacher strode to the bar and pulled a beer for himself.

"Look out!" The warning shout came from Nifty Bates in the doorway.

Preacher spun on one heel to see Algie Bloore pull a long, single-barrel, caplock pistol from his waistband. Now, Preacher had been willing to oblige when the pair of frontier trash yanked steel on him, but he figured this was going too far. Recently outfitted with a pair of .44 Walker Colts, Preacher unlimbered one. He smoothly cocked the hammer as the muzzle cleared leather and snapped his elbow inward to elevate the barrel and level it on the target.

For all of his getting started last, Preacher's bullet reached the target first. Algie Bloore's head snapped backward from the impact of the 200-grain ball. A fist-sized chunk of his skull erupted from the left rear and showered the wall with gore. Reflex triggered his pistol and sent a ball into the front of the bar, close by Preacher's leg.

Enraged beyond caution by the swift death of his partner, Big Nose Harper dragged out a pair of double-barreled pistols. He thumb-cocked one awkwardly and swung it in the direction of Preacher. His first barrel discharged and put a ball into the wall beside Preacher's head a split second after Preacher put a .44 slug from his Walker Colt in the center of Harper's forehead.

Ears ringing from the confined detonations, Preacher

examined his handiwork. Thick layers of powder smoke undulated in the cool interior of the saloon. Shakily, Nifty Bates entered. He walked over to Preacher and wrung his hand in gratitude and relief.

"I ain't never seen such fancy shootin' in my born days. Drinks are on the house, Preacher. Dinner, too. This pair's been nothin' but a misery and torment to me the past three days."

Up in the Blackfoot Mountains of Montana Territory, a huge gathering of warriors whooped it up around a large fire. The entire carcass of a bison, cut into quarters, turned on green-wood spits over separate cookfires. Off to one side, three Blackfoot braves handed out shiny new rifles from wooden crates at the back of a wagon. Each man gifted with one of these received a bag of a hundred lead balls and a horn of powder. For the time being, they would not be given the percussion caps. Four older men, seated around a large drum, hit the final double beat and concluded their song. The warriors stopped dancing and gathered in a wide semicircle around a startlingly white buffalo-hide lodge.

A young-looking man stepped out of the entrance and struck a pose before them. Although in his mid-thirties, he had the look of a man in his early twenties. His coppery face was elastic and unlined. He wore ankle-high moccasins, beaded and quilled in traditional Blackfoot design, a knee-length loincloth and an abbreviated, soft, pliable, elkskin hunting shirt. Over that was a most unusual item of garb, which lay in turn beneath a second, larger hunting shirt. Hair-pipe bracelets adorned his forearms and a breastplate of bison teeth, hair-pipe beads and brass cones covered his chest. He raised his arms above his head to command attention. The silence, immediate, became profound.

"My brothers, there are many among you who say Iron

Shirt is too young to make strong medicine. You say that
I have been a medicine man for only ten winters. Yet, I
say to you that I have the strongest medicine. I received
it in a vision when I visited among the Paiute. My spirit
guide appeared to me and showed me a hidden valley.
'Dig here' the spirit said, pointing at a low mound. 'You
will find the power of White Buffalo. You will learn the
ways of making the medicine that will bring back White
Buffalo and drive the white-eyes from our land forever.'
I dug there, and I found what the spirit wanted for me.
Then I was shown the dance we have just danced, and
much more. It makes me safe from any white man's bullets. It will work for you also. The day is coming soon
when the white men will fall to the earth like soft hail-
stones. I bring you rifles, the newest and best. Plenty of
bullets, too. When you have finished the ritual of Iron
Shirt, you will be stronger than any bullet."

"You say the white man's bullets cannot harm you,
Iron Shirt. Prove it and we will follow you," a doubter
among the experienced warriors challenged.

Iron Shirt looked at his detractor contemptuously for
a moment, then forced an amiable expression on his
face. He was, after all, selling something. He pointed
with his chin at one of his earlier converts.

"I ask Bent Trees to step to the far side of the fire.
Take your gun in hand and point it at my chest." Bent
Trees did as bidden. When he was in position, Iron Shirt
continued. "When I say so, shoot me."

Gasps of surprise and shock arose among the Blackfoot. "He will not aim at Iron Shirt," one brave stated
flatly.

"The gun is not loaded with a bullet," opined another.
"It is a trick."

Another convert sought to disabuse them. "No, it is
the power of Iron Shirt's medicine. Watch and see."

"Now, Bent Trees."

With a sharp crack, the .60 single-shot pistol discharged.

A black hole appeared in the outer hunting shirt worn by Iron Shirt a split second before he violently rocked backward, his face twisted in pain. Several Blackfoot rushed forward. Iron Shirt held up a hand to stay them.

Carefully he reached into the hole and worked his fingers a moment. He came out with a flattened .60-caliber ball. Yips and whoops of victory broke out among the spectators as he held it high and slowly turned full circle. When the jubilation subsided, he spoke again.

"You will be shown the secret of this medicine when you complete the ritual to become part of my Iron Shield Strong Heart Society. Death to all white-eyes!"

Seated inside the lodge of Iron Shirt were three white men, dressed as Blackfoot. One, Morton Gross, with thinning, mousy brown hair and eyes that looked like chips of blue ice, smoked a cigar. All three looked inordinately pleased with the progress being made. The nominal leader of their cabal nodded to Gross.

"It's fortunate that you have important friends in high places, Morton. Nice to get advance warning that a regiment of troops is on the way, and that it would be guided by an experienced frontiersman."

Morton Gross made light of his informant's importance. "He's only a clerk. The really important ones are so high up they don't dare make direct contact with us, but my informant was able to read the letter sent to the former mountain man, Preacher."

Praeger beamed as he bragged to his companions, "And now, if the men we sent to watch the Santa Fe Trail only do their job, our goal is in our hands."

2

A day's ride from Bent's Fort, Preacher sipped from his first cup of coffee in night camp. Orange shafts slanted over his right shoulder and the night birds and katydids were gradually tuning up for their serenade. They suddenly went silent and Preacher stiffened a moment, then moved with studied casualness as he set aside the tin cup and draped a hand over the butt of his right-hand Walker Colt. A moment later a man's voice rang out from among the trees.

"Hello, the camp. We done smelled coffee."

Preacher looked up in that direction. "Howdy to you, stranger. If you be friendly, come on in. There's plenty for both of us."

"We be two if that's all right by you?"

"Fine as frog hair. Come sit a spell."

Two men entered the clearing on foot, leading their horses. The one in front had a broad, ample girth, chubby arms and legs, and a moon face. The one behind him had a skinny frame, gaunt as a scarecrow's, with flat, dull eyes and big ears. He wore his hair in a boy's "soup bowl" cut, Preacher noticed. The friendly voice came from him.

"They call me Fat Louie, though I can't for the life of

me figger why. Ain't put on a single pound since before my voice changed. This lump o' lard be my pard, Yard-Long Farmer. I reckon you can work out why the name," he concluded with a wheezing cackle.

Yard-Long Farmer joined in the laughter. "Yup. When I was ten I had me the biggest tallywhacker of any kid under fifteen in our town," he offered in the event Preacher could not puzzle through the nickname.

"Name's Arthur," Preacher responded evasively. He had heard of this pair and kept alert. "Sit a while."

He poured coffee around and broke out some corn-bread and a pot of molasses. While they munched and sipped, Fat Louie spoke flatteringly to Preacher.

"I tell ya, Arthur, you're the very best we ever saw. We didn't cut no sign of you whatsomeever. We wouldn't have found this camp if we hadn't near stumbled right into it. You been in the Big Empty long?"

"Since before my voice changed," said Preacher dryly, mocking Fat Louie's earlier turn of phrase.

Fat Louie seemed not to notice. "It certain shows. Say, that's a mighty fine horse you've got. Looks like he could go a long ways, rid hard and put up wet, an' not be harmed. Must be worth a pretty penny."

"He's out of a shaggy mountain mustang," Preacher deliberately belittled his sturdy stallion.

Over the next half hour the conversation went much the same way. When Preacher came to his boots to pour more coffee, Fat Louie cut his eyes to Farmer. The chubby thug nodded slowly. Fat Louie agreed. They had this Arthur off his guard. At once, both rogues whipped out pistols and drew down on Preacher.

"Don't get goosey, Arthur. We'll just be takin' all yer gear an' yer horses an' those fancy irons yer wearin'."

Having been credited with inventing the words *gun-fighter* and *fastdraw*, this did not faze Preacher in the least. He had known of this pair's reputation for years, knew them to be cowardly trash who would kill him in a hot tick. He slowly turned toward the louts threatening him.

He spoke in a soft, flat tone. "I don't think so."

Fat Louie smirked over the barrel of his pistol. "Oh? What makes you say that?"

"Because you've got yourselves a little problem here. Most folks don't call me by my given name. They call me Preacher."

Yard-Long Farmer's eyes went wide and he let his jaw drop before he gulped out a frightened, *"Oh . . . hell!"*

Between the *Oh* and the *hell,* Preacher unlimbered a Walker Colt and shot Fat Louie in the center of his breastbone. Louie's pistol bucked in his hand and he put a ball through the side-wing of Preacher's long, colorful *capote.* Then his legs went rubbery and he sank to his knees.

Preacher immediately turned on Farmer and put a .44 ball in the hollow of his throat. Yard-Long went down, gargling his blood. His finger twitched and he fired one of the pair of pistols he held, sending the ball into his left calf. Pain sounded through his gurgles.

"Why? Why me?" he managed to choke out.

Preacher stepped over to him and removed the unfired pistol from his hand. Right then he heard the click of a caplock mechanism. Fat Louie had not yet gone off to meet his maker. Ignoring the question for a moment, Preacher turned to his right and fired in an almost casual way. His bullet went in one ear and out the other, ending forever the nefarious career of Fat Louie LaDeaux. Then Preacher dropped to one knee beside Yard-Long Farmer.

"You know, it's too bad you and yer partner chose the wrong path to walk. Best you make your peace with the Almighty. You ain't got much time."

* * *

When Preacher reached Bent's Fort, he encountered two old friends, Antoine Revier, a half-breed Delaware, and Three Sleeps Norris. Former mountain men who, like Preacher, could not leave the mountains after the fur trade collapsed, they moved like ghosts from one old haunt to another. Three Sleeps Norris burst out through the stockade gate with such animation that dust boiled up around his moccasins.

"I'll be danged if it ain't Preacher. Still got his hair, if he has growed a little potbelly."

Preacher dismounted and they embraced, then danced around and around. "I don't have a potbelly," Preacher protested. "And I keep my hair by stayin' on the watch for those who would lift it." He stopped their caper and held Three Sleeps out at arm's length. "I will say that you have grown a mite rounder since I last saw you."

Three Sleeps faked a pout. "I ain't no rounder. It's these clothes."

"Sure, sure, of course it is. Anybody else around from the old bunch."

"Antoine Revier is inside now. Also Pap Jacobs is mendin' from a broke leg. Nobody else at home but a couple of stuffy soldier-boys."

Preacher frowned. This was embarrassing. "They're waiting for me."

Three Sleeps cocked his head to one side. "What? Preacher hangin' with soldier-boys?"

"Not exactly hangin'. I got some papers for them. To be delivered. Back in Washington City."

Three Sleeps gave Preacher a knowing wink. "Couldn't be that you're signed up to actual work for the Army?"

Preacher swallowed hard and rushed his words. "We'll-talk-about-that-later. Now I want to wash the trail dust out of my throat."

"Wal, come on. Old Turner has him a new spring

house where he keeps his beer barrels. Like to crack yer teeth it's so cold."

The Bent brothers had long since departed from the private fort named for them. Currently a man named Ransom Turner occupied the trading post and saloon, and the immigrant's store. The fortifications had deteriorated badly. The Arapaho were no longer a threat, and the Kiowa raided farther east. Turner, more a businessman than a frontiersman, had not bothered with repairs. One of the gates, Preacher noted, hung from a single huge iron hinge. They strode across the small parade ground to the front of the saloon to encounter another warm welcome for Preacher.

Seated at last at a table in the plank-floored saloon, Preacher drank contentedly from a large stein of beer, which he used to chase swallows of some whisky of dubious origin. He easily saw why his present companions preferred the beer. Across from him, Antoine Revier leaned toward Preacher. Beady, black eyes glittered with merriment under Revier's thick mane of black hair and bushy brows.

"*Sacré nom*, it is good to see you again, Preacher. When was the last time?"

Preacher studied the traces of gray shot through Revier's hair at his temples and in his luxuriant mustache. A lot of time had gone by. "The 'twenty-eight rendezvous, as I recollect."

Antoine slapped a big hand on the tabletop. "You are right. It has been at least that long. What have you been doing of late? Met any of the other trappers?"

"Not in awhile. I did get crosswise of Fat Louie LaDeaux and Yard-Long Farmer jist the other day."

Revier scowled. "Those two are bad business. They rob the dead—people they have just shot in the back."

Preacher's eyes sparkled. "Not anymore. They tried their game on the wrong feller."

Revier and Norris sniggered. "Now that 'wrong feller' wouldn't happen to be called Preacher, would he?" Revier prompted. At Preacher's nod, he went on. "Good riddance."

Three Sleeps Norris tapped the side of his long nose. "I don't mean to pry, but what brings you this far south, Preacher?"

"Like I said, Three Sleeps, later."

Before Preacher could be asked more, the soft thumps of moccasin soles in the doorway drew their attention. A grizzled mountain man, one not known by any of the three. He nodded to the trio and crossed to the bar.

"Whisky," he ordered. "You hear the latest, Ransom?"

"What would that be, Ev?" asked the proprietor.

"There's word on the wind that a wagon train of pilgrims have been led astray somewhere up to the northeast. They was last seen along the Platte River." Evan Butler turned to include Preacher and his companions. "What do you think, boys? I say we've got more than enough flatlanders shovin' in around here. Present company excepted," he added over his shoulder to the relative newcomer, Ransom Turner.

With his tongue, Preacher worried a scrap of jerky that had caught in his teeth. When he freed it he spat it on the floor. "I say half of those who have come into the High Lonesome are more than enough. Why, them that don't want to tear up the sod and plant crops are Bible thumpers and Psalm singers. Most of them can't button their trousers of a mornin' without retraining, nor know which foot their boot goes on. Give me another beer, Mr. Turner," Preacher said in an aside. "Them lost pilgrims out there can rot for all I care." When the beer came, he quaffed a long draught and smacked his lips.

* * *

Quinton Praeger arose from the fragrant pile of pine boughs on which he had slept and stretched his long, lean frame, toughened by years of living out of doors. He was of an age with Morton Gross, yet he knew himself to be in far better shape. Years as a mining engineer had conditioned him to sleeping on the ground, and for him, unlike the rotund Gross, the Blackfoot bed of buffalo robes and boughs was a luxury. He reached down for his clothing and nudged the bare flank of the young woman who had pleasured him the previous night. She turned on her side and opened blue eyes. When she focused on Praeger, her expression registered disgust. But, as a slave to the Blackfoot, this white woman had no choice, Praeger knew.

Although he would have preferred a young, barely nubile Blackfoot girl, his host had offered this one and he would have offended by refusing. She'd been good, though, he had to admit. At least once he had gotten her suitably warmed up. They would be moving on today. Iron Shirt's Traveling Medicine Show, Praeger reflected with amusement. Three more bands of Blackfoot to visit, then they would go to the Cheyenne. Before long they would have the entire frontier aflame.

Over a rack of open pit-roasted bison ribs, Preacher finally acknowledged that his earlier assumption had been correct. He could not nursemaid a battalion of baby Dragoons all the way to the Big Empty alone. He indeed needed someone to come along. So he began to fabricate an elaborate tale to spin for his friends. Licking grease off his fingers, Preacher tossed away one rib bone and cut off another.

"Now that our bellies are full and we're feelin' good, I'll tell you all about what I come here for. Three Sleeps is right, I gave them papers to the soldier-boys. An' . . . though it galls me to admit it . . . I done signed on for a

job with the Army. You see, there's this new-formed
battalion of Dragoons . . ." Preacher went on to describe
what he expected to find when he reached Jefferson
Barracks. After talking of the well-known hazards of the
vastly unforgiving mountains, he concluded with his
sales pitch.

"'Course I knowed right off that it was gonna take
men of courage and powerful wisdom to shepherd those
green soldier-boys to Wyoming. I'll have to be real careful and choosey as to who I pick."

"Why, that's the stupidest thing I've heard," Three
Sleeps Norris exploded. "Them greenhorns would be
out there all alone. The nearest white settlement is
more miles away than I can count, even if I take off my
moccasins. Wyoming, plumb crazy."

"Oh, I agree. No man in his right mind would pick
that wild and wooly country for putting up a solitary fort.
'Course the government is gonna pay in gold, and plenty
of it. They wrote me that I could pay three dollars, gold,
a day for any who sign on."

"Three dollars?" Norris and Revier chorused.

"Yep. That's right. The way I see it, it'll take the entire
summer to get the job done. That comes to a total of two
hundred seventy-six dollars."

Antoine scratched his head. "Well, now, they sure are
generous. Out here a man can live a whole year on that
and have some left over. And it beats competin' with a
dozen other fellers over every dinky little bit of work that
comes up. If you'll have me, Preacher, I think I'll come
along."

Three Sleeps nodded in agreement. "What you said
about the competition for jobs out here is right, Antoine.
Seems as how Preacher has got himself into a bear cave
the first day of spring. Might be a couple of good fellers,
like ourselves, could save his bacon for him. Count me

in." He extended a hand to Preacher, who shook on the bargain. Then Norris signaled for another round.

Preacher beamed at them with sincere gratitude. "I've done seen the soldier-boys, and they took off lickety-split back east. We can light out first thing in the mornin'."

3

Night swiftly came on again at the edge of the Wyoming Bad Lands of the Great Divide Basin. Eve Billings hugged herself with tired arms. They ached from driving a team of six mules all day. Only two days previously had they found a way out of the Medicine Bow Mountains, at least that's the range in which she believed them to have been. Eve teetered on the verge of losing her battle with despair.

How much more must she endure? How much could she ask her children to take in stride? First the loss of her husband, killed a month and a half ago by a war party of Sauk and Fox in Iowa Territory. Next, their captain and his trail guide had led the wagon train into a blind canyon in the Medicine Bow range. There the scoundrels had robbed and abandoned the settlers. When at last the party had found their way out of the mountains, this stark desert rolled over to the horizon to daunt them.

Resolutely she spoke aloud her foremost thought. "We have to move on."

There was scant water for the stock, blistering heat, although it was only the end of May, and terrible chill at night. However could they find their way? In the distance, a coyote called for his mate, to be answered by half a dozen yaps and yelps. Eve shuddered and tightly clutched the barrel of the Model 40 Bridesburg Arsenal rifled musket her husband had so prudently provided as a necessity. A thin sliver of moon hung in the east, while the western sky still was washed in orange and magenta by the afterglow. Her eldest child, Charlie, came up to her and tugged at her apron as he had done as a babe.

"Mom—Momma, I'm hungry. Anna is cryin' again and wants to eat. What are we goin' to have?"

"There's some bacon, and a few potatoes left."

Charlie wrinkled his nose and twisted his ten-year-old face into a mask of repugnance. "Ugh! The bacon's all green and slippery on the outside."

"I'll trim it. That's all we have."

"Why can't we just go back?"

Eve's heart ached at the misery and pleading in the expression of her son. "We can't, Charlie. It's two months' journey back to New York State. In two months we'll be in the Oregon Country. A new home, a new life."

Charlie rubbed one bare foot over the other. "I don't want a new home. I don't *want* a new life. 'Sides, who's gonna lead us to Oregon? Mr. Tate? Mr. Labette? They can't find their way to the outhouse."

A scowl formed on Eve's high, clear forehead. "That sort of talk will get your mouth washed out with soap, young man. You are not old enough to fail to show respect to your elders. Mr. Pruitt seems to know what he is doing. At least he can hitch his mules without someone showing him how to do it."

"Big help that is," Charlie jeered, then dodged the swat Eve aimed at his rump.

"Back to the wagon, Charlie." When she turned back, the stars shone brightly in the bowl of the sky. Maybe tomorrow help would come.

* * *

Twenty-four naked Blackfoot warriors stood in a solemn rank on the bank of the Bighorn River. Monotonously, two drummers struck the surface of the big drum with their milkweed and sacred pollen padded buffalo-hide strikers. *Thummm* and *thummm* the skin stretched over a large section of hollowed tree trunk sounded. The close-by walls of the Bighorn Mountains reverberated with the drumming. Before the men stood Iron Shirt, stripped of his loincloth and moccasins. For a man of such ambition and power, he had surprisingly average endowment. He raised his bare arms above his head to capture the initiates' attention.

"My brothers, you are about to learn the mysteries behind my great medicine. First you must be purified. Part of that has already been accomplished in the sweat lodges. Now your fear of the white man's bullets must be washed from you so that you are reborn into the society of the Iron Shield Strong Hearts."

Here he paused and stepped backward into the shallows of the river. His bare feet found purchase among the rocks that lined it. The water was aching cold, though he showed no effect. He beckoned with both arms to the first two in line.

"You two come forward into the water." When they did so, his instructions continued. "Turn around and face your brothers." Once in position, four of Iron Shirt's closest followers joined the Blackfoot. Tipping them backward, they lowered each candidate into the water until fully immersed.

Iron Shirt raised one hand over each in benediction and solemnly intoned, "I command all wickedness and fear to abandon you, for you to renounce the power of the white man's bullets, and I baptize you in the name of the three-faced god, the Father and the Son and the Holy Ghost. Arise my brothers in Iron and go forth to be warmed by the coals."

Obediently, the pair waded clear of the river and

walked to where a long, narrow trench had been prepared. The air above it shimmered with distortion from the heat given off by a deep bed of coals. They stood near, letting the radiant waves warm their chilled bodies. While they did, Iron Shirt continued until all the remaining initiates had been baptized. Then he joined them at the firepit. Again he spoke the ritual words.

"To walk safely through the blaze of the white man's bullets, you must first walk through this earthly fire. Prepare your bodies and spirits for this ordeal by praying to the Great Spirit for the strength of the Sky Legend; Firewalker. When you are ready, I will lead you across the abyss of flame."

Iron Shirt waited a hundred heartbeats, then positioned himself at the lip of the trench. He stuck out one foot and made contact with the bed of coals. With a firm, unhurried tread, he walked the length of the shimmering embers. On the far side, he strode ten paces from the pit and raised first one foot, then the other, to reveal not the least damage. The candidates had followed close on his heels and emerged now in the same condition, until the twenty-second in line.

Suddenly that unfortunate warrior let out a pain-wracked shriek and leaped to one side. He fell to the ground to reveal feet of a cherry-red hue, puffed and badly blistered. He had not enough faith. Iron Shirt turned to him. He made a gesture of sympathy.

"Go and have Red Elk dress those feet with bear grease. Know that you did not gain dishonor for your failure. When your faith grows stronger, come again and make the sacrifice, that you may join us." When the injured man had been helped from sight, Iron Shirt gestured to the others. "Come, my brothers of Iron Shield, gather around. It is time for me to reveal the mystery of my medicine's power."

They did, eager as small boys around a strange animal. Iron Shirt reached down and pulled up the hem of his outer hunting shirt. It revealed a complete set, front and back, of chain mail. Although dented in places and rusty in other spots, its sturdy construction and latent protection awed them all. Iron Shirt turned slowly so they could examine the all-encasing war garment, then lowered his shirt and retrieved his loincloth and moccasins. The initiates did likewise, silent throughout. At last, Iron Shirt addressed them again.

"And would you now like to test your new power?" To their enthusiastic agreement, he added. "To the south and west of us, there can be found many rolling lodges of the whites. We shall ride there and kill them all. It is a true thing, I tell you. Not a one of us will fall."

They had circled the wagons for the night. Asa Wharton peered out into the ruddy glow of the setting sun and wondered at what fools they had been. To believe that they could make their way to the Oregon Country on their own should be enough to put them in the asylum, he thought with chagrin. We are too far north, his musings prompted. We always have been. It had been as much his fault as anyone else's. Worse, his voice had been one of the loudest, insisting that the Brothers not bring along any firearms.

"We are the children of God," he had declared. "We must show that we come in peace."

A lot of good that will do. There are Indians out in the hills all around us. He could feel it in his bones. He strongly doubted the savages would spend much time listening to anything they had to say. For the first time since childhood, Asa Wharton wondered what it would be like to die. He shuddered when he recalled the hoofprints he had seen in the loose soil.

He had been riding ahead of the slow-moving wagons when he came upon them. They angled down one slope and crossed the trail. From there, they disappeared over the ridge to the south. By the time the first wagon arrived, a stiff breeze had wiped out any sign of them. *Why had he not told the others about them?*

Because he did not want to create panic. Now it was too late. Asa sighed and turned away. He had taken only one step when the eerie, seething hiss of an arrow registered on him before the projectile winged between a pair of nose-to-tail wagon boxes and buried to the fletchings in Asa's back. The bloody point protruded, dripping, from his chest. Blackness engulfed him.

Iron Shirt led his Strong Hearts silently across the scrub-studded plain. They came within fifty feet and loosed a flight of arrows. Screams of terror and shrieks of pain followed moments later. Young Blackfoot boys, apprentice warriors, held the horses while the braves streamed forward on foot. The only shots fired came from the rifles in the hands of the Blackfoot. They had devastating effect. Seven men fell in the seconds after the death of Asa Wharton.

Whooping Indians broke through the barricade and rushed toward the stunned people. With tomahawks and war clubs they slammed into the helpless whites huddled beyond the fire. Iron Shirt stood back and watched with growing satisfaction. Given another moon, he would have an invincible force. The Cheyenne would join. The Sioux would be next.

Then, he thought, his mind filled with darkness, he would deal with the white men who masqueraded as Blackfoot and run the war against all whites his own way. How good that would be. Beyond him, within the circle of wagons, the slaughter grew terrible. Children, he contemptuously labeled the men and even the women who fell without offering the least resistance.

When the last white died, Iron Shirt came forward. A

quick check showed him that there had been no survivors. And better still, the Blackfoot took no losses.

Early the next morning, Preacher and his companions set out together along the north fork of the Santa Fe Trail. Hard-packed and rutted from much past use, it let them make good time. Near mid-morning, they came upon a packhorse trader. He had three animals on lead, their packsaddles heaped with tin pots and pans, shielded tin lanterns; one loaded with patterned pressed panels for ceilings.

He hailed the trio enthusiastically. "Howdy, fellers. good to see a friendly face. I'd be obliged if you'd ride along a spell. You're more than welcome."

Preacher considered it odd the peddler was headed the same way they were. "Don't mind if we do," he responded. "M'name's Preacher. These two are Three Sleeps Norris an' Antoine Revier."

"Pleased to meet you. I go by the name of Tinman, but it's really Morris Lorson."

"If you don't mind my saying so, them goods of yours looks like something bound for Santa Fe," observed Preacher.

"It is—it is. I just came from there. I got turned away, you see."

Three Sleeps gave him a puzzled look. "How's that, Tinman? I thought those Mezkins was all-fire hot for American goods."

"They are, usually. Only lately things aren't so cordial for Americans. Not since the Texicans won their independence back in 'thirty-six."

Preacher furrowed his brow as he thought this over. "That's old news, and didn't have anything to do with us Americans. What's got into 'em now to get riled at our people?"

Tinman Lorson gave Preacher a knowing look. "Didn't

you hear? For the last couple of years there's been talk about the Texicans wantin' to join up with the United States. An' the folks in Washington City are pushin' for them to do it. You can see how that don't sit well a-tall with the Mexicans."

"That a fact?" Preacher responded, then tuned out the peddler's chatter.

They made camp late in the afternoon. Around coffee, after ample plates of broiled grouse—provided by Antoine with his delicate, slender-barreled shotgun—fatback and beans, Tinman Lorson studied his impromptu fellow travelers. After several moment's consideration he hesitantly explored a subject of great interest to him.

"If you don't mind, I surely don't wish to pry, but would you tell me how you got that name—Three Sleeps?"

"Wal, it ain't nothin' much. It happened a long time ago."

"No, really, I'd like to know. I . . . ah . . . collect nicknames and the stories behind them. It's something to pass the long hours shared with others along the trading path. Please, indulge me if you will."

Preacher inserted himself in the conversation. "Three Sleeps is too modest to brag on hisself. I'll be happy to enlighten you."

Lorson brightened. "Yes, do."

Preacher thought a while, then began his tale. "Like Three Sleeps says, it happened a long time ago. He was a youngster then, hardly old enough to wet his throat with good whisky. As it happened, he was doin' just that one fine day when this notorious brawler slammed into the tradin' post where young Archibald Norris stood at the bar. As it happened, this bear-wrastlin' lout was spoilin' for a fight. Hadn't thumped on anyone for a couple of days and was feelin' out of sorts.

"So he eyes Arch here and says, 'Who let this skinny little puke in here?' Now Arch happened to be sensitive about his size at the time," Preacher went on with a chuckle. "He turns to face . . . ah . . . what was his name?"

"Travers. Meat Hook Travers," Three Sleeps provided quietly. He gave a little shudder.

"Yep. That's the one. Meat Hook Travers. Anyhow, ol' Meat Hook stomped up to the bar while Archibald formed the words he would say. Meat Hook thumped Arch on the chest and bellowed to the barkeep. 'Somebody answer me.' Archibald had his words gathered by then and decided it was up to him to speak. 'I brought myself in on my own two legs, and I reckon to leave the same way.' For Meat Hook, that was too hard to chew, let alone swallow. So, he rears back and bellows at Archibald. 'You'll go out of here on a plank.'" Preacher paused for a swallow of coffee.

"An' that's where ol' Meat Hook got a big surprise. Young Archie came at him like a buzz saw. He walked up Meat Hook with his fists and down t'other side. He booted that tub of muscle and lard in the butt and when Meat Hook turned with a roar, Arch mashed his lips with a solid left—or was it a right? Never mind, he moved fast as a wasp with a busted nest. Archie was quick and he was sneaky. He landed five punches for everyone Meat Hook connected. Then Meat Hook tried to catch Archibald in a bear hug.

"Archie was havin' none of that. He danced back and kicked Meat Hook in the belly. That did it. Meat Hook sank to his knees. Arch here waded in. When he got done, Meat Hook was stretched out on the dirt floor, cold as an iced-over lake. Arch rubbed his sore knuckles and stepped back to the bar. 'You'd best put some distance between the two of you,' the bartender advised. 'Not a problem. I think I'll finish my whisky and have a little brew,' Archibald responded. The fellow in the apron had good advice. 'He'll come after you for sure.' All calm and collected, Archie swallowed down his whisky and gestured for a beer. 'There's plenty time to make tracks. The way I see it, he's good for about three sleeps.' And, by jingo, if the name didn't stick. I know for certain it happened that way because I was the only witness beside the barman."

Slack-jawed, Morris Lorson stared into the fire. He did not know, for all his experience at collecting names and legends, if he was having his leg pulled or not. Then something that had been nagging at him all day went off in his mind. He looked up at the weathered features of the narrator of the tale.

"Are you the same Preacher who single-handed cleaned a nest of thieves and cutthroats out of a trading-post saloon a decade ago?"

"Friend, it's been at least a dozen saloons I've cleaned out by myself," Preacher enlightened him. "Not to count the Injuns I've fit and the personal squabbles with other mountain men. You've got the right one, sure enough, if your claims for me are a mite more modest than some."

Lorson beamed. "Then it's a pleasure to be counted among your associates, if only for a short while. And I have me a new nickname and the story behind it. I'm obliged." He rocked back on his heels.

"An' I'm for gettin' some shut-eye," announced Preacher. "Daylight comes mighty fast in these parts."

Along about what Preacher judged to be ten-thirty in the morning, he and his partners parted company with Tinman Lorson. They spurred their more lightly loaded mounts and rode ahead, to soon lose him from sight over a ridge. Shortly after that, Preacher began to pick up sign of an Indian presence.

A trimmed, decorated eagle feather stuck an inch or two above the ridge to the south. Bird calls, which had been plentiful moments before, had dwindled to a few. Those that came did not sound entirely true. A tiny puff of dust drifted upward suddenly from beyond the swale to the north. Preacher reined in abruptly and dismounted. His friends did likewise.

After a quick look around, they formed a close square with their mounts and the packhorse. Antoine cut his eyes to Preacher. "I noticed them, too, *mon ami.*"

A second later, a small party of howling Kiowa warriors broke the southern horizon and thundered down toward the white men behind the improvised barricade.

4

"Watch our backsides, Three Sleeps," Preacher instructed calmly while he sighted in and cleaned one Kiowa from the saddle with his rifle.

Quickly, Preacher reloaded. He changed his point of aim and put a .54-caliber ball through the shoulder of another warrior. Beside him, Antoine fired his trusty .36-caliber squirrel rifle and plunked a ball through the center of a screaming Kiowa's forehead. His war whoop ended mid-yelp.

Behind them, Three Sleeps Norris downed another warrior with a gut shot. "You were right, Preacher, they're comin' from the north now."

By then, Preacher and Antoine had reloaded. It would be their last rifle shot for this charge, they knew. The Kiowa braves had come within twenty yards now. Preacher fired first. He split a buffalo-hide shield and shattered the forearm behind it. The warrior ignored it, his left arm flopping uselessly amid a shower of blood. Antoine ended the life of another savage with a ball through the throat. Then Preacher drew one Walker Colt. He made a quick check of the percussion caps, found them secure on the nipples. Then he raised the heavy revolver and eared back the hammer.

A fat cloud of smoke enveloped the defenders when the big .44 fired. Preacher quickly recocked the revolver and got off another round. A shout of pain answered him. The light breeze slowly blew the obscuring cloud away. Another round from Preacher's Colt took a warrior in the side. With that, they had enough.

A shrill bark turned the Kiowa and they swung away from their target. They quickly galloped out of range.

"They'll be back," advised Preacher.

Several minutes passed in an eerie silence. Then the Kiowa came again, this time from the east. Preacher had counted twenty warriors at the outset. Now four lay dead on the ground and three had been severely wounded. That left a baker's dozen. Three rifles spoke with deadly authority and reduced the number to ten.

Still the Indians would not leave off. Their blood was up, their friends killed or wounded. They badly wanted these white scalps. Once again they recoiled from the blaze of Preacher's six-shooters.

Running Bull could not understand it. Had they come upon a party of the Texicans called Rangers? He knew of no others who possessed the fast-shoot hand rifles. If so, why did the others not use theirs? From the reverse slope of the rise to the east, he studied the besieged white men with keen eyes.

They are only three, he thought with confusion. How could they kill so many so quickly? A quick glance left and right showed his warriors poised for another attack. He also detected signs of nervousness. They, too, could count.

Running Bull raised his voice in exhortation. "This time we do not turn away. Ride over them, wet your lances in their blood. Are you women that only three frail white men can stop you?"

Blood lust boiled over and the Kiowa set the mounts

to a fast trot up and over the ridge, to thunder down the incline. Ahead waited the fiery death of the white men. Not a one of them lacked fear; yet they knew it to be a good day to die.

"*Sacre bleu!* Here they come again," Antoine spat out as he raised his rifle to take aim.

At extreme range, Preacher sighted in with his Hawken and put a ball in the chest of a warrior, piercing the right side. Undaunted, the Kiowa raised his lance and charged on. Preacher set aside the .56-caliber rifle and put the slender buttstock of his French Le Mat to shoulder. The finely made .36 sporting arm had served him well before. Now he honed the sights in on the face of his enemy.

Hair-fine, the second of the double-set triggers let off the round with ease. Smoke belched and blew away in time for Preacher to see the black hole that appeared where the tip of the warrior's nose had been a moment before.

At once, his lance sailed skyward and the Kiowa did a back-roll off his laboring pony. He hit with a thud and bounced only once. Preacher reloaded swiftly, only to be caught with the ramrod down the barrel of his Le Mat when the distance between him and the warriors closed to less than twenty feet. He lowered the muzzle against Tarnation's heaving flank and drew the reloaded Walker Colt. With what precision he could muster he emptied it into the mass of Indians in front of them, and yet they came on.

A lance thudded into the ground so close to his leg he felt the pressure of the shaft. Preacher holstered the Colt and drew the second one. He spent two rounds before the Kiowa warriors reined around and beat a hasty retreat. A quick count showed Preacher that only five remained alive.

"Stubborn," he told his companions. "Plain damn stubborn. They coulda quit a long time ago. I'd been willin'. What about you?"

"*Qui.* Without a doubt," Antoine panted.

Preacher turned to the horses. "We'd best be movin' on. We don't want them to work up the spit to make another try."

One fine afternoon, three days later, Preacher and his two friends rode along the trail with the sparkling waters of the Arkansas River to their right. Chubby barrel cactus and wicked-tipped Spanish bayonet abounded on the rolling sand hills ahead of them. Abruptly, Preacher raised his hand for a halt.

From a distance ahead came the dull thumps of gunshots. They all had heard them, and had halted to try to make out what they meant. With the recent Kiowa attack fresh in their minds, Preacher and his companions suspected a war party.

It had to be a large group under attack, or both sides had firearms, Preacher decided a moment later when the rate of fire escalated. This country did not lack for human trash that would prey on the law-abiding. He drummed heels into the ribs of Tarnation and rushed forward. Antoine and Three Sleeps came right behind.

Over the next rounded dune, the sounds of shots grew clearer. Preacher drew his revolver. Antoine and Three Sleeps loosened pistols in the holsters slung over their saddlehorns. Dust mingled with powder smoke had risen high enough to be clearly seen before they topped the grade. Preacher halted them again.

"Let's not blunder in, boys. I'll take a peek first."

He dismounted, removed his floppy summer hat and approached the ridge in a crouch. Slowly he raised his head. A moderate-sized freight train came into sight first. Preacher raised up a little higher and focused on

some twenty white renegades, several of whom fired on
the teamsters from an outcropping of boulders south
of the trail. Others milled back and forth on horseback,
apparently prevented from circling front or rear of the
caravan due to concentrated fire at those points. It
looked to Preacher like those freighters could use
some help.

Quickly he returned to the others and explained the
situation. Mounted again, he led the way up and over
the ridge. Pistols in hand, they dashed down on the
unsuspecting outlaws. The surprise arrival of three
more fighting men cleared four of the ten saddles
before the bandits knew that help had come for the
teamsters. Quick to realize that relief had arrived, the
teamsters began to rally. Preacher heard a voice raised
over the tumult, singing in a sweet tenor.

"'At the risin' o' the moon, at the risin' o' the moon, the
men and bies will gather at the risin' o' the moon.' Give
'em hell, bies, there's help on the way. C'mon, ye soldier-
bies!"

That galvanized the outlaws. Those who could whirled
away and ran a murderous gauntlet along the length of
the stationary wagons. Those afoot in the rocks turned
and tried to make a stand. Preacher sighted in on one
and reined sharply to send a .44 messenger on the way.
The letter it carried was death.

Shot through the mouth, the highwayman fell backward in an awkward sprawl. Preacher emptied the last
round from the Colt into the stomach of another hardcase. He changed weapons quickly and sought another
target. A ball cracked past close enough that he heard
its ominous moan. The shooter died an instant later,
shot through the heart by Antoine Revier. To his left,
Preacher heard the sound of increased resistance.

Bullwhackers fired and loaded and fired again. Rifle
balls snapped through the air, whined off rocks and
brought forth screams from human targets. Several

more outlaws died in this withering fire. Ahead of Preacher, wounded men crawled toward their horses, desperate to escape. Churned-up dust began to obscure the scene. Preacher fired at a fleeing man and missed. He turned Tarnation and sprinted to the head of the wagon train.

He reached his goal in a growing silence. Gradually the crackle of gunfire had diminished. At the lead wagon Preacher saw half a dozen highwaymen spurring frantically until they disappeared beyond the next swell.

A big, red-faced man came out from between two wagons and walked Preacher's way. He was a bull of a man, with bulging muscles and ham hands. When he spoke, his mouth became a black hole in his heavily bearded face.

"Right on time, lads, that ye are. Good work. Sure an' where's the soldiers you're scouting for?"

Preacher gave him a curious look. "At Jefferson Barracks. We haven't joined up with them as yet."

Momentarily stunned, the lead bullwhacker worked his mouth soundlessly. Words returned with a sputter. "Y-y-you mean there's just the th-three of you?"

"That's right."

"Well, truth is you fight like a whole company of soldiers. They call me Big Tom Lawson. This here is my strong right arm, Brian O'Shea, an' we're obliged to you."

Preacher gave them a nod. "Big Tom, Brian, my pleasure. I answer to Preacher, and these be Three Sleeps Norris an' Antoine Revier. Any idea why those road agents picked your train to raid?"

"None that make sense. What we're haulin' is too heavy to take off on horseback and these wagons would leave a trail a blindman could follow." Finally Preacher's name registered. "Say, you ain't *that* Preacher are you? The one in the penny dreadfuls?"

Preacher's cheeks carmined. "To my eternal torment, I be. What foolishness them idiot writers can dream up would gag a maggot. What you read in them things ain't true a-tall. Except I may have been in some of those places at the time they said I was, and I may have had something to do with what happened to some of those fellers they claim I done for. Jist may have, mind you."

Big Tom made a wry face. "Sure an' I don't buy none of that at all. Never mind. You are a gen-u-wine legend in yer own time. A living hero, you are. We'd be over-joyed to have you join us in our trading expedition, full share for all of you. Lord knows, you just earned it."

"No," Preacher replied politely. "We have to push on to Jeff Barracks. Gave my word. In writing, at that."

Big Tom looked greatly disappointed. "I understand contracts right enough. The least you can do is stay a spell and take supper with us. We'll lay on a right regu-lar feast. Why, we even have a fruitcake along. All sopped up in brandy." He gave a big wink. "I figgered to use it to mellow the Governor General in Santa Fe. What ya say, Preacher?"

Patting his flat, hard belly, Preacher produced a euphoric smile. "I never could resist fruitcake. 'Special if it's got itself drunk."

Once started out onto the Great Divide Basin, after long, heated debate, the wagon train ran into disaster after defeating disaster. Mr. Ledbetter had three mules die. After acrimonious exchanges, in which accusations of selfishness flew like snowflakes in a blizzard, it was decided to draw straws to see which two wagons would "voluntarily" give up a mule so that Ledbetter could keep up. Eve Billings drew one of the short straws.

No sooner had that predicament been solved than another sprang up. One day five precious water barrels had sprung leaks or broken apart. The next day, three more became useless. With much shouting and gesticulating, the decision was made to turn back. Eve had nothing to tell her children.

"Mom, are we really going home?" Charlie asked eagerly when it became apparent to him that they were retracing their steps.

"Only part way, dear," Eve told him tiredly.

"But why?" His button nose wrinkled in the effort to understand these adult mysteries.

"We aren't ready to go on as yet. We need a guide, someone who can take us out of this wilderness. Without water, the livestock will die, like Mr. Ledbetter had happen." She did not add the obvious, that people would die as well.

"I want to go all the way home."

"Don't start on that again, Charles Ryan Billings."

Charlie instantly lapsed into silence. He always knew when he was in trouble; his mother used his proper first name. When she used his middle name, too, he knew he was up to his neck in it. Charlie heaved a defeated sigh and scampered over the rumps of the mules to his favorite spot on the back of Jake, the lead animal.

Eve watched her son move with agility and assurance and then lifted her gaze to the horizon. She estimated they had another day of travel, back to the old camp.

A storyteller's high, singsong voice rang out across the camp in the Bighorn Mountains. He related an ancient tale of the grandfather times. One in which the Cheyenne and the Blackfoot were allies. It had to be a long time ago, Cloud Blanket thought as he watched the historic meeting from his place in the Cheyenne council circle.

Less than a moon ago, he would not have believed this gathering could happen. The Blackfoot had come under a white belt of truce. They had a great story to relate. About a young medicine man and the power he possessed. When the council gathered, the talk quickly turned to war against the whites. That greatly disturbed Cloud Blanket, though he could not name the reason why. All he could say was this was not the time to fight the white men. Suddenly he found the talking stick offered to him. He took it and came to his moccasins.

"You say that this prophet's medicine is so strong none of you fell in the battle which was described to us?" Two Moons nodded in the affirmative. "That may be so. It could also be that the whites did not carry long guns with them." His eyes twinkled with secret knowledge. He might have seen forty winters, might be past his prime, but he was not helpless or ignorant. Cloud Blanket had his sources of information, and one of them had told him of the attack on the unarmed whites. How odd, he thought, that anyone would not carry weapons. Did they not know there were tribes hungry for war? He suddenly realized the Blackfoot named Two Moons had responded to his jibe.

"The great prophet will come among you soon," Two Moons repeated when he saw the Cheyenne chief's attention had returned. "He will show you his medicine. It is true that he cannot be killed by normal bullets. His medicine is strong, the most powerful. We have been given his shield," Two Moons stated emphatically.

Cloud Blanket remained unimpressed. "I have seen far too often what the bullets of the white men can do."

Too hot in his zeal, Two Moons snatched up a rifle that lay beside a Cheyenne. "If you doubt me, take this, shoot me. Go ahead. I will not be killed."

"If I believed that, I would shoot you." Cloud Blanket shook his head resignedly. "I have heard of such medicine before. It has always failed its user. Leave us now, the council will reach a consensus and let you know. I am but one man, my voice is not listened to as much as it once was. Perhaps you will win an ally after all."

After the Blackfoot delegation withdrew to eat and nap through the afternoon, the Cheyenne spoke heatedly about the issue. Several agreed with Cloud Blanket: it would be a bad idea to make a pact with the Blackfoot. Had they not been enemies for longer than the storyteller could remember? In the end, Cloud Blanket prevailed on that point. He lost on the other. He felt obliged to take the word to the Blackfoot. He found them in the lodge that hosted them.

"Our council has come to a consensus. We will not ally with you at this time. You can send your prophet, Iron Shirt; we will listen to his message."

5

Preacher, Three Sleeps and Antoine spent the night at the Cottonwoood Crossing on the Santa Fe Trail. There, they underwent inspection by two disreputable characters, one with wispy strands of mustache that drooped below his jawline in Oriental style. His brown skin marked him as a Mexican. His partner had wild-straw hair that stuck out at all angles, buck teeth and pale, hollow cheeks. The pair slouched into the saloon of the trading post shortly after Preacher and his companions arrived.

Preacher nodded in their direction. "Now there's a pair to draw to."

Three Sleeps sniffed the air. "I wonder if they know what the word *bath* means?"

Antoine nodded agreement. "How about 'soap'?"

Preacher chuckled, a low, throaty sound, and leaned closer to them. "Way I rec'llect it, ain't neither of you could lay claim to bein' in the Every Saturday Night club." He drew in a lungful. "Though I will admit they've got a certain ripeness about them."

For the next hour, the surly pair nursed pewter mugs of beer and paid considerable, though covert, attention to Preacher and his friends. Then they settled their tab and stomped out. Preacher watched them through the open door as they settled down some distance off from the tavern and inn that had sprung up at the crossing to accommodate stagecoach travelers.

"Not overwhelming sociable, are they?" Preacher observed to his partners.

"I ain't gonna lose any sleep over it," remarked Antoine.

Preacher stroked his chin. "I wonder which way they're goin'? That's a pair it would do a body good to keep track of."

Three Sleeps narrowed his eyes. "You thinkin' they're trouble, Preacher?"

Preacher nodded. "That I do. I could smell it on them plain as that sweat stink. I may be wrong, but I could almost swear I saw the towheaded one with that bunch what attacked the freight wagons."

Although up well before dawn, Preacher noted that the unwashed pair had already departed. He saw to making a pot of coffee and was soon joined by Three Sleeps. The frown on the forehead of Norris indicated that he had noted the absence of the human trash.

He gestured with his chin. "They ain't gonna be missed. Not by this mother's son."

"Like I said, it'd pay to keep them in sight, or know what they might be up to."

"You've been alone too long, Preacher. That makes a man suspicious for no reason."

"You turnin' womanish on me, Three Sleeps?"

"Nope. C'mon, I'll lend a hand with that packsaddle. After we eat we can take right off."

"Now that's a good idea."

After a plate of fatback and beans, Preacher downed the last of his coffee, used the dregs in the pot to quench the fire and scuffed dirt over it. In the saddle, they made their way eastward. The trail ended at Independence,

Missouri, but there were supposed to be good roads through the state. At least as far as Jefferson Barracks, Preacher had been told. Two hours down the Santa Fe, Preacher's keen hearing picked up what sounded like thunder.

He looked around at a clear sky and produced a puzzled frown. "D'you hear thunder, Antoine?"

"Yep, sure sounded like it, but there's not a cloud up there."

Yet, the sound persisted and grew louder. Then the creak of wood on leather springs and the jingle of harness explained it to Preacher. Laboring up behind them came a six-up of spanking bays. Foam lathered their flanks and around their collars. Seated above them the driver sawed on the reins and called to his team.

"Gee up, there. Keep it brisk or no corn for you tonight."

Clouded in dust, the stagecoach grew in Preacher's vision. They must be closer than he thought to Muddy Creek Crossing, the mountain man thought to himself. Otherwise that feller would not be runnin' them horses like that. He turned in the saddle to watch the team draw up alongside. A scowling man, armed with a Purdey percussion shotgun, eyed the three mountain men with suspicion. Preacher removed his slouch hat and gave a cordial wave. The express guard acknowledged it with a curt nod.

"Well, he ain't bein' paid to be friendly," Preacher opined to his companions.

"You got the right o' that, Preacher."

"How long's it been, Three Sleeps, that the stage lines have had to run a guard on their coaches?"

Norris scratched the top of his head. "Leastwise ten years. An' it's gettin' worse, I'm told."

Preacher pondered a moment. "It's types like those yesterday that's behind it. Law's too easy on them."

"They still have hangings, don't they?"

"Oh, yeah, Three Sleeps. Used to be a man kept the law himself. Now, with law dogs mixed up in it, if a man shoots a thief, likely he'll be the one winds up in jail."

In the Black Hills of the Unorganized Territory, a young Red Cloud refused to even listen to the emissaries of Iron Shirt. Little good it would do. Since he had not yet seen twenty winters, he would not have been listened to anyway. Oh, the elders on the council would have made a show of hearing him out, but their ears might as well be plugged with wax from a bee tree. So frustrated had he become that he jumped on his favorite pony and rode out as the council gathered to hear the message of the prophet. Red Cloud sat atop a knoll and looked down into his village.

He knew every lodge. There, the one of his friend, Runner. Over close to the big drum lived White Knife. They had grown up together, hunted, then gone off to war the best of friends. White Knife had lost a little finger to a Pawnee war club while fighting at the side of Red Cloud. Now he added his voice to those clamoring for the council to approve bringing Iron Shirt and his medicine to the Lakota.

Red Cloud spat on the ground. A great shout reached his ears. The council had decided. From the looks of it they had decided in favor of the cursed Blackfoot and his iron medicine. Drums began to throb, and from every lodge, the women brought pots and baskets of food to feast the Blackfoot men. Red Cloud's lip curled in disgust.

What hurt most was his grudging admission that the time would soon come when the Lakota would have to fight the white men, but the time was not now.

* * *

A week and a half had passed since their first disastrous attempt to cross the Great Divide Basin. Fear of the unknown and indecision had kept the abandoned wagon train stranded at the same small spring that had previously provided their scant water supply. Eve Billings opened her flour barrel, and a momentary bolt of panic shot through her. She could see the bottom in places.

Provisions had run short for everyone. Eve knew she wasn't alone in this predicament. So many people had killed or run off the sparse game in the area, the men had to ride for miles to get even a few rabbits. She crumbled yeast into the bowl and began to add water to the flour. When she looked up, there stood Charlie.

The thin film of perspiration on his bare, sun-browned shoulders and sides under the straps of his overalls made his skin glow. He fixed big, cornflower blue eyes on her face. She wondered if her worry lines had become permanent. From the looks of Charlie, they must have.

"Mom, what are we having for supper?"

"Fried bread with molasses and potato soup," she answered, painfully aware of how inadequate that sounded.

Charlie's usually smooth, childish features twisted into an expression of misery. *"Again?* That's what we had last night."

"And the night before. Be grateful we have that. And that Mr. Tate shared his rabbits with us on Sunday."

"I want meat tonight!" Charlie stubbornly insisted.

"Well, we simply don't have any."

Charlie took on a coy, wheedling expression. "I could get us some. At least some rabbits. I'm a good shot, you know that, Mom. Please, let me take my rifle and go after some rabbits. I won't go far, and I know better than to shoot in the direction of the wagons."

He had already robbed her of her two best arguments. She swore that the boy would become a lawyer, or a politician some day. Or worst yet, both. What could she say to counter his intentions, good though they might be? Carefully, she framed her sentences.

"What horse would you use? The grass is so scarce that your pony's too weak to carry you."

Bright enthusiasm lighted Charlie's face. "I can always use Jake."

"A mule? One not broken to saddle at that, Charlie. I don't think it would be safe."

"I ride his back every day we're on the trail. An' when I take the others out to graze. He knows me an' he don't mind. Really, Mom."

Eve sighed. Rabbit would taste mighty good. A deep, vertical furrow formed between Eve's brows. "If you go— and mind, I said if—you would have to stay within sight of the wagons."

"Mo-oom," Charlie enunciated with exasperation, small fists on hips. "There aren't any rabbits within sight of the wagons. I'll be all right. After all, you said I would have to be the man of the family now. Please let me prove I can do it."

What could she say? What could she do? With a suppressed sigh, Eve swallowed her mother's fears and relented. "All right. But you take your father's pocket watch with you, and you be back here in two hours exactly, or you'll never go again."

Charlie abandoned his mannish stance and leaped up to wrap arms around his mother's neck. "Oh, Mom, thank you, thank you. I'll bring us rabbits, I promise. Enough we can share."

"And wear your boots," Eve added as Charlie turned from her.

When the boy scampered off to get the watch and his rifle, powder horn and bag of balls, Eve stood staring after him. Her son complaining about small portions and the lack of real meat. His little sister with a slight fever and runny bowels. What more could she endure? A sudden thought came to Eve.

Could it be the water? Painfully aware that they were far from the established trail, the specter of everyone falling victim to some terrible sickness arose to haunt her. Surrendering to a moment of despair, Eve began to suspect that no one would ever come along to lead them out of this desolation.

While Eve Billings battled with her dejection, Preacher and his companions took their nooning at Muddy Creek Crossing. The coach that had passed them had also stopped there. While the hostler changed the horses, Preacher watched the passengers descend to take their meal in the shade.

A chubby, moon-faced Osage woman, wife of the stage agent, and her gaggle of youngsters, stair-stepped from about thirteen to seven, brought out heaped platters of fried chicken, bowls of baked squash and beans, stewed onions swimming in butter and cold, boiled potatoes. All this bounty came from a large, well-tended kitchen garden that Preacher saw behind the ramshackle stage station. For the hefty sum of ten cents each, Preacher and the mountain men also sat down to the feast.

For that purpose, the relay station had trestle tables set out under a large, gnarled old cottonwood. A young woman passenger took note of Preacher's handsome features. Pursing her lips, she fixed her violet eyes on his profile and batted long lashes flirtatiously.

Antoine nudged Preacher in the ribs. "You got an admirer, I see."

"Huh? Who'd that be?"

"Over to your left. There's a purty young thing givin' you the eye."

Preacher cut his eyes quickly to the left and caught a flutter of long, black lashes. The woman brought a fan up to cover her face and uttered a brief titter. Preacher looked away. For several minutes he dedicated his attention to a chicken leg. Three Sleeps kicked him on the shin. Preacher jumped as a result.

"She's at it again. Givin' you the big ol' come-on eye. A right toothsome lass, you ask me."

"Then you flirt with her," Preacher grumbled.

Three Sleeps Norris sniggered "Wouldn't mind at all."

Suddenly the older woman with the flirtatious one caught her at it. This ample-bosomed dowager took an abundant pinch of forearm and hissed loud enough to be heard by Preacher and his friends.

"Agatha, for shame. I'll thank you to conduct yourself like a lady."

"But he's sooo handsome."

Her visage turned to stone, the elder companion took another pinch, this time of cheek. "You disappoint me, Agatha Sinclaire. That frontier trash isn't fit to shine your shoes. If you cannot behave in a refined manner, I'll see that you return to the coach." That said, she turned her acid tongue on Preacher. "And you, you unwashed barbarian, I'll thank you to keep your lustful eyes off my ward. It's your kind that have sullied this beautiful country. Those uncouth louts with you are no better. Have they no shame? It's scandalous the way they smirk and waggle their heads. Why . . ."

Her invective slid off Preacher like water ran off a duck. When the older woman finally ran down, Preacher removed his floppy hat and scratched his head, as though looking for lice. He ran his tongue around the inside of his mouth and came to his boots.

"Well, now, ma'am. I allow as how the girl is a tooth-some bit, right enough, but me an' my friends have important business at Jefferson Barracks and I can't take the time to dally."

With a squawk of indignation, the dowager abandoned her meal, grabbed the wrist of her charge and hauled the two of them off to the coach. Seated at another table, the same two scruffy ragbags from the previous day took in all that transpired. They exchanged meaningful glances and rose to silently slip away.

Preacher took note of that and stored it for later. He stared long after their rapidly retreating backs. They, too, were headed east. He and the other mountain men finished their food and started off for the Lost Springs Station. Something told Preacher it would be a long afternoon. One he might live to regret.

A grinning Charlie Billings returned to the wagon train with four plump rabbits strung over the neck of Jake. His slender-barreled .36-caliber squirrel rifle lay across his thighs. For all her elation over the fresh meat, Eve still noticed with irritation that Charlie had ignored his boots. He had also fastened a length of rope around his waist and slipped the shoulder straps of his overalls, so that he rode bare-chested as a wild Indian.

"Charles Ryan Billings, you put up the bib of those overalls right this minute. You're a scandalous sight. You look like a heathen red savage." Part of her irritation came from the memory of the four reports she had heard distantly from beyond a hill.

She had bitten her lip at hearing each shot. Worried that Charlie had injured himself, that he lay bleeding and near death, she could hardly contain herself, remain at the wagon and knead her bread dough. Now he shows up, looking like a brown-skinned imp of Satan, grinning and showing off his hunting skill. Abruptly her irritation fled and an ocean of love swelled up in her chest.

"Look what I've got, Mom! It was easy."

It took all her will not to run forward and embrace him, and she failed to keep from blurting her thoughts.

"My wonderful boy. We'll share them with the Tates and the Warners."

Charlie produced a pout. "I thought we'd smoke 'em and have meat for all week."

Eve put her hands on her hips and glowered at her son. "We have been gifted by others, now we can return their generosity. I'll fix you a hind leg and a chunk of loin."

"All right," Charlie agreed. He reined Jake to the right and rode to the Tate wagon.

Eve nearly called him back; he had done nothing about adjusting his clothing. "I swear, that boy would go bucknaked if he could get away with it," she said aloud to herself.

"Why, Mommy?" Anna asked from the spot of shade under the wagon.

Startled, Eve turned to her. "Because he has your father's orneriness, sweetie. Now, do you feel strong enough to help make dough balls with me for the fried bread?"

"Yes, Mommy, but my tummy hurts some."

"Oh, Anna, Anna," Eve spoke through a tight throat as tears welled in her eyes.

6

Preacher and his mountain man friends decided to spend the night in the dormitory-style hotel east of the stage station at Lost Springs. The Spanish had named the location during the Coronado expedition in the sixteenth century. The climate had been entirely different three hundred years earlier. The springs they had located and marked with tall stakes and flags had disappeared on their return from a fateful encounter with the Pawnee. They had called them The Lost Springs. Preacher explained the reason behind his suggestion to stay over a sit-down meal in the tavern.

"We're gettin' into country where people get suspicious of fellers campin' under the stars. Makes 'em edgy. So we might as well start gettin' used to a roof overhead."

"Sounds reasonable," Antoine Revier agreed. "Say, the feller who owns this place has got himself one powerful good cook. Who would have ever thought someone way out here could do a proper soufflé?" He smacked his lips in appreciation. His spoon paused over the gold-brown dome of the fancy corn pudding, which chose that moment to collapse.

Three Sleeps sniggered and Preacher pointed at the soufflé disaster with his chin. "It supposed to do that?"

Defensively, Antoine dug into the dish. "It's the thought that counts. My pappy. Now there's a man who could cook a perfect soufflé."

Preacher raised his brow. "That's right, your pap was a Frenchie, a *voyageur.* "

"*Mais oui.* He was also a great cook. A chef. A master in the kitchen."

Three Sleeps Norris waggled his head. "Cookin's women's work."

Antoine bristled. "Not so! The world's greatest cooks are men. Why, back in the days of knights and noble ladies, women were not even permitted to serve the food, let alone cook it. My friends, you are entirely too limited in worldly experience. Now, leave me to my soufflé in peace."

Three Sleeps sounded wounded. "It's part ourn, too."

Nose rising in the air, Antoine passed judgment on that. "You haven't the taste to appreciate it."

"Even if it is flat?" Preacher inquired.

Antoine relented, at least a little. "Awh, dig in, Preacher, it's ruined anyway."

After their evening meal, Preacher and his companions staked out floor-level, straw-stuffed mattresses and then went in search of distraction. Antoine and Three Sleeps found the bar, where a curious fellow worked fast and skillfully at charcoal sketches of some of the patrons. They watched in fascination while the features of a stolid Osage seated at one table emerged on the stretched canvas. Antoine nodded toward the Indian and his likeness.

"Right clever. D'you mind if I ask what yer doin' that for, mister?"

The artist looked up from his work. "I am preparing my canvases to do the subjects in oil."

Three Sleeps gaped at him, unbelieving. "You're gonna boil all these fellers in oil?"

Chuckling, the artist disabused him of that idea. "Far from it, my friend. I am going to paint them."

That set Three Sleeps back a bit. "Oh, oh, yes. You're an . . . an artist?"

"Just so. Would you like me to do you and your friend here in oil?"

"How long'd it take?"

The artist took a second to consider that. "An evening to do the sketch. Two, three days to finish the portrait. Then you could take it with you."

"Hmmm. Sorry, we got to keep movin' east. Be gone at first light tomorrow.

"That's a shame. Perhaps another time. My name is Catlin. If we meet again, I hope you have the time for me to paint you."

For Preacher distraction turned out to be a gaming table. Five men sat around the green baize circle when he approached.

"Evenin', gents. I answer to Preacher. Oh, no," he hastened to add when one man produced a black scowl. "I'm not going to give you a sermon on the evils of gamblin'. Matter of fact, if there's room, I'd be obliged for an invite to join the game."

Abandoning his scowl, the pudgy, soft-handed man produced a welcoming smile. "The name's Jessup. I own this place. These gentlemen are noble followers of the bullwhacker calling. Sit right down, Preacher. Your money is as good as any man's."

Jessup had his hair slicked down and smelled of bay rum. He had small, close-set eyes that missed meanness due to a warm, friendly twinkle. He and the others completed the hand while Preacher dumped a stack of gold pieces on the table. Jessup passed the deck to the man on his right, who nodded to Preacher.

"Among the teamsters, I'm known as Long Tom. What's yer pleasure?"

Preacher did not lack in card-playing etiquette. "You

name it, Tom." Introductions went around the table, and Preacher met Billy Green, Hank Lupton and Frank Spence.

Long Tom shuffled and announced, "Five-card stud."

Preacher played tight and smart. He folded after the third card. Jessup stayed to the bitter end with a bluff, Preacher noted. The next dealer called for five-card draw. Preacher was dealt a pair of queens, a ten, eight and deuce. He stayed and drew two cards. That gave him two pair. Jessup ran another bluff, raising the bet every time. Hank Lupton folded the first time Jessup did that. Billy Green's hand hovered over his stack of coins before he saw the final raise. Again Jessup lost. Preacher had the winning hand.

It soon became apparent to Preacher that Jessup should keep to his trade of tavern-keeper. He proved to be a terrible gambler. In one complete round at the table, he'd failed to take a single pot.

When it came Preacher's turn to deal again, he leaned forward and prefaced his call of game with an explanation. "There's a game I learned off a river boat captain up on the Platte one time. It's called seven-card stud. Played jist like five-card, but with three down cards, stead of one. Makes for an excitin' game."

He dealt it, watching Jessup closely. The man had a terrible hand, not even a pair or good face cards showing after two up cards. Why didn't he fold? He was truly awful. Someone real good could come along and clean him out, Preacher speculated. No matter, Jessup kept calling the bets. After the third card, he had a possible flush. A straight flush at that, Preacher noted. The bets, raises and cards went around. Preacher blinked.

Jessup had bettered his hand. This time he raised the bet. The final card went around, down. Only four players remained. Preacher had folded on his third card. Billy Green held the high hand in up cards. He bet a five-dollar gold piece. Jessup doubled it. When the pot was right, Jessup turned over his cards to reveal the straight flush.

Looking much relieved, he raked in the pot. Play resumed with Jessup dealing. He played badly over the next two hours. Preacher made it a habit never to count his stack of gold until the game ended. He did not like the idea of playing to scared money. This night proved his habit unnecessary. When he left the game, his poke bulged considerably more than when he had entered.

"Thank you, gents, for a right entertaining evening. Now I need some shut-eye before the sun catches me by surprise. Good night."

"Have a nightcap, Preacher. On me," Jessup offered.

"Thank ye kindly, but no thanks. I do need my sleep."

Makepeace Baxter had been badly misnamed by his doting parents. As a child, he had made war on small animals, tormenting them until they died. He loved to pull one wing off of several flies and watch them crawl around in circles until they dropped over from starvation. Another favorite was to pull the legs from frogs and toss them in a water trough to drown. His absolute favorite was to catch a cat on the tines of a pitchfork and watch as it writhed to a horrible death.

When he entered his teens, his tastes had become more refined. He tortured children smaller than himself, and threatened to kill them if they told. Once, at the age of fourteen, he went too far. A child died and he ran away from home, to live the next three months in terror of being caught and accused. Makepeace never went back. Over the ensuing years, he had found his niche among the lowest of the low, in the ranks of criminals.

He robbed, and often maimed, drunks for what money they might have. Lately, in this forsaken part of Indian Territory, he had taken up with the pair who sided him tonight. Now a hulking eighteen, he crouched in the sagebrush at the edge of the clearing on the southeast side of the creek created by the lost springs, which flowed sweetly from clefts in the rocks which formed a portion of the bank. With him were his best friends. His *only* friends, truth to be told. Youthful louts actually, who could stomach his sadistic ways. Lights had been lowered in the hotel portion of the stage station and the only sign of life came from the tavern.

Makepeace literally slobbered with anticipation. A bright, tall rectangle bloomed when the door to the tavern opened and out came that salty mountain man. "Him. He's the one," Makepeace Baxter whispered to Nate Glover and Wally Slaughter. "He won big in that game."

Preacher turned in the direction of the hotel and was striding toward the entrance when the three pieces of human debris made their move. They rushed at him, visions of gold discs filling their undoubtedly deficient brains. This would be easy. Their target looked completely unsuspecting. Makepeace Baxter growled like a dog when he leaped at the man in buckskins. He had not even made contact when he ran into a fistful of knuckles and learned that their victim had not been as unsuspecting as they would have liked him to be.

Makepeace landed on his butt. He dimly saw the man he attacked raise a leg. Pain exploded as Preacher kicked him square in the chest.

"Lookin' to bushwhack me, boy?" Preacher hissed, his face close to the pain-wracked one of his attacker. That was when Nate and Wally joined in, grabbing hold of Preacher by both arms.

An instant later they went flying as Preacher flung his arms wide. They fared somewhat better than Makepeace. Preacher slammed a fist into the side of the lout's head, which made his ear ring. By then Nate had regained his balance and gone for the mountain man again. Preacher met him with a grin on his face, dodged a wild left and put a looping right into the pudding face of the twenty-year-old thug. Nate came to a sudden stop. His arms sagged and Preacher gave frightful punishment to his ribs. When the man from the High Lonesome decided his opponent had been softened up enough, he went back to work on the face.

Blood spurted from Nate's broken nose. His lips stung as Preacher mashed them into his teeth, loosening two in the process. Nate tried to raise his arms to cover his head only to have his ribs explode in exquisite agony. He flailed wildly at Preacher to no avail. Preacher finished him with a sharp uppercut that clapped Nate's mouth shut with a loud ring. Nate sighed softly and settled in the dust. By then, Wally Slaughter had screwed up his courage and come at the wildcat they had cornered. Preacher let him approach, then sidestepped and whacked Wally in the side with his forearm. Next, Preacher grabbed the youthful bandit by the hair, which was long, blond and greasy, and yanked backward.

Wally's feet went out from under him and he went down hard. A screech of pain came when his tailbone fractured. Whimpering, he crawled aimlessly around on the ground like one of Makepeace's flies. Preacher paused and looked around himself, well pleased. That's when Makepeace Baxter got back in the fray. He came at Preacher with a knife. Moonlight gave the edge a wicked, blue glint.

Preacher had his own Greenriver in hand in an instant. The knife fighters squared off. Makepeace lashed out, a testing gesture. Preacher ignored it and began to circle.

"C'mon, stand still an' fight like a man."

"I am, you little bastard. You ever been in a knife fight before?"

"N-no."

"What's your name?"

"Why you wanna know?"

"So I have it right on your gravestone."

"It's Baxter. Makepeace Baxter, an' you're the one who's gonna die."

Preacher chuckled. "I reckon you'd best make some of that peace with the Almighty, 'cause you're gonna meet him real soon."

Makepeace could no longer contain himself. He launched forward. He swung his knife, now a blur, in front of him, left-right, right-left. Preacher backstepped and circled in the other direction. Makepeace followed him, his breathing harsh gasps, born of desperation as much as exertion. Preacher's moccasin landed on a loose pebble and caused him to stumble. At once, Makepeace rushed his opponent. He made a powerful slash and sensed the contact his blade made.

Preacher grunted and took a backstep, then plunged his Greenriver to the hilt in the chest of Makepeace. An expression of utter surprise formed on the suddenly pale face of the boy. He dropped his knife and closed his hands, gently as a lover, around Preacher's, which held the haft of the Greenriver.

Baxter's attempt to speak brought forth a river of blood. Then he gained enough of an opening. "You killed me."

"You didn't leave me much choice."

"Who . . . who are you?"

"They call me Preacher."

A mournful groan escaped the bloodied lips of Makepeace Baxter. "Oh, Jesus. I . . . I been done in by the best."

"That you have," Preacher told him without false modesty. He turned the blade slightly to break it free and pulled it from the dying youth's chest. Makepeace fell to the ground.

Preacher watched the young thug's dying throes, then turned away. He felt a lightness at his waist and reached down. During the brief fight, Makepeace had slashed open his money pouch. Half his winnings lay scattered in the dusty station yard.

"Damn, oh, damn, now I'll have to crawl around and pick it up like a beggar." Tomorrow, he speculated fervently, just had to be better.

7

Eve Billings tried once more to reason with the hard-headed men of their wagon train. "We must move on. Several children have taken a fever from some unknown source and even more are likely to."

"Fever's fever. We don't have to know what caused it." Gus Beecher stated stolidly.

"If we knew what caused it, we could avoid it. I suspect the water is tainted somehow. I have been boiling all of mine before giving any to my children. Little Anna is improving rapidly. No more stomach pain and the fever is lower."

Beecher remained adamant. "I say we should stay where we are. No one knows what's out there."

"Yeah," Enos Throcker inserted. "Look what happened when we tried. We got plum lost."

Eve was ready for that. "Send out scouts."

Throcker shook his head stubbornly. "They'll never find their way back."

Determined, Eve pressed her point. "There are several older boys and young men who are levelheaded enough. They can tell north from south and read sign. They could mark the trail for us in piles of stones."

Gus Beecher rejected her suggestion. "Wouldn't do. What if we wandered off between the piles of rocks?"

Eve thought that over a moment. Somewhere she had read something that might work. What was it and who had done it? It came to her after a long pause in which the men began to hope they had silenced her.

"There is a way. Do any of you know the story of the Llano Estacada? The Staked Plains down in Texas?" She received no answer and went on. "When the Spanish explorers first went there, they found a vast desert. Not a tree to guide one, no way to layout a trail for others to follow. The leader had an idea. He had soldiers ride back to the last stand of tall, young saplings. They cut poles from them, hundreds of them, oh, maybe fifteen feet high. To these they attached big flags. The leader had one set up at the edge of the rolling area of sand and rocks. Then they started off, taking the other poles with them.

"When they reached a spot nearly out of sight of the first pole, they erected another. Then they moved on and put up more flags." Eve paused, to make certain the men followed her. "Each staff was numbered, so if they wandered, and came upon one, they would know where they were and which way to go. And it worked exactly like the leader said it would. They crossed that barren, waterless wasteland and went on to found Santa Fe."

Enos Throcker was not buying any of that. "When'd they do that?"

Eve had her answer ready. "Almost three hundred years ago."

Throcker snorted in derision. "There, you see? Old-fashioned ideas like that won't get us anywhere."

Unable to abide such stupidity, Eve let go. She stomped her tiny, booted foot. "That's plain crazy. If we sent out the older boys and some young men, with arms to protect themselves and a wagonload of poles and flags, they could mark the trail the same way. Even come back if they needed more, or if they ran into trouble. After a couple of days head start, the train can load up on water and any game we can get, and follow the markers."

Silence answered her. Eve looked around, her features set in grim determination. "What about you, young Honeycutt? Do you think it would work?"

The adenoidal sixteen-year-old cut his eyes to his father, who shook his head in the negative. Then David Honeycutt took a deep breath and made his bold first venture at independence. "Yeah—yeah, I do. And it would be a great adventure." He turned to a cluster of his peers for support. "What do you think, fellahs?"

"It'll work, Davey, I know it will," a defiant Eb Throcker encouraged. His father took a menacing step in his direction. "Leave it be, Paw. We ain't gettin' anywhere just sittin' here eatin' up our supplies."

It quickly got out of Eve's hands. With the prospect of something, anything, to do besides sit around, the young men clamored to go. The decision made, those who would take the risks decided to set off that afternoon to find and cut a wagonload of lodge-pole pines. Meanwhile, their mothers and sisters would fashion flags from any bright material they had at hand. They would start off within two days, taking the wagon and three saddle mounts.

Hunkered down in a tall stand of wild mulberry, the spikey-haired lout who had dogged the mountain men along the Santa Fe Trail stared out at the deeply rutted roadway. Any time now, Amos Scraggs reckoned, the excitement growing. He itched. He twitched. Uneasily he cut his eyes left and right. His ace-boon runnin' pard, Miguel Lopez, sheltered behind a fallen tree to the right. Five others were closer in by the road.

Strung out on both sides of the trail were the surviving dozen of the gang that had attacked the freight wagon train. They had been paid well to locate and kill

the mountain man known as Preacher. They had attacked
the wagons out of greed, but their specific charge had
been to see that Preacher, and anyone with him, never
lived to reach the Missouri side of the river of the same
name.

Now their chance had come. Only the three mountain
men had broken up their raid before, Amos Scraggs
recalled. Could it be they could do it again? He stiffened
when he heard the distant thud of hooves. Four horses,
he figured it to be. It had to be them. Amos saw the one
called Preacher come into view first. He lined up his
sights, as he tried to quell the quiver in his hand. Slowly
he squeezed off a round.

A loud crack shattered the pastoral calm of the morning. Big mistake! the mind of Amos Scraggs shouted at
him as in the next instant the mountain men exploded
into a deadly fury.

Bright sun no longer slanted into Preacher's eyes
when he reined in. Shadows had grown so short they
had become pools around the bases of the objects that
made them. He estimated their morning's travel had
brought them close to Diamond Springs Crossing.
Another four days should see them in Missouri. He had
traveled the Santa Fe Trail three times before and felt
confident with that assessment. He turned to share that
with his friends when a shot blasted to silence the
warbling of the meadowlarks. Preacher put heels to
the flanks of Tarnation as he slid his Hawken from its
scabbard. The words that left his mouth had nothing to
do with their destination.

"By dang, we're bein' ambushed!"

Three Sleeps Norris grumbled agreement. "I figgered
that out for myself. I see some of 'em over there." He
fired as he spoke, sent a ball in among the high stand of
wild mulberry, and went for his powder horn. Preacher

loosed a round. A scream answered. To his right, Antoine emptied his Hawken into the screaming face of a pasty-skinned outlaw who broke from cover, confident that their numbers and surprise would carry the day.

He died without knowing the flaw in his judgment. Antoine quickly drew one of his single-barreled pistols from the saddle holsters and chopped a hole through the underbrush with a double-shotted load. His second pistol brought a groan and an enemy ball discharged skyward. Quickly Antoine holstered the empty weapon and drew one of two double-barreled pistols from the wide, red sash around his hard, flat middle. He cut his eyes to his companions and saw Preacher unlimber one of his wicked Walker Colts.

Three fast shots downed two more of the ambushers. Preacher looked at Antoine and nodded. They worked well together, the gesture seemed to say. With a roar, a squat, ugly thug stormed at Three Sleeps Norris, who had a cap fail to fire. Preacher wheeled around in the saddle and put a .44 ball into the jaw hinge of the attacker. He staggered three steps closer, enough so that Three Sleeps dropped him with a butt stroke to the top of his head.

"Obliged, Preacher."

"My pleasure."

By then they had ridden in among those who had laid the ambush. Preacher struck one down with the barrel of his Colt, then shot another who sprang upward to fire wildly. The bullet cracked by Preacher's cheek and struck a resin-slicked pine a foot away. A shower of amber moisture slapped the back of Preacher's neck. He'd play billy hell getting that out of his hair, he thought crankily, while he exchanged Colts.

Stunned by the incredible firepower of the mountain men, the border trash fell back as their intended victims kept coming. In rapid order, their number had diminished to a mere seven. Yet, they still outnumbered the men they had come to kill by two to one. Preacher and Antoine quickly reduced that advantage by two.

Antoine pulled a sad face as he advised Preacher. *"Par hasard*, I have shot myself dry, my friend."

By chance, eh? Preacher thought. "You got a war hawk ain'tcha?"

Antoine brightened and brought forth a wicked-looking iron-bladed tomahawk. The thug in front of him paled and threw a wild shot. The ball made a red line along Antoine's ribs, but failed to prevent him from splitting the skull of the hapless bandit. Preacher heeled Tarnation to one side, and fired one of his remaining three loads.

Mouth puckered in a soundless howl, the ruffian who took that .44 ball bent double and toppled to one side. A second later, Preacher held his fire as a fear-stamped face popped out of the underbrush. He was not surprised to recognize the straw-haired rascal who had been dogging their trail since Cottonwood Crossing.

"Don't shoot. I give up. I'm hurt bad," wailed the young outlaw.

Another disreputable creature crawled into the open. His usually coppery complexion had turned a sickly gray-green. Thin wisps of mustache were matted around his face by sweat. He dragged a bloody leg with a bullet-shattered thighbone. *"Yo tambien*. Don't kill us, *por favor."*

Preacher and his friends surrounded the defeated pair. Preacher chuckled softly. "Now ain't this something?" He leaned low in his saddle. "Haven't we met someplace before?"

Groaning, the towhead with the spiky hair licked dry lips. "You know damn well we have. You gonna stop this bleedin'?"

Preacher examined the wound in the side of the ruffian without moving from his horse. "We might, if we get some straight answers. Like, to start, do you have a name?"

Anger flared a moment. "Of course, everyone has a

name. Mine's Amos Scraggs. This is my pard, Miguel Lopez. But, we don't know nothin' about nothin'."

Preacher pursed his lips. "Now I believe that."

"You do?" a surprised thug blurted.

"Yep. Back some years we had us what we called the University of the Rockies in the High Lonesome. I learned me a lot of grammar there. What you did was use a double negative; 'don't know nothing' you said. Well, what rules we've got for English says a double negative is a positive. In other words, you small piece of buffalo dung, you know a whole lot we'd like to hear from you."

"What if we don't tell you?"

"We leave you here to bleed to death."

"You'd never do a thing like . . ." Then Amos Scraggs read the deadly message in Preacher's steely eyes. "What do you want to know?"

"This jist another fling for you? Like that freighter train?"

"N-no. We—we were sent to see that you never reached Missouri."

"Who's we? That include that scruffy lot you rode with?"

Scraggs' eyes strayed from Preacher's face. He forced a tone of indignation into his voice. "No. We weren't no part of them," he lied. "Ask Miguel. That bunch was pure trash. Miguel an' me joined up for that raid on the freight wagons only to make more money."

Miguel, who believed incorrectly that the artery in his thigh had been severed, and he was about to die, sought to absolve himself before he met his Maker. He motioned to Preacher. The mountain man dismounted and squatted down beside the Mexican bandit.

"What is it?" he asked.

Heat flared in Amos. "Don't tell him nothin'!"

Miguel whispered urgently, his eyes alight with the

fear of death. "I will tell you the truth, Señor Preacher. The whole gang had been paid well to keel you."

"Who paid you?"

"Three men. They are called Gross, Praeger and Reiker."

"You done good, Miguel. I'm sure the Almighty will take that into account."

"*Por favor*, please, I want a priest. I want to make my confession."

"We'll see if we can find you one. First off, we've got to bind up that wound and fix your partner."

Sergeant Stalking Elk of the Osage Tribal Police rode up to the Diamond Creek Crossing relay station. That young Ryan boy had come like a whirlwind. Had two prisoners and a whole passel of bodies to take care of. Stalking Elk wondered how Finn Ryan and his boys, both under fourteen, could have stood off so many as made up the pile of corpses outside the tavern door. He supposed he would find out soon.

Three tall, lean men in buckskin stepped out into the dooryard. The one in the middle, with a square jaw and a far-off look in his eyes, introduced himself as Preacher and named his friends. Stalking Elk nodded toward the bodies.

"Do you want to tell me about it?"

"Don't mind if I do." He went on to describe the ambush, eliminating only the purpose. Then he added, "There's two inside who need medical treatment, if any's available."

Stalking Elk pulled a wry expression. "Our medicine man is all that's near."

"That'll have to do. I've been put back on the rosy side of health more than once by a medicine man. If these two don't cotton to it, tell 'em they can walk to the nearest white doctor."

Stalking Elk studied the toes of his moccasins for a moment. "From what you tell me, they're due for a hanging under white law."

"That they are."

"White man's law does not apply out here. We don't have courts or hangmen. When an Osage kills another of his tribe, he is beaten and turned out of the camp. That is most likely what will happen to this pair."

Preacher puckered his lips and worried his tongue around his mouth a while. He didn't like the idea of exile. "It'd be a shame if they died of their wounds, then."

Sergeant Stalking Elk cut his eyes to the pile of corpses once more. Thoroughly impressed with the fighting prowess of the mountain men, he offered up a bit of embarrassing news. "I read a book once about the legendary mountain man called Preacher. Never thought I would meet him in person."

Preacher blushed hotly. "Aw, shucks, them things is pure fancy. I've never done half the things they put in there. It's jist stuff and nonsense."

"We will see to your living pair. I don't suppose they will go adventuring again. Mr. Ryan can bury the dead. There is money from your government for such needs."

Preacher extended his hand. "Thank you, Stalking Elk. We'll stay and lend a hand."

"May I ask where you are bound for?"

Keeping a straight face, Preacher saved himself from a lie by only a light exaggeration. "We're set on seein' Independence, then go on to Jefferson Barracks."

"Safe journey, then."

Takes Rain and Gray Eagle looked downslope at the laboring of the draft animals. A mixed train of mules and oxen trudged through the roiling red-brown dust of a sage-choked basin near the banks of the Yellowstone River. Soon they would stop to take food, Takes Rain knew. That is when the Blackfoot would take something else. A cold smile lifted the corners of his mouth. Before long his Bison Eaters society would test the power of the medicine given by Iron Shirt.

"Wagons . . . Whoooooa-UP!" came faintly on the light breeze that blew from the direction of the train toward the Blackfoot warriors waiting to strike.

Those words had no exact meaning to Takes Rain. He only knew that it was what they said when the leader wanted the wagons to stop. Obedient to them, the rolling lodges began to slow and swing into a half circle. Women dismounted and their birdlike chatter lifted on the wind. Time to strike. Takes Rain cut his eyes to Gray Eagle and nodded. Both men came to their moccasins and released their ponies. Swiftly they mounted. Thirty other warriors did the same. Takes Rain raised the new rifle he had been given by the followers of Iron Shirt and waved it over his head.

"*Ki-yi-yi-yi!*" he keened to sound the attack.

Startled white faces looked up at them. Then the warriors hidden around the wagons, in the thick covering of sagebrush, opened fire with bows and arrows. Rifles cracked also. Three men went down, one gagging and clutching at the arrow that stuck out from his throat, front and rear. A woman shrieked and dropped the pot of beans she had saved from breakfast. A red stain spread on her ample bosom around the gruesome exit wound a .56-caliber ball had made.

Shouting their war cries, and profane insults, thirty Blackfoot warriors thundered down the slope to flow through their comrades and bring more death and destruction. Several oxen went slack in their harness and sagged to their knees. A mule erupted in agony, its rump pierced by two arrows. Stunned by the suddenness of the attack, the immigrants finally began to react.

Several men grabbed up rifles and returned fire. Their bullets seemed to avoid all the mounted Indians. Another volley had as little effect. Five men died before they could reload. Children screamed and ran in panic. Whooping warriors rode in among them, oblivious to the crack and moan of white men's bullets. The Blackfoot bent low and scooped small boys and girls off their feet, then whirled away from the scene of battle.

Seizing a flaming brand from a cookfire, Gray Eagle hurled it into the rear of a wagon. Screams of terror came from within. The flames quickly licked up. A woman with graying hair and two barely nubile girls tumbled out. The woman died from a lance thrust, the girls were dragged aside to provide later amusement for the aroused warriors. Unable to reload in the swirl of battle, Takes Rain slung his fine new rifle over one shoulder by a rawhide thong and drew his tomahawk.

Horror filled the face of the white man who watched the grinning warrior with the war axe descend on him. Blackness quickly replaced the sight of the savage as the keen edge of the 'hawk blade sheered through the pilgrim's forehead and mangled his brain. Then a man with a shotgun found one howling savage within range and gave out a load of 00 buckshot. Five of the nine .32-caliber pellets pulped the chest of one Blackfoot, after shattering his hair-pipe bone war vest.

Dismayed, the warriors nearest him looked on in disbelief while he slumped dead over the neck of his horse. This wasn't supposed to happen, Takes Rain thought, his stomach churning. Maybe the medicine was not good against the many-balls guns. Sensing the loss of faith among his companions, Takes Rain signaled for the braves to follow him as he streaked away.

They took the young women and small children with them. Only two adults had survived the attack. They stood in numbed despair as flames licked at four wagons. Slowly they looked around at the scene of slaughter.

From over the rise they heard the shrieks and wails of the young women and girls as the savages used them in cruel and lustful ways. Helpless to do anything about it, the man and woman could only hug each other and weep.

The torment went on for a long time. At last the Blackfoot had been drained of their urgent sap and split the skulls of their abused captives. Then they rode off with the children. Silence slowly returned to the banks of the Yellowstone River.

8

At an isolated trading post on the North Platte River, Praeger and his partners received a message from Washington City. Instructions written on the outside had told the proprietor to hold it until called for. Praeger, whose aggressive qualities and dominance had propelled him without dissent into leadership, split the wax seal, and opened the thick, three-fold paper. He read it quickly and then raised his mottled-blue eyes, the slight cast in the right one disconcerting as always, and smiled.

"It is short and sweet, gentlemen. We are informed that arrangements have been completed for stage two. Those involved will be on their way within . . ." He consulted a calendar on the wall beside the bar. "A week from now."

Morton Gross rubbed pudgy hands together. "Wonderful. How long will it take them to get out here?"

Praeger considered that. "I would imagine six weeks to two months. Unless they take the mail packet or some other steam-powered riverboat."

Gross worked his thick, rubbery lips in and out. "And our little . . . ah . . . impediment?"

"You mean Preacher? By now I assume he has been

taken care of. Come, this calls for a celebration. Barman, do you have any champagne?"

Mouth a black O in his thick, ebony beard, the bartender blinked in disbelief. "Any what? I ain't seed no champagne since I moved out here." He pronounced the word champ-ag-nee. "Never saw none before that neither."

"Do you have a good rye?" Praeger asked suspiciously.

"I got a small barrel from the Cumberland Gap country."

"That will do quite well." To the others, Praeger said, "We have to get Iron Shirt to move faster on enlisting the Cheyenne. They are the key to the whole thing."

Across the Missouri now and drawing nearer to Jefferson Barracks each hour, Preacher felt downright uneasy. He spared no effort putting his discomfort into words.

"It's too crowded around here. Why, there's actually more than one house per' mile. Not fittin' nor healthy for folks to live all shoved up against one another like that."

Intrigued, Three Sleeps chimed in. "What do you consider comfortable living space, Preacher?"

Preacher did not even hesitate. "I reckon one per ten or twenty miles. That be the absolute limit I can tolerate. Among white folk, that is," he elaborated.

"Don't keep them from being ornery," Three Sleeps observed as he indicated a group of armed men who sat astride the high road. The bulk of their horses blocked the advance of the mountain men.

A big, ugly brute, with orange-red hair and matching beard, in the middle of the ragged formation, raised a hand and pointed one thick finger imperiously at Preacher. "What you fellers' business?" he demanded.

Preacher gave it a moment's thought and decided what he had told Sergeant Stalking Elk would serve in this case equally well. "Why, friend, we're on our way to . . . ah . . . Independence."

Thunder clouds writhed in the scowl produced by their interrogator. "It be back the way you came. So, you'd best turn around an' light a shuck out of here. There ain't no room for frontier riffraff the likes of you three among civilized folk here in Missouri."

Preacher had heard all he needed to. He worked his mouth a bit and produced a cud of Redman Premium Braid. "Well, then," he observed as he spat the wad of tobacco at the hooves of the delegation's horses, "we'll just have to make room."

In a flash the fight was on. Preacher leaped like a panther from the back of Tarnation. His powerful arms looped around the leader of the welcoming party and dragged the bigger man from the saddle. With a lithe twist, Preacher turned them in midair so that the carrot-topped brute landed on his back, with Preacher atop him.

Wind knocked from his lungs in a loud grunt, the unfriendly lout went cross-eyed while Preacher sawed the lapels of his hairy cowhide vest across his throat.

"Gah . . . gah . . . yer chokin' me."

Preacher smiled down at him, his expression conveying that he was fully aware of that. "Now, we might not be the most sartorially splendid fellers you've ever seen, that I'll allow. But you an' yer friends are no prize winners yerselves. I'd appreciate it if you could find it in your heart to be more cordial in your greeting."

While this exchange went on, Three Sleeps Norris let out a whoop and sprang toward the pair nearest to him. His point of aim was a space between them, which he swiftly filled by a quick reach and grab. Then Three Sleeps swung his arms inward and filled the opening with their noggins, which made a loud *clunk!* as they met in midair. On the opposite side of Preacher, two of the local, lowbrow social arbiters had decided on the use of deadly force.

Their hands barely touched the stocks of their rifles when they heard the double click of hammers. They looked up, startled to see the twin muzzles of a double-barreled pistol pointed levelly at them. Antoine Revier gave them a wide, knowing smile.

With a roar, the huge man under Preacher heaved upright and freed himself. He drove a fist into the face of his opponent, which caused stars to explode in Preacher's left eye. Preacher let the force of the blow carry him up and over. He hit on heels and shoulders and bounded upright.

By then the brute who had dislodged him came at him with ham fists. Preacher dodged backward, only to come up against one of the pair Three Sleeps had dealt with. The groggy man stirred and then reached out with both hands to cling tightly to Preacher's ankles.

"Get him, Red," he urged.

"Thanks, Barney." Red came after Preacher with punishing punches to the mountain man's face.

Preacher's lips stung and swelled. His tongue explored and felt several loosened teeth. His left eye was almost closed. Then Red shifted weight to put a finish to the interloper. Preacher seized his chance.

He put his shoulders and hips behind each smashing blow he drove into Red's chest and gut. Although padded by fat, Red felt each one, and with increasing intensity. His arms drooped slightly. Enough so that Preacher could go to work on his face. Red's lips split and his nose became a rose blossom before the bully could draw a refreshing breath. Knifelike pains filled his chest.

Preacher sucked in air and spoke lightly to his friends. "I'd appreciate it if one of you would unwind this snake from my legs."

Three Sleeps sprang to the task. He hauled the slighter built Barney away from Preacher's legs and spun him. His moccasin collided with the seat of Barney's trousers and propelled the leech back down the road in the direction of home. Stumbling, Barney recovered quickly and turned on Three Sleeps.

Norris set himself for the rush. When it came, he side-stepped and smacked Barney on the side of the head. Staggered, Barney turned in the wrong direction. Preacher popped him in the mouth and sent him on around to Three Sleeps.

Laughing now, Norris pegged Barney on the left hinge of his jaw and the Missourian went rubber-legged. He collided with the flank of his horse when he went to the ground. Red roared again and reached for Preacher, while Three Sleeps walked over to one of the mounted men and yanked him from the saddle.

"Reckon I can put this away," Antoine speculated aloud.

He released the hammers and did just that. Then he dismounted and hauled the other thug from his horse. Knuckles met flesh and a new brawl was on. By then, Red had brought himself upright and planted a fist between Preacher's shoulder blades. It staggered the mountain man, who turned as he jolted forward.

"Some fellers never learn," he grumbled as he blocked a punch and answered with a short right.

It gradually dawned on Preacher that fists would simply not do it with this brute. When Red bore in again, Preacher flexed his legs, cocked the right one and slammed the heel of his moccasin into Red's exposed belly. Eyes bulging, Red did a pratfall that jarred his teeth. Preacher turned slightly and kicked Red in the side of his head. Bells and birdies went off inside Red's skull. His eyes rolled up and he fell backward, arms widespread. His body stirred up puffs of dust, and he let out a soft snore.

"Welcome to Missouri," Preacher panted and the trio of mountain men chuckled sardonically. Then, "Think they've had enough?" Preacher asked his companions.

"Just about," advised Antoine as he drove a hard left to the jaw of the last standing Missourian. His target flopped onto the ground and lay still. "Now they have."

It worked for them like it did for the Spanish on the Llano Estocado. Eve Billings thrilled at the sight of the fifteen foot shafts, their colorful cloth pennants fluttering in the hot breeze that blew across the sandy soil of the Great Basin. From the ridge where her wagon rested, she could see a line of them leading back to their starting place and on into the distance beyond. Progress had been slow at first.

They'd barely made seven miles a day the first three days because the neophyte scouts frequently dashed back with alarms that proved unfounded. Such a misgiving had stopped them at the saddle of this ridge not half an hour ago. Davey Honeycutt had galloped a lathered horse back, his eyes as enlarged as his mount's.

"Injuns!" he had shouted. "Injuns not five miles ahead."

From the color of his face one would suspect they were the ghosts of Indians. A party of armed men rode forward to investigate. Eve could see them returning now, small, black specks against the blasted earth. Beside her, Charlie stirred on the seat and shifted his rifle.

"They're not wavin' a red flag, Mom." Charlie sounded disappointed that the agreed-upon signal to warn them of hostiles was not fluttering above the riders.

"We can thank the Lord for that," his mother responded.

"Aw, Mom, I want to shoot an Injun."

Shocked, Eve almost slapped the boy's face. "No you don't, Charles Ryan Billings. You don't want to shoot any human. Hunting for food is a necessity, killing someone is a horrid crime."

"Even if they are tryin' to kill you?"

That left Eve speechless for a long moment. "You're just a boy, Charlie. Leave those sorts of things to grown men."

Some of the less alarmist among the travelers started their wagons out toward the approaching men. There would have been shots, after all, had there been Indians. Overall, Eve remained highly pleased at their progress. Even better, the game which had been absent on their first attempt now seemed to have come back in abundance. Anna was growing stronger every hour, and Charlie had become quite an expert shot, adding to his credit deer and antelope as well as rabbits. She put the Bridesburg Arsenal rifle aside and turned to Charlie.

"Put your rifle up, Charlie. We're heading out."

"Can I take Star out and hunt a little?"

"No need today, son. Remember those plump rabbits Damion Brewster brought us?"

Charlie did not sound enthused over that. Damion, an acne-riddled youth with a crush on his mother, was a pain in the butt. "Oh, yeah, those."

Charlie replaced his rifle in the wagon bed and scampered out to his usual place, astride Jake. His bare heels bounced with the churning rhythm of the stolid animal. Once again Eve surveyed her world and found herself entirely at peace. Then she looked up from the rumps of her team to see a solitary Indian sitting on top of a close-by mound.

Sudden cold clutched at her heart. Could he be the forerunner of the Indians the Honeycutt boy thought he had seen? If not, where had he come from? She tensed and reached for the rifle at her feet when the Indian slowly began to raise his lance. Extended to full arm's length, the Indian moved his lance from side to side.

Fearing that to be the signal for an attack, Eve filled her lungs for a cry of alarm, only to realize that it was only a friendly wave, backed up by a broad smile.

At Jefferson Barracks at last, Preacher found the situation and the troops even sorrier than he expected. The

Dragoons turned out to be raw and green, barely aware of what was expected of them. While Preacher and his companions walked their horses through the gate, sergeants bellowed at the hapless soldiers, their faces scarlet with their fury.

"No, damnit, Mallory! Far the love of Jazus, how many times do I have to tell ya? Ye mount so yer facing the same direction the horse is, ye do."

Mallory made the mistake of whining. "I don't know why I get so mixed up, Sergeant Muldoon. Honest I don't. Maybe I ain't a horse person."

Battalion Sergeant Major Terrance Muldoon threw down the riding crop he carried and strode to Mallory's side. He shoved his face to within an inch of Mallory's and bellowed. "It's Sergeant Major, ye dimwit. It is. Ye'll go get yer knapsack. Ye'll fill it with rocks, ye will. An' ye'll report back here to me on the double."

"I know what's gonna happen then, Sergeant Major," Mallory recited, his stupid face alight. "I'm gonna run around this big ol' field here."

"*Parade Ground* goddamnit! Parade Ground."

Mallory looked puzzled. "Ain't seed no parades go by since we been here."

"Yer a sorry son of a . . . Aw, what the hell. It's no use, you're no use. Sure an' sometimes I think I'm of no use, I do. Get that knapsack."

"Yah, sure, Sergeant Major."

Preacher approached the infuriated noncom. "Excuse me, Sergeant Major, could you tell me where I can find Colonel Danvers?"

BSM Terrance Muldoon turned to Preacher with a sour expression. "In Saint Louis."

"May I ask what he is doing there?"

"Who be ye?"

"They call me Preacher, this be Three Sleeps Norris an' Antoine Revier. We are reporting in as guides for this battalion through the Injun country."

Fists on hips, feet wide apart in a belligerent stance, Muldoon introduced himself. "Battalion Sergeant Major Muldoon. An' fer yer information, the good colonel and those young gentlemen officers of his wanted a last fling among the ladies an' the sparklin' wine before makin' their great sacrifice fer God and country."

"They left you in charge?"

"No, Mr. Preacher. We've got us one officer with his brains in his head, not in his pants, we do. Captain Edward Dreiling is commanding at present, he is. Ye can find him at battalion headquarters. Across the parade ground there, it is."

"Thank you, Sergeant Major." Preacher turned to leave as Mallory returned.

The knapsack bounced viciously against his shoulders and back as he began to run. The black visor of his flat-topped bill-cap slid slowly down his forehead until it obscured his eyes. Preacher stared at him as though seeing a creature from another planet. Then he began to laugh. At his side, an amused Three Sleeps questioned BSM Muldoon.

"Does it do any good?"

"Does it now? Not with that one, sure an' it doesn't. There's some's fine lads, smart and quick to learn. But that one has to take off a boot to count to eleven, he does. I fear what will become of him out there." He gestured to the west.

Preacher and the other mountain men walked to the headquarters building. Inside, an orderly told them that Captain Dreiling could be found on the firing range on the far side of the cantonment. Preacher got exact directions and led the way to the sound of erratic firing.

Seated on a canvas-backed camp stool, an officer observed while sweating, swearing sergeants conducted firing exercises. The captain wore the split-tail, regulation blue uniform coat with thick, shaggy, brass epaulets at the shoulder points, matching insignia of rank—three horizontal strips—on the high, tight collar. His trousers, with the gold stripe down the seams, covered the high tops of his black boots. His shako style hat, of black, patent leather, complete with horsehair plume that drooped over the front, sat squarely on a round, blond head.

Somehow he managed to seem cool and comfortable, while the NCOs and enlisted men showed wide rings at their armpits and long wet smears down their backs. Their appearances made even Preacher feel uncomfortable. Captain Dreiling had no difficulty in recognizing the newcomers. He rose and extended a hand.

"You must be our guides. And, I would say that you are Preacher." He unerringly picked the right man.

"That I am. You'd be Captain Dreiling?"

At six foot even, the broad shoulders, full chest and narrow hips gave Dreiling a handsome cut by anyone's standards. He answered Preacher with alacrity. "Yes. However, on informal occasions, you may call me Edward."

Preacher prefaced his remarks with a softening smile. "An' you can call me Preacher. I don't mean to pry into Army business, Captain, but may I ask why you did not join your associates in the pleasures of Saint Louis?"

For an instant, Preacher thought the expression of contempt that darkened Captain Dreiling's face was intended for him. "Bloody damned children, you ask me. Most of these rabble cannot yet tell right from left foot, let alone conduct themselves as soldiers, and the ones with the responsibility to hammer them into shape go off skirt-chasing."

To emphasize his point, a Hall Model 43 rifled carbine discharged loudly in their direction. The ball from the breech-loading weapon cracked past close enough for Preacher to feel the wind. Immediately a sergeant burst forth in a flurry of profanity.

"You goddamned idiot! You'll get the effing lash for

that. I said to clear all weapons before leaving the line."
A fist lashed out and knocked the offender sprawling.
The sergeant kicked him in the ribs twice.

"Excuse me," said Dreiling politely before turning to
the sergeant. "Enough of that, Sergeant Peters. Extra
duty for Emmons and four punishment tours should suffice. No one was injured."

Suddenly rigid in the position of attention, Sergeant
Peters saluted smartly. "Yes, sir. Very good, sir. It will be
done as ordered. Now, you worthless reprobate, keep
that muzzle downrange at all times, you hear."

A fair-minded man, as well as conscientious, Preacher
thought to himself. The rest of the day's tour of the battalion established some strong opinions in Preacher. At
the stable area, soldiers tried rear vault and running side
mounts, most falling in the dirt over and over. Sergeants
screamed and cursed. Those who could ride, Preacher
soon learned, could not hit a bull in the ass with a bass
fiddle, let alone score on a target from the prone position with their weapons.

Which left him with a rather dim view of Colonel
Arlington Danvers, the battalion commander. If the
other officers, save Captain Dreiling, are as ill-concerned
about the readiness of their men, they could all be in for
a hell of a time out in the High Lonesome. Instinct told
him to seek out the Battalion staff in St. Louis at once.
Logic told him to wait here, lend a hand where he could
and hope for the best when the errant officers returned.
Whatever came of this, Preacher promised himself, he
would sure as hell never take a job with the Army again.

9

Lieutenant Colonel Arlington Danvers and his officers returned to Jefferson Barracks five days later. To the expert eyes of Preacher and his mountain-man friends, they all looked powerfully hungover and sadly dissipated, an all-around surly lot. By the lights of the mountain men, based on the harshness of the noncoms and the appearance and deportment of Lieutenant Colonel Danvers, the colonel was a martinet and thorough popinjay. This opinion was reinforced when they reported to Danvers in a borrowed office, intended for some of the permanent staff. The colonel looked up and his lip curled with contempt and disgust.

"You're a scruffy-looking lot, I must say. Do you ever take baths? You'll have to in this Army."

"Pardon me, Colonel," blurted Preacher. "But we ain't in 'this Army.' We're just hired to guide you to where you want to go in the Big Empty."

Nattily dressed in a freshly pressed uniform, Danvers looked Preacher up and down. Preacher had a classic shiner, all purple, yellow and blue. He had a cut on his chin, and a red mark on one cheek. Danvers worked his mouth as though he wanted to rid himself of some foul-tasting object.

"You have obviously all recently been in some sort of drunken brawl. From now on, until the completion of your employment, you will all refrain from spirits—liquor of any sort—and you will clean up your clothing and present a well-washed appearance at all times. Your hair is to be cut to regulation length, and all facial hair is forbidden.

"You are to ride out before dawn each morning, scout the territory ahead and send back reports." Danvers' arrogant tone continued while he ticked off each point on long slender fingers. "You will not fraternize with the officers, noncommissioned officers or the enlisted men of my command. You will negotiate safe passage for us with any savages you encounter. You are to make certain that the path we take is wide enough to accommodate mounted troops—four abreast, with our field piece at the center of the column—and wagons, two wide to the rear."

Preacher bristled. He'd heard all of the "You will" and "You are" that he could swallow without getting a sore stomach. He raised a hand to cut off the tirade.

"Now whoa up there a second, Colonel. Exactly who are to be the guides for this expedition?"

Danvers blinked. "Why, you three, of course."

"Well, then, don't the colonel think that the men in charge should have some say in how the soldier-boys will march?"

Lieutenant Colonel Danvers countered at once. "Regulations cover that quite nicely, I believe."

Fire fanned in Preacher's eyes. "Ain't no regulations out there in the High Lonesome. An' as for the trail, dependin' on which way you intend to go, there ain't no real trail at all. We just have to find the best way through, over or around the rocks, rivers, gorges and hills as we can. And do it without breaking every wheel or upsettin' any loads.

"Now, marchin' four abreast might be well an' good on a wide street or grassy meadow, but not out there.

There's cactus with thorns long and sharp enough to pierce a horse's hoof to the cannon bone. There's prairie-dog holes jist waitin' to bust a leg." Preacher paused for a breath, which he took, swallowed deeply and went on. "Then you have bison who'll stampede at any loud sound, and rattlesnakes that can fell a horse as easy as a man. Not to mention Injuns by the thousands. Nope, two men to a file, an' they alternately walk and ride their mounts. Another thing. No horn tooting or drum banging. That's the surest way to attract some unpleasant Injuns. Those fancy sabers yer so fond of has got to be padded and tied down so they don't rattle, an' all tack and loose gear also. An Injun can hear the noise they make a mile away."

Filled with equal parts of bluster and indignation, Danvers protested hotly. "We absolutely must have trumpet calls and drums to convey orders. Typical civilian ignorance," he summed up.

Preacher cocked an eyebrow. "Ever hear of arm signals? The Injuns have used 'em for ages and get along jist dandy."

Danvers continued his resistance. "And field music is essential for morale."

"I wonder how serious you are about getting there and getting your fort built before you take on the hostiles? If you have your soldier-boys practice arm signals while we're still in friendly country, they'll know them when they need 'em. Me, I say it's the smart thing to do."

"They are Dragoons, Mr. Preacher. Dragoons."

No matter what Preacher proposed, Lieutenant Colonel Danvers balked at adopting. At last, Preacher had reached his limit. "Here's my final word on this, Colonel. We're gonna do it my way, or I quit the job and hand the money back to the government."

Realizing that this assignment was his last hope of providing for his future, Danvers knew he had no choice. He had been passed over for promotion too many times, so his career would soon be at an end. If this did not go the way he had been told it would, the years ahead would be bleak indeed. Mustering his will power he suppressed his outrage and caved in.

"Very well, it will be as you say."

With a single drum marking time, the column moved out early the next morning. To Preacher's surprise, the troops had improved greatly. They sat their horses straight and tall, all of them required to be no less than five foot ten to six foot two in height. Not a one fell off his horse. Not even simpleminded Mallory mounted backward.

On the highroad outside the barracks ground they rode four abreast. For all their smart appearance, Preacher sensed something odd. He rode in a relaxed slouch with Three Sleeps and Antoine some two hundred yards ahead of the battalion commander and his staff and flag bearers. Cardinals warbled and woodpeckers kept up a steady *rat-a-tat* on hollow trees. Preacher glanced constantly behind them, his gaze resting long on the files of men and horses. At last, he decided to confide in Three Sleeps.

"D'you feel it, too? I got me a strong sensation that something is mighty wrong."

Three Sleeps Norris showed indifference. "I don't follow you."

"I don't know exactly how, but these greenhorn soldier-boys—er, excuse me—Dragoons have done messed up the works somethin' powerful."

"We'll find our eventual." Three Sleeps stifled a yawn, then swatted at a huge horsefly that had lined up an enticing spot on the neck of his horse.

Preacher cut his eyes to the column again. "I certain sure hope it's soon enough."

* * *

"Sure, an' what do you mean they were left behind, Hadley?!" roared BSM Muldoon.

Preacher and his companions turned to see what caused the outburst. Slanted backward from the glowering, red face of the Battalion Sergeant Major, who leaned over him, the Quartermaster Sergeant, Hadley, gulped hard before answering. "That's what happened, Sergeant Major. Four of my teamsters reported to sick call this morning and there was no one to drive the wagons."

"An', why wasn't I told of this?"

"Y-You were. I reported four men confined in the infirmary."

BSM Muldoon poked a thick finger into Hadley's chest to emphasize each word. "But . . . you didn't . . . tell . . . me . . . four . . . wagons . . . didn't . . . have . . . drivers!"

Sergeant Hadley looked like he was about to be sick all his shiny boots. "I . . . I thought you'd figure that out for yourself, Sergeant Major."

"Yer flirt in' with insubordination, Hadley, b'God ye are. An', Lord love us, we'll have to send men back to recover them." He spun on one heel. "You there: Collins, Masters, Pickerel and Sawyer. Can you drive a wagon?"

"Yes, Sergeant Major!" they chorused.

"Then mount up and ride like hell back to the barracks. Ye'll find four of our supply wagons there. Bring them up with the column right quickly, lads."

"What about evening chow, Sergeant Major?" Corporal Collins asked.

"Take food enough with ye for two or three meals."

Sergeant Hadley tugged urgently at Muldoon's sleeve. "Bu-but they're not teamsters."

"Sure an' I don't give a damn if they're old-maid schoolteachers. We need those supplies."

Preacher turned away in disgust. "Here we are; haven't

made fifteen miles the first day and we have lost half of the supplies. At this rate, we'll make the North Platte come December."

Far from the foothills of the Ozark Mountains in Missouri, at a large, well-tended trading post on the North Platte River, Quinton Praeger sat at a table with his coconspirators and their chief henchman, Blake Soures. All four men lapsed into silence when a large platter of roasted bison hump arrived at their table.

They ate heartily, pleasurably chewing slabs of the layered meat and fat along with boiled turnips and onions, squash and chili peppers, all washed down with tankards of beer. Not until the last morsel disappeared did Praeger bring up business.

"Everything is going according to schedule. The money is starting to roll in from back East. The Dragoons are to have left Jefferson Barracks yesterday." He paused and wiped greasy lips with a soiled napkin. "We should have us a tidy little Indian war before too long."

Always a blunt, direct man, Blake Soures spoke his mind. "Exactly what is behind this plan to stir up the Indians? That is, after all, a dangerous thing to do."

Morton Gross looked amused. "How is that, Mr. Soures?"

"A feller can be their friend and ally one day, an' the next they'll lift his hair. They're . . . changeable, moody."

"The idea is to get rid of them once and for all," Praeger explained patiently. "And the best way to do that is to get an Indian war started. We can count on the Indians doing their part through Iron Shirt. He has tremendous influence among the Blackfoot, and now with the Cheyenne. His power grows daily."

Soures frowned. "That's the part I don't like, what I'm tryin' to warn you about. I've got seventeen good men ridin' with me. Then there's you three. Twenty-two guns don't amount to a fart in a windstorm if Iron Shirt decides he don't need us anymore."

Aaron Reiker gave Blake Soures a condescending smirk. "I think you are overestimating his capacity for duplicity. We provide him with rifles and ammunition, and we brought him out of obscurity and made him famous. No, friend Soures, we can trust Iron Shirt."

"But why get rid of the Injuns at all? That's what I want to know."

Morton Gross answered, his voice sugary, as though talking to a dolt. "The East is getting crowded. The land these Indians occupy will be valuable in any westward expansion. Certain high-placed interests in Washington City have a desire to lay claim to that ground. At least, once the savages have been eliminated."

Soures produced an expression of concern. "But, ain't it Injuns' land?"

Praeger turned a condescending gaze on their chief gunman. "Our friends in Washington City are paying exceedingly well to see that it no longer is. Well enough to assuage any conscience."

Soures frowned. "What's that mean, ass—assuage?"

"To pacify, Mr. Soures, to calm."

None of the conspirators mentioned the presence of gold in the mountains of Montana. Instead, they directed him to an assignment as backup to the men sent to stop Preacher.

"There is only one impediment, one man who might be able to prevent an all out war of extermination," Praeger pressed on. "His name is Preacher, and he is known and respected by both sides. Only, if all went well, he should be out of the picture by now. If he is not, it will be your job to remove him."

True to Preacher's prediction, a whole lot was wrong with the expedition. Trouble began before the troops got out of Missouri. After the four supply wagons joined the column, they made better time. A lot of good that did them.

BSM Muldoon came to Preacher one evening in camp. A harried-looking Dragoon had just ridden in on a lathered horse. He must have galloped the animal for a good ways. What he revealed, sent Muldoon to seek help from the mountain men.

Now Muldoon stood contemplating the three rugged guides, his bristly red hair and florid complexion making a torch of his head. "Gentlemen, I come to you with a . . . wee problem, it is. Now mind, I could send some of me sergeants to deal with this. But then it would become an official matter, it would."

Preacher laughed softly at this circumlocution. "Spit it out, man."

"The thing is, it is, that some of the lads have taken it to mind to slip off from our encampment and indulge themselves in some spirituous waters." Muldoon's perpetually rosy nose gave testament to his own fondness for such diversions. "In the process, so's to speak, they have got themselves afoul of some of the local citizens." He paused and cleared his throat, as though the words bore thorns. "The fact of the matter is, there's one hell of a fine brawl goin' on between some eight Dragoons and some sawyers from a nearby mill, that's what."

"And you would appreciate some small gesture of aid from the three of us?" Preacher got to the point.

"Sure an' it would avoid the messiness of a court-martial and the need for punishment."

Preacher gave him a hard eye. "We'd not be taking sides. We'll bust anyone who gets in our way."

"It's skinnin' yer knuckles on all comers, is it?" Muldoon clapped his hands together in approval. "Then, so be it. I'll be accompanyin' ye buckos. Though not in an official capacity. Thing is, we don't need any floggin's before we get beyond civilization. That's how I see it."

"'Floggings'?" Preacher echoed.

"Aye. That's the usual for such infractions. Six of yer best, laid on with a will."

A thunderous frown creased Preacher's brow. "By damn, I'll not be party to any of that."

"So it's the four of us, is it?"

Preacher gave a curt nod. "Right, Muldoon. We'll head out now."

Screams, curses, and the crash of furniture could be heard from two hundred yards off when Preacher and the cleanup squad reached the tavern. They trotted up to the tie rail outside and looped reins over the crossbar. Preacher looked up at a particularly loud, tinkling crash and saw a man fly bodily out through a window. He grunted and cut his eyes to take in the others.

"Looks like we have a job of work on our hands."

Three Sleeps nodded enthusiastically. "Yer not lyin' there, Preacher."

With determination, the four men stalked to the door. It flew open in their faces and two men, wrapped in a mutual bear hug stumbled out. Being nearest, Preacher reached out and grabbed both miscreants by the hair and slammed their heads together. They went down like heart-shot elk. BSM Muldoon bent and separated the Dragoon from the lumberman and dragged him to the hitch rack. The three mountain men entered the establishment.

It had been a nicely appointed place, Preacher noted, before the fight began. Now splintered tables and chairs floated like driftwood in a tidal pool of beer which had come from a ruptured hogshead. There had once been a mirror behind the bar. It lay in diamond spears of brightness amid overturned bottles and small casks. One of the ceiling supports had been snapped in two, the roof sagged dangerously above it. Showing even worse signs of wear, eight men remained on their feet, flinging fists with wild abandon.

One of those went down as the mountain men gained the

doorway. Preacher stepped through and took the knuckles of a huge sawyer at the under edge of his right eye.

"Aw, hell, now it's the other one," he grumbled.

Then he set his feet and pile-drivered a steady rain of punches to the sturdy frame of the sandy-haired man who had hit him. It seemed all too easy to Preacher. The man went down and was out at the first pummeling Preacher gave him. Three Sleeps and Antoine waded in behind him and the three started picking Dragoons off their opponents and hauling them toward the door.

"Take yer damn hands off me," one snarled.

Three Sleeps released the complaining soldier and raised both open hands, in a gesture of surrender. "All right, all right." Then he swiftly closed his right hand into a fist and popped the Dragoon flush in the mouth.

With all the rolling muscle of his powerful shoulders behind it, the blow decisively felled the private. His boot heels bounced off the rough boards of the floor. Three Sleeps grabbed him by the collar and dragged him out into the dooryard. Then, with a grin, he turned about and went back for more.

"By Jaazas, those mountain fellers sure love a fight. They must be Irish," Muldoon said to the unconscious Dragoon. Then he added the young soldier to the stack growing by the tie rail.

Preacher hurled another protesting Dragoon out the door and Muldoon saw the spitting, cursing lout stumble toward him, then quickly corrected that with a hard left to the jaw.

A furious bellow came from the mill workers inside the tavern. "You let us at those soldier-boys. We'll tear them limb from limb."

Preacher's voice sounded. "Calm down. We're takin' 'em all back where they belong."

His words were followed by the loud click of a hammer being cocked and the sharp report of a single-barreled pistol.

10

Following instinct and training, the remaining Dragoons dropped to the floor the instant the shot went off. Preacher and his companions did not. Antoine reached down and felt a hot, burning gouge along his ribs that oozed blood. That made both sides. Damn, he'd be sorer than a fresh-gelded hound dog for more than a month. He reached for one of his double-barreled pistols, but Preacher beat him to the draw.

A big Walker Colt appeared in Preacher's hand and the hammer dropped on a percussion cap. The fat ball sped across the short distance and pinwheeled the belligerent sawyer in the breastbone. "Yer lucky to be alive, Antoine. He was a lousy shot."

None of the Missouri lumbermen had ever seen a revolving pistol before. They stared at it in wonder. One, who had gone for the butt of a small pocket pistol, let go of it with all the speed of a cat making contact with a cookstove. Preacher cocked the weapon and put a menacing look on his face.

"Unless any of you is eager to argue with my friend, Mr. Walker here, I'd advise you forget all about tearing anyone limb from limb."

"You kilt Tucker Blake," accused one of the less intimidated mill workers.

"Didn't know his name. That don't matter. What matters is, your Mr. Blake drew first. What's more, he shot a friend of mine. I don't take kindly to that. Though I will say I'm sorry your friend is dead."

Unmollified, the talker challenged. "You won't get away with this. We'll get the sheriff on you."

"It was self-defense, any fool can see that."

Three Sleeps Norris stepped up and touched Preacher on the arm. "Not any Missouri fool, Preacher," he said tightly. "I suggest we send for the sheriff ourselves and let him hear both sides of the story."

Preacher eyed the mouthy sawyer. "How far off is your sheriff?"

"He's right here," came a hard voice from the doorway. "I'd put that smoke-pole up if I was you."

The man who entered the tavern was a size with Preacher, though he carried authority and power with him enough to make him ten feet tall. "Bill Parker." He introduced himself as he gave the corpse a casual glance. "What happened here?"

All of the lumber company men began to speak at once. The one who had challenged Preacher overrode his friends. "This stranger came through the door, bold as brass, and shot down Tucker Blake in cold blood."

"Yeah, that's right. That's what he did, all right." A chorus of agreement.

Shrewd enough not to be deceived by men whose thick noggins he had thumped more than once, Sheriff Parker pursed his lips, eyed the scene again and then spoke. "If that's the case, George, what accounts for the pistol in Tucker's hand?"

Stunned at having his version disputed, and by a fellow Missourian at that, George gaped a moment before he could find new words to butter his lie. "He . . . uh . . . one of his friends put it there. Ain't that right, boys?"

Sheriff Parker turned and eyed Three Sleeps and Antoine. "Was that before or after this feller got his ribs skinned?" He whirled back to face the sawmill men. "My maw didn't raise any stupid sons. What do you take me for? That's Tucker's pistol, I've had to take it off him enough times when he got drunked up. I was on my way here when I heard the shots. Kylie Burks came by to tell me there was a big fight goin' betwixt you boys and some soldiers. I'd have been in here sooner if I hadn't stopped to have a word with the sergeant out there."

"That's Sergeant Major, if ye please, Sheriff. Battalion Sergeant Major Muldoon," said that worthy from the doorway. "Now, if ye don't mind I'll be takin' my lads and our brave frontier guides back to our camp."

Sheriff Bill Parker made a mock bow. "Go right ahead, Sergeant Major Muldoon." Then, to Antoine, "I'd get that patched up right quick. Might fester."

Antoine cocked an eyebrow. "Thank you for good advice, Sheriff."

Outside, Muldoon surveyed the subdued but conscious, and the unconscious Dragoons. "Thank the Virgin an' all the saints, their horses are right at hand. Be a thankless task rousin' them all to walk that far."

"We'll lend a hand getting them across their mounts," Preacher offered.

"That won't be necessary. There's enough of them with their wits about them to do that."

Not to be denied the last word, mouthy George stood in the doorway and shouted to them. "If I was any of you, I'd get me as far and as fast out of Missouri as I could. We've got friends."

No sooner had the errant Dragoons been returned to the camp near Sedalia than Lieutenant Colonel Danvers summoned the necessary members for a drumhead court-martial. Having been assured that he had acquired a second shiner and more sore ribs for the purpose of avoiding this very event, Preacher had his curiosity piqued. He went along to witness. Naturally, his companions accompanied him.

Preacher could not believe the abrupt nature of the proceeding. All eight of the disobedient Dragoons were hauled before a lantern-lighted barrel head, over which Danvers presided. He read off a list of charges, including desertion, absent without leave, public drunkenness and inciting to riot. He did not ask how the accused pleaded.

"Now, as regards Corporal Evers, and Privates Fields, Smith and O'Banyon, the charges of desertion and absent without leave are dismissed. On the counts of public drunkenness and inciting to riot, the above-named soldiers are fined two-thirds of a month's pay for three months. Now, Privates Babcock, Upton, Venner and Killeen, you are sentenced to be stretched upon a wagon wheel and given six strokes of the lash."

"Are ye not givin' them a chance to plead their case, Colonel, sor?" BSM Muldoon burst out, unable to bridle his umbrage.

"Contain yourself, Sergeant Major," Danvers said in an aside.

"But, Colonel, sor . . . it's . . ."

Lieutenant Colonel Danvers snapped at him in black humor. "Would you like to join them at the grate?"

Captain Dreiling leaned close to Lieutenant Colonel Danvers and whispered in his ear. "Regulations, Colonel. You are always saying that. And in this case, regulations will not allow you to flog the Battalion Sergeant Major without a full general court-martial."

Lieutenant Colonel Danvers swelled and seemed ready to burst, then sighed until deflated. "Yes . . . yes, you are right, as usual, Captain. Much to my regret, I might add. He should never have gone after those fools."

Then back in his judicial role, "Sentence to be carried out at once."

Although outraged by the barbarity of the punishment, Preacher remained to watch it carried out. Afterward, he fetched a jug from a parfleche on his packhorse and, regulations be damned, got riproaring drunk along with his friends and BSM Muldoon.

Two wagons had broken down that day. Eve Billings was beginning to have second thoughts. After the past three days of soul-searching, she had made up her mind to go to Isaac Warner, who had been elected captain for their attempt at crossing the basin. She put aside the last of the dishes from supper and walked reluctantly to his wagon. Eve had hardly begun when Warner interrupted her.

"I have an idea what it is you want to say. And I want some of the other men to be here to hear it." He gave a wave of one arm to Damion Brewster to summon him from his family cookfire a third of the way around the circle of wagons. When the youth arrived, Warner gave him curt orders.

In short time, Renard Labette and Hiram Tate ambled up. They were immediately joined by Gus Beecher and Cecil Brewster. Tate gave a polite nod to Eve and asked, "What's up, Isaac?"

"The Widow Billings here has something she wants to tell us. Now, go ahead, don't be shy," he prodded Eve.

Cheeks crimson and hot from his patronizing manner, Eve glanced at each man in turn. "You know about the breakdowns. Not only those today, the others. They are taking a heavy toll."

Warner jutted his chin defiantly. "Yep. Said that was what would happen. Go on."

"Also, game and water are growing scarce again. I

feel . . . it seems to me the time has come to examine our
decision to try making a crossing."

"What you're gettin' at is?" prompted Warner.

Eve wanted to shout. Out of pure spite this pompous
man was forcing her to say every bitter word. Nervously
she cleared her throat. "Those of us who favored the
attempt had no idea how strenuous it would be. It is perhaps time to consider the possibility of turning around
and following the stakes to the edge of the basin and
then going beyond to fresh water and plentiful game."
There, she had said it and they could smirk all they
wanted.

To her utter frustration the same men who had stubbornly insisted upon that course of action from the
outset now objected to the idea with perfectly straight
faces.

"I say it's the wrong thing to do," Isaac Warner snapped.

"Yes. We've come this far, there can't be much more like
this," Gus Beecher added with a taunting smirk.

Eve's torment and humiliation lasted a long time,
while the men wrangled over what should be done. Her
patience at last exhausted by their circular reasoning,
Eve slipped away. Dredging up new hope, she went to
seek out the wives. The first was Hattie Honeycutt, to
whom Eve recited what she had pointed out to the men.

"We have to make them see reason," she summed up
to Mrs. Honeycutt. "There has to be a way."

"But we're mere women. Our menfolk have total sway
over us."

An idea forming, Eve countered quickly. "Not in all
things."

"Name me one," came the challenge.

Eve leaned forward and whispered in Hattie Honeycutt's ear.

Eyes wide and mouth in an O of astonishment, the portly
woman sputtered a while before regaining her tongue.
"That would never work. Why, they would just . . . just . . ."

"No they wouldn't, not if we all stuck to it. And not if we slept with a loaded gun at hand."

"My word. It's such a strange idea."

Eve went from wife to wife, explaining their womanly rebellion. Whenever she was told it could not possibly work, she smiled enigmatically and dropped the final gem of her argument.

"It has worked before. It happened back in ancient times. There was this woman named Lysistrata . . ."

After that it became easy. One by one the women approached their husbands and whispered in their ears.

"You'll what?" bellowed Isaac Warner. His wife told him again.

Several other men repeated Isaac's shocked response on being informed, only to be assured that their wives meant what they said. Visibly shaken, by nooning the next day, they began to admit that maybe that pushy woman, the Widow Billings, might be right for once. If they did return to the foothills, they would have graze for the livestock, fresh water and a chance to hunt for their food.

Independence, which they had skirted on the way to Jefferson Barracks, teemed with people. Droves of wagons appeared to be bound for destinations at every point of the compass. Men, women and a surprising number of children swarmed the streets, bustled in and out of stores and shops. Few of them took time to stop and stare at the column of Dragoons who rode their mounts at a walk down the main street to the distant docks. Only the night before had Preacher learned that he and his companions were in for a rare treat.

Lieutenant Colonel Danvers had summoned Preacher to his tent, yet he would not directly meet the eyes of the mountain man. "Due to the delays," Danvers began, clearing his throat frequently, his embarrassment clear in his posture, "I have decided that we shall negotiate this portion of our journey by riverboat. It will cut a month off our travel time."

Hiding his surprise and pleasure, Preacher spoke sincerely. "That's mighty smart thinkin', Colonel. I'd never have come up with it myself, what with bein' used to crossin' the mountains by horse or shanks' mare."

"No : . . no, I suppose not. Advise your assistants and be prepared to board tomorrow when we reach Independence."

Now they did just that. Two by two, the Dragoon horses went aboard a livestock barge, to be towed by the rearmost of six steam packets requisitioned by Lieutenant Colonel Danvers. They had been paid for by voucher drawn on the Department of the Army. Danvers, who oversaw the operation from beside Preacher, turned to the mountain man.

"Due to your positions as scouts, you hold ranks equivalent to a captain's and to lieutenants'. Therefore you will be billeted aboard the lead vessel with myself and the other officers." His expression told how little he liked that.

Preacher beamed with insincerity. "That's plum considerate of you, Colonel."

Danvers's expression became pinched. "It is not out of consideration, believe me. It's—"

Preacher stifled a guffaw. "Yeah, I know. It's *regulations.*"

"Well put," Danvers replied tightly.

"It'll be a pleasure for all, I'm sure," Preacher concluded as he turned away.

Steam Packet *Prairie Spirit* shrilled a lively blast on its tall, brass whistle and pulled away from the dock in Independence at three-thirty that afternoon. On board were the battalion commander, his staff, the captains commanding the four squadrons and the three scouts. Also one company of Dragoons. The blunt prow nudged into the Missouri River's brown water and began to struggle to overcome the current to make way upsteam. The huge side-mounted paddle wheels thrashed the water and sent off a fine mist of spray. Rainbows formed in a nimbus around each churning wheel.

More steam-whistle blasts and then everything began to settle down. The fifteen civilian passengers left the rail and went to their staterooms to open trunks and prepare clothing for dinner. Several of the men made their way to the Gentlemen's Salon. Preacher and his companions located their accommodations and dumped their belongings in the corners.

Preacher confided in his friends. "I don't know if I'm gonna like this. Outside of the time it will save, of course."

"Why is that, Preacher?" Antoine inquired.

Preacher studied his moccasin toes. Embarrassment pinked his cheeks. "I've never felt entirely comfortable on the water. Nothin' I can put a finger on, but it jist don't seem . . . natural. Water's for fishes and beaver."

"What about small boys?" asked Three Sleeps. "Didn't you like to swim when you were young?"

Preacher looked up at them. "Tell you the truth, I was over twelve an' livin' with the Cheyenne before I learned how to swim right proper like. Up to then, I jist paddled around like a spaniel after ducks. An' not likin' it much, either." He sighed. "It's funny. I put money in Mr. Fulton's steamboat works, an' this is only the third time I ever rid one of the contraptions."

Antoine turned an anxious face to Preacher. "I have heard that the boilers blow up sometimes."

Preacher nodded, which did little to allay Antoine's worry. "That they do. Usual it's because the stokers over-fill the fireboxes or the metal is old."

"How does one tell if the metal is old?"

"Antoine, my friend, I don't know. I jist have to hope the captain and the engineer have some idea."

* * *

They changed into cloth suits and boots and took dinner at seven o'clock, an hour before the sun went down. That only served to amplify Preacher's uneasiness. The truth that Preacher would not admit to was that prolonged travel over water made his stomach queasy. Although he did not suffer dizziness and nausea, it did make him develop gas. Preacher soon found himself out on the foredeck, a hand gently pressing his belly.

He was still there, the rumbles somewhat subsided, when a conversation among three fellow travelers advised him that there were card games in the Gentlemen's Salon. Despite his precarious internal state, the lure of the pasteboards drew him like a dead critter attracted flies.

After sitting in for an hour, Preacher's situation made it understandable to a reasonable person that he grew increasingly edgy when an oily fellow with a remarkable deck of cards made deep dents in his "government money," paid in advance for services rendered.

Beauregard Calhoon, still slim and dapper, with a thin, pencil line of a mustache and manicured fingernails, gave a shark's grin as he raked in yet another pot. He laid a particularly offensive sneer on Preacher, who had lost steadily. Preacher allowed as how he must keep an eye on Calhoon and discover the source of his unusual luck.

"Y'all seem to be havin' a terrible run of luck," the fashionably overdressed Calhoon observed to those at the table. "I learned to court the lady at a tender age an' I never fail to pay her homage."

Preacher's words had a coating of ice. "'Pears to me that her favors have been phe-nom-inal."

Calhoon gave Preacher a fishy eye. After three more hands, two of which were won by Calhoon, Preacher deliberately discarded an ace of clubs during the next, which he discreetly creased with a thumbnail. Sure enough,

Calhoon won again. His full house of aces and tens contained the ace of clubs.

Before Calhoon could pick up the hand with which he had won, Preacher came to his boots, leaned across the table and clamped a hard hand over Calhoon's wrist. His composure broken, despite his oily, black hair neatly parted in the middle and his fancy, shiny boots, the gambler could only splutter.

"See here, there's nothing to be gained by this sort of conduct. Release me, my man."

"I ain't yer man, nor any other's. I find it right interesting you won that hand with the ace of clubs. Special since I discarded that same card in the draw."

"You can't prove that," Calhoon gulped.

"Oh, yes, I can. You see, gents," he addressed the entire table. "I took the trouble to crease that card with a thumbnail before I dropped it on the table. By that time I had got myself the idee that this particular deck had a special set of marks Calhoon, here, can read."

Preacher squeezed tighter as Calhoon began to squirm. It caused the voice of the tinhorn gambler to rise two octaves. "I must protest. You'll not find a crease on that card, suh."

Preacher shook his head. "Nope, I don't reckon I will. But, I am willin' to bet I'll find the crimped one up your sleeve, or in a vest pocket. Somewhere anyway. You saw what I was gettin' rid of an' couldn't resist the urge to put another one into your hand to improve it."

"Are you calling me a cheat, suh?"

Preacher's eyes bored deeply into those of Calhoon, while his free hand delved into the sleeve of the fancy suit Calhoon wore. Deftly he produced the card in question. "That's exactly what I'm sayin'."

"Then, I demand immediate satisfaction." With these words, Beauregard Calhoon thrust his left hand under the wing of his coat and came out with a small, .36-caliber, double-barreled pocket pistol.

11

Preacher responded with the speed of a puma. His open hand, still holding the evidence, flashed across his body. Preacher's shoulder rolled when he made powerful, backhand contact with the exposed cheek of Calhoon. The impact could have been a thunderclap. Beauregard Calhoon shot back from the table, spun slightly and reeled drunkenly toward the bar. At the last moment, before he made violent impact, he remembered the pistol in his hand.

Fighting to control the movement of his body, Beauregard swung the small .28-caliber, four-shot, revolving-barrel pistol to bear on Preacher. One hammer fell on a cap. A thin stream of smoke spurted from the nipple an instant before detonation of the small powder charge. Several gentlemen gasped as the little ball made a loud *thock!* when it struck the wide, thick, bull bison-hide belt Preacher wore around his middle. Immediately Beauregard rotated the barrels and fired again. And hit Preacher again.

Concussion from the two slugs bulged Preacher's eyes and stabbing pain doubled him over. Air shot from his open mouth. For a long, spellbound moment, no one moved. Then Preacher straightened shakily, erased the agony-drawn lines from his face, and extended his right arm. The hand at the end held a Walker Colt, its hammer full back and ready to drop. This gun Preacher pointed steadily at the center of Calhoon's chest. He fought for air and, at last, spoke in sepulchral tones.

"You done played yer last hand."

Stunned by the incredible staying power of his target, Beauregard Calhoon only then recovered enough of his wits to turn, cock and aim the third barrel. This time, Preacher beat him to the mark.

Flame lanced from the muzzle of the .44 Colt, as it bucked and snorted in Preacher's hand. The round, two-hundred-grain ball sped across the small distance to the center of the exposed chest and smashed bone and tissue with destructive force. Flattened slightly now, it ploughed a wide furrow through the aorta, only slightly off center, and into back loin muscle, before blasting one of Beauregard's vertebrae into fragments.

Reflex jerked the trigger of the pistol in Calhoon's hand. The woefully underpowered ball shattered the glass chimney of a wall-mounted lamp and rang musically off the inside of its brass shade. Gleaming shards tinkled to the deck in the silence that followed. A thick layer of powder smoke undulated in the space between Preacher and the dead cheat. Slowly, Preacher reached down and plucked one of the little balls from the thick leather of his belt. A worried player hurried up to him.

"Neither one got all the way through," Preacher informed him. "But I'm gonna be sore as hell for a week. Awful bruise, you can bet."

Awed, the well-dressed man spoke for everyone in the salon. "You've been saved by a miracle."

Preacher shook his head. "Nope. Buffalo-hide belt. That little popgun didn't have a chance."

Another of the men who had been at the table spoke from where he crouched beside Beauregard. "He's dead."

"I didn't aim to only tickle him some."

A cluster of onlookers at the doorway gave room for the first officer to enter, buttoning his jacket as he crossed the room. "Someone tell me what happened?" he commanded. "Oh, and put away that revolver."

Preacher complied while the man at his side made explanation. "I'm Norton Babbott, Babbott Bobbin Company. This gentleman caught a cheat in our game. The scoundrel pulled a gun on him. Shot him twice. The rest you can see for yourself."

"I know this man," the first officer declared. "It's Beau-regard Calhoon. We've had complaints about him before." He paused, cut his eyes to Preacher. "You're a brave man to have faced him down . . . or a fool."

Preacher winced and unconsciously touched his aching middle lightly. "Right now I feel more the fool."

"It happened as Mr. Babbott said?"

Preacher shrugged. "More or less."

"How did you manage to detect him cheating?"

"I spend as much time watching the players as I do the cards in a game. Calhoon had a marked deck and he used hold-out cards, too."

Turning to look at Calhoon, the first officer spoke over his shoulder to Preacher. "I'll explain to the captain. He may want to speak with you. You're not planning to disembark soon, are you?"

"Nope. Not until I get these baby soldiers to the upper North Platte."

"And your name, sir?"

"I'm the one they call Preacher."

Eyebrows rose. "So that's why you're standing and he's not. Yes, I see, now. Very well, Preacher, from here on, it's merely a formality."

Far up the North Platte River, after an uneventful passage, the squadron of Dragoons disembarked. While the long, tedious process of unloading the horses, wagons and equipment progressed, Preacher consulted with the captain and river pilot. The latter showed Preacher a map of the river's course. With a stubby finger he pointed out their present location. Preacher nodded with satisfaction.

"This is where we are now. It's not much of a town, called North Platte. End of the line this time of year. I reckon you'll be heading northwest, through the small settlement of Scottsbluff. Nice folks there. Last trip, we brought them five ton of flour in barrels. You can resupply there without any problem."

Preacher studied the sparse details on the map. "Don't see why you can't get on up there. The map shows the river runnin' all the way into the Wyoming country."

"Too shallow. Why, by August, most of the river west of here will be dried up into a series of mudholes connected by a foot-wide trickle. No, sir, this will be our last run this far. Next trip will be no farther than the town of Grand Island. There's two hundred folk livin' there now. Makes for profitable hauling when the river's up."

Preacher matched the map's representations to images in his mind. They would still have close to two weeks travel to reach the part of the Bighorn Mountains Danvers had selected for his fort. He thanked the river men for their assistance and strode off onto the dock.

A small warehouse fronted the river at North Platte. In its tiny office, Preacher approached the factor. A portly, bald-headed man with an open, friendly face and jolly manner, the manager greeted Preacher affably.

"You came with the soldiers?" he inquired.

"That I did. Anything goin' on in these parts that I should know about?"

"Nothin' much. Except that the Pawnee have been kicking up their heels a mite."

"Do tell. Never could abide nor trust a Pawnee. Go on, if you please."

"They've made periodic attacks on the trail. Burned a

small settlement west of here. Scared hell outta the folks in Scottsbluff. Matter of fact, they did a good bit of scarin' around here."

"When's the last time they hit?"

In an unconscious gesture left over from when there was something to scratch, the factor rubbed fingertips on his bald pate. "About a week ago. Least, that's the last we've heard of here in North Platte."

Preacher split his darkly tanned face with a grin. "That sounds good. Don't imagine they'd be eager to take on a squadron of Dragoons."

"I wouldn't say so. You be settin' up a fort around here by any chance?"

"Nope. We're headed way northwest."

"What? The whole frontier is on the verge of a massive uprising and those idiots in Washington City send troops clear the hell and gone into where?"

Preacher answered him, his voice somber. "Northeast corner of the Wyoming country. Someone's got a wild idea that a fort out in the middle of nowhere, supported by nothing, will scare the breechcloths off the Injuns."

"You ask me, mister, a person has to be certified to have no brains at all to qualify to be a politician. I mean them all, an' I can say that 'cause I'm neither Whig nor Democrat."

Preacher clapped a big hand on the factor's shoulder, and winced at the pain in his bruised belly. "I have to agree with you there, friend. What else can you tell me?"

"There's talk flyin' around about some hotshot medicine man amongst the Blackfoot talkin' a holy war against us whites. Though I doubt you need to be told that. Part of the reason they're puttin' that fort out there, ain't it?" He gave Preacher a conspiratorial wink.

Preacher replied in kind and added, "Government secrets. Ask our illustrious squadron leader, he'll tell you it's to show the flag to the Sioux and Cheyenne. Whatever that means."

They jawed over other matters for a while and then Preacher departed to rejoin the column of Dragoons. He found them on the edge of the tiny village of North Platte. As usual, Lieutenant Colonel Danvers was in a foul mood.

"I have heard that the Pawnee are raiding in this area."

Preacher cocked his head to one side. "I hear the same, Colonel. We'll likely find evidence of their prowlin' before long."

"Such as what?"

Studying the officer closely, Preacher drawled an answer. "Oh, broke arrows, burned buildings and wagons, bones. The usual Injun leavings."

"Would they attack us, do you think?"

Preacher raised an eyebrow. "Not unless they've plum taken leave of their senses. We're too many and we have that little cannon."

Not entirely convinced, Danvers took on a belligerent posture. "I'll remind you of that in the event the need arises. For now, head out and scout ahead of our line of march." Danvers emphasized his order with a crisp snap of his riding crop.

"I'm sure you will," Preacher muttered, stung by the implied lack of confidence.

"What's that?" snapped Danvers.

"I said, I'll get the long view from the top of that hill." With that he wheeled Tarnation and sprinted off, leaving the colonel with an open mouth.

"Forty miles a day on beans and hay," turned out to be more than a boast Preacher soon discovered. The first day on the trail, the Dragoon squadron made twenty-five of that. Even burdened down with eight huge freight wagons and a field piece, the column covered fifteen miles by midday. They also found the first sign of Pawnee raids.

A well-established trail paralleled the North Platte River, which some were already beginning to call the Oregon Trail. It being wide enough at this point, Preacher relaxed his double-file formation rule and let the troops move along four abreast. In a hidden defile, which kept them from sight on the rolling prairie, Preacher and Three Sleeps came upon the blackened remains of three wagons, along with the bones of the owners.

"Look over here, Preacher," Three Sleeps called to his friend. "Arrow shafts. Most broken, some with the feathers burned. They've had the heads removed."

"Thrifty folks, those Pawnee," opined Preacher.

He studied the ground a while, found little clear and easy to interpret due to time passed. He estimated the attack to have happened at least a week ago. With that established, Preacher remounted and rode back to report to Lieutenant Colonel Danvers.

The colonel heard of the attack with mounting fury. "We have a treaty with the Pawnee," he exploded. "It has been in force for twenty years. Their chiefs should have stopped this outrage."

Patiently Preacher explained. "Among the Injuns, the chiefs have no absolute power. They ain't rulers, Colonel. They lead, give advice, represent the tribe or band with others. An' yes, make treaties. But the folks they represent don't have to obey them or hold to any agreement made in their name by the chiefs."

"Why . . . why, that's preposterous. What sort of leadership does that represent? The Army would get nothing at all done if the troops were not required to do as I order them."

"There might be somethin' good in that," Preacher observed in a muttered aside.

"What did you say?" demanded Danvers.

"I said, there's more to it than that. Most likely the chiefs who signed that treaty are dead now or replaced by someone else the folks are more willing to follow. And so, the people are free to decide whether or not to continue to honor the treaty."

"But they can't do that!"

Preacher could no longer stifle the guffaw that climbed his throat in a rush. "Oh, but they can and do, Colonel. They have always followed their way—it's their law, for want of a better word."

Colonel Danvers made it clear that he was unimpressed and definitely not amused. He addressed Preacher with dismissive authority. "We'll push on. The scene of this massacre would be too depressing a place to camp."

Hump Jaspar had survived the fury of the mountain men by the simple expedient of running like the devil was after him when the ambush failed. He had headed north, robbing folks occasionally to build up a stake. When he reached the North Platte, after running three horses to the ground under him, he took passage on a riverboat for as far as it would take him. Then he started out West on horseback.

Jaspar stopped in his quest only long enough to inquire at trading posts about Praeger and his partners. He had to find them. No matter that the news he brought would probably send them up like July Fourth rockets, he knew he might receive some benefit from it.

Hump had never heard of the old tradition of kings killing the bearers of bad news. So, when he found Branson Naylor, one of his friends who had joined the gang run by Blake Soures, at a trading post far up the Platte, he learned that Praeger could be found in a Blackfoot camp not far from the Bighorn Mountains and rode there with all speed. Only to face the fury of Quinton Praeger.

"*You* got away? Only you? How many men did you say sided with Preacher?"

"Two." The smallness of his voice startled Hump Jaspar.

"Impossible! Three men killed twenty-five?"

"Yeah. But it was in two fights."

Sarcasm enveloped Praeger's words. "Only two fights? Only two? Why in hell did it take more than one to finish off three men?"

"The first fight wasn't against Preacher."

"Then kindly tell me about its purpose?"

"We . . . ah . . . we decided to rob this train of freight wagons."

Quinton Praeger went white. "In the name of all that's holy, what in hell possessed you to do that?"

"We . . . thought we'd make some quick money."

Praeger could not suppress the shudder that came from a foretaste of doom. "I see. Yes, I really do. But you said you fought Preacher there?"

"Yes, sir. He and these two fellers came along and broke up our attack on the wagons. Only at the time we did not know it was him."

Eyebrows arched, Praeger ran a finger along the knife scar on his left cheek. His voice purred with feigned reasonableness "That explains it all. And the next time you met, he finished off all the rest, right?"

Hump Jaspar forced an expression of wide-eyed innocence. "Yes, sir. All except me."

"Thank you, Mr. Jaspar. Now that everything is in a shambles around my feet, I feel constrained to correct the one error Preacher made."

Puzzled, Hump Jaspar asked a fateful question. "Uh, what's that, Mr. Praeger?"

Praeger drew a compact .60-caliber, Miquelet Spanish pistol from under his coat and cocked the hammer. "Killing you," he replied a moment before he squeezed the trigger and shot Jaspar through the heart.

* * *

Praeger was still furious when he reached the council lodge. Iron Shirt showed his usual irritation at being summoned forth. He stood with arms folded over his chest, face black and in a glower.

"I was discussing important matters. What is it you want? We hear soldiers are coming. Is this true?"

"Yes. They are all a part of the plan. Right now I must speak with you and the war chiefs. It is an important issue."

"We will meet with you when we are ready."

Anger flared again in Praeger's chest. "Listen to me. I made you what you are. I gave you that iron shirt. I made up the ritual you use. Without me, you are nothing. When I want a meeting you will see that it happens. Is that clear?"

Iron Shirt's lips curled in contempt. "White man, you are a flea trying to bite a bull bison. When we are ready to listen, we will send for you." He turned on the heel of one moccasin and stomped back inside the lodge.

White, shaking with rage now, Quinton Praeger fought back a hot burst of profanity. Slowly he realized that his time with Iron Shirt had come near the end. Every day, every hour, had to be balanced with utmost care. Starting with regaining the dependency of Iron Shirt, he acknowledged. So, he smiled and waited.

Three hours went by before a young warrior came to summon him to the council. When he entered and went through the formalities, Praeger quickly explained the situation with Preacher. He concluded with a suggestion that when Preacher arrived with the squadron of Dragoons, the Blackfoot kill him themselves. To their credit, Quinton admitted, the war chiefs listened politely and with interest. Then they began to respond.

To his surprise, Praeger soon began to understand that the ferocious Blackfoot did not seem the least eager to face the living legend. When the last speaker's words had been translated for him, Praeger could not contain his profound exasperation.

"But we can't let him interfere with your war to drive out all whites," he blurted.

Two Moons rocked forward and came to his moccasins. "Why is it," he asked, "that you and the other two white men are so anxious to stir up war between our two peoples?"

Praeger worried that question a while, then made an oily, evasive answer. "I have learned your ways and have come to love and respect them. I wish to live as one of you after the whites are gone from this land."

Two Moons, as did the other chiefs, carefully kept his features neutral, in order not to reveal that they did not believe a single word of what they had heard. If it is true that ignorance is bliss, Quinton Praeger left the council lodge a misinformed but happy man.

12

Lieutenant Colonel Danvers had even less reason to be happy the next day. Antoine Revier came fogging back to the column at a quarter past ten with news that electrified the battalion commander and his officers.

"Colonel, we cut sign of a Pawnee war party about three miles ahead."

Danvers blinked and took a backhand swipe across his forehead. "Preposterous. We are at peace with the Pawnee." The last thing he wanted was to have a hostile force at his back when they settled in to build a fort.

Antoine gave him a mischievous eye. "Maybe this bunch don't know that. Preacher recommends that the tro— ah-Dragoons be mounted 'til this is worked out."

"We shall proceed afoot," Danvers decided aloud, ignoring the good advice. "Please inform Mr. Preacher that I wish him to extend his scouting activities over a much wider area."

With that dismissal, Antoine rode back to the point. The colonel waited until he had ridden out of hearing, then turned to call over his shoulder. "Captain Dreiling, flankers out, if you please."

"Yes, sir. Lieutenant Brice, take Sergeant Holcomb and twenty men to form flankers."

"Yes, sir. Holcomb, divide the platoon. You take the right flank, I'll take the left."

"Right, sir. First and Third Squads, follow me."

Lieutenant Brice wasted no time. "Second and Fourth, you're with me. Platoon . . . prepare to mount. . . . Mount."

With a flurry of dust from two hundred hooves, the flankers moved out smartly. Danvers watched them go in grim-lipped silence. He did not want to stir up trouble with the Pawnee. His orders were explicit. They were to proceed to the Bighorn Mountains, avoiding hostile engagements, and establish a cantonment area sufficient to house a regiment when completed. He had other orders as well, which he preferred not to think of. Sighing, he took up his reins, raised his arms and signaled for the column to advance. The Dragoons remained on foot twenty minutes later when the Pawnee raised up, seemingly out of the ground, and attacked the column.

Blind Wolf looked to the west, down the shallow slope of the rolling prairie. How foolish these white men. To go afoot when they had perfectly healthy horses to ride. More so for doing it in this country where death awaited them at every turn. This would be easy. Once his hidden warriors had them halted and confused, he and the rest of his brave Pawnee would sweep down on them at a gallop and ride the length of the column, killing many. He squinted to see the lead soldiers start up the next swell. He raised his feather-decorated rifle and gave the shrill call of a hunting eagle.

Responding to the signal to attack, Pawnee warriors came out from under their dirt-covered blankets and quickly sent a flight of arrows into the unsuspecting whites. Here and there a rifle cracked. Other braves, risking certain death, rushed forward to flail with their blankets and bison robes to frighten the horses of the white men. Even at his distance of a quarter mile, Blind Wolf saw several mounts' forehooves pawing the air.

Two even broke free of their owners' hold and bolted away from the noise—war whoops, shots—and the ghostly song of arrows. Any time now, he thought. Some of the soldiers had recovered and began to fire at the attackers. Blind Wolf knew he could wait no longer.

Raising his rifle again, he looked left and right, then brought it down smartly. At once he and twenty-five mounted warriors streaked forward. Swiftly, they closed on the wagons at the rear of the column.

An arrow made its uncanny moan past the ear of Lieutenant Colonel Danvers. Another thudded into the valise cover behind the cantle of his Grimsley saddle. A third bounced off the pommel of his adjutant's saddle. Instinct drove Danvers to take cover behind the stout forequarters and neck of his horse. This gave him a clear view of his holster, with its sheepskin cover.

To his credit, the Dragoon commander was the first to get off a shot. He threw back the tube of sheepskin and drew one large, unwieldy .44 Dragoon pistol and fired two fast rounds, one of which entered the screaming mouth of a Pawnee warrior who rushed at the horses with a flopping blanket.

Off went the left rear quarter of the brave's head as the flattened ball, now approximately .60-caliber in size, burned through brain and blew away bone and scalp. A Model 43 Hall, breech-loading carbine went off close by and Danvers flinched involuntarily. The hot wind of expanding gases from the foreshortened rifle brushed his cheek. Another flight of arrows seethed through the air.

One found a home in the forearm of Private Sawyer, who screamed as the point pierced the skin of his inner arm and protruded toward the forestock of his Hall.

Corporal Collins, who'd gone back for the wagons left behind, came quickly to Sawyer's side, Danvers noted.

Deftly, the NCO broke off the shaft of the projectile and pulled the remainder through the wound. He quickly had Sawyer bound with a light blue neck scarf he had pulled from the open collar of his uniform jacket. Seemingly unfazed, Sawyer calmly reloaded his weapon, seated a percussion cap on the nipple and took aim on another screaming savage. Sergeant Simmons and the other lead NCOs bellowed commands to restore order among the milling, confused troops.

Gradually more of the Dragoons unlimbered their weapons and returned fire. For a moment, the Pawnee rush faltered. Then the thunder of pounding hooves attracted the attention of everyone to the rear of the column.

Gunfire crackled out as another swarm of hostiles raced along the eight freight wagons, rifles blazing. Unable to reload on the run, the Pawnee slung their rifles over their shoulders and resorted to more conventional weapons. Now the teamsters and their swampers plied their firearms. At a rate of fire three times that of muzzle-loaders—three per minute—the breech-loading carbines poured a steady stream of lead in the direction of the Pawnee attackers. In a short time, the scene became obscured to the Dragoons and their enemy alike.

Blind Wolf had seriously underestimated the firepower of these flashily dressed soldiers. He had never encountered a breech-loading weapon before, had no idea of the speed with which they could be loaded and fired repeatedly. When the moan and crackle of balls thickened, and the reports of the short rifles grew to a deafening volume, he gave the signal for his warriors to pull back.

"We have hurt them. We will come again," Blind Wolf

told his son, Tall Raven, a boy of sixteen winters, who rode at his side.

Fired with the excitement of his first raid as a warrior, Tall Raven showed his disappointment. "Why not now, Father?"

"They are too many. They have shoot-fast guns we know nothing about. But, see, two of them are down, never to rise again. I count two hands of those who have felt the sharp teeth of the Pawnee. Soon again they will be off guard. It is then we will hit them."

Lieutenant Colonel Arlington Danvers rode the length of the column, inspected the damage and spent a minute with each of the wounded. Upset over the losses and the speed and surprise of the attack, he wore a deep frown. Beyond him, the flankers appeared over the swells to north and south while the Pawnee streamed away to the east. Danvers watched with mounting anger as the security details drew closer.

When Lieutenant Brice reported, the colonel icily cut him off in mid-recitation. "Explain yourself, mister. Why did you not get here in time to strike the hostiles from the rear?"

Brice stiffened. "No excuse, sir. But, for the record, we were pretty well spread out, screening for hostiles, sir, and it took some while to regroup and return, sir."

Realizing the correctness of this explanation, though loath to admit it, Danvers delayed his response. "Quite right, Lieutenant Brice. We will maintain flankers, only this time, they are to remain within visual contact of one another, and work in teams of two."

"Yes, sir. We'll go out at once, sir."

"Keep a sharp eye. Those savages caught us quite by surprise the first time," he grudgingly added.

"You expect them to come again?"

"Oh, yes, Lieutenant. Indians never give up with a single attack."

Brice and his platoon of flankers rode off to their assigned areas. A moment later, Preacher and Three Sleeps Norris cantered over the rise ahead of the column and located Lieutenant Colonel Danvers.

"We heard the ruckus, Colonel. Thought we'd best come see what went on."

"We were attacked by hostiles. Pawnee, I believe."

Preacher bent and retrieved an arrow. "That's what this says. Pawnee markin's right enough. They're fierce devils. Can't figger why they broke off so soon."

Danvers produced a satisfied smirk, recalling the surprised and confused expressions of the enemy. "I imagine they had never encountered breech-loading weapons before. We put out a volume of fire nearly triple that of older arms. I have flankers out. I think we can expect a return call from the Indians."

"Oh, yes, that you certain can. You want us to stay back with you, Colonel?"

Danvers considered it. "The warriors seemed to rise up out of the ground. Total surprise for us. I think it best if you do stay with the column, work out to the edges. Maybe you can detect another such shock tactic."

Preacher had more bad news. "One thing sure, Colonel, they won't play the same trick twice. The Pawnee have a whole bag full."

Blind Wolf bided his time for the second attack. The soldiers had made another five miles before the mounted Pawnee rushed over the lip of a ravine to the left of their route. Driving hard, they rushed down on the flank of the column. From his vantage point, Blind Wolf watched with satisfaction as the soldiers once again reacted slowly.

Faint shouts in the white man's language, which Blind Wolf understood only poorly under the best conditions, came to his ears. The soldiers wheeled left and lifted short rifles from where they hung on the saddles. A faint smile lifted his full lips and flickered momentarily. Then he raised his arm and waved it left and right.

A flight of arrows soared upward from beyond the edge of a high creek bank to the right of the mass of soldiers. Before they landed, the left flank disappeared behind a wall of smoke. A moment later, another volley crashed across the prairie. Blind Wolf's lips compressed and his eyes narrowed. He had expected this. Yet, he ached for each of his brave men who fell in the withering fire.

Short of the soldiers by only three pony lengths, the Pawnee reined in, those with rifles fired, then they wheeled and galloped away. Another flight of arrows went aloft from the creek bank. Orders shouted in a thin, high voice turned half the mounted troops in that direction. Two heart-stoppingly fast volleys ripped into the verge and chewed chunks out of the bank. Rifle in hand, Blind Wolf extended his arm and pumped it up and down.

Again his mounted warriors charged. Their ponies pounded down on the stationary ranks. Shrill whoops came from strong, young throats. The short rifles crashed again. Several braves flew from their saddles. Inexorably, the opposing forces grew closer together.

Then three buckskin-clad, white demons cut diagonally across the advancing warriors. Their gunfire rippled across the waving grass, the aim incredibly accurate. First one, then a second of Blind Wolf's leaders slipped from the backs of their ponies. In a flash, the surprisingly disciplined charge of the Pawnee warriors dissolved into a confused, milling mass.

With hardly any pause, the soldiers changed the shape of their defense. Alternating groups turned their horses left or right and began to move toward their attackers at a walk. In five heartbeat intervals, the walk became a trot, then a canter, then a gallop. With a raw roar from parched throats, the Dragoons charged.

By sheer volume of fire, the Dragoons stopped the Pawnee in their tracks. Then, while the men reloaded, Preacher and his companions dashed between the contesting forces, firing with their multiple-shot weapons. Preacher downed a leader, then wounded another. Antoine Revier killed a second subchief. That did it. The leaderless warriors turned, scattered. Cursing the showoff stunt of the mountain men, Lieutenant Colonel Danvers suddenly realized that it gave him the opportunity he sought. Now he could bring a decisive end to this. He stood full in the stirrups and issued commands in his high-pitched voice.

"By alternate companies, form as skirmishers, left and right. Draw pistols. Prepare to charge. Trumpeter, sound the charge!" As the crisp, tingling notes sounded, Danvers drew his saber. *"Chaaaaarge!"*

Haunches flexed, the big Dragoon horses bounded forward. Clods of turf flew in the air around them. Snorting and grunting, they increased their pace with each step. Quickly the Dragoons closed on their enemy. Suddenly, frightened faces turned toward them. Isolated islands of resistance formed here and there. The big, broad-shouldered soldiers in the two-tone blue uniforms grew huge in the eyes of the Pawnee. At extreme pistol range, the chilling order came.

"Take aim . . . fire! Take aim . . . fire! Take aim . . . fire!" On they thundered. "Fire at will!"

At that point, the flankers returned and struck the enemy in the rear. Quickly the huge, six-shot Dragoon pistols turned the tide. The Pawnee held fast for a moment, then broke in wild disarray, to be swept from the field. Within minutes, the battle ended. Silence settled over the field, save for the groans of the wounded. Abruptly, Preacher stormed up to Danvers.

Seeming furious, he lashed out verbally. "I thought I said no damn trumpets." Then he grinned broadly. "But it sure was a sweet, purty sight."

Danvers relaxed his usual brittle, disapproving attitude toward Preacher. "Yes, it is. A full-out, Dragoon charge is awe-inspiring." Then he frowned. "I see only one advantage coming out of this fierce, protracted fighting. It has blooded these green troops." He had not finished with that.

"This skirmish could have been, should have been, avoided. I want a plan drawn up that will insure we are not delayed by such actions. Those savages are supposed to be on friendly terms. What can we expect when we encounter real hostiles?"

It had been intended to be rhetorical, but Preacher took delight in answering. "More'n likely you'll git yer hair lifted."

Despite himself, Danvers cut his eyes to Preacher and acknowledged the remark, which made it more to the point. "That is not amusing. Any more delays like this will make us seriously overdue on our arrival in the high country."

Preacher considered the colonel's upset over the raid to be excessive. Yet, he bided his time for the present. What would come, would come.

Early in the afternoon, the forsaken wagon train arrived in what was seen as a safe haven tucked into a fold of the northeast slope of the Medicine Bow Mountains, a lush, gentle valley spread along a buttress of the foothills. The clear water of the Platte River ran in front of their hidden vale. Their tired eyes explored the bounty and found it good.

Isaac Warner halted his wagon at the entrance and

repeated his instruction to all who came by. "Go on in, find a likely space and settle in. We'll organize a hunting party soon as everybody is unhitched."

Each family quickly staked out areas of the belly-high grass for their draft animals and saddle stock to graze on. The women set about preparing firepits and rigging lines to air out long-confined clothing and blankets.

With her chores completed, Eve Billings ambled over to the site selected by the Honeycutts. Eve spoke her innermost thoughts to Hattie as she approached. "What a pure delight, all the water we want."

"And pure, too," Hattie added with a shake of her gray-streaked auburn hair. She had started the trek with uniformly coppery tresses.

"There will be plenty of game. And the chance for our livestock to fatten up for a long haul." She saw the older woman strain to move a boulder that she wanted elsewhere. "Here, let me help you with that."

They worked together for the better part of an hour. Eve soon noticed that neighborliness had once more come to life all over the encampment. Gone was the bickering and petty spite of the trail. It took far less time than usual to establish comfortable living areas. With the work out of the way, and the animals at graze, everyone seemed to decide at once that the time had come to wash away the dust and grit of the sun-blasted Basin.

While the adults and older youths decorously washed themselves in the shallows of the North Platte River, Eve watched as Charlie joined the other boys under fourteen and, along with the others, gleefully threw off his clothes and leaped into the chill water of the river. Eve could only cluck her tongue and shake her head. Not a streak of modesty in the lot of them. How like his father as a boy Charlie is, she thought.

Sudden tears sprang to her eyes at thinking of the man she had loved so dearly and who had died in her arms. She lowered her head to conceal her private grief from the others. Slowly her suppressed sobs, changed from gulps to sighs, and at last into long, slow, deep breaths. Eve looked up to see a sparkling, naked Charlie leap from a slippery boulder into the water in an awkward dive. A worried mother's words escaped her before she could cut them off.

"Charlie! Look out!"

A deep rumble of thunder came from the northwest to drown out her appeal. Swiftly, the temperature dropped fifteen degrees. The children ran shouting from the water to hurriedly wipe themselves down and dress. Eve chuckled softly. At least there was something that would get Charlie into clothes without an argument. If only Howard could see him now, she thought with fierce pride. This time, fond, loving tears filled her eyes.

She glanced up to see a blurry figure on horseback across the river. Curious, and wary, Eve wiped away mistiness to discover the same Indian she had seen nearly a week before. Behind him were foothills and huge columns of boiling black clouds. Again he raised his lance in a salute and smiled at her. Mystified, Eve stood, the hem of her dress dripping, and watched him until he turned and slowly rode away.

13

Celestial keglers made strike after strike ahead of the route of march. From north to south, the horizon had turned a boiling black. Skeletal fingers, edged in orange, lanced through the obsidian stew. With a swiftness known only to denizens of the West, the towering, anvil-headed cumulonimbus arched out to engulf the whole dome of the sky.

Preacher had been watching the approach of the storm. He prudently exchanged his hunting shirt for one of faded green flannel and his fringed buckskin jacket for an oiled-skin *capote*. His floppy felt went into his saddlebag along with his skins. A spanking new, stiff-brimmed one took its place. Preacher used a fist to punch the crown into a faint resemblance of its original shape.

While he industriously made these alterations in his clothing, the thunder rumbled, increasingly louder. To his dismay, when he looked back at the column, the Dragoons appeared to ride along in blissful ignorance.

"Them fellers is gonna get a first-class soakin'," he confided to Three Sleeps.

Norris nodded. "I reckon so. They've got them those fancy India-rubber *capotes* they use for ground sheets.

I wonder why nobody's given the order to break them out?"

Preacher's face twisted into an expression of sudden enlightenment. "Now, that's the entire trouble with the Army. Somebody's always got to tell you what to do. They yell and cuss at a body until he forgets how to think for hisself, an' then they don't let them anyway."

Three Sleeps removed his coonskin cap and scratched at a thick thatch of silver-blond hair. "I *think* I understand what you jist said, but I ain't gonna answer any questions on it."

Preacher started to make a wounded reply when the light breeze that had been in their faces dropped to dead still. That held for several heartbeats; then a strong, cold blast rushed at them out of the east. At once, the temperature plummeted ten degrees and continued to fall.

Preacher tightened the chin strap of his hat; the brim fluttered wildly. "B'God, here she comes."

A tremendous peal of thunder came right on the heels of a searing, white tongue of lightning that slammed into a pile of boulders a hundred yards from the trail. The ground shook with the violence of it. Despite the powerful gust of wind, the air tingled with the scent of ozone.

Insubstantial shouts came from the column. Preacher looked down to see the Dragoons halted, dismounting now, and digging into the cylindrical valises behind their saddles. From them, the troops hurriedly took their water-proof ponchos and donned them.

"That seems to have got their attention," he said dryly.

Widely spaced, huge, fat drops made silver streaks in the air. Another blinding flash and boom. The thunder erupted directly overhead and continued to grind and growl across the sky. Echoes of its passage bounced from the sun-baked ground. More rain fell, thicker now, with the main downpour close behind. It arrived with a seething hiss and swept like a giant's broom across the ridge where Preacher and his friends sat their mounts.

Tarnation made wall-eyes and twitched his ears. His hide followed suit when the heavenly cannonade fired another battery of forked electricity at six wide-spaced places in rapid succession. Down below, Preacher saw the Dragoons had a lot of trouble with their horses. Having dismounted, they could barely control the animals in the fierce teeth of the storm.

"Those boys are gonna lose some horses," opined Antoine Revier.

Preacher nodded agreement. "I reckon they will." Another near miss by a sizzling bolt put Preacher in motion. "Let's quit playin' target for that stuff."

Halfway down the grade toward the column, the rattle and drumbeat of swiftly approaching hail reached the ears of Preacher. He drubbed heels into Tarnation's ribs and streaked for a low, spreading plain tree that stood in valiant isolation in the shelter of a gully. He reached it only seconds behind his companions.

Shredded leaves fell in green confetti around them, while out in the open, the Dragoons did not fare so well. Two horses, painfully pelted with fist-sized ice stones, squealed and reared. Rain-slicked, the reins slipped through the hands of the Dragoons who held them. At once, the frightened, hurting animals bolted.

In spite of orders to the contrary, their hapless riders ran after them. In no time, the Dragoons and their mounts disappeared over a low swell. Preacher spat on a fallen leaf.

"There goes a couple of damn fools."

"You got the right of it, Preacher," Antoine Revier agreed.

"Any bets as to who'll have to go after them?" Three Sleeps Norris put in.

Preacher grimaced. "None at all. Soon's this downpour ends, we'd best be making tracks."

For all its violence, the storm had been a welcome sight for the unfortunate members of the wagon train. Eve Billings had hurried back in time to gather in the bedding and clothes she had out to air. The rain, when it came, was warm and inviting. At the insistence of her children, Eve relented and erected a screen of spare wagon-top canvas. Within its confines, Charlie and Anna cavorted, bare as the day they had been born. The only protest the youngsters made was when Eve produced a bar of soap.

"Mind you do your ears, Charlie Billings," she admonished.

Smiling and humming an old tune, she sat out the tempest in the shelter of the wagon box. Blue-lipped and shivering, Charlie and Anna had held out to the last drop, then had oohed and aahed over a rainbow that formed on the northern end of the storm's back. At last, they climbed, dripping, over the tailgate. Eve toweled them dry.

"Ow, Mom, that hurts," Charlie complained of the stiff, prickly cloth.

"Yeah, that hurth," Anna lisped.

Another sacrifice of the trail. Eve had been able to wash clothes in the water of streams they had passed, many of which were rich in lime and iron particles. Her supply of bluing had long since run out, and she regretted the stiffness her efforts put into the items she had washed. She would have given anything to capture barrels of that marvelously soft rain water.

Now that the tempest had rolled away to the east, the leaves of beech and oak, and pine needles, dropped, as if doing a slow dance, into puddles that had formed on the long-dry ground. The pioneers began to stir in their wagons. Eve reflected on her mystery Indian as she laid a fire from dry wood that she'd sheltered from the elements in a net sling under the floor of the Conestoga.

Obviously he was not hostile, she told herself. Why was it he only appeared to her? She had mentioned him after the first sighting, but none of the men had admitted to seeing the lone figure. Gus Beecher had even snidely suggested that she was seeing things. Maybe she was, her mind mocked.

Dismissing that, she knelt by the pyramid of sticks and pulled a tuft of oily wood tinder from the brass box. She struck sparks from flint and steel and gently blew an orange spot in the kindling into lively flames. Careful not to burn her fingers, she shoved the lintwood in under a mound of shavings. They reluctantly ignited and sent larger, hotter tendrils of fire among the larger pieces of wood. She looked up as Charlie approached. He was dressed as usual, shirtless, in his one-piece overalls, bare toes squishing in the mud.

"Mom, I want to go with the hunters. I'll get us something good."

"I'm sorry, but no. It's not safe. Some of the men can't . . ." Eve cut herself off short. She had admonished herself not to criticize the men in the group after Charlie had repeated her scathing evaluation of their abilities weeks ago. It did little good this time, as Charlie provided her opinion of their marksmanship.

"Hit the broad side of a barn."

Mad at herself more than the boy, Eve spoke hotly. "Charles Ryan, what have I told you about speaking ill of your elders?"

"Oh, boy, am I in trouble?" His lower lip protruded in a pink, wet pout.

Eve looked down on his sweet face and could only shake her head in the negative. Then she had to turn away to keep from breaking out in gales of laughter.

* * *

After two hours of searching, Preacher had nothing to show for it but some muddy hoofprints. Again he cursed the Army, and Lieutenant Colonel Danvers in particular. The muddle-headed nincompoop had insisted that at least some of the guides remain with the column. His idea of some turned out to be all save Preacher. Well, Mrs. Houghton's little boy Arthur had not turned out dense.

Preacher figured it was Danvers's idea to get him killed by the Pawnee, which likely had happened to the idiots he attempted to track. He sighed heavily and urged Tarnation forward. While the miles ticked off, he grumbled about the stupidity of officer-type soldiers or gnawed on a strip of jerky which he had softened between saddle and blanket.

With only three hours of daylight left, he at last found the missing men right enough. A big cloud of bluebottle flies led him the last fifty yards to a dry wash that cut like a knife slash across the prairie. They made quite a sight, one that wrenched even as experienced a stomach as Preacher's.

They had been stripped, staked out, mutilated, killed and scalped. Though not necessarily in that order, Preacher noted. One had been slit from sternum to groin, and had his private parts stuffed in his mouth. The other had been cut deeply from crotch to ankle of both legs and armpits to wrists. It had been done slowly, Preacher reckoned from the contorted condition of the unfortunate fellow's muscles.

Cautiously, Preacher looked around the scene. His keen eyes took in everything. First, he noted that there was no sign of their uniforms, weapons or gear. There was plenty of sign of Pawnee warriors. Oddly enough, one of the dead men's horses placidly chomped grass at the bottom of the ravine. It had been stripped of all equipage.

"Damn an' double damn," Preacher swore aloud.

Moving with care, he walked to Tarnation's side. There Preacher fetched a short length of rope from a latigo tie and fashioned a crude hackamore. He approached the Dragoon mount with patience. When the creature's bulging eye first registered his presence, Preacher began to coo to it and speak softly.

"There now. There, nobody's gonna hurt you. Good boy. Stand still, ya hear?"

Step by mindful step, Preacher's moccasined feet took him up to the heaving flank of the horse. He touched the animal lightly, ran his hand along the curve of its back to the neck. Another pace forward, a second. Murmuring platitudes, he raised the makeshift halter. Then, with a deft movement, Preacher slipped it over the muzzle.

Only a slight jump came from the creature. Preacher patted his arched neck firmly and blew gently in a cocked ear. Then he carefully led the beast away from the patch of grass.

"Come on, boy, you've got an unpleasant task to do."

After adding a lead rope to the hackamore and fixing that to a ground anchor, Preacher cut free the dead Dragoons. He wrapped them in his ground sloth and an old blanket and slung them over the back of the captured horse. A nervous twitching rewarded his efforts. With a grunt of acceptance of a bad job done the best he could, he mounted Tarnation and took up the lead. Mindful of the bodies he brought, he put the noses of the horses in the direction of the column. He did not relish making a report to Danvers on what happened.

Preacher had predicted the result accurately. Lieutenant Colonel Danvers stomped back and forth in his tent, cursed and railed, then concluded his tirade with a wholly uncalled-for accusation.

"Why did you not get to them sooner?"

Preacher cocked his head to one side. "I don't put up with that kind of talk from you or anybody. What did you expect me to do? I counted sign of fully sixteen Pawnee warriors around them bodies. I ain't fool enough to ride in among 'em and pass the time o' day, or bargain for the release of those idiots what ran after their mounts in hostile country. Besides, I don't think it would have done much good. They looked to have been dead since shortly after the storm passed by. Now, *Colonel,* I'll accept your apology, or I'll demand satisfaction right here an' now."

Surprise painted Danvers's face. "Duel with you? Why, you're not even a *gentleman.*"

Preacher looked astonished. "I didn't intend on no duel. Death's a serious matter." He turned abruptly and started for the front flap of the tent.

"Then what did you have in that primitive brain of yours?"

"I jist figgered to tom-turkey stomp the shit out of you, Colonel. But I've cooled off some. We'll forget it . . . for now. Good night, Colonel."

"Wait!" Danvers started after Preacher. "What are we going to do to stop these treaty violations?"

Preacher stared coldly and levelly at the colonel. "These incidents will continue unless the Pawnees learn not to mess with us. The best way to do that is to raid their villages, burn their lodges and supplies, run off their ponies, kill a few warriors."

"That's madness, man!" Danvers went on to protest vehemently. "There is a treaty. These are not the Indians we came out here to fight."

Preacher's amused expression turned to one of intense curiosity. "What Injuns are you supposed to fight? The way I understand it, we didn't come out here to fight any

Injuns. Jist to 'show the flag,'" he tossed the pet phrase of Arlington Danvers back in his face.

Danvers paled, cognizant that his mouth had overstepped his reasoning. "Yes . . . yes, you're right about that. The fort is to enforce the peace, not incite war. Yet, I must maintain that nothing can be gained from pushing a dispute on the Pawnee."

Preacher grinned and gave the colonel a wink. "I can think of something. It will provide excellent trainin' for yer baby Dragoons, that it will."

Grudgingly, Danvers saw the sense in that. Reluctantly he agreed to allow Preacher and one other guide to observe any Pawnee camps or villages in close proximity to their route of march.

Over the next two nights, Preacher and Antoine Revier scouted as many Pawnee villages. Preacher had reasoned correctly that such a large number of warriors could not come from a small raiding band on the warpath. It took him only to the second night to find what he sought. He would make a third foray to verify what he had learned.

Preacher squatted behind a stunted, wind-twisted bristlecone pine and looked down into a village. Flickering firelight turned the scene a Dantesque orange. His ears soon picked up the spine-chilling throb of drums and the eerie, wailing of the Scalp Dance, a song he'd painfully learned long ago and had lived to remember. From the gyrating shadows projected onto lodge covers, he estimated that at least six of the marauders lived in this community. At the time, he did not realize he had missed the count by ten.

After half an hour of careful study, Preacher slipped away into the night to rendezvous with Antoine. The first thing the French-Delaware mountain man said was: "You saw it, too?"

"Yep. The Scalp Dance."

"I counted eleven of 'em got the hoop with the scalps on it passed to them."

"You did? I marked it as six. My eyes must be goin' bad. Or I left too soon."

"May have. From the other side I could see real clear. Made my blood run cold."

"We'll check that other village tomorrow night, then tell the good colonel where to hit."

"I'm for that."

Together, they turned their mounts to the south and started for the trail of the Dragoon column. On the way, Preacher began to formulate a plan of attack.

After the third night's visit, Preacher completed his strategy on the ride to the Dragoon camp. He explained it to Lieutenant Colonel Danvers and to his utter surprise, the constantly critical officer agreed entirely. He did make a couple of changes and offered a suggestion.

"Standard Dragoon tactics call for keeping one element of one's force in reserve. In this case, I think they should be deployed. They can act as a screen, at some distance, to see none of the hostiles escape us."

"You're sure gonna make life hard for those Injun folk. I reckon we can work it out right smart."

Shortly before dawn the next day, the Dragoons eased into position to attack the slumbering Pawnee village. When all was in readiness, Danvers gave the signal. Howling like banshees, the Dragoons stormed in among the lodges. Some of these they set afire. Others they pulled down. Rearing horses trampled firepits and cooking pots. Yapping dogs bristled in challenge, only to be shot down by Dragoons. Preacher took his own course to enter the encampment.

Shocked, he felt a tangible chill along his spine when he saw the horse herd had disappeared. Sudden premonition caused Preacher to try to shout a warning. The first words had barely left his mouth when disaster struck.

Suddenly the tables turned on the Dragoons. Howling Pawnee warriors attacked them from outside the village. Whooping war cries and screaming insults, they charged into the bewildered soldiers.

14

Panic struck the green troops on the outer edges when the Indians appeared so suddenly. It rippled inward to those still occupied with trashing the village. Entire companies milled about in confusion. Who was it shooting at them? There weren't any Indians. Those furthest removed from the Pawnee menace had no idea of the terrible death that threatened them.

Preacher put heels to the ribs of his stallion and drove a wedge through some Dragoons paralyzed by fear. "Spread out an' get them weapons workin', damnit! There's Injuns right over there." He pointed the way and his calm, purposeful demeanor broke the spell.

First by ones and twos, the Dragoons opened space between one another and brought their Hall carbines into action. An arrow hissed past Preacher's ear and he jinked his head to the side automatically. A Walker Colt filled his right hand, and he fired almost point-blank into the chest of a Pawnee warrior. With a final shriek, the brave rolled backward off the rump of his pony.

Preacher sought another target, to find himself face-to-face with Three Sleeps Norris. "Muldoon is over on the other side, tryin' to organize some sort of defense."

Preacher assimilated the information and nodded.

"Antoine is right over there. I'll send him to Muldoon. You an' him can keep us in touch."

BSM Terrance Muldoon found himself alone in the command structure. Two young lieutenants had gone down in the first bevy of arrows to descend on the unsuspecting troops. Both officers took only wounds, but one was serious. No sign of Captain Dreiling, the most reliable and steadiest of the company commanders. None of the others had been on this side of the village. After the initial shock of the swift, swirling assault, Muldoon shouldered his mount into that of one Dragoon after another and shouted loudly enough to break their glazes of shock.

"Get that damn rifle to workin', soldier!"

"Bu-But the Indians," one had blathered back at him.

"Sure an' they ain't bulletproof, ye idiot."

By the time he had bullied enough of the wild-eyed troopers into a passable defensive formation, with every other man dismounted, the Pawnee had disappeared into the tall grass to prepare for a second rush. When the seed clusters at the tops of the stalks began to weave in snakelike patterns, Muldoon spoke low and reassuringly to the men he commanded.

"Easy now. Let 'em come to us. Be ready, stand fast, lads. Standing men kneel. Prepare to fire by volley. Hold yer fire. Take aim . . . Kneeling rank . . . fire!"

Lighted by the muzzle flash of fifteen carbines, the predawn murk turned to orange sunrise. "Reload. Mounted rank . . . take aim . . . fire!"

Again the sun rose in the south for the Pawnee. "Reload. Kneeling rank, take aim . . . fire! Reload. Steady, lads, steady. Mounted rank, take aim . . . fire! Reload. Kneeling rank, take aim . . . fire!"

Seemingly oblivious to the hail of balls that snapped through the air in their direction, the warriors came on.

At each volley, ten to twelve Pawnee fell in the grass, killed, stunned or wounded by the Dragoons. After the third volley, the distance between them and the soldiers had narrowed enough that the Dragoons did not have time to reload their carbines.

Muldoon judged the situation well. His voice rang calm and clear over the defenders. "Replace carbines. Draw pistols . . . Fire at will."

A wave of staccato reports rippled along the file of Dragoons. The sheer volume of fire sent dread through the swarm of warriors. In disarray, they thrashed their way back into the concealing grass.

"Keep it up, bies, that grass can't stop a bullet," Muldoon cheered on his rag-tag band of soldiers.

"Muldoon's checked them on the north," Antoine Revier reported to Preacher after he rode up in a fog of dust.

Preacher gestured to the empty plain that stretched from the village to a deep gully. "They ain't showin' themselves so free and easy over here. I found a couple of the company commanders. They got their troops outta their daze and blasted hell outta the Pawnee a short while back." He beckoned to Three Sleeps. "Git yerself over to Muldoon, take some of this surplus of officers we've got here with you. Tell him I expect the next charge will come at this side any time now. I'm gettin' tired of runnin' this show for the Army. Time to let the one's supposed to do it." He paused and looked around, a puzzled frown creasing his powder-grimed brow.

"Speakin' of which, where in daylights is Colonel Danvers?"

"Don't see him anywhere," Antoine remarked.

Then Preacher replayed the first moments of pandemonium when the Pawnee attacked. He pursed his lips and slapped a thigh with an open palm. "As I recollect, when the hostiles fu'st hit us, Danvers disappeared into one of the tipis still standin'. Funny thing, I ain't see him since."

Antoine was full of helpful suggestions. "Let's go see if we can find him."

"We will, soon's I figger out which one he went to."

Preacher and Antoine drew blanks on the first two lodges. At the entrance flap of the third, Preacher found a private standing post as though on garrison guard duty. He poked his head inside and found Lieutenant Colonel Arlington Danvers.

Seated on a camp stool that Preacher sometimes thought must have grown out of his ass, Danvers directed his officers by way of messengers. One of the latter saluted smartly and stepped hurriedly in Preacher's direction. Taken aback by the unreality of what he witnessed, Preacher stared in disgust. At last he found control of his vocal cords and stomped into the lodge, Antoine right behind. Danvers' high-pitched voice elevated more in complaint.

"I don't understand why we have not heard from the north side of the village. Has Captain Dreiling taken leave of his senses?"

Preacher stepped in front of the colonel then and spoke with an obvious effort to control his loathing. "Might I suggest, Colonel, that if you were out there, where the fighting is goin' on, you could learn firsthand what is going on and why. You might even be able to personally direct your subordinates, which would free up all these messenger-boys to take part in the battle."

Danvers tried to wither Preacher with his most contemptuous stare. "That's what company commanders and platoon leaders are for," he told Preacher coldly. "Company commanders are supposed to observe, supervise and direct."

That he failed to intimidate became immediately obvious. Preacher turned partway from the prim, icy-eyed colonel, then swung back, fists balled and eyes turned to steel. "My point is, Colonel, that you sure as hell can't see much cringing inside a tipi like a yeller-bellied cur."

He stomped to the entrance to the lodge and was bending to exit when a shrill roar came from Danvers, only to be drowned out by war cries and explosions of Hall carbines from outside. Preacher made for the fight at once.

Warriors from the other villages had to be in on this, Preacher reasoned correctly. Even if all sixteen of the braves involved in the torture and killing of the Dragoons lived in this camp, there simply weren't enough lodges to account for the number of Pawnee who surrounded the troops. A man usually figured three warriors to a lodge. By count of tipis, this village should account for some fifty-four warriors.

Hell, Preacher thought, that many had already been killed or knocked out of action. And, he recalled, the other two villages had been larger by half than this one. Ruefully he acknowledged that the sneaky Pawnee had gotten one up on him again. Time to worry about that later. Preacher took aim and shot a lance-wielding warrior off his pony. Quickly he reloaded his Hawken. There had to be a better way of ending this, he told himself.

During the next assault, an idea came to Preacher. When the lull that followed the charge extended far longer than the previous ones, he decided to put it to use. To do so, he sought out Antoine Revier. He found Antoine standing in the shade cast by a lodge, loading his pistols.

"Antoine, ol' friend, I think we're overdue in bringin' an end to this mess. Get that long-range Frenchie rifle of yours an' let's go out an' change the odds."

Antoine turned a beaming countenance on Preacher.

"I think I know what you have in mind. We should have done this sooner."

"They hadn't settled down enough. I'd say they was gettin' some grub right about now. Should work perfect."

Ten minutes later, Preacher and Antoine Revier slipped out of the besieged village and headed due east. A mile from the circles of lodges, they turned north, skirted the Pawnee flank and worked their way to within half a mile of the enemy. Both mountain men spent a tense fifteen minutes in concentrated study of the hostiles through long, brass telescopes. Satisfied that they had identified the proper individuals, they moved in a bit closer.

Being long-range sporting arms, both Preacher's Le Mat and Antoine's Alouette had been fitted with simple, unsophisticated telescopic sights. At ranges up to six-hundred yards, they could reasonably be expected to hit a man-sized target with every shot, and cause a fatal wound three out of five times. At least, in the hands of these expert marksmen that was possible. They used Y-shaped metal barrel rests that came with the weapons, carried in the stock, behind hinged butt-plates. After easing their way into suitable prone positions on a gentle upslope, they settled in and sought their targets.

Preacher found one first, took careful aim and pressed the set trigger. Then his finger curled around the firing trigger, and he fined his sight picture. A gentle squeeze and the .36-caliber rifle fired. At that range, he had the weapon clear of the stand and the old cap off the nipple before the head of a tall, wiry Pawnee with a face split by black and white war paint, snapped backward slightly and a geyser of gore spurted from the back of his crown.

Preacher had the powder charge rammed home by the time the other Pawnee reacted to the startling sight. Muffled by distance, the report of his Le Mat did not reach them until nearly two seconds after the ball that killed one war leader. A stiff crosswind had disbursed the powder smoke. Confused as to how and from where this blow had come, the Indians milled about, providing Antoine a target as easy as Preacher's had been.

His man went down rubber-legged a moment before Preacher fired again. A third war leader died. "I reckon one more each and we'd best get out of here," he advised Antoine after the latter had fired his second shot.

"*Mais oui.* Or we will leave our hair with the Pawnee."

Their guns reloaded, they sought out fresh marks and fired simultaneously. Another pair of war leaders clutched their chests and keeled over, their hearts pierced by deadly metal. Quickly, Preacher and Antoine folded up their gear and crawled off through the tall grass to where they had left their mounts on the far side of the low swell.

Six most important men killed in less than three minutes did it for the Pawnee. Muttering darkly about bad medicine, they abandoned the fight and rode off toward the other nearby villages. Even the inexperienced Dragoons knew that the battle had ended long before Preacher and Antoine rode into the battered encampment.

Iron Shirt stood before the assembled councils of the Northern Cheyenne. Many had journeyed far to hear the message of the Blackfoot messiah. Not all, though, were captivated by his promise to drive out the whites and bring back the old days. Some, including Cloud Blanket, privately believed, like the Crow, that some means must be found to live alongside the whites in peace. Cloud Blanket had heard appeals such as Iron Shirt's before.

They had failed to impress him then, and still did. He winced as Iron Shirt reached the part about how his secret medicine would make ordinary red men proof against the white man's bullets.

"Not a man shall die of white bullets after joining in the ritual of the Iron Shield Society. Some of you may have heard of how some warriors died from the white man's many-balls gun. Recently the Spirit who guides us revealed to me what needs to be done to make my medicine proof against even these."

What nonsense, thought Cloud Blanket. At close range, a shotgun—yes, he knew the proper name for it—could bring terrible destruction. An old friend among the whites, Preacher, had once told him that it was the awful shock to the body from being hit so many times at once that killed. Unless, the mountain man had added, a man took a load in the heart or got his head blown off. Iron Shirt had reached the climax of his boastful speech, the exhortation to join.

"I want ten double-hands of brave Cheyenne warriors to step forward and become brothers in the Iron Shield Society. All is in readiness for the ritual. Those who do not join us are asked to leave now."

It heartened Cloud Blanket to see so many turn away. Yet, some eighty stood as though enchanted by the words of Iron Shirt. This would be a bad thing for the Cheyenne, Cloud Blanket admitted to himself. He turned to an old friend, Four Bears.

"I am thinking of moving my band toward the Black Hills. Iron Shirt is like a stick of green wood in a fire. It spits and pops and throws sparks in the air. But sparks are not a blaze . . . unless they land in your sleeping robes."

Four Bears nodded thoughtfully. "You are right. I will ask my people to do the same."

Back on the march again, the Dragoons seemed more confident and at ease, though somewhat subdued. Five of them had been killed; more than thirty took wounds. Most bore only minor injuries, and wore their white swatches of courage with noticeable pride. The six serious cases rode in wagons, under the care of Major Claire Couglin, the company surgeon. Troubled by the condition of his charges, Major Couglin left the wagon in which he tended three of them, and on his dapple-gray mare rode to the head of the cavalcade.

"Colonel, I am greatly concerned for the recovery of the seriously wounded men. I urge you to slow our pace. At this rate of march, the wagons are doing more harm than the Pawnee did."

Danvers snorted. "Nonsense, Doctor. We need to put as much distance between us and the Pawnee as we can, in order to avoid any more such . . . incidents."

The balding Major Couglin raised his eyebrows in astonishment. "I'd hardly call a pitched battle an 'incident,' Colonel."

Danvers gave him a hard, level stare. "Officially, that is what it has to be. Otherwise, we might be charged with violating the treaty."

Couglin scratched his chin. "Preacher has given me to understand that it is highly unlikely we will have a repeat of hostilities."

Snorting, Danvers glared in disdain. "Preacher? What does he know about it, *Major* Couglin?"

In a quiet voice, the doctor added his clincher. "He's lived out here for thirty years."

It had little effect on Danvers. "I regret to inform you that we cannot slow the pace, Major Couglin."

The major bristled. "Need I remind you that in matters of the health and well-being of the troops, I have authority to supersede your decisions?"

Fire flamed in the eyes of Danvers. "Your objection is noted—and rejected. In the presence of hostiles, my decisions alone are binding."

Defeated, Couglin tried one final appeal. "At least, let me have a suitable escort so that the wagons can proceed at a rate consistent with the best interests of the wounded."

Lieutenant Colonel Danvers relented. "Very well. You may have two platoons. This discussion is concluded."

From a short distance away, Three Sleeps Norris had overheard the entire exchange. He muttered to himself his heartfelt opinion of Lieutenant Colonel Arlington Danvers: "Heartless, miserable son of a bitch." Had he heard it, Norris knew, Preacher would have agreed.

15

Blooding the troops had side benefits born of their increased confidence. Preacher soon noted that the Dragoons' smart deportment made the old saw about forty miles a day solid reality. On one fine afternoon, he found the Medicine Bow Mountains on his left. He had seen their matte-black ramparts over the previous three days. Now sure enough they had gained the red-orange pinnacles covered with tall stands of lodge-pole pine, juniper and fir so dense that had the Black Hills of Lakota country not been seen first by white men, these would have borne that name. What Preacher did not expect was to come upon a mounted white man, who appeared suddenly out of one of the deep folds on the northeast face of the Medicine Bows.

A cry of surprise reached Preacher's ears a fraction of a second before the stranger energetically waved his arms in a show of peaceful intent. He spurred his horse and came on fast. Preacher urged Tarnation toward the approaching rider. Face alight with hope and relief, the newcomer reined up in a shower of turf.

"Mister, am I glad to see you. Thank the good Lord you've come at last. How many in your party?"

Preacher blinked and studied the man in an attempt

to determine if he was addle-pated. "There's nigh onto two hundred."

That startled the stranger. "Lordy . . . lordy, that's the biggest wagon train I've ever heard of."

"Not a train. I'm guide for a squadron of Dragoons. Folks call me Preacher."

Face glowing with joy, Isaac Warner introduced himself, then added, "You have no idea how grateful we are to see you. Many of our people have given up hope."

Preacher rubbed his chin. "Maybe I should ask how many there are of you folk?"

"We number seventy-three souls, Mr. Preacher. Two of those are in danger of departing if we can't get medicine."

"It's jist plain Preacher, no mister about it. An' we've a surgeon along, so your sick can get help."

Warner raised his eyes to the sky. "Praise God, Preacher. Now we have a chance."

"That'll depend more upon Colonel Danvers than on me, I'm sorry to tell you, Mr. Warner."

Warner looked perplexed. "Surely he is a compassionate man. He'd not leave children stranded in this wilderness?"

Preacher pulled a long face. "Oh, it's entirely possible, Mr. Warner. To put the best light on it, he could be said not to have much use for what he calls 'civilians,' present company included."

"He's a harsh man?"

That had been amply proven with the flogging of the four Dragoons, to Preacher's way of thinking. "That's about the right of it."

"Wh-what sort of man can he be?"

"I'd say you would most likely say he resembled the north end of a southbound jackass."

That left Warner without a reply. After a moment, he broke the strained silence. "I had better show you to our encampment. Everyone will be so excited."

Preacher pulled a droll face. "Oh, I've no doubt of that. Even Colonel Danvers."

On the ride into the lush valley, Isaac Warner explained to Preacher how they had come to be abandoned in such an, as the pilgrim saw it, unforgiving land. When the perfidies of their guides and captain had been revealed, he concluded with a plaintive remark.

"So, we're not sure where we are, or how to get where we were going."

"Where might that be, Mr. Warner?"

"Why, the Northwest Territory, of course, to Oregon."

Preacher sighed regretfully. "You're about two hundred miles too far north for the Northwest Trace."

Warner frowned. "What's that?"

Preacher called on all his patience. "The trail you should have been on. The one folks are takin' to callin' the Oregon Trail."

"We're that far off?"

"Yep. And intentional, I'd judge. It's an old game. Lead a party out into nowhere, rob them and leave them for the coyotes and buzzards. I'm surprised they didn't take your livestock as well."

Warner shrugged. "I suppose we were too many, too well armed. They snuck away in the dead of night."

Preacher turned philosophical. "No accountin' for some folks." A moment later, the sheer volume of cheering, waving and hugging that greeted him left the mountain man utterly speechless.

"Absolutely not!" High as his voice might be, Lieutenant Colonel Danvers still managed a bellow. "Civilians," he spat out the word like an epithet. "Complaining, dragging their feet, whining, they'll hold us back, make us a month late reaching our goal."

Preacher tried calming words. "Come, now, Colonel. We're only five to seven days from where you want to build that fine fort of yours. Even if they cut our daily advance in half, that's only two weeks."

Danvers slammed a small fist on the table. "I say leave them to their fate. They were fools enough to come out here without proper guidance, they should get what they deserve."

Chillingly, Preacher heard his own words thrown back in his face. He'd said the same thing at Bent's Fort. Coming out of the mouth of Arlington Danvers they sounded dirty and mean. That served to make him more determined.

His eyes narrowed as he pressed his argument. "Am I correct in believing that part of your purpose in being out here is to protect settlers moving through?"

Danvers paused before he fired off another hot retort. "Yes, yes, we have that assignment. It is secondary to keeping the tribes at peace."

Preacher cocked a brow. "Wouldn't it serve your purpose better to protect this partic'lar group of settlers? If you leave them here an' there's a massacre, the howl that's sure to go up back East will light a fire that'll singe your fingers way out here."

The colonel could not deny the truth in that. With a visible exertion of will, he toned down his demeanor. "Perhaps you are right, Mr. Preacher. Like it or not, I don't suppose I have any choice. Say, I thought you had short shrift for these immigrants?"

Shrewd ol' pup, Preacher thought silently. "Now, that's true. I've had me more'n one belly full of pilgrims. Damn fools the most of them. But that was then, and this is now. An' we got them on our hands. It's up to you an' me to do the best for them we can."

Danvers threw his hands in the air and walked away. Outflanked and defeated, he didn't want to admit it. Preacher spent no time gloating over his victory. Instead, he went directly to Isaac Warner. With Warner, he found a young woman. A particularly good-looking young woman.

"Preacher, this is Eve Billings. She and her two children have a wagon in our train."

Remembering his parlor manners, Preacher removed his hat and extended a hand. "Pleased to meet you, ma'am."

"Please, it is Eve. I came to find out what the colonel has decided."

Preacher found himself liking what he told her. "We're gonna escort you as far as we're goin'. When the fort is built, you can winter there and go south toward the Oregon Trace next spring, join another train."

In a gesture that harkened back to childhood, Eve clapped her palms together and did a couple of dance steps. "Oh, that's just wonderful. You're a . . . ah . . . minister?"

"No, that's jist what they call me in the High Lonesome." Preacher seemed uncomfortable to his friends. Three Sleeps sniggered.

"This calls for a celebration. I'm going to cook a regular feast for you and your fellow guides, Preacher. My son got us a deer today. You'll meet Charlie and Anna and . . ." Eve realized she was chattering and cut it off abruptly. "You'll be there? Good. An hour before sundown."

While his companions whooped and slapped each other on the back, Preacher stripped to the buff and entered the water of the Platte to wash away his accumulated grime. Following his ablutions, he dried, donned fresh, clean buckskins, tied back his hair with a strip of tanned rabbit hide, the fur still in place, and slid into his fancy pair of beaded and quilled moccasins. Three Sleeps and Antoine howled with laughter. They found his preparations uproarious.

Preacher did not share their mirth. "You two could stand a good douchin' off, ya know," he grumbled.

"Me? Three Sleeps gasped. "Why, I smell sweet as a May flower."

"Road apple's more like it," grumped Preacher.

Eve Billings greeted them warmly, an apron around her slender waist, a big spoon in her hand. "We have venison stew, and I made pot pies from the kidneys and sweetbreads. You must take some along for your noon- ing tomorrow. Ah, here are the children," she gushed, then gulped back her flow of words and proceeded at a slower pace. "Preacher, Mr. Norris, Mr. Revier, this is Charlie. He turned ten two months ago. This is Anna. She's eight. Children, these are our guides, who are going to find a way out of here for us."

"I hope they're better than Mr. Beecher."

"Charles Billings, you watch that mouth of yours," his scandalized mother cautioned.

Preacher squatted to put himself on Charlie's level. "Don't you think it'ud make a body cross-eyed, watchin' his own mouth? Without a lookin' glass, that is."

Charlie had a giggle fit, and Eve surrendered in the presence of these carefree men who obviously knew this country so well. By the time she served up supper, with the help of Anna, Preacher and Charlie were fast friends. Eve exerted constant efforts to curb her bab- bling. To his companions, it soon became obvious that Eve had eyes for Preacher. She batted them at him throughout the meal. While totally oblivious to this, the object of her attentions enjoyed himself thoroughly.

During the next day's nooning, Lieutenant Colonel Danvers summoned Preacher back from point. "I trust you are aware we are making only half the speed today we did in the past two weeks," he said.

"Yep. That's what I said before. Half the pace will take us two weeks to make the Bighorn Mountains."

Danvers had a dire prediction. "It will get worse, mark me on that. With these wagons hanging on our backs, we will have all the problems and delays of any of their kind."

Preacher considered a moment. Ten miles a day would be disastrous for the pilgrims, too. Not to count the effect on the morale of the troops. Too many good-looking gals among the civilians. But not enough to go around.

"I can go to them and force more speed, but not a whole lot. And I think I can avoid a slowdown to ten miles a day. There are ways to trim time off all sorts of things."

"I certainly hope so," Danvers snapped.

Preacher went to where the immigrants cooked and ate at some distance from the soldiers. Several looked askance at him. Puzzled, he found a stump near the center of the circle of wagons. He jumped up on it and raised an arm to draw attention.

"Gather around, folks. There's some strips of stringy meat we've got to chaw on." When those who had finished their meal and those who had not started the cleanup had formed a semicircle around him, Preacher went on. "I've been told by the colonel that we're not makin' good enough time. He feels that the blame falls on you. Now, I don't take to that entirely. But there are some things you could do to speed us up."

Fully expecting it, Preacher at first absorbed the torrent of complaints and excuses that rained on him. "Our wagons will break down," Renard Labette objected.

"We can only move faster if we lighten our wagons."

"That means we'll have to abandon precious possessions," Martha Brewster blurted, near to tears.

Gus Beecher came up with what he thought to be the

clincher. "It'll be too hard on our livestock. They'll start to die off."

Isaac Warner took a more personal outlook. "The soldiers will just have to move at a pace we can keep up with. It's their duty to protect us."

Preacher waited out the storm, arms across his chest. Then he jutted his jaw and laid out the alternatives. "Fact is, the soldiers do not have to do more than leave a small escort with you. They have their orders from the War Department. They have to carry them out. Colonel Danvers wants to leave you behind. He has every right to do that. If you can't keep up, if there are more delays, it will result in you being abandoned again. If that is the case, the Indians will find you. You won't be able to defend yourselves. Not even if the colonel leaves a company behind. On the other hand, if you exercise some imagination you will be able to keep up."

Fists on hips, Gus Beecher spat truculently. "Says you."

"Yes, says I. You have two choices; adapt and keep up, or be left behind."

Beecher wasn't ready to leave it alone. "Somethin' tells me we were better off before you came along. Might know you'd side with the Army."

Suddenly Eve Billings appeared beside Preacher. "Listen to him. He's fought hard against the colonel's determination to leave us to our fate. He must know lots of ways to help us save time."

Good girl! Preacher wanted to hug her. "That I do. For instance, buildin' fires and cooking meals at noon slows the whole column. From now on you might try cooking enough in the morning, or the night before, to provide for the noonin'. In this climate, meat cooked over a smoky fire will last several days. Biscuits will hold a week or more. If you have any cornmeal along, or dried corn that can be ground into meal, you can make mush.

"Warmed on a hot rock," he went on to explain, "it can be mighty tasty dipped in a little molasses at noon.

Another thing, I see you have firewood slings under yer wagons. Send your kids along the route of march each day and have them collect deadfall. Stow it while yer rollin'. Then you don't have the hankering to stop early to gather wood. Those of you with spare draft animals, change 'em off at the noonin'."

"We still can't move as fast as the soldiers," Gus Beecher objected.

"Not unless you lighten your loads. An' I've already heard all the sad stories about grandma's treadle organ half a hundred times. For instance you, Mr. Beecher. I notice you have a whole lot of heavy iron things in your wagon."

"Of course. I'm a blacksmith."

"Thing is, it makes you lag behind the other wagons. I'd suggest you dump yer anvil and a lot of other stuff. They can be had off the ships that call on the Oregon country."

"I'll do no such thing. My life's work is in there."

Preacher planted a glower on his face and bent forward so he came eye to eye with Gus Beecher. "Mr. Beecher, you can either voluntarily lighten your load now, or you can have it done later by the soldiers at gunpoint."

Beecher turned red-purple. In a blink, he swung at Preacher's jaw. Preacher blocked the blow with steely fingers coiled around the offending wrist. He pivoted with the force of the swing and carried Beecher past him. All the while he squeezed tighter on the wrist. Beecher's hand opened and turned the same dark color as his face.

"Mind yer manners, friend. I've got no reason to give you real grief, unless you insist."

For all his great strength, the blacksmith could not take control of the situation. Defeated in mind as well as body, when Preacher let him go, he stumbled through those gathered to listen and headed to his wagon.

"Sorry for the little interruption, folks. Like I was sayin', it's up to you. If you have any questions me an' my friends will be proud to help."

Snaking silently through the aspens, a large party of Blackfoot and Cheyenne, armed with the mystical power of Iron Shirt and aided by his modern rifles, closed on an Arapaho village. Located in the foothills of the Bridger-Teton Range, along Little Sandy Creek, the Arapaho band had long enjoyed a peaceful existence. That ended suddenly in the keening war cry of the Blackfoot leader.

Swift and deadly, the warriors swarmed in among the lodges to take women and children for slaves, horses to build their importance in their tribes. Only belatedly did the Arapaho men begin to offer resistance.

16

Screaming, a portly Arapaho woman ran behind a brood of frightened children. She shooed them before her like a flock of chickens. Suddenly she stumbled and lurched forward when the head and half of a lance shaft entered her back between the shoulder blades and burst out her chest in a welter of scarlet droplets. Yipping his triumph, the Blackfoot warrior who had run her down yanked his weapon free and turned to overtake another fleeing Arapaho.

"This is easier than we thought, Black Hawk," he shouted to a companion.

Black Hawk agreed. "The Arapaho have become women. They do not fight."

"They do not have these fine new rifles, Gray Otter."

Gray Otter's face clouded a moment. "Yes. That is true, but the fancy-dressed soldiers have even better weapons than we do. They load without a ramrod, and fast, too. They punished us badly three suns ago."

Black Hawk copied Gray Otter's frown. "Men died. Is the medicine of Iron Shirt not as strong as he claims?"

Gray Otter spoke what would, under other circumstances, be considered blasphemy. "I do not think his is good medicine at all. For all its power, it seems to follow the way of the dark spirits."

Black Hawk looked worried. "Do not let Iron Shirt hear you say that. He will have you stripped of the medicine and made a target for all men."

For a moment Gray Otter could not believe what he heard. "Do you mean he would have me killed?"

Nodding thoughtfully, Black Hawk revealed something else to the new recruit. "It is possible. Iron Shirt has three white men for council. They wear our clothes, but they are white. I have seen them."

"Then what do we do, Black Hawk?"

"Fight, and watch. The Great Spirit will show us what to do when the time comes."

More screams attracted their attention, and they turned to join in the final roundup of the children. In the distance, the stolen pony herd kicked up a dense fog of dust. Flames flickered from several lodges. Moments later, a sharp, clear peal of brassy notes alerted Black Hawk and Gray Otter to an unexpected danger.

Preacher sent back word when he first heard the rifle fire. There should not be anyone out here, he reasoned. Twenty minutes later, he topped the ridge he now sat upon and looked down on what appeared to be an Arapaho village. What were they doing this far north? Never mind that for now, he decided. Another, bigger problem faced him.

Someone had attacked the Arapaho. Preacher could do nothing. He and the other two scouts could not turn the tide. A large force had swarmed into the village to kill, loot and carry off captives. In the distance he saw a large cloud of dust that had to be the pony herd. This would be a matter of waiting it out, or taking the entire battalion in to drive off the raiders.

To his credit, Lieutenant Colonel Danvers brought

the column up smartly and wasted no time in bluster or examining options. "We'll deploy as skirmishers and charge. From the sound of those rifles, I'd say we have encountered some of the renegades we've been informed of."

"I reckon you're right, Colonel."

"Very well, Mr. Preacher—"

Preacher winced. "It's jist *Preacher*, Colonel."

"Yes, as I was saying, Mr. Preacher, take your fellow scouts and reconnoiter our route of approach."

"Which will be?"

"Straight down this slope and have at them."

A fleeting smile turned up the corner of Preacher's mouth. "Sounds good. The sooner the better, they're stealin' the children down there."

When it came, Preacher saw the charge to be every bit as awesome as the first time he'd witnessed it. It caught the looters and slavers by surprise and riveted many in place, their hands coiled in the braids of small girls and boys. Several died that way before the spell dissipated and the survivors raced for their ponies. A dozen courageous ones formed a rear guard while their companions removed the captives. Then they swung astride their mounts and whirled away across the prairie. For once, Preacher found Danvers ready for continued battle.

"We should go after them, chase the savages down."

"That's not all that good an idee, Colonel," drawled Preacher. "When troops split up and go in pursuit of a war party that size, there's good odds they'll be ambushed. Injuns love to run away, only to spring a trap. No, sir, if you don't want to wind up staked out like those fools who chased their horses, you'd best let the Blackfoot get away with their new slaves."

Three Crows Walking, a young Arapaho war chief, came up to the gathering of officers. He recognized the cut of the buckskin-clad trio, if not their faces. Accordingly, he addressed himself to them.

"The Blackfoot do not fight like themselves." Then, in the best English he had, he repeated himself to make certain they understood. "The Blackfoot fight like crazy men. Not afraid of bullets, not afraid of arrows. Fight like Great Spirit watch over them. Crazy men."

Preacher nodded and cut his eyes to Danvers. "What is it you had on this Iron Shirt feller?"

"He is promising to drive out all whites, bring back the white buffalo. He is supposed to have some sort of magic that makes him bulletproof."

"Not 'magic,' Colonel. Medicine. Powerful medicine," corrected Preacher. "An' I'm willin' to bet he's told his followers that if they keep to his ritual, maybe eat an' drink certain things, or don't eat or drink some others, they'll be jist like him. It's big stuff among the Injuns."

Danvers made a puzzled frown. "We've killed them, haven't we?"

"We've been fightin' Pawnee. These are Blackfoot, accordin' to . . . ah . . ."

"I am called Three Crows Walking."

Preacher nodded. "Accordin' to Three Crows Walkin'. And, accordin' to these here . . ." Preacher bent to retrieve two arrows with red paint markings. "There was some Cheyenne mixed in among 'em. This thing is spreadin', Colonel. I think you've got your first job already cut out for you."

More than you know, Lieutenant Colonel Danvers thought to himself. "Are you suggesting we interrupt our march to pursue, round up and punish these renegades?"

"Naw, Colonel. Nothin' like that. Partic'lar we got these pilgrims with us. We'll jist go along, keep a sharper eye and see what develops."

"What about the behavior of these Blackfoot in the face of armed resistance? Have you ever encountered anything like that before?"

Preacher considered a moment. "Nope. Not personal. I've heard of Injuns chargin' into the mouths of guns like that some while back. Comanche, it was, down south in Texas. They had them a war chief name of Iron Shirt, jist like this one, who wore one of those Spanish iron breastplate things."

Captain Edward Dreiling stepped up to provide the correct term. "Cuirass. It's called a cuirass."

"Whatsomever, he could stop a ball from a flintlock musket, even some of the earlier caplock rifles. Feller who stopped him, he was a Texas Ranger, shot him right betwixt the eyes. His medicine didn't work too good against that."

Captain Dreiling had a question, which the colonel should have asked. "Preacher, do you think that is the answer in this case?"

"Sure enough. If you can get these grass-green youngsters to hold steady and hit what they aim at. Now, we'd best be doin' what we can for the survivors. Most special, that includes a big pot of coffee."

"Very well. Then we will push on in the morning."

Eve Billings hastily removed her stained apron and dabbed at a smudge of flour on her nose. She rinsed her hands and walked quickly to where the guides had their small gathering, putting on her best smile and patting back a stray strand of auburn hair. When the men looked up from the coffee they shared with two fierce-looking Indians, she repressed a shudder and spoke lightly, trying not to reveal in her tone the importance the invitation held for her.

"Preacher, it would greatly please me if you would take supper with my children and myself this evening." Before he could make reply, she stumbled on. "There will be another guest. Captain Edward Dreiling has graciously accepted an invitation."

Preacher rolled that around in his head a moment. "Well now, there's a couple of things I'd like to take up with him, he bein' the only officer in that outfit with a lick of sense. I thank you for the invite, and I'll be pleased to be there. What time?"

"Oh, say an hour before sundown. I've made a dried apple pie."

"Yer a treasure, Miss Eve. I'll bring along a little jug to wet our whistles." Preacher gave her a big wink.

After she departed, Three Sleeps Norris and Antoine Revier rolled on the ground, holding their sides in merriment. "Well, lah-di-dah! Formal invites from the little lady," Norris choked the words out over laughter.

"Best look out," advised Antoine. "She's set to make you the rooster in her henyard."

For a moment, Preacher looked thunderstruck, contemplating the future *that* promised. He rejected the notion out of hand. "I don't believe that for a minute. Naw, sir, not for a minute. She's only bein' friendly."

Antoine would not let it go. "Last time, when we all went, *that* was being friendly. Mark me, Preacher, she's got her cap set for you."

Preacher remained adamant. "Not by a long shot. You wait and see. That gal's jist bein' nice."

Preacher timed his arrival at Eve's wagon to coincide with that of Captain Dreiling. Eve greeted them warmly, showed them to straight-back chairs she had dug out of her household goods and had had Charlie dust to a suitable turn. Playing the good hostess, she accepted a very watered-down whisky from Preacher. The mountain man and the Dragoon officer took theirs straight and tall.

"Are we far from where you are going?" Eve asked to make conversation.

"Only a week or so, give or take a few days," Preacher responded, distinctly uncomfortable after the ragging given him by his companions.

"I must admit, I am grown quite weary of living in a

wagon. What will it be like going on to the Oregon Country?"

Edward Dreiling smiled weakly at Eve Billings. "I'm afraid I can't help you there. Army travel is quite different."

"As I have observed," Eve answered, then added to soften the snippy sound of her words, "Riding free and easy on a horse, living in a tent. It seems so . . . romantic."

"Believe me, Miss Eve, it is far from that," Dreiling felt compelled to advise her. "Even for us, accustomed to going on horseback, it took a week after leaving the steam packets to rid ourselves of saddle sores."

Eve's light laugh rang musically. "My, sir, the image that presents. Should I be scandalized?" she asked rhetorically. "No, I think not."

As the evening progressed, Eve flirted with them both outrageously. She secretly wanted to strike sparks of jealousy from Preacher. To all outward appearances, her plan failed miserably. Preacher was charming and gracious, and entertained all present with tall tales of his trapping years. When the time came to end the gathering, Charlie asked permission to accompany Preacher to his fireside.

Once the boy had the mountain man out of earshot of his mother's wagon, he crooked an index finger to draw Preacher down to his level. Preacher hunkered down. Then Charlie spoke earnestly, in a low whisper.

"You'd best look out, Preacher. My mom's tryin' to kindle the fires of romance in your heart. I know so, 'cause I heard her tellin' Mizus Honeycutt."

A low chuckle came from Preacher's throat. "Why, shucks, son, I know that. Women have been hatchin' such schemes since the first Eve kissed a snake."

Charlie widened his eyes in shocked indignation. "But, don't you just hate it? How can you abide a woman who'd sneak about and plot behind yer back?"

"No problem at all. Truth is I sorta hanker after the affection of a pretty woman now and again. That ain't all that bad, is it?"

Hesitant, Charlie studied his toes. Given his age, his first response was predictable. "Girls ain't good for anything." He paused, considered a moment. "No . . . I guess not," he replied. "If—if you don't mind."

"How about you, son? Would you object to my bein' around your momma somewhat?"

Feet forgotten, Charlie glanced up with a bright, happy expression. "Oh, no, sir. Not at all. I'd like to have you around more."

"Well, then, don't let all of it fret you. Ol' Preacher can manage for himself right enough. Now, good night."

Early the next morning, the Dragoons prepared to move on. The wails of the mourning Arapaho women, those few who were left, trembled in the air. Tight-faced, Three Crows Walking and five braves, one slightly wounded, came to Preacher.

"If you would have us, we would come with you, help to scout. Maybe we find the ones who did this."

Preacher hid his smile behind a pensive pose, hand over his mouth. "Now, I don't know about that. You'd have to provide eats for yerselves. Army won't feed you. Won't pay you, either. But, I might find a few coppers, some silver you can rub together when this is over."

Comprehension brightened the face of Three Crows Walking. "You would pay us? White man's wampum?"

"You do a good job, I sure will."

Three Crows Walking explained to his fellow Arapaho and they all produced expressions of eager approval. With that settled, they mounted the ponies they had managed to save and fanned out ahead of the column which was forming. They rode out of sight to the northwest.

Preacher gave them half an hour, then he and his

companions mounted, ready to set off. But not before Lieutenant Colonel Danvers had his say. "Mr. Preacher, I trust you have made it entirely clear to the immigrants that the same fate as befell these peaceful Arapaho will be theirs if they fail to keep up?"

Preacher could not keep his disregard for Danvers out of his expression. "They've got eyes. I didn't need to put it quite that way. They'll keep up, be sure of that."

For all his assurances, by nine o'clock in the morning, a considerable gap had developed between the Army freight wagons and the civilian train. Something about the specter of the Arapaho village must have influenced Isaac Warner. He became more aggressive in setting the pace for the cumbersome vehicles. Constantly, he urged greater speed. At times his shouts to his mules could be heard far ahead by Preacher, in the stillness of the high plains.

By the nooning, it took only ten minutes for the pilgrim train to catch up to the Dragoons. After stretching their legs and working the kinks from their backs, the civilians ate in the shade of the Conestogas and drank water to wash down the food. Warner actually had his charges ready to depart before the soldiers had completed their meal.

To Preacher's surprise and satisfaction, he calculated they had made fifteen miles. shortly after Preacher and Antoine Revier took their places ahead of the column, which had gotten under way without complaint or delay, a faint ripple of gunfire came from the rear. Preacher had a sinking sensation that it was not hunters out to bag fresh game for the evening meal. His suspicion was verified shortly when a messenger came pounding up from the head of the column.

"The Blackfoot. They've come back."

17

Warriors of the Iron Shield Society raced their ponies along the high-sided wagons of the immigrants. Fired with confidence by the medicine of Iron Shirt, they abandoned any of their usual caution. It came as a total surprise to two of them when young Davey Honeycutt leveled his side by side, 10-gauge Greener and pumped thirty 00 buckshot pellets into them.

Instant fire erupted in the lungs and belly of the first Indian Davey shot. Shock-borne blackness swept over him and he slumped forward onto the neck of his churning pony. The right side of his chest and face shredded, his jaw hanging from a single hinge, the other Blackfoot flew off his mount when Davey loosed his second load.

Ahead of the Honeycutt wagon, rifles began to crackle as the well-armed Blackfoot poured a stream of lead into the stout vehicles of the immigrants. After several con- fused minutes, it appeared the hostiles would buy an inexpensive victory. Eve Billings had been caught up in the middle of the fighting. Huddled low behind the three-inch-thick oak sideboards of the Conestoga, she made good use of the Model 40 Bridesburg Arsenal rifle and a shotgun. Hunkered beside her, Charlie industriously reloaded and handed the weapons to his mother as she fired at the Indians.

"Faster, Charlie, there's a whole lot of them out there."

"Sure, Mom, I know that." He paused in the act of ramming a ball home in the Model 40 as a warrior leaped at the open front of their wagon.

Swiftly, Charlie snatched up his .36-caliber squirrel rifle and popped a cap on the invader. A small, black hole appeared in the left side of the Blackfoot's chest and his grip on the dashboard relaxed. Screaming, he fell under the steel-tired wheel on the right front.

"Oh, sweet Jesus, Mom, I shot him," Charlie wailed. Eve didn't consider this the time for commiseration. "Good boy."

Control came out of the confusion as Preacher and his companions, accompanied by Captain Dreiling and some of his company, turned back and fell on the Blackfoot. The hostiles saw them coming and those in the lead on both sides of the column reined in sharply. Several fired at the soldiers, while others reared their mounts and turned about. Few cared to run the gauntlet of the settlers again, yet the prospect of clashing with the soldiers held even less appeal. Preacher quickly pointed out their apparent milling confusion and hesitation.

"We got 'em bottled up betwixt us," he shouted to Captain Dreiling.

"Looks like it. I only hope those amateurs know enough to shoot at the Indians and not us."

Preacher quickly allayed his concern. "We'll be pushin' the Blackfoot hard. Likely those pilgrims won't have time to shoot at anyone."

Within a breath's span, the mountain man and those with him clashed directly with the hesitant Blackfoot. Their faltering ceased abruptly when face-to-face with the white troopers. Unable to reload, the Blackfoot soon discovered themselves to be at a terrible disadvantage. Armed with a dozen immediate shots each from the big

Dragoon pistols, the soldiers blazed into the faces of the enemy. Preacher, too, unlimbered his Walker Colt and fired point-blank into the eagle wing-bone breastplate of a screaming warrior.

Another came at him, screaming defiance, tomahawk raised. Preacher turned to meet the threat.

Short Tail and three others took the brunt of the Dragoon charge on the opposite side from Preacher. Led by Three Sleeps Norris and Antoine Revier, the soldiers under the command of Lieutenant Brice swept along the rear of the Army column and caught the Blackfoot by surprise. Short Tail made to swing away, only to find his way blocked by a grinning man in buckskin.

"Gonna run out on yer friends, eh?' Three Sleeps asked Short Tail in incomprehensible words.

"May your mother's Entrance to the World, through which you came, rot and fall off," Short Tail cursed back in Blackfoot.

Three Sleeps knew only enough Blackfoot to catch the drift of the insult. "I love you, too, you horse's patootie." Then he shot the tomahawk wielder through the breastbone.

An expression of consternation and disbelief washed over the warrior's face. How could this be? He is a white man, his bullets can do no harm. A moment later Short Tail learned that the truth ran radically contrary to his belief.

Three Sleeps sidestepped his mount as the Blackfoot fell dead at the side of his pony. He turned in the saddle and triggered off the second barrel of his pistol. The big, .60-caliber ball shattered another brave's shoulder joint, rendered his left arm useless and sent his pony in a frightened sideways dance ending in a frantic dash away from the sounds and smells of battle.

Two Moons witnessed the swift, sure deaths of eight of

his warriors. Quickly the number of wounded mounted to thirteen, with another two dead. He could not believe that this could be happening. What of Iron Shirt's medicine? Had the shaman lied to them, deceived them as to how much power his rituals, dances and dunkings in the river contained? In a tortured half minute, fanatic belief changed to repudiation. Hooting the recall signal, Two Moons rallied his warriors and led the way from the sure and certain death that prowled among them at the hands of the bluecoats and their plainsfolk allies.

Charlie Billings stood on the outside edge of the night camp, legs widespread, body bent forward and down. His stomach cramped, lurched and shot forth another spew of bitter, slimy liquid. Tears of shame and misery coursed down his face. The misery came from his appalling sorrow over having taken a human life. The shame came from his reaction to what he had done.

He had actually killed one Blackfoot, shot him right through the heart. He had wounded two others; one of them had spewed blood from his mouth as he fell away from the wagon.

God, this is awful! Whimpering like a sissy, Charlie thought desperately. How could he ever face himself, or anyone else, again? He tensed as he heard the rustle of a footfall in the leaves behind him.

"Takin' it hard, are you, son?" The warm, gentle voice of Preacher flowed over the boy who fought to hold back a sob of relief.

Misery returned in an instant. "Don't look at me."

"Why not, Charlie? D'you think you're the first and only man who's been upset by killin' someone?"

Preacher's praise—he had called Charlie a *man*—was unmarked by the boy. "Yeah, but, I'll look like a sissy to everyone, *especially you.*"

"'Yeah, but,'"—Preacher put the words back on the

boy—"do you think I didn't puke my guts out the first time I killed a man? An' I was four years older than you."

Amazement arrested Charlie's anguish for a moment, "You did? You were?"

Preacher took a slow step forward, reached down and put an arm around the boy's shoulders. Gently, he raised him to an upright position. "Yes. You might not believe it to see me now, but I went through everything you're experiencing. Trust me, it's never an easy thing. You saved your mother's life, and your sister's. You should stand tall Charlie, be proud. Yer a man now."

Charlie blinked his dark eyes. "I am? I mean . . . I am. I really am. I . . . I . . . ah . . . thank you, Preacher. I was so scared. I wanted to throw up all the time we were fighting. I wanted to run away and never hear a gun go off again."

"That's natural."

"But I . . . thought there wasn't that much difference between killing an animal or a man. That it would be easy."

Preacher patted him affectionately. "You had best thank yer God it wasn't easy for you. Those what find it like snappin' their fingers are plum crazy. They're bound to meet a bad end."

"Really?"

"Yeah. I oughtta know. I've brung more of 'em to that bad end than I care to count. Now, come on, yer maw has supper ready."

After the meal, Eve confided in Preacher. "That was the worst thing that's ever happened to us. Those . . . those Indians didn't seem to care. They kept coming, no matter how many of us shot at them."

"They believe themselves to be bulletproof. It's some crazy, Injun medicine thing," he dismissed the fanaticism of the followers of the Blackfoot messiah.

"Please, don't misunderstand, Preacher. It's not that I fear for myself. It's only . . . only if some harm came to my children I could not bear that. I've heard the stories. H-How the savages use children in horrid practices. They have their way with girls as young as seven. Anna is eight. Some, I've been told, even use boys in the same manner."

Keyed to the intensity of her emotion, Preacher could still not refrain from being truthful. "I've never seen or heard of such-like happening to the younger children. An' it's only a few tribes practice such vile things. Mostly, the younger ones, like Charlie and Anna, are used as slaves, or to take the place of a child who has died for one reason or another. Especial if the kids show some spirit. Why, the way Charlie fought off those warriors, he'd be a prize to them Blackfoot. One of them would adopt him, certain sure, an' have him in a loincloth and moccasins, with a pony of his own, an' his hair in a braid in no time."

That prospect registered more horror on the face of Eve Billings than the possibility of abuse and eventual murder. Quickly, she put her emotions into words. "What a terrible fate! How could he possibly endure such a miserable life?"

He'd take to it like ducks to water, Preacher wanted to tell her, but refrained from doing so. "You gotta understand, men are kings amongst the Injuns, even when they're little kids. Most boys who are captured don't want to give it up when they've got the chance. They have ponies of their own, which makes for how rich a body is among the savages, and they learn to use a bow, set snares, all sorts of things civilized folk have forgotten how to do."

In a sudden shift of mood, Eve nervously tittered, then spoke. "That's not exactly reassuring, Preacher. You've described my Charlie exactly."

Preacher showed surprise; then his lips turned down. "Well, I was only tryin' to show you that somethin' else could be at hand in such an event."

"And bless you for it. It's only . . . only that I—I'm so frightened for my children."

Although he still did not fully understand, Preacher recognized her position and acted with alacrity. When tears brimmed in her eyes, he took her protectively into his arms to calm her trembling. Eve let go then. She stifled harsh sobs against his broad shoulder. Unconsciously, she pressed her body tightly against his.

Awkwardly, Preacher stroked her long, auburn hair, circled her trim waist with a strong, reassuring arm. Instead of tensing, as did so many women in the arms of a powerful man, Eve melted into his chest. Slowly her sobs diminished, grew less violent, to finally cease. She gasped for air and fought inwardly to regain composure.

Her eyes still shone from the recently shed tears when she tilted her head upward to gaze into Preacher's eyes, alight with concern. At a loss for words of appreciation, Eve rose on tiptoe and placed her lips on those of Preacher. It started out as an expression of gratitude, then quickly changed into a long, hungry kiss that sent tendrils of fire through both of them.

When it ended, both were breathless. Eve said not a word, only freed herself from Preacher's embrace and hurried into her wagon. His lips tingling, Preacher walked off to his blankets, thoroughly confused. That had been the best kiss he had shared in . . . what? Maybe ten years? Yeah, that was it. There had been that Cheyenne gal . . .

Camped alone for the first time in six months, Praeger, Gross and Reiker experienced an overpowering sense of relief and safety. They paid little attention to the splendor of the Bighorn Mountains. What commanded their concentration glowed dully in the light of a coaloil lantern. Its main attraction centered on size. Fully as large as the third knuckle of Praeger's middle finger, the gold nugget lay on a square of black velvet that perfectly set off its splendor. Praeger reached out and caressed its smooth, warm surface. Then he nodded to the chunk of gold.

"It weighs a bit over six ounces."

Avarice glowed in the eyes of Morton Gross as he spoke. "Where did it come from?"

"The area I told you about before. It came out of the Lolo Range of the Rocky Mountains, near the Continental Divide. There are more like this, lots more," Praeger assured his partners.

A sudden rustle at the tent flap drew their attention and Quinton Praeger quickly concealed the nugget. Blake Soures, dressed in Blackfoot garb, entered. "The men are ready to ride out, Mr. Praeger."

"Where this time?"

"There's a clutch of Psalm Shouters nestled down to the east of here. Near the headwaters of the Tongue River. I figgered we ought to pay 'em a visit. We'll leave enough living behind to swear it was Blackfoot who did it."

Praeger beamed and came to his boots to shake the hand of Soures. "Excellent. Be sure that no one knows you are white men. That could be a disaster."

Brother Frankel could not sleep. He sat alone by the dying embers of the central fire in the circle of wagons. Behind him, the mules and horses of their wagon train milled about in drowsy stubbornness. None wanted to lie down and sleep. Like himself, the good brother thought.

Not a man familiar with the ways of horses, Brother Frankel failed to note when the animals became silent at the soft whuffle and stamp of hoof from the most dominant beast. Two more laid back ears and stomped the ground in warning. Still it went unnoticed by him.

Reacting as though to an invisible pressure from beyond the circle, the livestock began to move inward. They exerted increasing pressure on the single strand of rope that restrained them.

At last, Brother Frankel looked up, affected by the unrest that emanated from the usually placid creatures. A yellow-orange streak suddenly arced through the blackness of night. A shooting star, Brother Frankel thought at first. While he was in the process of eliminating that due to its closeness to the ground, three more arcs of fire fluttered through the air. Two struck a wagon's side and the canvas top burst into flame. Jerkily, Brother Frankel came to his boots. Throat churning, he fought to get out the words.

"Indians! We're under attack. God protect us."

For two long minutes nothing happened. Brother Frankel continued to cry the alarm, though with little response. Then six burning brands shot through the night and struck two wagons. Shouts of alarm came from the three burning Conestogas. From beyond the crude stockade came raw yelps—war cries—followed by a steady stream of war paint-decorated savages who flowed into the unprotected center. One, armed with a rifle, took time to aim and fire a bullet at Brother Frankel. It pierced his skin low in the belly. He went down with a shriek of incredible agony.

By then, his fellow evangelists had roused from the stupor of sleep. Yelling in fright, the men and women poured from their rolling homes to spill onto the ground. There they cowered in the dirt, quaking in absolute terror. They died that way, cut down by arrow, tomahawk or bullet. Screaming children, the younger ones, peered out over tail gates to have their brains dashed out by war clubs and already bloody 'hawks.

Only at one point did some resistance show. The train captain, scouts and cook took up firearms and fought a desperate, no-win engagement. By the light of burning wagons they clearly saw their enemy. The attackers looked to be Blackfoot, the experienced frontiersmen agreed. Three of the savages died in less than a minute after the trained men returned fire.

"Stupid goddamned fools, I told them they needed guns out here," the captain spat out in useless anger.

"Lot of good that would do," the cook retorted. "Chances are, they'd try to pray these heathen scum into peacefulness." He took careful aim with a Hawken and shot another Blackfoot off his feet.

"Ain't no prayin' gonna get us out of this," a surly guide scoffed.

More howling Blackfoot shoved into the melee. The horses and mules had broken free and added another hazard to the confused struggles of the nonviolent missionaries. It did not take the invaders long to subdue the wagon folk. The slaughter was fierce and methodical. When it ended, the only evangelists left standing consisted of the nubile girls, those newly ripe, and those not long in that state. Under the rough direction of one big, burly savage, they were herded aside.

Once the livestock had been gathered and corralled again, the raping began. The screams and wails, sobs and moans of the young victims filled the night, bearing witness to the unending horror of the brutalized girls. Unnoticed, one of the guides, the cook and the captain slipped away into the night while the raiders wallowed in their lust. One of the rapists, who would be heard by no one in the attacked party who would be left alive, commented on the object of his bestial attention.

"Mighty sweet. I sure do thank you, Blake, for lettin' me be first to pleasure myself with this one."

"Think nothing of it," Soures responded. "You did a good job, you deserve a reward."

When the gang of murderous whites had expended

their churning appetites, they fired all the remaining wagons, took the livestock and rode off. Blake Soures made certain that ample items of Blackfoot manufacture remained to be discovered by those who found the remains of the unfortunate missionaries.

18

Lieutenant Colonel Danvers counseled with Preacher and the mountain men at noon the next day. "We are to turn northward after our mid-day meal and head for the Powder River. Our objective, as I have explained before, is where the Powder cuts through the lower foothills of the Bighorn Mountains."

One long, soft, artist's finger pointed to a spot on the crude map. "Right here. There's supposed to be an ideal bluff on which to build the fort."

Preacher knew the country well. He studied the indicated location, gave it several moments' thought, then shook his head. "Nope. I wouldn't recommend it. Trees are scarce in those parts."

"Why, I've been assured the trees grow right down onto the bluff."

"May well be true. But, after you build your fort, you'd be required to go outside every day or so for firewood. An' another thing. From what this map shows, that bluff is exposed to higher ground on all but one side. Well, one side, an' part of a second. A feller could fire right down into the fort. Won't matter much for a while. Only consider this: what happens when the Cheyenne get their hands on some of those new rifles like we took off the Blackfoot t'other day?"

Danvers raised his voice. "That is not your concern. Your job is to see we get there."

"True. Only pointin' out some things. Like for instance, unless you don't want to dig a well down sev'ral hundred feet, you'd have to take the livestock out daily to water at this little creek that feeds into the Powder, an' haul more water to have some for people."

"That's nonsense. You don't know what you're talking about. I've been given assurances from the United States Survey Office, backed up by the highest authority. They have assured me there is ample wood for lumber—and for cooking and heating—lush grass and easy access to water."

Preacher agreed readily. "Sure, so long as you don't rile the Injuns. That's Cheyenne country, an' the land of their cousins the Sioux. Now, they don't look on owning land the same way we do, but they're mighty territorial jist the same. An' I ain't even mentioned the Crow and Blackfoot."

Danvers loftily dismissed that argument. "Savages are savages. We will be prepared to take them in stride. Let it suffice that this is the location chosen at the War Department, and it is where we will build."

All through the next day, Preacher and his companions found plentiful Indian sign. It took little time to come to the obvious conclusion. They were being watched. Three Crows Walking returned to the column to report the same.

"What do we do now?" the Arapaho war chief asked.

Preacher had an answer ready. "Make real certain of every lump you see on the ground. Some of them might breathe." Three Crows nodded knowingly. "Also, I'd have my weapons at hand ever' minute. Never can tell."

"My thoughts exactly. We already keep watch on dust clouds in the sky."

Preacher reached over and clapped the Arapaho on the upper arm. "Good man, Three Crows. With you as our eyes out front, we don't need to worry."

For the rest of the afternoon Preacher rode along in higher spirits, though not oblivious to the plentiful sign of a Blackfoot presence. After camp had been made for the night, he walked away from the bustle of soldiers and pilgrims to find a little solitude for himself. He had only pulled a twisted, black, dry-cured cigar from the pocket of his buckskin shirt when he looked up and spotted three Cheyenne warriors on horseback. Silhouetted against the ruddy ball of the setting sun, they sat at ease, one bent forward with a hand on his bare knee. Preacher's eyes narrowed as he studied them.

Each wore two feathers at the back of his head, the frizzed and fox fur-trimmed tips pointed upward, a sure sign of being on the war trail. Slight motions of the watching Indians revealed that they both carried lances. Preacher jerked his gaze away from the Cheyenne at the sound of a footfall behind him. He turned cat-quick, with a hand on the butt of a Walker Colt.

Little Charlie Billings stood there, eyes wide with shock at the swift movement of Preacher. He swallowed hard and rubbed a bare foot against his overalls leg. "It's only me," he squeaked.

"Sorry, Charlie. Somethin' out there spooked me."

For the first time, the boy looked beyond Preacher. His eyes went round and white, and his jaw clapped shut. Before he could speak, he had to swallow hard.

"Are those Injuns Blackfoot?"

"Nope, Charlie. They's Cheyenne. An' done up for war. No reason to keep the truth from you. Yer man enough to handle it, an' I trust, man enough not to spread alarm amongst the rest of you pilgrims."

Charlie nodded solemnly. "Yes, sir."

Preacher clapped the boy roughly on the shoulder, nearly dislodging Charlie from his feet. "Good. You do me proud." No one who observed them, except his mountain man cronies, would have suspected how much discomfort Preacher experienced relating to small children. "Now, Charlie, what did you come out here for?"

"Mom told me to ask you to come to supper tonight." Charlie looked unhappy. "But now, with those Injuns out there, I don't suppose you can."

The prospect of a good meal, and good-looking companionship, pleased Preacher. "I don't see why not. Only, if I were you, Charlie, I'd sleep with your shotgun beside you tonight."

Dressed in white men's suits, Quinton Praeger, Morton Gross and Aaron Reiker sashayed into the most elegant saloon that graced a large, prosperous trading post on the south fork of the Powder River. All three paid token deference to current custom with the wide, brightly colored sashes around their middles. That the red one worn by Praeger, the green cloth strip on Gross, and the electric blue chosen by Reiker concealed at least one pistol each was a given. Several roughly dressed individuals at the bar gave them cold, inhospitable stares as they took a table to one side.

"Friendly sort, aren't they?" Morton Gross observed fastidiously. "Two months back they fell all over us, offering to buy the drinks."

Praeger shrugged. "We were dressed like they are then. I doubt if they recognize us, let alone remember how hard they tried to be hired on to work with Soures."

Reiker sighed. "We had us some times then, didn't we?"

A huge man with greasy, long, black, curly hair and a matching mustache pushed himself away from the bar and turned in their direction. He had thick, rubbery lips that shone wetly and made it obvious he had been drinking heavily. Waving a huge, ham hand, he encompassed the well-dressed trio.

"Hey, fancy-boys, this here's a man's bar. They call me Dandy Spencer, an' I want you to know we don't allow no prissy Eastern folk to come in and spoil the at—atmos . . ."

"Try *atmosphere*, my good man," Praeger suggested.

Spencer's face flushed dark red. "I ain't your 'good man,' nor any other's. I'm my own man and proud of it. Talk like that could get yer head busted out here."

"Are you challenging me, Mr. Spencer?" Praeger asked, his voice suddenly cold and menacing, although the tone went unnoticed by the bully.

Dandy Spencer rose on tiptoe and began to rock back and forth. "You goddamn' right."

"Well, then, since I'm the challenged one, I have choice of weapon, time and place, right?"

A puzzled frown creased the bull head of Dandy Spencer. "That's a mighty useless way to go about it, ya ask me. Around these parts, we jist open the dance and set to clawin'. You ain't got sand for that, turn tail and light out of here."

Quinton Praeger maintained an air of amiable civility. "Oh, I can understand the faint customs of such drunken louts as yourself without explanation, Mr. Spencer. My point is that I wish to make clear the terms of our duel."

"D-Duel? What duel?"

"Why, the one you challenged me to," Praeger tossed out lightly. The whitish cast in his right eye gave him a piratical mien.

Dandy could only splutter. "I didn't challenge you to a duel. I said I wanted to rip your sissy head off."

"Good enough. Same thing. You want to fight with me, I have agreed. Thus, the choice of weapons, place and time are mine. It's only fair."

Insulted, Dandy Spencer set things straight. "Ain't never fought fair in my life."

Praeger appeared unfazed. By far the toughest of the three partners, one more than willing to kill when necessary, the cold glint in his eyes betrayed to all but the dullest, which included Dandy Spencer, the hidden strength he possessed. "I can believe that. You want a fight, I accept. Now, I pick how we fight and when. I see you have a pistol, so I choose pistols. And for the time and place; right here and now!"

With which, Quinton Praeger snatched a short-barrel, fifty-caliber pocket pistol—made by Deringer and Sons in Philadelphia—from inside his sash, cocked it and put a ball into the right elbow joint of Dandy Spencer. Dandy, whom fate had decreed to be left-handed, completed his draw in spite of the pain that flared up his opposite arm. Gritting his teeth, he swung the muzzle in the direction of Praeger and triggered a round.

His ball went wide. Quinton Praeger let his empty pistol drop to the tabletop and whipped out a second deadly Deringer. This ball he put between two ribs, low on the left side of the chest of Dandy Spencer. A stentorian roar came from the huge man, who absorbed the fatal shot with all the outward sign of having been bitten by a mosquito. His coach gun hit the floor and Dandy groped for another one.

"This one's a bit hard to finish," said Praeger in an aside to his companions. By then, they had come to their boots and drawn pistols to cover the rest of the room. Praeger took a third pistol from partway around the sash and brought up the barrel.

By then, the message sent by his body reached the tiny brain of Dandy Spencer and informed him that he was dead. Shot through the heart, he went slack-legged and flopped forward over the table occupied by the conspirators. Praeger returned the pistol to its proper place and hailed the bartender. "I say, we need someone to remove this trash. And I'll stand a round for the house."

"Yes, sir, anything you say, sir."

Dawn found everything safe and sound. The Cheyenne did not attack. Accordingly, the column set out again on what could best be described as an uneventful journey. So confident had Lieutenant Colonel Danvers become that he urged Preacher to ride at his side. Preacher found that not at all a pleasant prospect. While they rode along, Danvers waxed almost eloquent. Waving a gloved hand at the fluttering grass on the uptilted prairie slope, he drew a deep breath and launched into his theme.

"Those Cheyenne did not attack us, as you can now see. They sat quietly and watched us, without any show of hostile intent. Perhaps they were curious. With their childlike minds, that could be expected."

Knowing it to be rude, and not giving a damn, Preacher interrupted. "Them 'childlike minds,' you refer to have planned and carried off some of the slickest ambushes you'll ever see. As to their 'hostile intent,' Colonel, them braves had their feathers upright. Those feathers are symbols of their valor. They're fixed in a beaded disc, and are worn in different directions for different reasons. Down, toward their left shoulder, means they're lookin' for no trouble. Down, to the right, says they're lookin' to do some courtin'. Up, like they had 'em, means they're ready for war.

"The biggest mistake most whites make about Injuns is that since they live different from us they ain't got any smarts." Preacher cocked his head to one side. "Never fall into that pit, Colonel. It could be the death of you."

Danvers had a pensive look. Albeit he spoke stiffly, his tone lacked the icy sarcasm of earlier exchanges. "Believe me, I've learned that lesson already. I still can't find a reason why the Pawnee were so hotheaded."

Preacher sighed. To him it was entirely obvious. "Because the Blackfoot and Cheyenne are worked up. There's war talk—and raids all over the high plains. For all their lack of modern communication, word gets around the tribes mighty fast."

Danvers retreated to his orders for inspiration. "Our purpose in being here is to induce a calming effect."

Preacher shook his head. "Seems to me we're doin' jist the opposite." For a long time, he could not fathom the meaning behind the enigmatic smile with which Danvers answered him.

In the short term, Preacher soon found himself with a lot more to occupy him. By midmorning, the column had made ten miles, a new record since adopting the abandoned wagon train. It had been accomplished with no end of grumbling by the pilgrims. When Gus Beecher cantered up to the head of the column for the third time, Preacher knew he was in for more.

"Blast and damn, this pace is killing my mules," the burly blacksmith complained. "You have to slow down."

The colonel would not deign to address whining civilians. Instead he cut his eyes to Preacher in a silent order to the mountain man to handle the situation. Preacher sighed and made reply.

"We don't have to do anything of the sort. I can't see a reason to have to explain this again, but here goes. This is a military expedition. It is under orders to git along the trail at the convenience of the Dragoon Battalion Commander. That be Colonel Danvers here. He says we gotta make better time, we make better time. You may not like it, I may not like it. But we ain't got any say in it. I told you before, Mr. Beecher, to get rid of some of that heavy load yerself or do it at gunpoint. If I was you, I'd hightail it back to that wagon and start heavin' heavy things out as you go."

"You can't do this to me. I—I'll protest."

Finally, Danvers bestirred himself to partake in the exchange. "To whom?"

"Wh-why to the War Department."

"Go right ahead," Danvers challenged in a brittle tone. "I estimate the next post will run through here in about fifty years."

Gus Beecher muttered that he would hold a meeting, circulate a petition. Lieutenant Colonel Danvers put on a nasty smile. "Oh, you do that, Mr. Beecher. I *love* to read petitions."

Instantly deflated, Beecher uttered a muffled curse and turned away. He had ridden halfway down the column when, suddenly, a force of over a hundred Blackfoot braves in war paint rushed down on the cavalcade from one side and the rear. Women and children, out gleaning deadfall firewood along the way, dropped their bundles and ran, screaming in terror. Rifles cracked among the Indians and a slight-built boy of twelve went sprawling. At once a shrill howl of anguish came from the rear of a wagon.

"My boy! They've killed my Jimmy."

An arrow thudded into the tail gate in direct line with her body and she was violently thrust back out of sight. Nearly every Indian had a rifle, which they fired at once, with much enthusiasm, albeit little accuracy.

19

Whooping and howling, the Blackfoot rode just inside range and loosed a flight of arrows. Commands had been shouted up and down the files of Dragoons and the troops immediately responded with a furious volley.

"Reload!" More order came to the troops as their unseasoned officers gained control. "Volley by Companies! . . . Company A, take aim . . . fire! Reload. Company B, take aim . . . fire!"

So it went, down the line of the four companies. Forty rifles crackling in answer. Then, yipping, the Blackfoot rode away. A final volley raced after them. A dozen rifles fired a parting shot from the rear of the column and the Indians departed. Silence returned to the cavalcade, except for the sobbing of the woman whose son had been killed.

Their respite lasted only a short while. The hostiles swarmed down on their white enemy once more. This time the discipline drilled into them by Iron Shirt and his closest followers dissolved when six warriors toppled from their saddles. Hooting and shrieking war cries, the braves turned their charge into a scramble for individual honors.

It became a pigeon shoot for even the most inept

Dragoons, a source of deep disillusionment for the Blackfoot as one after another of the braves fell dead from their ponies. Time enough had gone by to calm troops and civilians alike. They now brought withering fire on the hostiles. Preacher took time, while reloading, to pose a question to Danvers.

"Might be none o' my business, but I wonder why you didn't put out flankers today."

For an instant, the colonel stiffened; then he forced geniality into his voice. "You're right, it's none of your business. The truth is, I grew overconfident. Are these some of your friendly Cheyenne?"

"Nope. Blackfoot, though I'm damned if I can come up with a reason for them to be so far east. Unless . . . that prophet of theirs got them all riled up and is out smokin' the war trail."

Danvers spoke darkly, as though privy to some secret. "That had better not be the case."

Dangerously close to the wagons, within twenty-five yards, the Blackfoot lost their nerve at last. They scattered up a red-orange slope, so many coppery leaves in a whirlwind. Bullets followed them, though only Preacher's, his companions', and BSM Muldoon's scored in flesh. Not to be daunted, Danvers issued fateful orders.

"First and Second Platoon, C Company, pursue the enemy. Lieutenant Brice in command. Move 'em out!"

"I woul—" Preacher made to dissuade the Dragoon commander, then cut off his words at sight of the wild light in the colonel's eyes. Stubborn man, Preacher thought, let him learn the hard way.

With a full platoon at left and right, Lieutenant Brice led the charge from the middle. The big, powerful Dragoon horses churned up the rise and hesitated only a fraction of a second before plunging down the reverse slope. They had barely gone out of sight when all hell broke loose.

Preacher did not wait for the realization to come

over Danvers. Driving heels in the ribs of Tarnation, he shouted to Captain Dreiling. "Come on, Cap'n, bring the rest of yer company. Let's go get your men back."

With Danvers sputtering alone at the head of the column, the entire Dragoon battalion broke ranks and charged over the rise. In the lead, Preacher took encouragement from the continued crackling exchange. It had to be a small ambush to keep the troops alive so long. The big-chested, Morgan-cross, Tarnation, ate ground at a dazzling pace.

Preacher and the two remaining platoons of C Company slammed into the surprised Blackfoot war party before the Indians could react. The thunderous crash of Hall carbines drowned out their shrill war cries. To Preacher's right a Blackfoot swung around and fired his rifle one-handed. For all his lack of accuracy, the ball moaned past Preacher's head close enough for the mountain man to feel its wind. Preacher rode low now, the reins in his teeth, and the Hawken bucked in his grip. His shot hit the Blackfoot high in the chest, on the center line. Knocked to one side, the warrior disappeared under the hooves of his companions' horses.

With the Hawken dry, Preacher shoved it into the scabbard and pivoted at the waist to find another target. Plenty presented themselves. The Walker Colt spat lead and creased ribs on a youthful Blackfoot not yet out of his teens. Bone and meat flew in a welter of blood, and Preacher reckoned that the man-child would have a fist-sized depression on that side for the rest of his life. Preacher cocked the hammer as another Blackfoot swung his empty rifle at the head of the mountain man.

Powder smoke obscured the scene, so Preacher could not see the results of his hasty shot. The rifle butt did not meet his chin, so he rightly assumed he'd scored a good hit. Suddenly, the remaining Indians swung away from the onslaught of so many soldiers and rode swiftly out of range. Preacher took quick count.

Six Indian bodies littered the ground, and only one soldier had been killed. Seven had suffered minor wounds, though. Lieutenant Brice, his youthful face begrimed by greasy powder residue, dismounted and surveyed the scene. Then, Danvers cantered up, his saber drawn, and glowered at Preacher and Captain Dreiling.

"I demand to know who ordered that charge."

Dreiling cut his eyes to Preacher, who winked at him. "I do not know, sir. I did not. It . . . sort of . . . just happened."

Danvers surveyed the scene. "We'll not go after them. Mr. Preacher, your point about ambushes is noted and stored for reference." He turned to the Battalion Sergeant Major. "Sergeant Major Muldoon, return the men to the column."

Talking Cloud was decidedly unhappy. The medicine of Iron Shirt had deserted them. Of the number of warriors with which he had started—one hundred and seventeen—he had five hands killed and seven hands wounded. He directed the survivors to the big war camp to the west. There he went directly to Three Horses who listened to his complaints with obvious indifference. It only served to inflame Talking Cloud more.

"How could Iron Shirt's medicine have failed us?" Talking Cloud demanded hotly.

"They did not believe enough in the medicine, or they would be alive," Three Horses concluded about the dead. "Or they were not purified enough."

"You did not hear me. Twenty-five men killed, thirty-five wounded. Not that many could be impure or doubtful at the same time. That means we will not be able to guard our village from the Shoshoni this winter."

"Then take your people to the Bighorn Mountains."

Not satisfied in the least with this, Talking Cloud went in search of Iron Shirt. He found the visionary medicine man in the process of initiating a group of twenty-five Cheyenne. Talking Cloud viewed the proceedings with far less conviction than before. When the rite had been concluded and the mail shirt exposed, Talking Cloud took Iron Shirt aside. He wasted no time on diplomacy.

"Why is it that your rebirth in water and the gauntlet of coals did not purify the warriors killed so far?"

Iron Shirt cocked his head to one side, to show his disbelief. "You have had men die?" he asked in a chiding tone.

"Twenty-five," Talking Cloud shouted. "In one battle. They went down like aspen in a whirlwind."

Iron Shirt nodded thoughtfully, then gave Talking Cloud essentially the same answer Three Horses had given. After so doing, he suggested, "I think another Strong Heart ceremony is needed." He took on a cheerful expression. "Gather your men and we can do it while the coals are still hot. Then you will see."

That evening, when the nervousness and strain of the attack had eased, Eve Billings sought out Preacher, who sat with his companions, a plate of fatback and beans in his hands. She looked at the concoction with unease and forced a smile.

"You didn't come to supper tonight. I know Charlie relayed my invitation."

"Yep. That he did. An' nope, I did not. Too much good cookin' makes a man soft." He set the tin plate aside and pinched his flat, hard abdomen. "Why, I reckon I've gained five pounds spongin' off your generosity. I thought I'd take a day or two away from the delicious table you lay, so's not to make a habit of it."

Smiling, Eve reached out a coaxing hand. "I wouldn't mind if you made a habit of it. Matter of fact, I'd like that a lot."

Preacher sighed and roused himself. He joined Eve and they ambled off toward the southern edge of the large encampment. There they found the peaceful vista of a moonlit, rolling sea of grass that stretched out before them to the south, east and west. Eve sighed languidly and took Preacher's right hand in both of hers.

"It's so tranquil out there. You'd never know those savages are lurking out in the dark."

Preacher shrugged. "I don't reckon they are. They were Blackfoot. That means they were loaded up with that hokum of Iron Shirt's. When we killed a passel of 'em, they had to think the medicine failed 'em. They get spooked at that, so it's likely they'll go off an' lick their wounds."

"I hope you're right."

They stood silently for a long while then. After the stillness grew strained, Eve started haltingly. "About the other night. The . . . kiss. It was—it was brazen of me. But . . . I—I think it was . . . wonderful."

She did a step turn and faced Preacher, her arms wide. He paused only a moment before he reached out and drew her into a firm embrace.

Iron Shirt stood before his lodge and scowled as Quinton Praeger and his two associates rode through the rings of lodges that made up this large encampment of Blackfoot, Cheyenne and some Pawnee who had left their country to the east to join in the battle against all whites. The Sioux would come to him soon. He believed that in his heart. Which intensified his displeasure at the return of these renegade white men.

"They should stay away," he confided to Bent Trees who stood beside him.

A ghost of a smile flickered on the face of Bent Trees. "We could *make* them stay away."

Iron Shirt put a restraining hand on the forearm of

Bent Trees. "The time is not right to do away with them as yet, my friend. We must get the last of the weapons they promise, the powder and balls, the caps. Without them, we cannot win."

"I heard about Talking Cloud. Will he stay after the new ritual?"

"I do not know. If not, we lose eight hands of warriors. It would weaken us."

"The Cheyenne and the Sioux?" Bent Trees made the common plains sign of a slash across the throat to signify the Lakota.

Iron Shirt nodded. "They'll come. Not all, as we had hoped. Cloud Blanket has taken his people away."

Eyebrows elevated, Bent Trees pointed out the obvious. "If Talking Cloud leaves us, then we will be too weak for the final battle."

A sudden flare of anger darkened the face of Iron Shirt. "No we will not. We will drive the whites past the Big Water river. My spirit guide tells"—a shaft of reality pierced his mind when he reminded himself of the source of his spirit wisdom—"me this is true."

Bent Trees grunted. "Would that he told me the same."

Startled by this lack of faith, Iron Shirt blurted, "You doubt my vision?"

"No—no. Only I think you should fast and visit with your spirit guide again. *We* do not know him. We have not heard him speak. Our strength, our faith, comes from you."

Iron Shirt put a hand on his friend's shoulder. "Perhaps you are right. I will think on it. First we must impress on our white friends the need for more rifles."

After another three long, satisfyingly uneventful days, Preacher guided his fledgling soldiers to the spot selected by Lieutenant Colonel Danvers. It was situated on a nice promontory overlooking a deep valley and the ringing peaks of the Bighorn Mountains. Tents went up with many joyful sounds of relief. Even in their permanent situation, Preacher noted, the civilians kept to themselves, erecting their spare wagon covers for tents. A surveying crew set up and began to layout the fort. Gus Beecher started to assemble his smithy, leaving his family shelter to his wife and daughters to prepare.

With the only direct, easy approach up a draw and along the wide, sloping finger of land that led to the site, the main gate would be there. Also the only stockade. That bothered Preacher. He left the details of their camp to Three Fingers Norris and Antoine Revier and went in search of Danvers. He found the commander with the surveyors, in shirtsleeves, gesturing with wide, emphatic swings of his arms. When Danvers completed his vehement discussion, he turned to find Preacher patiently waiting.

"Pardon me, Colonel. I figgered now was the time to remind you of a few things. You may want to put up a stockade all around this place. Look there, over my shoulder. That's a mighty high peak back there. I know it's kinda steep. Even so, hostiles could come sweepin' right down there and behind this wall. That'd trap you folks in back of your own device. Then there's the water. This spine is pure granite. I don't think you can dig a well. More likely a cistern would be the best you can do. A big pit, blasted out of the rock, an' covered over could give you a good supply of rainwater and snowmelt. But not enough for year 'round. An' for trees to make buildings and yer stockade, you can see that outside that little stand over there, the nearest are out of range of your best riflemen. They'll have no protection."

Lieutenant Colonel Danvers gave Preacher a long, cool look up and down as though inspecting a tramp discovered in his backyard. "Your job with the Army is ended, Mr. Preacher. I have these problems in mind and can handle them adequately. If you so choose, you may leave."

Preacher's eyes narrowed slightly, and he pursed his lips to keep his true feelings from being spoken. "Is that your final word on this?"

"It most certainly is. Now, if you will excuse me?"

"Well, then, b'god, I jist might pull out after all. Me an' my friends."

Danvers hastily informed Preacher, "Oh, but there is work for them if they wish to remain."

Close to loosing the iron grip on his anger, Preacher responded tightly. "I think I can answer for them. Thanks, but no thanks." With that, he stomped off.

Preacher felt duty-bound to explain his decision to Eve Billings. He went to her and stood, hat in one hand, over his heart, and informed her of his decision to leave the next day for his favored country in the Colorado Rockies. Eve's eyes went wide when she understood what his rambling phrases meant.

"Oh, but you can't," she protested. "You have helped us so much. We would never have made it without you, dear, dear Preacher."

And that was part of it, too, although a small part, Preacher told himself. He was beginning to feel entirely too fond of this wisp of a girl. No, he corrected himself, this stalwart young widow—and her children. Why, hell, he had no use for children. Even those he had sired among the Indian camps mattered not a jot to him. At least not until they grew old enough to go hunting, trapping and fishing with him. Nope, the settled life held no appeal to him. Only how to tell Eve that in a gentle way?

"Er, the colonel don't want me around anymore. He as much as told me to pack my saddlebags and haul out of here."

"You are your own man, aren't you? He is bound to

protect civilians within the range of the fort. You could . . . could join us and he would be obliged to put up with you."

"No—no, ma'am . . . er, Eve. I couldn't do that."

"And why not?" Eve spun on one heel and called loudly. "Charlie, Charlie Billings, come here at once." When the boy arrived, she gave him clear, quick instructions. "Go find Mr. Warner and Mr. Tate. Bring them here. Mr. Beecher, too. Tell them it is very important."

"Yes, ma'am," Charlie replied and scampered away.

Preacher tried to derail her juggernaut. "Now, Eve, there's no call to cause a fuss."

Eve gave him an impish, though determined, look. "It's not a fuss I'm figuring on. You must be convinced that we need you here, to teach us things to help us survive when we set off for Oregon Country again."

"Shoot, anybody can do that for you. Don't have to be me. The way I figger it, I've got about enough time to git back to the High Lonesome, stock up on supplies, then make it to my winterin' place and settle in."

Equally stubborn, Eve Billings put her hands on her hips and leaned toward Preacher. "Are you always this selfish? Don't you ever consider giving others a helping hand?"

Preacher bent even closer. "Nope. I al'ays had to make do for myself. An' I've observed that those folks who get ahead in this world have done the same."

"Why, that's awful. It's so un-Christian."

"I don't recall layin' claim to bein' a Christian."

Shocked by this admission, Eve arched her eyebrows. "For shame, Preacher!" Then her mind exploded with a realization. "Are we . . . are we having our first fight, Preacher?"

Suddenly robbed of his self-defensive pique, Preacher abandoned his aggressive stance and began to chortle. "By dang, I think yer right. Looks like that's what it is."

Relaxed, and no longer feeling threatened, Eve joined Preacher in his laughter. He reached out for her and put one arm on her shoulder. They remained in a chaste, semi-embrace when the wagon-train leaders stormed up.

Beet-faced, Gus Beecher made the first complaint. "What's so all-fired important to take me away from settlin' in? I've my smithy to finish. We've a cave to dig, and sod walls to put up, a sod roof to add." Then he cocked a gimlet eye at Eve Billings. "Or is it that the Widow Billings has chosen now to announce her engagement?"

Scandalized, Eve covered her mouth with one hand for a moment before she spoke. "What stuff and nonsense, Gus Beecher. Preacher is talking about leaving." She went on to relate what he had told her of the confrontation with Lieutenant Colonel Danvers and his decision to leave.

That changed the tone of the men, except for Gus Beecher. "He can go any time he wants, for all I care."

Hiram Tate saw it differently. "Preacher, you can't leave us like this. There's so much we need to learn. And, how can we ever get along with Colonel Danvers?"

"I reckon much like porcupines make love—very carefully." Then Preacher blushed slightly and nodded toward Eve. "If you'll pardon my language, ma'am. As to goin', I figger I'm free to do so when I take a mind."

Isaac Warner made an open plea. "You'll leave us helpless. Look at all you've done so far. We've learned how to make better time, how to effectively fight Indians, better ways to cook for the noonin'. Oh, so many things. An' there must be more. How to better track and take down game, what to avoid on the trail. Such things make you a gold mine to us. Please, at least take a day or two to think it over. We haven't much left, but we can pay you for your advice. Won't you at least give it fair consideration, Preacher?"

Erasing the scowl on his high forehead, Preacher spoke quietly. "I'll think on it some. No promises, mind, but I'll let you know."

20

By mid-morning the next day, the surveyor and his crew had driven stakes to set out the dimensions of the stockade and its headquarters. Also the corral and two outbuildings. Favorably noting this rapid progress, Lieutenant Colonel Danvers ordered felling crews to be detailed to cut down trees in the thick stands of pine down near the base of the fingerlike promontory. Hearing of this, Gus Beecher came to the colonel and, toadying up as was his want, offered his services to forge hinges for the gate, along with bolts, spikes and other iron products as needed, at a reasonable price of course. To his credit, Danvers let his face show his distaste for the man, though he did hire him on a by-the-job basis.

The colonel learned of three men among the civilians who had sawmill experience. He interviewed them and, satisfied, hired them at once. "You are to inspect, set up and operate the portable saw that accompanied us from Jefferson Barracks. I expect a preliminary report by this afternoon." He soon learned the full extent of the bad news.

Shortly after two o'clock that afternoon, the three sawyers came to Danvers. The eldest, Tom Quigley, who had been a foreman, revealed the results of their studies. "The blade made it through nice as can be. Same for the other parts. The belts could stand a good oiling an' they'll be supple again. Only one problem."

"What is that?"

Quigley wiped a damp brow. "How are we goin' to power the saw? That blade has to be movin' a fair clip to cut through wood, especially green wood."

Danvers scowled at this setback. "I was given to understand that everything necessary had been included. Surely, you've overlooked something."

"Nope. Not a blessed thing. Oh, it's all there, disassembled and the parts numbered. Ya see, Colonel, this mill was designed to be run by a waterwheel."

Suspicion registered on the face of the colonel. "There was no wheel with the saw parts."

"Nope, we have to build it. The metal fittings are all there," Quigley informed him.

"How's it all operate?"

"Well, Colonel, there's this big ol' flywheel that attaches to the spline of the waterwheel, and a little one that goes on the shaft of the saw blade. The problem is we've got to have a water source to use it."

Danvers slapped the gloves he carried in his left hand against his outer thigh. "I am constantly beset with obstacles. Why is that, do you suppose, Mr. Quigley?"

Quigley ducked his head in embarrassment. "I wouldn't rightly know, sir, bein' I ain't been in the Army. But, from those I know what have been, it seems that's the way of it, Colonel. If it ain't one thing goin' wrong, it's six others."

Lieutenant Colonel Danvers produced a warm, genuine smile, the first, save those he gave to Eve Billings, he had ever given to one of the settlers. "Quite right, Quigley, quite right, indeed. That has been the bane of my existence since I attended the military academy. Not once has anyone put it so succinctly. But that's not my immediate problem. Why did those idiots in the

Quartermaster Corps provide us with a water-powered sawmill when we were coming into this godforsaken country?"

Quigley shrugged. "It is mountainous, sir. Maybe they thought you'd find a waterfall, which would be dandy for this kind of mill."

Danvers grunted. "Those fools have never seen beyond the west bank of the Potomac, let alone the real West. Can you convert it to a treadmill?"

"Not easily, nor likely, Colonel. Best bet is we dam up that creek down below to build pressure and put the mill wheel in the spillway."

Danvers seemed doubtful. "Can that be done?"

"Easy as can be. Your engineer officer an' someone with knowledge of artillery could do the figgers and draw up what's needed. The surveyors could lay it out."

"Then, get to it. I'll assign the men you asked for to your supervision. We need that mill operative as soon as possible. By all means, long before winter."

Preacher decided to take one more look around at the operation Danvers had put in motion before making his final decision. What he saw only convinced him further of the folly of the entire project. The fellers had moved a good three-quarters of a mile from the site of the fort. Well out of range of covering fire, the only protection they had came from half a dozen Dragoons assigned to them. Already the detail assigned to limbing the logs and dragging them down to the area of the stockade had run into trouble.

Dragoon horses, unaccustomed to working in harness, rebelled against the strangeness of heavy loads that pulled against their necks. They clashed into one another, reared, whinnied and occasionally balked. For most of their journey, they remained out of rifle range from the fort as well. Preacher found Captain Dreiling watching the neophyte lumberjacks through field glasses.

Preacher addressed him in a low, confidential tone. "Jist betwixt you an' me, Edward, this is one hell of a mistake. Those fellers out there are as exposed as a baby's bare bottom on birthin' day. You're all near a thousand miles from any other soldiers, jist about as far from any white man. Supply will be difficult, impossible in winter, and the colonel's plans for water are nonexistent, or plum silly at best."

Dreiling turned to Preacher. "Are you wound down now, my friend? For all the good it'll do, I agree with you absolutely. Putting a fort here, on this impossible plateau, in the middle of Indian country, is what I call downright suicidal."

Preacher shrugged. "I told the colonel he'd be wise to make a large cistern in the middle of the fort area. That'd give you a reliable supply most of the year. If he ran that stockade around the whole place, it would even be safe to draw water durin' an attack, too."

Dreiling brightened over that. "A cistern would work? Tell me about it."

For the next half hour Preacher enlarged his idea. Although in conclusion he returned to his main theme. "The smartest thing to do would be to get clear the hell away from here and set up somewhere else."

Later in the afternoon, Preacher had opportunity to point out to Lieutenant Colonel Danvers all he had discussed with Captain Dreiling. The colonel barely suppressed his irritation. He did make one concession.

"All right, Mr. Preacher. I'll agree with you on one point. I have been studying the approach routes to the site. I'm ordering other palisades to be erected along the south and west faces. I've come to the conclusion that without them we are entirely too exposed. I'm certain that the sheer walls to the east side will take care of any threat from that direction."

"I'd give that second thought, too, Colonel. 'Cause even if the walls are sheer, including being too steep to climb safely, unless they're completely concave, there won't be no such word as *can't* in the heads of Injuns fixed on climbin' up here."

"I'll consider it, but it won't be at the top of my list of priorities."

"Mayhap it had better be, Colonel. Because I'm sure it's on their minds." With a slow movement, Preacher raised his arm and, like the Specter of Doom, pointed a long finger at the figures of some forty mounted Cheyenne and twenty-five Lakota warriors watching in ominous silence from the hilltops in the near distance.

Eve Billings could not believe the emotions that surged through her. At one moment, a girlish giddiness flooded her. The next, she sank into deep shame that she could imagine such thing so soon after poor Howard's death, only to find herself awash with gloomy despair that she would never have what she so dearly wanted. Then euphoria surged again. She would hum old ballads, put a dance step in her walk, a sparkle in her eyes and a silly smile on her lips. Abruptly she broke off her self-examination to give Charlie's shoulder a hard squeeze.

"Charlie, sit still. I'm trying to cut your hair evenly all around."

"I don't want my hair cut," replied Charlie in a surly tone. "I want it to grow long so I can braid it."

Amazement washed over Eve's face. "Why, Charlie, whatever for?"

Charlie's lower lip came out in a pink crescent of pout. "Indian boys have their hair braided."

"Charles Ryan Billings, your hair is as auburn as mine, and your complexion as fair. You are not an Indian boy."

Conscious of having gone entirely too far, Charlie could not meet her eyes. He inspected his feet, which in gratitude and relief, Eve saw were now covered. Although by moccasins he had acquired who knew where. "I wanna be."

"What put that notion in your head, son?"

"I've been thinkin'. Indian boys get to ride and hunt and fish and swim whenever they want to. Preacher's told me so." Then he cut his dark eyes to his mother. "Preacher also told me that Indian boys' folks don't spank them."

Eve studied her son, conscious that he had aged beyond his years, yet remained emotionally a little boy. "Have you done something you think you might be spanked for?"

Shock registered on Charlie's face. "No! Yes. Er . . . I mean, I don't know."

"Do you want to tell me about it?"

"I can't. I promised. It's a secret. Between him an me." Whenever Charlie Billings suffered from guilt feelings, he spoke in short, incomplete sentences.

"Who? Preacher?"

"No, Mom. Not him. Someone . . . secret."

One hand on her hip, Eve shook her head in resignation. She would learn about it sooner or later, she knew with a mother's certainty.

A week went by with the logging detail required to go farther from the rudimentary fort each day. The present party of eighteen, twelve loggers and six guards, had only ridden out of sight when Preacher heard the thin, high keen of a war cry, followed by the muffled pop of gunfire. Quickly, he ankled his way across the crudely marked-out parade ground. He went directly to the large tent located in the center of an area that would become the future headquarters.

He brushed past the sentries and strode straight to the

desk behind which sat Lieutenant Colonel Danvers. "Sorry to bother you, Colonel, but from the sound of it, your loggers are gettin' attacked."

Voice almost a squeal, Danvers bounded from his chair. "What! That's impossible. They have an escort."

Had the situation not been so serious, Preacher would have laughed out loud. "I don't think that means much to half a hundred Cheyenne."

Before Danvers could work up a reply, a mounted man thundered up to the tent. He shouted through the canvas. "Colonel—Colonel, we're under attack. Injuns are swarmin' all over us."

"Here?" Danvers mouthed rhetorically.

The wild-eyed Dragoon, his face slicked with fear sweat and mottled with dust burst through the flap. "It's the detail, sir. There must be a hunnerd Injuns."

Surprising to Preacher, Danvers responded quickly. "Borden," he snapped to the commander of Company A. "Assemble your men. Form a relief column. Extra cartridges for all. Be ready to ride in five minutes. Mr. Preacher, will you scout?"

Preacher stifled a groan. "I reckon so, Colonel."

Dust and powder smoke boiled up from beyond the near swell on the breast of the Bighorn Mountains. Preacher ignored the rough trail already cut into the soil and took the most direct route. Streaming behind him in a column of twos, Preacher noticed with satisfaction, the Dragoons pounded hard over the ground. Seven minutes later, they came upon the rear of the left flank of a two-sided Cheyenne attack.

Startled Indians in the grass turned at the sound of pounding hooves. Two of them started to swing their rifles into line as Captain Borden bellowed; "Echelon left and right, draw carbines . . . aim . . . fire!"

Four warriors went down before a scythe of lead.

Three others took wounds that disabled them. Preacher noted that a Dragoon sergeant had learned his lessons well. He skidded his mount to a halt and covered the injured Cheyennes with his revolver. Preacher faced front in time to drive the buttplate of his Hawken into the face of a snarling brave.

"Pour it on, boys! Help's come," sang out the voice of Lieutenant Gresham of Company B.

Gresham had been in charge of the logging detail, Preacher recalled. Quickly he cut his way toward the stalled wagons, his hand filled now with a Walker Colt. Gresham reared up and fired at a warrior who lunged from the back of his pony toward Preacher. Preacher's .44 ball reached his attacker at the same time as Gresham's .54-caliber Hall carbine round. In the next second, the complexion of the battle changed entirely.

With a hundred-twenty Dragoons rushing down on them, the forty-three remaining Cheyenne warriors lost interest in their no longer easy prey. They abandoned the attack and raced through the waving grass, to disappear down a draw. Odd, Preacher thought to himself, he could swear he had seen some Blackfoot among them. The two tribes had been enemies for hundreds of years. Preacher would have never believed he would see them fighting side by side.

The Cheyenne might listen to the message of Iron Shirt, but Preacher could not believe even such a powerful prophet could weld a lasting alliance. Yet, he felt certain he had seen a Blackfoot pattern on a shield and in the decoration of a feathered lance. When the last warrior had left the field, Preacher trotted Tarnation over to Lieutenant Gresham.

"You lose any men?"

"No, thanks be. Not that they didn't try damned hard. We're going to have to take a larger escort."

"It'd be smarter if you didn't go out at all. I've talked

myself blue in the face tryin' to get Colonel Danvers to see that. Don't do much good, but I'll try again."

"I wish you luck. And . . . ah . . . thanks for gettin' the relief here so fast."

"You're welcome. Ain't your fault you've got yer neck stuck out a mile. Next time, you might not be so lucky."

Back at the fort, Preacher stormed directly into the headquarters tent to confront Lieutenant Colonel Danvers. So exacerbated had he become, his face bore the likeness of a thundercloud. He found himself forced to stand in impotent silence while Danvers dallied over an inconsequential report. When at last the colonel glanced up indifferently, Preacher used every bit of will to curb his temper.

"Colonel, according to what those fellers in Washington City writ to me, I was to advise you in all matters regarding the frontier, including Injun fighting techniques and the habits of the tribes. For the last two months, that is what I've been tryin' to do. Only you seem determined to ignore what I say.

"Now, unlike me, these boys has got to do as you say." Preacher paused, then delivered his suspicions in clear and cogent speech. "What I wonder is why you remain so blind to the formidable danger everyone is being subjected to? Don't you care? My point is, we have hostiles where there were none when I left for Jefferson Barracks. That could be exceedingly costly in the lives of these young men."

Put off balance by Preacher's erudite delivery, Danvers gaped a moment before he waved a hand in easy dismissal. "They volunteered for the Army, every man jack of them. As for my lack of surprise, I must say that after all, I didn't expect the savages to come down and greet my troops with open arms. I learned that from you on the way out here. It is something we all have to take in stride, or get out of the game. Now, is there anything of importance you have for me?"

Preacher bit off his furious reply. "I want to scout that raiding party, see where they're goin' and what they're up to."

"That's quite all right with me. Be ready to make a complete report when you return. And leave at least one of the other scouts for duties around the fort."

An hour later, Preacher and Antoine Revier left the fledgling fort. They traveled light, with only what their saddle- and possibles-bags could carry. Once clear of the finger of land and out of sight of the fort, the wilderness swallowed them. To some, the silence and vastness would be intimidating. Not so the mountain men, for Preacher and Antoine, a welcome blanket of tranquillity settled over them.

They picked up the trail of the fleeing Cheyenne easily and began to follow it. Conscious that they were being watched every inch of the way, Preacher had an intense itching sensation between his shoulder blades.

21

Preacher and Antoine trailed along behind the war party at a leisurely pace. That way it took two days to catch up. Preacher saw the first sign of the hostiles. The point and part of the shaft of a feather-decorated lance seemed to float on the horizon. Within a few strides, a mop of black, braided hair rose into view. A single eagle feather protruded upward from the back of the head. Preacher made a sign to Antoine Revier and they reined in their mounts.

Preacher cupped his chin in one hand. "We've found 'em, right enough. Now what are we gonna do with them?"

"I figger you've got an idee or two up yer sleeve, Preacher. Me, I could use a nice snooze between now and full dark."

"Right. We eat now and wait 'til nightfall to move in closer."

After staking out their horses to graze, the two mountain men leaned against their saddles, which they propped against the thick trunk of an ancient oak. They gnawed on strips of softened jerky. Cold biscuits and a pot of beans, provided by Eve Billings, filled out the meal. Preacher's jaw continued to work as, with a slender wild onion he had pulled from a bunch that grew nearby, he pointed in the direction taken by the Cheyenne.

"Them fellers ain't gonna throw out a welcome blanket for us. So, I figger we need to get in real close tonight and find out what they're talkin' about. Get the lay of the land, so's to speak. Then we can decide what to do."

Antoine washed down beans with cold water from the creek. "Suits. I ain't exactly anxious to go mix in with them. How's yer Cheyenne?"

"Good enough, though a mite rusty. I reckon I can make out what they're sayin' among themselves."

"Good. How's it feel to be away from those soldier-boys an' on yer own for once?"

Preacher heaved a long sigh of relief. "I ain't felt this good in three months. Jist about got the stink of white folks out of my lungs. Why is it there's so many of them has such an aversion to keepin' clean? A good Injun nose could smell 'em comin' a good quarter mile away."

Antoine snorted, amused at the image he had created. "Can you imagine the mess it would make in a crick if all them soldiers, an' the pilgrims, took a bath every night?"

Preacher wrinkled his nose. "Never thought of it that way before. Might be you're right. All that soap and stench floatin' downstream would tell an Injun jist where to look. No matter, it's good to be out here. Now I'm gonna pull me a tomcat and catch a few winks."

Only the pale, frosty light of the stars broke up the black blanket of a moonless night later on when Preacher and Antoine fastened their horses to ground anchors and eeled through the tough, wiry grass to within twenty feet of the Cheyenne camp. Low, small lodges had been set in a semicircle around a large, central fire. Preacher extended his spyglass and swept the rows of seated men.

Sure enough, he was not pleased to note, there was more than one Blackfoot among the Cheyenne. One of them stood before the assembly and harangued them in their language. His Cheyenne was imperfect, and Preacher found it hard to understand. What he did make out alarmed him.

"When Iron Shirt and our people join you and your cousins, the Lakota, it will be easy to kill all the white men on the bluff. Then we will sweep across the plains with rifle and firebrand and drive the rest out of the country of our brothers forever." He paused to strut proudly in front of the rapt Cheyenne.

"In two sun's time, all of the Iron Shield Society will join us here and the massacre will soon follow. Those who died in the attack on the wagons did not have strong enough faith in the medicine of Iron Shirt. Look about you. The faces you see are of those who, like you, believed. With strong hearts like yours, we cannot fail."

Preacher had heard enough. He tugged at the sleeve of the hunting shirt worn by Antoine Revier. When Antoine cut his eyes to Preacher, the latter motioned for them to draw back. Cautiously they began to move away from the Cheyenne camp. They made it halfway to their horses without incident. Then, as he crawled past a large sage bush, Preacher found himself looking at five pair of coppery knees.

Slowly he raised his gaze to take in the warriors, all of whom competently held modern rifles, pointed directly at him. He froze and sucked in a deep breath. From beyond the obscuring brush he heard the soft voice of Antoine Revier. "Preacher, dang me, but I think we're caught."

Preacher's heart rate increased rapidly, driven by the fight or flight reflex, as adrenaline pumped into his system. Suddenly he lashed out at the nearest pair of legs.

* * *

Thrashing sounds across the sage told Preacher that Antoine had chosen to resist also. Preacher had the Cheyenne warrior off his legs in no time. He snatched up the dropped rifle and used it clublike to knock the knees from under another brave. Then the other three jumped him.

Preacher fought silently, and with a controlled fury that left one Cheyenne with a broken jaw. Another warrior came at him from the front, prepared to do a kick to Preacher's face. Preacher dodged and slapped the leg to the side. Then he came upright and split the upper lip of the unprepared Indian. Grunts and the soft impact of fist against flesh told him Antoine was holding his own. A knee to the groin toppled the bleeding Cheyenne.

Preacher started to follow up with a knockout punch, only to have his arms grabbed from behind. A sturdy warrior held him tightly while the last of the group kicked him in the belly. Stomach juices burned their way up Preacher's throat. He gagged and retched while he struggled to free himself.

It did little good. The next instant, blackness washed over him and pain erupted in his head from a blow with a rifle butt. His knees went slack and he hung from the grasp of the Cheyenne who held him.

Preacher and Antoine Revier came to in the center of the Cheyenne camp. Spread-eagled and staked to the ground, they had been stripped of their clothing and moccasins. A tidal surge of pain churned in Preacher's head. Through it, he vaguely heard a stirring beyond his bare feet. A blurred figure came into view and Preacher tried to blink his eyes into focus.

When the image came clear, it turned out to be a man Preacher recognized. "Swift Bear," he grated rustily in Cheyenne. The effort caused him another tsunami of pain.

"It is truly you, White Ghost?"

"Yes, it is, Swift Bear. Yer warriors caught me fair and square." With that admission, Preacher set out on a plan that had only begun to form in his mind. It was one he hoped would save their lives. After another hard swallow, he began to bargain.

"You know me, Swift Bear, an' you know I do not lie."

"That is so. What is it you wish to talk about lying there on the ground?"

Preacher stalled a moment. "Glad you mentioned that. I would feel better about it if I was sittin' upright, so I could talk like a man, instead of a deer laid out for dressin'. Could you do that, Swift Bear?"

After due consideration, the Cheyenne war chief nodded in agreement. "Since it is you, I shall allow it. Release his arms."

Now he was getting somewhere. When the rawhide thongs had been severed, Preacher flexed his fingers to restore feeling, and levered himself up into a sitting position.

Preacher made a nod of his head and proceeded politely. "White Ghost thanks Swift Bear. Now, what you've got here is two fellers who have been friend to the Cheyenne for many winters. Why, I even took me a Cheyenne wife, had two sons by her. 'Cept she got took off by sickness."

"The white man's curse," Swift Bear provided.

"Yep. Smallpox. Nothin' could be done about it. But, my boys are being raised as Cheyenne in the band of Cloud Blanket. It is as the Great Spirit sees best. What I'm gettin' at is that since we're friends, more or less, maybe you would cut us loose and let us go on our way?"

"We are a war party. And I have a band of my own now. I no longer listen to the words of Cloud Blanket."

Preacher cocked a brow. "You two at odds? That's a shame. What happened?"

"Cloud Blanket turned away from the Iron Shield Society."

"What is that?"

"A new warrior society, with powerful medicine. It was brought to us by a Blackfoot shaman."

"Oh, yes, Iron Shirt." Preacher cocked a brow and continued shrewdly. "But Iron Shirt does not speak for the Cheyenne, now that I know for a fact. An' I don't think he speaks for Swift Bear."

Swift Bear curled his lower lip outward a moment before replying. "We follow him in the great battle."

"What fight is that?"

"To rid our land of the white men. Iron Shirt leads us in that."

"But he doesn't tell you what to do with a friend."

"No. That is so. True though it is, I cannot simply release White Ghost. You were spying on a war camp."

Preacher put on an unhappy expression, then brightened with a show of hope. "There is a way, though, isn't there?"

A brief smile showed Swift Bear followed Preacher's logic. "You could . . . fight your way free."

"You mean, take on the whole mess of you?"

Swift Bear shook his head. "No. If you could fight your way past ten warriors, you could go on your way in peace."

"What about my friend? He looks a mite worse for wear. Could I fight for his release, too?"

Considering that a while, Swift Bear finally made answer. "You would have to better four hands of men for that." At Preacher's unhappy expression, he added. "Or you could fight one man to the death."

"I would have to fight any man you send against me?" At the nod from Swift Bear, he went on. "If I win, me an' my friend go free and unharmed?"

"That is so. And if you do not defeat my choice, let us hope you both die like men."

"What weapons will we use?"

"That will be decided by the council tonight."

Preacher had another, vital question to ask. "Who will I fight?"

Swift Bear remained silent, let his gaze roam over the gathered warriors. Then he made a gesture that summoned an important-looking Blackfoot. The two spoke too quietly for Preacher to hear. When they had decided, Swift Bear turned back to Preacher.

"I have asked my brother, Three Horses, who he thinks should uphold our honor. He has suggested that it would be fitting for Tall Bull to claim your scalp. Tall Bull is a Blackfoot, one who has taken the way of Iron Shirt and is immune to the weapons of the white man."

By the slightest value of intonation, Preacher managed to keep sarcasm out of his voice when he replied dryly, "Well, then, I don't think pistols would be a fair choice for weapons. I need at least a little chance to win."

"You will learn of our decision tomorrow. When the sun is high, the fight will begin."

Preacher and Antoine spent an uneasy night. In the chill mountain air, they soon found themselves stiffening and had to clench their jaws to keep their teeth from chattering. Tied to the trunks of a pair of saplings, they could not even layout full-length to sleep. When morning came, their muscles had grown knotted and sore.

Thoughtfully, Swift Bear had ordered them cut loose and, while food was brought to them, they worked out the kinks. They were kept under control by rawhide tethers around their waists. Preacher ate with his usual appetite; a stew made of some sort of meat he could not identify. Then he began to exercise lightly.

Relentlessly the sun climbed the sky while Preacher continued to stretch, bend and run in place. All the while, he tried to think through a strategy to insure he won. When he worked up a light sheen of sweat and his muscles seemed as smooth in operation as usual, he stopped and sat beside Antoine.

Lacking tact, Antoine brought up one of several old

acquaintances who had undergone such a challenge. "Remember ol' Kip? He had to fight for his life one time like this. Against the Arapaho, I believe. Too bad it kilt him."

"Now, that's a fact. How about French Jake, though? He came through it missin' only three fingers of one hand. Gives a feller real inspiration, that does."

Antoine had more encouragement. "How about ol' Jim Bridger? Seems he ran afoul of some excitable Paiutes. They was fixed to torture him and burn him alive, only he talked them into a fight, best man wins all. Now, you know the Paiutes is sneaky. He had to fight three men before they kept their word. Killed all three Jim did. With only a couple light cuts on his arms."

"Not to mention a slice on one cheek that near tooken out one eye."

Antoine cut a slantways glance at Preacher. "You sound like you're regrettin' this fight already."

Preacher slid his gaze to the whiskered face of his companion. "Now that you mention it, maybe I am."

"You want out of it?" probed Antoine.

"I want out of here. An' the only way to do that is go through with a fight."

Antoine offered a crumb of hope. "You coulda said no."

"An' we'd been killed on the spot. Nope, that's not for this child. I plan on livin' a whole long time after this affair."

"We've had some good times, haven't we, Preacher?"

"You goin' softhearted on me, Antoine?"

"Not me, *mon ami*. I was . . . only thinking."

"About what?"

Antoine sighed heavily. "We both know of more men that failed to get through such an ordeal than those who did. I feel responsible in a way. It is as though if I had not been along, you might have gotten away."

"Nonsense, my friend. You did not cause this. I failed to keep careful watch. They found us and nabbed us, an' here we are. But I think I've figgered a way out for us. It would be crazy to expect that I'll not get hurt some in the process."

Sincerity radiated from the respectful expression Antoine wore. "By *le bon Dieu*, Preacher, you have more sand than any ten men I know. God go with you."

Preacher swallowed hard at the lump that had suddenly appeared in his throat. "Thank you, Antoine."

Before they expected it, the time arrived for the mortal combat. Down the slope a way, the Cheyenne and their tenuous allies gathered in a large, loose circle around a bare spot of ground. Swift Bear and four of his warriors came for Preacher. Two of them escorted Antoine Revier while the other pair accompanied Preacher. To muttered insults, Preacher's captors shouldered a path through the crowd and delivered him to the center. Then they released the tether and stepped back.

A loud clamor rose as Tall Bull stepped through the ranks of spectators. His name suited him to perfection. He towered well over six feet, with thick muscles and tree-trunk legs. His hands were the size of a grizzly's paws and his head would not fit the largest hat size. He had Preacher by five inches and a good fifty-five pounds. Swift Bear came forward and handed each man a knife and a tomahawk. Relief coursed through Preacher when he found that the weapons were his own. Then the Cheyenne chief stepped back and motioned for the contestants to face him.

"This is a fight to the death. You will use no other weapons than those given you. If you lose both, you may use hands, feet, and teeth. It is in the hands of the Great Spirit, and up to your skill, to decide who will win."

With that, he melted back into the inner ring of onlookers and raised his arm. "Let the fight begin."

22

Warily, the two fighters circled, intent on studying each other's strengths and weaknesses. Tall Bull, with the advantage of size and weight, struck first. His tomahawk whistled loudly in a roundhouse swing. Preacher lithely sprang out of the way. Instantly he retaliated with a flick of his left wrist.

The keen edge of his Greenriver knife bit into flesh over the left eye of Tall Bull. A sheet of blood washed over the lid and obscured his vision. In the instant of hesitation that caused, Preacher lashed out with his war 'hawk and lightly nicked Tall Bull over the left hipbone. A heavier stream of blood flowed down the Blackfoot's leg. The spectators raised an angry roar.

Tall Bull stumbled twice, then flexed his knees and coiled his body for another attack. He came in straight, tomahawk whirring in a silvery blur before his face. Knife held with the edge up, he feinted for the proper opening and drove the blade forward. Preacher jumped high in the air and brought his 'hawk down on the haft of the one in the hand of his adversary.

Sharp pain radiated up the arm of Tall Bull and he nearly dropped his tomahawk. Then he shifted his weight and spun in a full circle. When he saw the hated white man again, he let out a howl and swung his knife with all his force. The stroke split Preacher's buckskin shirt from his left hip to his right shoulder. A thin ribbon of blood oozed from the chest of Preacher. Off balance from his effort to avoid the deadly steel, he stumbled over his own feet.

Down Preacher went, but not before Tall Bull charged forward and sank the sharp edge of his tomahawk into the thick muscle of Preacher's upper chest. By immediately going slack the blade did not cut through bone or pierce a lung. Preacher hastily rolled to one side. He recovered before Tall Bull could follow up his advantage. Panther quick, Preacher smacked the Cheyenne in the gut with the flat of his blade.

Groaning, Tall Bull doubled over. Preacher sacrificed a chance to get in another blow to return to his feet. Slowly, a plan began to form in his mind. Swinging rapidly in a figure-eight, Preacher made the blade of his 'hawk a continuous blur between them. Inexorably he edged Tall Bull backward, toward a large, old tree. Eyes fixed over the shoulder of Tall Bull, Preacher gauged his distance. When he had the Blackfoot in the proper position, he feinted to his left, then whirled right and ran around the slower-moving Tall Bull.

Seeing an opening, Tall Bull rushed in. His arm raised above his head, he was prepared to split Preacher's skull. The moment his opponent committed himself to the blow, Preacher dropped flat on the ground. Unable to arrest his motion, Tall Bull buried his tomahawk in the tree trunk up to the haft. Swiftly, Preacher cut a line across the exposed belly of Tall Bull, which released a river of blood.

Tall Bull choked back a howl of pain while he struggled to free his weapon from the wooden vise. Suddenly aware that Preacher was on the way up, momentary panic seized him. Unable to free his war 'hawk, Tall Bull abandoned it for his knife, which he changed to his right hand.

Making a shrewd surmise, Preacher tossed away his own 'hawk and shifted to his Greenriver. This gesture brought the first sound of appreciation from the spectators. Preacher stepped in and began to circle. Awkward and uncertain, his reservoir of cunning and strength bleeding out through his wounds, Tall Bull did likewise. Grimly, the fight went on.

Steel clashed on steel as Preacher parried an overhand thrust. Pain flowed through his chest like fire. Both men danced back and circled again. Tall Bull moved slower, his shoulders drooped and his head canted forward. He gasped in great drafts of air and vigilantly sought an opening. At last he sensed a flaw in Preacher's defense. With a deep grunt he lunged forward on his right leg and drove the tip of the blade toward Preacher's belly.

All at once, the knife in Preacher's hand showed up where it should not be. It deflected the blade of Tall Bull as Preacher spun away out of danger. Loss of his target sent Tall Bull stumbling to one side, bent over and vulnerable. The wound in Preacher's shoulder stung mightily as he tried to reverse his swing and plunge the Greenriver into the soft side of Tall Bull.

Having missed his lunge, Tall Bull knew the cold loneliness of desperation. Slowly he calmed his racing emotions. In sudden inspiration, he bent lower and snatched up a handful of dust and pebbles. Recovering his balance, he turned and hurled the contents of his hand into the face of Preacher.

Blinded, Preacher dropped low and did a forward roll. After two turns he crashed into the legs of the onlookers and, before Tall Bull could close on him, snatched a remembered gourd of water from between the nearest Cheyenne's legs. Quickly he poured the contents over his head and blinked his vision clear as he came to one knee. He managed it in time to keep from having Tall Bull's knife buried in his back.

Slowly Preacher yielded to the relentless pressure of the heavy, muscular warrior who had crashed into him. He shifted his feet and used the momentum of Tall Bull to throw the Blackfoot over one hip and send him crashing into the Cheyenne spectators. Immediately, Preacher regained his equilibrium and lashed out a foot.

His kick caught Tall Bull in the side of the head. Instantly groggy, Tall Bull momentarily lost sight of his opponent. Seizing his chance, Preacher dove in and made a quick slash that cut the throat of Tall Bull, who dropped to the ground, where he died before the gasping Preacher. A long, stunned silence followed.

Frowning, Two Moons stepped forward to clasp forearms with Preacher. "You have won fairly, White Ghost. Take your friend, your weapons and horses and ride out in peace. You will not be harmed."

Preacher and Antoine made the return trip to the fort in a day and a half. They paused only to dress Preacher's wounds and to rest their mounts. Preacher had grown feverish by the time they came in sight of the partly erected palisade. He rejected the suggestion made by Captain Dreiling that he see Major Couglin. Like most mountain men, he was wary of the medical profession.

"You never hear a pill-roller say he's *doing* medicine. They're all the time *practicin'*, which says to me they ain't got it right yet," he growled at the Dragoon officer's repeated insistence. Instead, he sent Antoine Revier and Three Sleeps Norris to find some special moss, leaves and spiderwebs.

When Eve Billings heard of his condition she came at once to the lean-to where Preacher lay. His forehead was dew-slicked with perspiration, and he had sunk into an uneasy sleep. His dry lips parted and he muttered unintelligible words. Eve knelt at his side and dabbed his mouth with a water-soaked cloth. Preacher moaned and shuddered reflexively.

Gibberish spilled from his tongue. "Ubbajubba."

By that time, his companions had returned with their shopping list filled. Eve looked up at them in an appeal. "Why didn't he go to the Army doctor?"

Three Sleeps answered her. "Stubborn fool won't have no truck with a doctor. Says a Cheyenne medicine man can cure a feller faster. An' a shaman won't cut anything off."

Secretly, Eve agreed. She saw as hopelessly medieval the popular assumption that amputation was the solution for nearly everything that would not respond to bleeding. Yet, Preacher obviously had an infection. The inflamed skin around the wound, the steady ooze of yellow matter from the broken scab pointed to no other possibility.

"We brought the things Preacher wanted." Antoine Revier offered the reed basket to Eve for her inspection.

What she saw made her nose wrinkle. "Do you know how to mix these?"

Revier, the half-French, half-Delaware mountain man answered eagerly. "Yes, ma'am. More or less that is. If Preacher was awake, he'd know the exact amount. We'll jist add a dab of this and a drop of that until it starts to pull the pus outta that wound."

A bullfrog croak came from the supine Preacher. "I am awake, damnit. Now listen." He went on to give the proportions of each ingredient.

Antoine mixed them while Eve hovered over Preacher. Then the jaunty son of a *voyageur* grew serious while he poured whisky over Preacher's wound and scraped away all of the scab with his knife. Next came the poultice, which Antoine packed deeply into the cut. Finally, while Three Sleeps lifted Preacher's shoulder and Eve held his head, Antoine bound the wound with a folded strip of cheese cloth he had purchased off Hattie Honeycutt, then wrapped a thin, thoroughly wet strip of well-boiled buckskin over that.

"There," he pronounced over his ministrations. "That should start to draw right nicely by this evening. Tomorrow, he'll be up and sassy as ever."

Not at all convinced, Eve asked, "Are you sure?"

Antoine considered it. "By noonin' time, at least."

Decidedly uneasy, Eve made an offer. "If you don't mind, I'll watch over him part of the evening, give you two a rest."

"Fine with me," Three Sleeps agreed. "I'm sure Preacher would rather wake up lookin' at your face instead of one of ours."

Regardless of the assurances given by Three Sleeps Norris, three days passed before Preacher awoke from his septic delirium and made conscious note of his surroundings. He forced a delighted smile, though too weak to sustain it long, when he found Eve Billings dutifully at his side with a damp cloth ready to salve his fevered brow. That his mind had not suffered became immediately clear.

"How long?" he asked.

Eve fought back the tears of joy and relief that formed in her hazel eyes. "Three days. You . . . you were very sick."

Preacher made little of it. "Weren't nothin'. A li'l bout of sweats is all."

"Preacher you nearly burned up with fever. Dr. Coughlin wanted to bleed you. I told him I'd take a shotgun to him if he tried."

Lips curled in a feeble smile, Preacher expressed his gratitude for that. "An Army sawbones is good for only one thing. Makin' a feller worse off." His voice gained

strength and a gentle warmth. "Thank you for lookin'
out for me, Eve. I'm much beholdin'."

"No thanks needed. Call it . . ." Go on, say it, her mind
told her. "Call it a labor of love." Then she stumbled on.
"Your friends took turns with me, watching over you."
Eve reached out and wiped Preacher's brow a final time.

A week went by before Preacher walked abroad unaided
in the fast-growing compound. The first floor of the
headquarters had been completed, along with a long,
low, warehouse sort of building for the quartermaster.
First to go up, Preacher had pointed out to him by
Antoine Revier, had been the sutler's.

"He has some near quality whisky," Antoine advised.

"Beer," Preacher corrected. "One beer is about all I
think I can handle."

"*Très bien!* Then let us go and get it now, before you
change your mind, or your nursemaid comes along and
forbids it. *Allez vite!*"

Two more weeks went by before Preacher pronounced
himself as fit as before the fight. He looked back on the
duel with Tall Bull as he surveyed progress on the fort.
He had not intended to kill the big Blackfoot. He had
used the ploy of throwing aside his 'hawk in furtherance
of that. But a Blackfoot was a Blackfoot. When Tall Bull
threw the dirt in his face, Preacher knew he might not
leave this circle of warriors alive. So, all bets were off.

Old news, Preacher thought as he discarded his reflec-
tions and watched the last of the split logs being
hammered into place on the second-floor roof of the
headquarters. Somehow, panes of glass had survived
the arduous trek to this promontory and amateur
glaziers were gingerly fitting filled sashes into the lower
floor's windows. The front stockade had been completed,
Preacher saw with relief.

It consisted of a double palisade of foot-thick pine

trunks, sharpened on the tops with a two-foot space of rammed earth between. Running the length of it, a five-foot-deep battlement had been installed, to provide for firing from the wall. The huge gates had been hung and now moved ponderously on thick iron hinges. Fully a third of the outer defenses extended along the west face. Some ten feet inside the main gate, a pounded ramp of dirt and granite boulders provided access to a platform of the same material at the top. The battalion's three-pound field piece could be hauled up there to give covering fire. It stood now beside a flagpole which had been erected in front of the headquarters building in a circle of whitewashed rocks. More of the chalky stones marked out the parade ground and walkways to and from the buildings.

"Danvers must have these poor devils working day and night," Preacher observed to Eve.

"Yes, he does. I overheard some of the soldiers talking. They said the colonel was setting a record in minor infractions' punishment. The men who break minor regulations receive extra duty details after retreat—whatever that means."

Preacher turned an amused smile on her. "I think that's when they fire off the little cannon and haul down the flag."

Perplexity lined Eve's brow. "Oh, yes. But, why do they call it 'retreat'? Isn't that running from the enemy?"

Preacher shrugged. "Same word, diff'rent meanings. That's the Army for you." They laughed together.

"You're coming to supper tonight?" Eve asked.

Chuckling, Preacher spread his hands in submission. "A team of a dozen mules could not keep me away."

Something had gone decidedly wrong with the alliance between the Blackfoot, Cheyenne and Sioux, as it often did in such meldings of one-time enemies. The Cheyenne had been slow in coming in. Three large bands, including that of Cloud Blanket, had refused to join at all. The Sioux had sent only token numbers from the Brule, Oglala and Teton subtribes. Notable among those absent were the members of Red Cloud's band. As a result, the planned great uprising did not happen on schedule. Iron Shirt fumed over it. At last he decided to take out his anger on the nearest whites.

Accordingly, he stormed into the lodge occupied by Praeger, Gross and Reiker. He studied them in silence a moment, smelled their sudden outbreak of fear. What puny creatures, he thought to himself.

"Where are your wagons of rifles? Where's the powder?"

"On the way, Iron Shirt," Praeger managed calmly.

Iron Shirt spat into the fire. "That is not good enough. We hold back and waste our energy in races and gambling. This war cannot begin without the weapons you promised. When will they be here?"

Coldly Praeger responded. "I don't know any more than you do. Besides, the other tribes have not come in as you expected. When the warriors get here, the guns will be here also. What you need is another show of big medicine. I think I might have just the thing."

Intrigued, Iron Shirt leaned toward the broadshouldered, lean white man, his eyes fixed on the knife scar. "What is that?"

"Give me time to get everything rigged up. Then, tonight at the dances, tell everyone that you are going to do a most potent dance. A spirit dance that will do wondrous things, like nothing they have ever seen. Use the dance you worked out last month, the one you were going to use as a victory dance when the white soldiers are destroyed."

Plentifully shrewd for all his lack of sophistication, Iron Shirt's eyes held a gleam of anticipation. "What is it I am going to make happen?"

"Tell them that you will make stars rise from the ground up into the sky."

Uncertain, Iron Shirt blurted, "Can I do that? I mean, what are you going to do to make it happen?"

Praeger gave him an enigmatic smile. "Wait and see. I promise you it might even have you wetting your loin-cloth."

Praeger and his associates, along with Soures and three henchmen spent the rest of the day well beyond the large encampment of Blackfoot, Cheyenne and Sioux. They had the last tube in place shortly before dark.

Praeger headed for the rear of one wagon. "We'll fix something to eat out here. No sense in going back and drawing attention to ourselves, then having to come back after dark. Someone might follow and spoil the whole show."

"You've got it all figgered out, Mr. Praeger," Blake Soures said, sincerely complimenting his boss. "Those Injuns'll think the world's comin' to an end, sure enough."

Morton Gross raised a cautioning hand. "'We do not want to terrify them into running away. This exercise is merely for the purpose of reinforcing the magical powers of our great prophet, Iron Shirt."

Aaron Reiker added his own praise. "Still, it was inspired of you to have ordered these pyrotechnics and to have had them shipped out here."

Praeger fought back a smirk. "We'll soon see, won't we?" He began to take food from a large woven reed basket and pass it around.

Two hours after darkness fell, Quinton Praeger roused himself. "Better get ready. That's the drum beat for Iron Shirt's fancy dance. It'll take about twenty minutes, then we let go the first shell."

When the time came, Praeger touched the glowing tip of a length of slow match to the short fuse near the bottom of a fiberboard tube. With a dull thud, a whoosh and a hissing roar the projectile leaped into the night sky. It burst when it reached the apex of its arc, showering the sky in smoky red streamers. By then the second star shell was on its way.

This one erupted in green and white, with bright spots at the end of streamers of smoke that crackled and popped as their internal fuses burned down to the small charges. Most of the fireworks Praeger had arranged for consisted of three-pound star bursts. For the finale, he had something special. Following a simultaneous discharge of six star shells, he and his associates ignited and launched five aerial reports.

Discs of white appeared one after another in the sky, each followed by a violent blast and an accompanying shock wave. When the awesome sound of the last one rolled away across the hills, Quinton Praeger heard the cackle of Blake Soures.

"That'll have them savages dribblin' in their drawers for certain sure. What a hell of a show, Mr. Praeger. I'd call it brilliant."

Those in the camp did not share the enthusiasm of Blake Soures. Unable to contain them, the guards stood helplessly by while the pony herd stampeded. Many of the warriors abandoned their immense pride to hide, shivering under their bison robes. Some fell to the ground, stupefied, in superstitious veneration. The Great Spirit truly spoke through Iron Shirt, others exclaimed to their neighbors.

Slowly the pandemonium subsided. Shaken to his core by the dreadful display, Iron Shirt had no words for those who gradually came to reaffirm their allegiance. He could only grip their forearms and nod and mumble. The coldly analytical part of his mind eventually asserted itself. Whatever the white men had done, it had restored his power over these fractious tribes.

He turned, smiling, to his most trusted subordinates, Two Moons and Bent Trees. "Trust me, my friends. With this great medicine, the mighty battle really will come."

23

Preacher had become downright itchy-footed. Another week had gone by and still no major attack by the hostiles. There had been skirmishes against wood and water details, the fellers had been shot at from a distance and the newly erected sawmill had been thoroughly riddled with .54 caliber balls on two occasions. Preacher considered the damming of the swift little creek and the locating of the mill on its banks below the obstruction to be the height of stupidity.

"Even dumber than buildin' this fort out where it's exposed to ever'thing," he had been heard to opine frequently. At least one of his worries seemed to have somewhat worked its way to a solution.

Every day, more of the pilgrims settled in to rest and wait out the year at the fort. Spring, they declared, would suit them fine to move on. They had listened to his tales and those of his companions about winter in the high country. None among them felt hearty enough to endure exposure to the elements in wagon boxes. Well and good, Preacher figured. It gave him more time to ponder on why the Blackfoot and their allies had not attacked in force.

An exception to the settling down of the immigrants

was the subtle campaign still waged by Eve Billings and Isaac Warner to get Preacher to commit to leading them through the wilderness. It manifested itself again that evening at a supper presided over by Eve and Rebecca Warner. After a satisfying meal featuring roast venison, Isaac Warner sopped the last of a rich brown gravy from his plate with a delicate, yeast-raised bread roll, leaned back and patted his fledgling potbelly.

"Yessir, I've come to see spring as the ideal time to move on. We can learn a lot in the meantime, and the animals will certainly be more fit."

Preacher accepted a cheroot from the wagon captain which he tipped toward his benefactor before he lighted it. "Couldn't do a better thing. By then, it might be this fuss with the Injuns will be ended."

Isaac touched a burning ember to his own cigar. "Only one thing is left undone, then. We will still be in need of a guide, competent scouts, that sort of thing."

Preacher tried to be evasive. "When word gets around about this fort, there'll be all sorts of folk drop by. You can find someone easy."

Warner was not to be put off so easily. "Fact of the matter is, myself and the committee are set on it bein' you and possibly your friends, Revier and Norris."

"Nope. Ain't possible. Soon's this Injun ruckus is over with, I'm on my way to the Shinin' Mountains."

"We can pay well. If not all in advance, then when we reach the Oregon Country."

Shaking his head, Preacher made to leave. "Sorry, Mr. Warner. I ain't in the guide business. I leave that to them that enjoys it." He gave his thanks for the good meal and walked away.

Eve excused herself and quickly followed. When she caught up to Preacher she scurried around his broad-shouldered frame and halted in his path. Every bit the auburn-haired image of determination, she came right to the point.

"Preacher, for the life of me, I don't know what you have against leading us to the Northwest. Mr. Warner said we could pay well. Forgive me for being far too bold, brazen even, but let me tell you this. Along with the monetary reward we can give you, there can be other, more pleasant rewards, if you agree."

Stifling a groan born of inner turmoil, Preacher put his big hands on her tender shoulders. "Eve . . . Eve, what's a body to do? By jing, the truth is, I'd plow an' plant a garden for one of your smiles. For a kiss, I'd do handsprings from here to the Grand Tetons. If . . . if I heard you right, for that, I'd take on those Blackfoot single-handed and whup them all. But I can't—I won't let myself be harnessed up and put in charge of a wagon train. I'm sorry. I know I'll regret it tomorrow. Only it's jist the way I am."

Disappointment registered in Eve's hazel eyes. "That's the longest, and most eloquent, speech I've ever heard you make. I'm sorry over your stubborn refusal, but I think I can understand. You've always been a free soul. Any sort of harness, and I'm afraid that includes matrimony, would only chafe. But, now that I've said it, Preacher dear, the offer remains open. Good night."

Five double hands of Lakota warriors had set up a camp near their Cheyenne cousins. In spite of their earlier promises, they had failed to join with the Blackfoot for a large raid on the soldier-place. Iron Shirt went to visit them, his patience at an end. They welcomed him warmly enough and, after the customary meal, got down to serious talking.

"We are coming. It has been decided, and we will be there," Spotted Horse, the Lakota's principal war chief stated patiently.

Iron Shirt barely held his impatience in check. "Yes, but when?"

Spotted Horse made a gesture of indifference with his bead-decorated turkey-wing fan. "When we get there. Why are you in such haste, Iron Shirt? Going to war requires deliberation and careful planning."

That loosed a spill of heated words. "The planning is done; there is nothing difficult about it. We must not let this soldier-place be built. Like all white men, once they come, they never leave. Do you want all of your bison killed? The soldiers will do that. They shoot them for trophies. As you know, I have three tame white men in my village. They tell me this is a true thing."

Spotted Horse nodded sagely. "I have been told they scratch the ground, tear up the grass to put in seeds."

"Yes, they plant for food, like the Navajo," Iron Shirt spat in disgust. "We must attack this evil place and burn it to the ground."

Spotted Horse pursed his full lips, then nodded curtly. "It is agreed. We will come at the next moon."

Exasperated, Iron Shirt sprang to his feet. No! It must be now. We leave for the soldier-place with tomorrow's sun. Meet us there."

For want of something to do, Preacher rode out with Lieutenant Judson of Company C the next morning on the water detail. The youthful officer, Preacher was willing to bet he did not shave more than every other day, had matured considerably since their encounter with the Pawnee. Lines had appeared on his forehead and cheeks, where none had been before. He didn't talk as loudly, nor move with nervous energy like a youngster in his teens. Privately, he shared Preacher's opinion of the water situation. With construction nearly complete at the fort, he felt secure in bringing up the subject to the mountain man.

"Our engineering officer, Major Vickers, has completed his tests for building a cistern. I for one will be glad when we don't have to come out every day to water the horses. For some reason, I can't shake the prickling sensation that Blackfoot eyes are watching my every move."

Preacher chuckled deep in his throat. "That outlook'll keep you alive a whale of a lot longer than some others I could mention."

Vickers read Preacher correctly. "Colonel Danvers certainly does have an optimistic attitude. Not that I'm criticizing, of course."

"Ain't for me to be bearin' tales, Tom. Right now, I'm jist an unemployed scout."

"Then why do you take these risks like the others?"

Preacher rubbed his square chin. "Keeps my edge keen. Fastest way to get yourself kilt in the High Lonesome is to take to thinkin' you're nice and safe."

"Is it really that wild out here, Preacher?"

"It is at times. Thing is, you never know for certain when those times have come around. Injuns is moody, and changeable. The closer you are to them, the more they give you cause to play guessin' games."

Lieutenant Judson cast a nervous glance around the hillside above the creek bed. "And we're mighty close to them down here."

"Yep. There's three Cheyenne watchin' us now, right up in them pines." Preacher jutted his chin to indicate the direction of the observers.

Tom Judson jerked as though wasp-stung. "I'd better alert the others."

A restraining hand went to his arm as Preacher drawled in a low voice. "Nope. I wouldn't get all stirred up and make 'em think we're the hostiles. If they had any thought to lift our hair, they'd not let me get an eye on 'em."

Judson cut his eyes to Preacher's face. "How can you be so sure?"

"I ain't. But I've jist never seen warriors sit their horses right quiet like that an' then attack."

"What should I do then?"

Preacher did not even hesitate. "We'll jist mosey right slow along the crick, tell the watering detail as we go. No hurry. Them Cheyenne ain't gonna leave until after we do."

Half an hour later, Lieutenant Judson heaved a heavy sigh of relief as the watering detail rode away from the creek. He reported their discovery to the Battalion Sergeant Major upon their return. BSM Muldoon doubled the number of the second detail to take horses out for water.

"It's Injuns now, is it?" Muldoon developed a faraway look in his blue eyes. With a limited supply of old John Barleycorn, his nose had lost much of its ruddy glow. He had leaned down some, also. Preacher noted the changes approvingly. Fat might be all right for a politician, but a man on the spare side moved faster in a fight.

"Three Cheyenne. One of them was a mere boy."

"But Mr. Judson said he never laid an eye on them, sure an' he did."

"*I* saw them, that's all that mattered, Muldoon."

"Right ye are, Preacher."

Preacher changed the subject. "Judson says the engineer is about ready to blast out a cistern."

"That he is. By all the saints, they're goin' at it backward as usual. What I mean is, what are we to do with all these winders in place? One mistake in the amount of blasting powder an' we'll have glass flyin' all over the inside o' this room, we will."

Preacher laughed. "Board them up, Sergeant Major."

Muldoon cocked his head to one side. "Ye ever see how fast a chunk of rock moves with a big bang behind it?"

"Ummm. You've got a point. All you can hope for is none of them powder men has got three thumbs."

"You goin' out with the new detail?"

"No. I've had an invite to take nooning with Eve Billings. She's promised something special."

Merriment twinkled in the eyes of BSM Muldoon. "Sure an' ye've the sound of a man that's been already caught."

A twinge radiated from the area of Preacher's heart. "Not in the least. I've been alone, on my own, for too many years to change my ways."

Laughing, Muldoon turned back to his paperwork. "Now, that'll be the day, it will."

Bored by lack of something destructive to do, Blake Soures and four of his henchmen decided to pay a visit to the sutler's store at the new fort. They had a hanker to try out some of the whiskey the government-contracted civilian merchant had in stock. They rode inside the stockade shortly after noon the same day, having noted the watering detail on the way.

"Somebody's mighty stupid around these parts," opined Eden Dillon. Yellowed, snaggy teeth made an unhealthy slash in the lower part of his mouth. "They ain't gonna git no water outta rock."

Blake Soures nodded agreement. "The thing for our Indian friends to do is catch them out in the open, watering horses. Be a regular slaughter."

They dismounted at a freshly built, raw, yellow pine tie-rail and looped reins. With his accustomed swagger, Soures led the way into the saloon side of the sutler's store. There, the first thing he saw was a large sign in bold, black, capital letters.

**HARD LIQUOR SALES PROHIBITED
TO ENLISTED AND NCO
PERSONNEL
(OFFICERS AND CIVILIANS ONLY)**

by Order of
Lt. Col. Danvers, Commanding.

Soures pointed it out to his subordinates. "Well, lookie here. Aren't you glad you didn't sign on to wear one of those pretty blue uniforms?"

Pete Price leaned toward Blake Soures. "I betcha we found out who thought up puttin' this place on a finger of rock."

"It ain't natural, that's what." Dillon was put out. "Not right to get between a man an' his whisky. Downright barbarian."

From behind the bar, a jovial-faced man urged them toward the planks. "Seein' as how none of you gentlemen are soldiers, step right up and enjoy a drink."

While the five outlaws settled themselves at the bar, the barkeep poured into large, fish-eye shot glasses. With a deft flick of his wrist, he distributed them to his new customers. "You're new here, so first round is on the house."

Soures answered him with a big grin and a hearty voice. "Now, that's mighty nice. Much obliged, my good man." He had listened intently to the conversations of Quinton Praeger and his associates and now often made a conscious effort to mimic their speech mannerisms when he addressed strangers.

With a good-natured smile, and a wink, the barkeep informed them, "The next one'll cost you double."

Soures eyed the man over the rim of his shot glass, which he had raised to his lips. "Sounds like a place I know of down in the French Quarter of New Orleans."

Entermann, the sutler, gave Soures an expression of innocence. "I've never been in N'awlins."

They shared a laugh and Soures downed his whisky. A moment later, Preacher entered the saloon. He came up short on the threshold and eyed the strangers with immediate suspicion. To the best of his knowledge, there wasn't a white man within two hundred miles. Except, of course, the ones rumored to be with Iron Shirt. Preacher broke his momentary freeze and crossed the plank floor to the far end of the bar.

From there, he could keep an eye on all five hard-faced men. For their part, they wasted little time before turning cold, killer's eyes on Preacher. Their threatening demeanors sent warning jangles along the arms of the mountain man. Ordinarily, he did not wear his pair of Walker Colts inside the fort, only he'd had no time after returning from the water detail to remove them, because of his noon invitation from Eve. Sight of these five set his fingers itching to close around the butt of at least one .44. When they had made clear their awareness of his presence, Preacher seized the main chance.

"You fellers is new around here. Might I ask what brings you to Fort Washington?" Recently, Danvers had grandiosely named his small compound after the Father of His Country.

Constantly on the prod, Pete Price made a snotty reply. "You might ask, but you won't get any answers. So, butt out."

Even more on guard, Preacher tried calming words. "Now, now. That's hardly the way to answer a polite question. Seein' as how I'm the unofficial welcoming committee, I only sought to make you feel at home."

"We don't need a welcome," snapped Soures. "Who are you to be pokin' your nose into our business?"

"Folks call me Preacher."

Thought of the thousand dollars in gold bonus for killing the mountain man named Preacher galvanized Blake Soures. His hand sped to his sash and the butt of a .60-caliber pistol while he shouted to his underlings.

"We got us a thousand dollars, boys! Get him!"

With his outside holsters, Preacher beat all five easily. A Walker Colt filled his right hand and he had the hammer falling before the speediest, Pete Price, could clear the barrel of his long single-shot pistol from his belt. A thunderous clap announced the detonation of the powder load in one chamber of Preacher's Colt.

A powerful fist slammed into the lock plate of Price's pistol and rammed it painfully back into his gut. He doubled over painfully and his finger reflexively twitched. An accomplished shootist, Pete Price had cocked the cumbersome firearm before drawing it clear. As a result, another loud blast filled the room and Price blew a fist-sized hole in his left thigh. He went down shrieking in agony while blood spurted from his femoral artery. Now, Preacher had only three to contend with.

Hot lead cut a painful path across the top of Preacher's left shoulder. An instant later the Walker spoke again. Its message went to a wooly-faced hardcase with mean little pig eyes and a smoking pistol in his left hand. He had fired too soon, Preacher noted. The muzzle was still high. He learned of his mistake when the messenger of death split his breastbone and ripped a hole through his left lung.

Preacher went to one knee, the .44 Colt erupting a third time. Glass tinkled when the ball shattered the chimney of a wall-mounted coal oil-lamp, after it exited the back of the head of surly Eden Dillon. Preacher cut his eyes to Blake Soures, who had taken refuge behind the bar.

Intent on making the perfect shot, Soures did not recognize the dreadful image of the Grim Reaper crouched before him in the person of Preacher. A fourth ball fluttered through the air with the leathery rustle of the death angel's wings. The lead pellet smacked through the bar front and ended in the hinge of Soures' right elbow. With a howl and a curse, he propelled himself backward, fumbled left-handed with the pistol in his waistband and drew it.

By then, Preacher had the fifth piece of frontier trash to deal with. Their weapons fired as one. Preacher immediately flattened out on the floor.

"You got him! You got him, Earl!" Soures shouted as he came full upright in time to hear the bad news.

"No, I didn'," Earl gargled out through the blood welling in his throat. "He . . . got . . . me."

Horrified, Soures cut his eyes to the floor. He focused at once on the black hole that formed the muzzle of Preacher's Walker Colt. Flame blossomed in that darkness, then a stunning agony seared through the chest of Blake Soures. He fired his pistol blindly. The slug put a shower of splinters in the face of Preacher, who fired his second Colt into the exposed gut of his would-be killer. Soures died before he hit the floor.

"Damned unfriendly fellers, I'd say," Preacher offered to a bug-eyed Hyman Entermann.

"B'God, Preacher, you are faster than a scalded cat."

"I've worked at it a mite. Now, I think I'll have me a beer. Gun-fightin' gives me a thirst."

A moment later, the Provost Marshal, Captain Preston, and three of the afternoon guard detail rushed into the sutler's store. "What's going on here?" the officer demanded.

"Nothin' now," Preacher answered laconically.

"How did these bodies get here?"

Preacher took a pull on his beer and made a sour face. "Preston, I swear, you don't have a sensible question to ask. What you should be findin' out is who started the shootin'." His annoyance rang in his voice.

"Well . . . who did start the shooting?"

Nodding toward the jumble of broken and spilled bottles and the body sprawled among them, Preacher spoke simply. "That one there did."

With almost a simper in his prim, disapproving voice, the Provost Marshal declared, "Brawling is prohibited in this establishment or anywhere at Fort Washington. Brawling with firearms is a flogging offense."

"You won't be floggin' this mother's son."

Captain Preston gauged the man he addressed. "Oh? And why not?"

"Take a look around you, Captain Preston. There's five of them here. An' they were ready for me. An' I've got four loads left for this revolvin' pistol here."

Hyman Entermann interrupted. "It was self-defense, Captain. This one back here said they would be paid a thousand dollars gold for killing Preacher. Then he went for his gun. Preacher beat him. End of story. Now please have your men remove this filth from my establishment."

Preacher beamed at the bantam rooster attitude of the sutler. "Yer a good man, Brother Entermann."

"There'll be an investigation," Captain Preston grumbled darkly. Then he made a curt gesture to the guards.

Preacher had the last word. "Don't count on it."

Three days later, Preacher awakened as usual an hour before dawn. He pulled on a long-sleeved flannel shirt against the morning chill and stretched out the kinks. He struck flint to steel, ignited the hat-sized fire he had laid out the previous night and put on water to boil for coffee.

He was working on his second cup in the pearly light of a peaceful dawn when the Blackfoot, Cheyenne and Sioux attacked.

24

Lieutenant Brice had the water detail for the Company horses. He kept in mind everything Preacher had told his friend, Tom Judson. For one thing, he never looked directly at anything in the shadows of the trees that grew along the gorges that formed the watershed for Goose Creek. Although he could not put a name to it, Brice had a particularly active itch between his shoulder blades.

It came as no surprise to him, then, when his roving gaze picked out feathers where there should be none. Neatly trimmed feathers at that. Controlling his urge to draw his Dragoon revolver from the saddle holster and fire, he brought up the nose of his drinking horse and ambled over to his platoon sergeant.

"Sergeant Meaney, pass the word quietly for the men to prepare to draw and fire a cylinder load into those trees over there on my command. Then we get these horses the hell away from here."

"May I ask what it is, sir?"

"Indians, Meaney. Too damned many of them for us to hold off on our own. I have me an itch that tells me they are all around the fort."

Sergeant Meaney nodded his understanding. "I have a sore gut that tells me the same, sir."

"Very well. Be careful about it, don't let the savages suspect we know they are there."

Throughout their exchange, Lieutenant Brice used all his will to keep from looking at the spot where he had seen the feathers. Now he rode with a tense back to the location, expectant of an arrow at any second. He reached the far end of the formation, told Corporal Grange about the hostiles and then looked back over the detail with every show of boredom.

To his satisfaction, he saw every man had his hand near or on the sheepskin covers of his pistol's holster. "All right, men . . . do it now!"

His own Dragoon pistol came free, and he had the hammer back before the muzzle centered on the area where the feathers had been before. "Fire!"

A thunderous roar swelled up in the creek bed, as twelve Dragoons emptied six rounds each from their pistols. Immediately they smoothly changed weapons. Lieutenant Brice stood in his stirrups.

"Back to the fort at the double. . . . Hooo!"

With exceptional skill, the platoon had the entire company's horses on the move and up and out of the creek bed before the hidden Blackfoot could recover from the blazing curtain of lead delivered by the Dragoons. They came on soon enough. Whooping and yipping, all of the Indians broke from concealment and splashed across the creek. In the lead, Red Elk, a Cheyenne, raised his rifle and fired blindly.

His bullet cracked over the heads of the trailing soldiers. It only served to move them faster. Thinking quickly, Lieutenant Brice put Sergeant Meaney at the head of the string of horses and turned back to hastily form a rear guard. The crackle of their pistols drowned out the war cries of the Blackfoot. The sudden, unexpected conflict triggered a premature opening to the battle.

While the Dragoons raced for a small sally port near the corral inside the stockade, a long line of Blackfoot warriors whipped their horses to a gallop on the long, steep slope beyond the fort to the west.

Fully a hundred Blackfoot warriors swept down the steep slope to the west of Fort Washington. An equal number of Cheyenne charged toward the main gate. Behind them loomed the Sioux. Frantically, the sentries labored to swing closed the gates. A bugle blared hysterically. Dragoons on fatigue details dropped their brooms and pitchforks and ran for their Hall carbines. Others spilled from their tents, drawing suspenders over their long-sleeved underwear. Half a dozen ran for the cannon. Preacher made for his lean-to to recover his rifles.

"Knew they would be comin'," he shouted to Three Sleeps Norris, headed in the same direction from their cookfire.

Three Sleeps spat a quid of tobacco from his mouth. "Damn right. Jist a matter of time."

Lieutenant Colonel Danvers' adjutant stood in the middle of the parade ground and bellowed orders. "Companies A and D to the west wall. Companies B and C to the north wall. Get that cannon moving!"

Dust boiled up inside the compound as Dragoons dashed back and forth, uncertain as to whether they should dismount and man the walls or form as skirmishers for a future counterattack. Gradually the officers calmed and directed them. Rifles crackled from outside.

Return fire started at once. Preacher heard Captain Dreiling's firm voice steadying his troops. "Hold your fire until they're well within range. Hold fast, men. Take careful aim. Ready . . . fire!"

A swath of lead balls flung thirty-five Cheyenne warriors from their saddles. "Reload . . . take aim . . . fire."

* * *

Two Moons had the contentment of a man whose dream had come true. He fully believed again in the medicine of Iron Shirt. Now that they traveled down the long-promised warpath to drive out all whites, the Blackfoot war chief banished all doubts. His warriors would be in the second wave to dash down the high mount. They had been given the honor of scaling the wall and fighting the soldiers hand to hand. The first surge, made up of braves from Iron Shirt's band, who were supposed to give covering fire, had already ridden half the distance to the high, pole barricade. Two Moons reflected on the past moon of difficulties.

It had taken a lot more effort than Iron Shirt's white men had expected. Not an easy task to get a warrior, proud of his individual feats of bravery, to work as part of a *team*. Even now the white man's word tasted strange in the mouth of Two Moons. What was a team, and what made it a better way to fight? Why was it superior to the way we have fought since the ancestor days? Where is the honor to be won if everyone holds back to shoot at the enemy from behind rocks and from the protection of gulley banks?

There was little glory in counting coup on a dead man. That was for boys beginning their seasons as warriors. Two Moons recalled the time when his sap ran fresh and hot. He had gone on a raiding party against the Cheyenne. They had stolen horses and ridden away without a scratch. The Cheyenne followed them. When the Red Top people came up to them, they offered challenge. A younger Two Moons had ridden out ahead of the line of his Raven Society brothers and shouted insults at the Cheyenne. He had exposed his manhood and waved it in the faces of the enemy while he told them what he would do with it when they had been conquered. Then he had charged directly at them, an arrow nocked and ready. The Cheyenne stared at him as though frozen.

Two Moons shot one Red Top warrior in the chest, then struck another with his bow. Two perfect coups, and right in front of his brothers! A line of fire ran across the point of his shoulder as a Cheyenne lance barely grazed him. He whirled and rode back, then all the Blackfoot charged.

The Cheyenne fought like Dark Spirits. One of them had a white man's fire-stick—no, a rifle—the older Two Moons corrected himself. With it, he killed two of the Blackfoot. Yet, when the fighting ended, Two Moons and his brothers rode away victorious, dripping scalps tied to their bows, and with more Cheyenne horses than they had started with. Now, the Red Top people fought with them, not as enemies. How the world had turned upside down. Two Moons shook his head in wonder.

From the tree line north of the fort, Spotted Horse could hear the solid thuds when the high gates swung together. The soldiers would be protected now, he thought. How foolish, the Lakota leader thought, for a man to lock himself inside a small place to fight. Only the clear, open plains suited a warrior's soul. Beyond him, on the narrow shelf that jutted out from the base of the foothills, the Cheyenne, led by Red Elk, raced toward where the soldiers waited. The *Sahiela*—the Cheyenne—our cousins, are brave and they fight well. Yet, only our braves can match the ferocity of the Blackfoot. Spotted Horse spat as he thought the word for their traditional enemy. How is it that we come to fight beside them?

Because of the medicine of Iron Shirt, he acknowledged unwillingly. He had seen with his own eyes men who died, even though they had been given the protection of Iron Shirt's medicine. Not all of our people agree, he recalled, mindful of the young hothead, Red Cloud. He had maintained that the medicine was fake. He had agreed with Cloud Blanket of the Cheyenne, and strangely, the elders agreed and stayed out of this fight. He himself had only changed his mind at the last minute. Gunfire erupted along the wall before him and the two sides joined. Spotted Horse readied his pony. Their time would come soon.

Red Elk pushed his pony to a full gallop and loosed one arrow after another at the high wall of the fort. Never had they fought against such a thing. He doubted that arrows would do much damage against the thick forest of lodge-pole pines that had been lashed together across their path. What a strange way to fight, he mused. Who would want to hide behind a barrier three times the height of the tallest man?

Where was the honor in that? From beside him, one of the rifles given them by Iron Shirt barked, and as the smoke cleared, Red Elk saw a white soldier rear up and fall backward. Maybe they had a chance after all. It would be their job to keep the blue-coats busy while their cousins, the Lakota, rushed forward and scaled the walls. Such a strange way to fight. Yet, Iron Shirt had assured them all that it had come to him in a dream. One small thought nagged at him: the Blackfoot have been our enemies since the grandfather times—why do they share their medicine with us now? He would soon see how it worked, of that he was certain.

From his vantage point outside headquarters, Battalion Sergeant Major Muldoon could see little of the hostiles. Here and there feathers and painted faces revealed frantic action beyond the walls. Farther back, more ranks of savages could be seen on the slope that overlooked the fort.

He turned to the young headquarters lieutenant next to him. "Sure an' it's just like Preacher said it would be. Th' heathen devils have got themselves up on that hillside and can look right down in here. If they knew a jot about artillery, we'd all be dead ducks, we would."

A tightening of jaw muscles gave clear indication of the effect of those words on the youthful subaltern. For all *he* knew, the Indians might well have a battery of field pieces. So far, none of the savages they had engaged conducted their battles like Indians were supposed to fight. For some reason, they used standard military tactics. That made it downright scary. From the next words spoken by Muldoon, he might have been reading the lieutenant's mind.

"Of course, when they be pressed too hard, they have always fallen back on their every man for himself ways and flung themselves at us with total disregard for their lives or those of their unit. That's when the advantage falls to us. Ye'll be sein' that here, I've no doubt, sor."

Shouted curses came from the parapet behind the wall and the rate of fire increased. "There's more of 'em coming!" Arrows sailed over the defenses to land harmlessly on the parade ground.

BSM Muldoon touched the edge of the shiny black bill on his cap in salute. "If ye'll excuse me, sor, I must go and take a better look at what's makin' up. Th' darlin' colonel will need to know."

A surge of relief passed through the lieutenant, and he made no offer to accompany Muldoon. "Right, you do that, Sergeant Major."

A flight of twenty-five arrows slammed into the ground all around, their colorful fletchings so many evil blossoms. Muldoon did not even flinch from them, instead he strode through their pattern with a light word on his lips. "'Tis a fine day for a stroll through the flowers, it is."

* * *

Not being paid to defend the fort, the immigrant men armed themselves and formed a protective screen around their portion of the inner compound. Not surprisingly, when the call for the men to rally had come, Charlie Billings had taken up his light rifle and started off. Eve caught her son by the scooped back of his overalls.

"Where do you think you are going, young man?"

Talking over one shoulder, Charlie explained himself. "They called for all the men to arm themselves. There's Injuns out there attacking the fort."

"That did not include ten-year-old boys. You can do your best service by staying here and reloading for me, if the Indians get inside."

Charlie's face clouded. "Aw, Mom."

"No arguments. The matter is closed. Besides, I thought you liked the idea of being an Indian."

His stubborn streak flaring, Charlie answered hotly. "That's different. These are bad Injuns. *Hostiles.*"

Eve would not be swayed any more than her son. "I want you to watch your sister in the meantime. And," she added to soften her refusal, "I think it would be wise for you to carry your rifle with you while you do."

Charlie brightened. "Sure, Mom."

When Charlie and Anna departed for the soddy that had been built for the family, Eve lifted her eyes to the heavens. "Dear God, don't let anything happen to them."

Preacher and Three Sleeps reached a portion of the revetment over the gate before the Cheyenne came into range. Both shared in the dismay of the lieutenant. Never had they seen such control and order among charging hostiles. Someone had found a way to train them and make it stick. At least for the present. Pick off a couple of war leaders and that would quickly change, he reasoned.

"There's hundreds of them, Preacher."

"Yer right, Three Sleeps. And more yet to come. D'ya notice they're fightin' like soldiers?"

"Yes, and I don't like it."

Three Cheyenne had ridden well inside range. Preacher took aim on one, Three Sleeps sighted on another. They fired a fraction of a second apart and the targets left the backs of their ponies for the Spirit World. Quickly, the mountain men reloaded. Preacher popped the last one at forty yards. Some twenty-five yards from the stockade, an irregular line of broken rocks and fair-sized boulders had been left behind by the Dragoons when the fort grounds had been cleared.

Preacher had cautioned Lieutenant Colonel Danvers about this slip in planning and had, as usual, been ignored. He pointed them out now to Three Sleeps as Cheyenne braves, who had ridden double, slipped from behind their friends and taken cover in this manmade barrier. "I told the colonel about those rocks. They'll hide a Cheyenne right enough."

An increased rate of fire from the west told Preacher of the arrival of even more hostiles. He took a quick look over the parade ground and saw the six Dragoons still trying to get the cannon in place. He shook his head.

"Ain't any of those dummies ever heard of a horse? That's half a ton of metal they're tryin' to carry on their backs. A couple of horses would pull that gun up the ramp in no time at all."

"There's a right way, and a wrong way, and—"

Preacher's sigh cut off Three Sleeps. "Yeah, I know, the Army way."

From the tree line came the foulest of Lakota curses. *"Hu ihpeya wicayapo!"*

Preacher's scowl held a bushel of misery. "Aw, damn,

the Lakota have got in this thing, too. Well, one thing certain, they ain't gonna use *me* like a woman."

"Not this chile, neither," Three Sleeps readily agreed.

Eighty-five Lakota warriors, painted and ready for war, rode out of the trees. Three Sleeps saw a brown shoulder between two large rocks and snapped a shot. A howl answered him and the now bloody shoulder disappeared. While he reloaded, he offered his observation to Preacher.

"It don't get much nastier than this."

"Right as rain, Pard. An' I got a feelin' it's gonna get worse before it gets better."

Being senior, by time in grade, Captain Dreiling commanded the defenses over the main gate. He watched with even greater trepidation than Preacher when the Sioux showed themselves and began the charge down the length of the promontory. Protectively, the Dragoons on the parapet had crouched down when the Cheyenne had taken positions in the rocks and begun a sniping duel. Now he found himself forced to go along the double rank of defenders and whack rumps with the flat of his saber to get the troops up to fire at the new hostiles.

"All right, ladies, this is not a quilting bee. Get loaded, get up and prepare to fire by volley. The Sioux have come to pay us a visit." Funny, he did not feel the least bit sarcastic. At the bottom of it, he knew himself to be every bit as scared as the greenest Dragoon out there.

There had to be one in every unit, and Private Finney was the one in Company C. "But, Cap'n, if we do that, those other Injuns will potshot us for sure."

Captain Dreiling ground his teeth. "Why do you think there are two ranks of you? The kneeling rank covers the rocks, the standing one fires on the approaching hostiles. Make ready, men, they are almost in range."

How vastly different from exercises in tactical defense of fortified installations taught at the Academy, Edward Dreiling mused as dust and powder smoke drifted across the ground below. There had been no bullets or arrows snapping past then. If anyone received serious injuries it was due to carelessness or stupidity. These red men swarming out there wanted to kill those in the fort.

From what he had been told they would not stay their hand if appealed to for quarter. The Indians knew no such civilized concept as taking prisoners for exchange. This day there would be many deaths.

Will I be ready for it? his mind mocked him.

25

By noon, two heavy, concerted charges by the hostiles had been repulsed. Preacher munched on a wedge of cornbread, passed out by the women of the sheltering wagon train, and examined the powder-smeared faces of the young Dragoons. To his relief and satisfaction, he saw only expressions of determination. They had gotten over their initial fear. Some of them had even gotten up a game of mumblety-peg. Now, if luck held, the Injuns would not think of the concave wall to the east of this finger of land. Preacher lifted a gourd pitcher to his lips to wash down the cornbread with water. It had tasted good. Someone had thoughtfully cooked bits of bacon into it.

Years of fighting Indians and living in the wilderness had conditioned Preacher to take advantage of food whenever the opportunity presented itself. He ran the tip of his tongue across his teeth and reached for one of two flaky biscuits that remained on his tin plate. When he lifted it, a pink-centered slice of roast venison appeared beneath. He nodded at his plate and spoke to Antoine Revier.

"Maybe we ought to fight Injuns ever' day. Those folks are sure feedin' us nice."

"The venison came from *you know who,*" said Antoine, who gave Preacher a poke in the ribs.

"Aw, git off my back, Tony."

A sudden stir broke out at the junction of the north and west walls. "They're comin' again!" BSM Muldoon bellowed. "Dragoons, stand to your arms."

Iron Shirt had lost his patience. So many warriors should have overrun that small number of soldiers long ago. They had followed orders well, at least until the volume of fire had rained down from those cursed walls increased to a steady roar. Then they forgot what they were supposed to do and went back to the old ways. He decided that a display of courage was needed. Taking up lance and rifle, he gathered his closest, most loyal followers and set out to lead the next attack.

First he harangued the warriors. "We must take this fort before the sun goes to sleep in the west. We cannot fail. Do you see that small knoll? If we do not carry the walls this time, I will be on the top, to make medicine and renew your spirits. One way or another we will kill all of the soldiers before darkness."

Revived, the Blackfoot, Cheyenne and Sioux formed new lines and made ready to attack. At the signal from Iron Shirt, they threw themselves at the walls again. For many, it took supreme effort to blank out the images of their dead brothers and friends, men who were now supposed to be protected from the white men's bullets.

Battalion Sergeant Major Muldoon had worked through the noon hour. At his direction, two sets of compound pulleys had been rigged at the top of the pounded earth ramp. Muldoon strung ropes through them and attached one end of each piece to the carriage of the three-pound cannon. The other ends, he gave to mounted Dragoons.

"Bend them around the pommels of yer darlin' saddles, if ye will. When I give the word, set off at a walk toward the stables."

Private Mallory scratched his chin. "But the stables ain't built yet, Sergeant Major."

One thing that had not changed during the journey here had been the woeful lack of intelligence on the part of Mallory. His patience already frayed by rampaging hostiles, BSM Muldoon got right up in the face of Mallory. "Sure an' they ain't gonna get built, ye idiot, unless we get this darlin' cannon into action and drive them hostiles off. Now, *do as I say.*"

Wooden pulleys creaked and taut ropes thrummed as the weight of the cannon came on them. Step by persistent step, the half-ton weapon rolled toward the base of the ramp. The lines vibrated wildly when the wheels started up the incline. Then one cord, which had been exposed too long to sun and heavy dewfall, snapped with a loud report.

Like a whiplash, it hummed through the air and viciously struck the rump of the horse ridden by Mallory. The animal uttered a very human squeal of pain, reared and dumped its dull-witted rider to the ground.

Muldoon exploded. "Damn yer black heart an' empty head, Mallory. Ye come a thousand miles and still can't keep yer seat. Harris, git over here with that horse an' another rope."

After another twenty minutes, the small field piece had been dragged into place. Quickly the crew milled around it, rammed home a bag of powder, a wad and a fist-sized ball. They all stepped back smartly and stood rigidly in a position of attention.

"Prick . . . prime," the gun captain commanded. Then he lowered a slow match over the touch hole. The little cannon went off with an ear-splitting roar.

The small, round projectile screamed through the air, to burst ten feet above a cluster of Blackfoot. Hot, smoldering shrapnel slashed into them and their horses. Shrieking, they went down together in a heap.

"Reload."

Out came a water-soaked brush, to clean the bore, then the loader placed another bag in the muzzle and the rammer drove it down to the breech. Next came a cloth patch, and another ball. The gun crew stood back and the piece barked again. Shrieking, the ball lobbed over the wall slowly enough to be almost visible from the side.

It burst above another clutch of Blackfoot warriors. The defenders' volume of fire increased, and confusion washed over the stunned Indians.

Although Lieutenant Colonel Danvers thought it better to have one of the mountain men on each of the completed walls, Preacher did not agree. If left together, their disciplined fire and superb, long-range marksmanship would have a devastating effect on the hostiles. Accordingly, he took Three Sleeps Norris and Antoine Revier to the west wall, where the Blackfoot had concentrated.

They began knocking riders from their horses at seventy yards. Perplexed, the Blackfoot soon gave evidence of their doubt. The medicine of Iron Shirt had failed them. Only twenty-five of the seventy who were supposed to do so ran forward to throw braided horsehide ropes over the barricade. Almost at once, three of them stumbled and went down from the well-placed shots of Preacher and his companions.

Preacher made an observation about their stubbornness. "They's still got it in their heads that our bullets can't hurt them. We've gotta make them think otherwise."

Norris nodded. "You know, once an Injun's got somethin'

in his head, it takes billy-be-damned to knock it out of there."

By then, six of the attackers had scaled to the top of the wall. Preacher reached out and smashed one in the head with the butt of his Hawken. The Blackfoot fell away without a sound. Then the little cannon opened up.

Its first round stunned to immobility fully a hundred of the enemy. Seven of them died along with their horses. None of them had ever experienced anything like it. The second detonation ignited fear in the hearts of many of the more prudent among the Cheyenne and Sioux. Wisely, they broke off their attack.

When the third projectile killed one and wounded seven Sioux, a general exodus began. Warriors streamed from the field, eyes wild with open fear that not even their enormous pride could suppress. Within ten minutes, not a single warrior remained within rifle range of Fort Washington.

"Well, that looks like it put the fear of the Almighty into them," opined Preacher. When he reported to Lieutenant Colonel Danvers, he summed up with an ominous statement. "They'll be back. Maybe not today, but give 'em time to whup up some more medicine an' they'll be on our doorstep bright and early tomorrow."

Preacher kept his plans to himself. He had a strong hunch that Lieutenant Colonel Danvers would strenuously disapprove of what he had on for tonight. Accordingly, he, Antoine and Three Sleeps left the fort quietly, by way of the sally port near the corral, well after dark. Lights out had been sounded by the trumpeter and the fort had settled in for sleep. Out on a small knoll to the west, a big bonfire blazed.

Preacher correctly judged that Iron Shirt would be whipping up more medicine. He'd have to, the mountain man reasoned, after the disaster of today's attack. The heartbeat throbs of the big medicine drum reached Preacher's ears as they headed toward the first target, their aim to create confusion and dread among the allies of the Blackfoot. For that purpose he had selected the Lakota encampment first.

With the soldiers bottled up in the fort, and their cousins the Cheyenne close by, the Sioux had not bothered with a night watch. Only the usual herd guards had been placed to prevent their ponies from straying. Preacher found one of them easily. The youthful Brule sat quietly on his pony, eyes fixed on the stars. His lips moved silently.

No doubt he's making a poem for a gal friend, Preacher speculated as he crept up close to the unaware sentry. He had approached from downwind so not even the piebald animal gave warning as Preacher raised up in the tall grass and swung with the flat of his tomahawk blade.

A soft clang came as fine steel met hard head. The teenaged Sioux slumped forward onto the neck of his mount and twitched slightly. Preacher sprang forward and dragged him from the pony. With rawhide thongs he bound the youth, gagged him and left him in a shallow draw. Quietly, he moved on in search of another guard.

Three Sleeps Norris all but blundered into the first of the herd watchers on his side. He surged up out of a gully and found himself not three feet from the broad, bronze back of a Sioux warrior. He recovered quickly enough and brained the warrior with a pistol barrel.

One less to worry about. Gliding on moccasins through the grass, Three Sleeps continued to skirt the horses. He had nearly completed his third of the circuit when he came upon another guard. This one showed wide-eyed surprise at suddenly being confronted by a white man.

"Wa—" he blurted a moment before Three Sleeps silenced him with a hard fist to the jaw. The brave went slack, then heaved himself upward from the ground.

Three Sleeps rapped him back into quiet with the flat of his tomahawk. In no time he had the Sioux bound and gagged. Then he started back, to cover the same ground and make certain he had gotten them all.

Antoine Revier slithered, belly down, through the grass. A chubby, moon-faced youth lounged against a tree trunk. His hand went constantly to his mouth and Antoine realized he was eating something. The French-Delaware cut to his right to circle the herd guard and came upon him from the rear. In the end it became all too easy.

Gnawing on the hind leg of a roast rabbit, the drowsy, fat, young man could not have heard the last trump due to his sensual absorption with food. Antoine's left arm circled his neck and choked off the air. Surprise caused the Sioux to suck fragments of flesh into his lungs. He began to choke and thrash.

Antoine silenced him with a doeskin bag of damp sand taken from the creek. The hapless sentry would have a lump the size of his fist on his head the next morning, provided he didn't strangle on his meal. The brave tied tightly and dragged out of sight into some brush, his assailant ghosted away into the night. There would be at least one more, Antoine thought grimly.

By prearrangement, the trio of mountain men met back at the spot where they had separated. Each had taken out two of the young watchmen. Being careful not to raise an alarm, they started to cut out ponies from the herd. When they had what Preacher estimated to be between twenty and thirty, they eased them away from the rest and headed toward the Cheyenne camp.

When they had come a safe distance, Antoine Revier whispered softly to Preacher, "I can understand, you bein' right friendly with the Cheyenne, why we'd not do any permanent damage, but why spare them cutthroats. The Lakota are bad news."

Preacher answered him readily enough. "Also they are allies of the Cheyenne, and considered to be cousins from sometime in the far-off past. No sense in riling them too much. Thing is to get them to break this alliance with the bloodthirsty Blackfoot."

"Well and good, Preacher, but for me, I'd as soon kill 'em all," Three Sleeps offered.

Preacher tendered his assurances. "I think we'll have us some fun this way."

When they drew close to the Cheyenne camp, Preacher and his friends slipped onto the backs of three ponies and whipped the others up into a gallop. Whooping and caterwauling, they soon turned the gallop into a stampede. Jolted out of their ruminations on lush sweet grass, the animals bounded toward the camp.

Pounding in among the lodges, the ponies created havoc. Warriors, dopey with sleep, struggled into loincloths and stumbled out into the path of the horses. Meanwhile, Preacher, Three Sleeps and Antoine overturned several hide tents and set more afire. Only a few stray arrows challenged them. Howling with laughter, they rode well beyond the Cheyenne village to where they had left their own horses.

Dawn brought back the warriors, boiling with anger this time. After a night of medicine dances, their faith had been restored in Iron Shirt and his Iron Shield ritual. The insults the Sioux and Cheyenne had endured at the hands of Preacher and his friends had not turned them from the alliance. Rather it had stiffened their resolve. They hurled themselves at the stockade with total disregard for personal safety. Braided horsehide lariats snaked over the pointed poles of the outer wall and found purchase on some.

"They're comin' up the walls!" shouted a nervous lieutenant in Company D.

"Shoot 'em off," Preacher grunted.

Fire arrows joined the arsenal of the Blackfoot. The smoking, flame-tipped, shafts whirred over the palisade and thudded into the ground. Two landed on the roof of headquarters, only to be extinguished quickly by the soldiers stationed there, at Preacher's suggestion, for that purpose.

Three Sleeps pointed in the direction of headquarters. "Those fellers are gettin' riled some."

Preacher inclined his head. "Let's hope they don't have too many of those."

With the scalers repulsed, the hostiles drew back a little and the battle became a protracted exchange of gunfire. Using all the speed they could, the Blackfoot and their allies reloaded and fired at the men on the walls.

Lieutenant Colonel Danvers called together the company commanders of Company A and D. "We can sweep them from in front of the gate with a counterattack."

Captain Bronston of Company D scratched at a bald spot on his head. "Do you think that's wise, sir? Once we're exposed, the massive force on the west could flank us and roll us up right smartly."

"Mr. Preacher assured me that when something went wrong for the savages, they would break off an assault and scatter. I'm confident they will do the same now."

Bronston had a ready reply. "Yes, sir, but haven't you noticed that they are fighting in a disciplined manner for once. It is as though someone has introduced them to tactical concepts. If that's the case, they will attack."

"We need to find that out, don't we? Prepare your

companies for a counterattack, gentlemen. The gun crew has come up with grapeshot loads from fifty-four-caliber balls we have in reserve. We can cover you with the cannon."

"Yes, sir. Sabers, sir?"

Lieutenant Col. Danvers considered Captain Bronston's suggestion a moment. "Yes, I think so. Leave your carbines behind."

It had been a facetious offering and the response took Bronston by surprise. Still, he replied quickly. "But the Halls offer us our best firepower."

"Your men cannot hold both in their hands at the same time. You'd only get off two shots at best. Pistols and sabers, Captain Bronston." He turned away.

Ten minutes later, the sally port swung open and the two companies charged out and around the flank of the Cheyenne and Sioux positions. Sabers gleamed in the sun as they descended on the unsuspecting hostiles. Only a few reared upward and fired their rifles at the fast-approaching Dragoons. Pistols barked, and those who resisted died where they stood.

Keen edges flashed deadly light as the Dragoons hacked and slashed their way through the massed forces of warriors. Faster than Captain Bronston imagined, the flank turned back on itself and Indians fell to both sides, wounded or dead. Word of the attack raced through the warriors. It took little time to rally the Blackfoot to come to the aid of their allies.

By that time, the Dragoon charge had come level with the main gate. With a roar of encouragement for the beleaguered, the Blackfoot swarmed around the corner of the stockade and rushed toward the soldiers. Arrows and rifle balls flew toward the mounted troops. Still they prevailed. With a sharp roar, the cannon detonated. Thin shrieks filled the air as the insubstantial leather sheath stripped from the improvised grapeshot. The balls rippled as they passed in front of the Dragoons. At once, some of the men among the Blackfoot began to scream in agony.

Captain Borden, who commanded the counterattack, raised his saber above his head. "Turn about! To the rear . . . Hooo!"

Back through the disorganized hostiles they rode. More of the Cheyenne and Sioux suffered from the pistols and blades in the hands of the Dragoons. Ahead of them, the sally port swung open and the troops streamed toward it.

Fighting dragged on into the afternoon. Preacher offered his opinion of the counterattack. "They lost eight Dragoons kilt an' another eleven wounded. Damn waste of time, I say."

Around three o'clock, nature intervened to disrupt the plans of Iron Shirt. Huge towers of black thunderclouds billowed up in the northwest. They moved swiftly across the Bighorns. Lightning flashed and crackled through the heavy air. The first sheet of rain swept over the finger of land toward Fort Washington at three-ten.

In seconds it turned to a solid downpour. Visibility shrank to mere feet. The three-pounder became inoperative. Already short on ammunition, the hostiles hunkered in the chill deluge and engaged in only desultory return fire. Another benefit the way Preacher saw it, the drencher softened the bow strings of the warriors, which rendered them useless.

Silently, they began to stream away from the walls of Fort Washington. Disappointed in this reversal, the Blackfoot, Cheyenne and Sioux did not even cast glances back at their relieved enemy. When the last of them plodded out of range, a shrill, worried voice came to Preacher's ears.

"Anna! Anna! Charlie, have you seen Anna anywhere?"

"No, Mom," Charlie Billings called back, sudden guilt burning his face red. "Where was she?"

"I . . . I don't know. I left her at the cave with you. When the storm came up, I thought she would surely stay."

"She's not here now."

Eve Billings saw Preacher on the wall and hurried to the stairs that led upward. Worry creased her brow when she approached the mountain man. "Preacher, Anna is missing. I can't find her anywhere."

"We'll look." Preacher grated the words out.

Twenty minutes later, every corner and nook of the fort had been searched without results. Preacher brought Eve the bad news.

"I don't know how, or why, but somehow Anna has gotten out of the fort."

"Oh, my God. You have to find her."

Despite the visions Preacher had about the appeal of a sweet-faced, blond little girl to a Cheyenne or Sioux warrior, he spared Eve that torment. "I'll do ever'thing I can. Don't you worry. It may take a while, but I'll turn over mountains to find her."

26

Not until Preacher passed well beyond the ground churned up by the Indians did he find any sign of Anna Billings. He suspected that she had become terrified of the constant fighting and later the crackling lightning and the boom of thunder. Somehow, in the midst of the furious storm, she had managed to slip away. The small door in the sally port had been found partly open. It stood to reason that the eight-year-old had drawn the latch and left the fort by that means. Preacher's major concern centered around the very good chance that she had been seen by some of the stragglers among the Indians and taken captive.

He found it encouraging when he came upon her small shoe prints in the mud, at a right angle to the direction traveled by the retreating hostiles. It did not eliminate the possibility of her capture. She could have escaped from her captors, Preacher speculated. If so, they would be coming after her. The wind diminished slowly as he followed her sign. Preacher quickly recognized the terrain. Her trail led down into the valley where Goose Creek ran through, made swift and turbulent by the dam and water wheel.

Preacher swung Tarnation northward to stay with her

steps as they led toward the mill. He surmised that the small building there had been her goal. Ahead of him now, he thought he saw a frilly, lace-trimmed collar and flaxen head. He urged Tarnation to a faster pace. Satisfaction glowed in Preacher's chest when he pushed through the tall grass and saw Anna on the bank of the treacherous stream.

Calmly, she went about unlacing her shoes. She was going to cross, Preacher realized. The creek bank looked insubstantial and slippery. He drummed heels into Tarnation's flanks. The hooves squished noisily in the sodden turf, the thump of their impact muffled. Not enough, though.

Anna looked up wide-eyed at picking up sounds of the rapid approach. Unable to recognize Preacher in the low light from an overcast sky, she saw only a huge horse looming over her, remembered the charging Indians, and panicked. With only thought of escape in her mind, the girl sprang to her feet and took a step toward the water. A second later, the saturated soil of the bank gave way under even her slight weight.

With a thin scream, Anna Billings toppled forward into the stream fully clothed. Swollen by the rain, Goose Creek ran swiftly. Anna wailed in terror as the current swept her quickly downstream.

Preacher shouted encouragement as he skidded Tarnation to a halt. "Anna! Hold on. I'm coming."

He took time only to shuck his heavy holsters and Walker Colts, his hat and moccasins. Then he dove into the roiling water. Anna's fair hair formed a dim halo on the surface as she was whirled away.

"Get on your back," Preacher shouted. "Try to float."

Anna tried, failed, and went under. She came up sputtering. "I can't. My dress pulls me down," she wailed. "Please help me."

Preacher drew closer with powerful strokes. "Take off your dress."

A deeper look of horror came on Anna's face. "I c-can't. I don't have a petticoat."

Preacher was barely over an arm's length from her. "Do it anyway. That thing could suck you under for good."

Small fingers tugging at the stubborn buttons, Anna undid her dress far enough to allow its sodden weight to drag it free from her body.

Two more strokes and Preacher reached her. He slid an arm under both of hers and across her bare chest. "Now we've gotta get out of this current."

One-armed, he pulled at the turbulent water at an oblique angle to that of the stream. It soon became hard work. Preacher strained until the cords in his neck stood out like whitened ropes. To his gratitude, Anna did not try to fight the water. He noted progress when a large rock flashed past. Preacher recognized its shape and knew it to be close to the near-side bank.

A few more stout pulls, legs scissoring to provide thrust, and Preacher felt mud and sand beneath his toes. He relaxed and stood upright. Gasping for breath he sized up their situation. Anna clung to him like a monkey. Staggered by the rush of water and his burden, Preacher made unsteady progress to a bar of pebbles and sand that extended into the creek. Once there, he put the girl down.

"You've only one shoe. Best that you take it off 'stead of limpin'."

Tears welled in Anna's eyes. "Thank you, Preacher. You saved me."

Preacher looked down, embarrassed. "It was me scared you into the crick in the first place."

"Did . . . did your horse run away?"

"No. He'll stay where I dropped the reins. We'd best be movin', get you a blanket."

When the naked Anna was wrapped warmly, Preacher handed her up onto the back of Tarnation, then mounted behind her. The girl gave not even a single backward glance at the stream that had come so close to claiming her life.

On the way, Preacher swung Tarnation down into a gully to keep off the skyline. They rounded a bend in the ancient, eroded riverbed and came face-to-face with five grim-visaged Cheyenne warriors.

"Oh-oh, missy, it looks like we've jumped into some trouble," Preacher told Anna calmly while he lifted and shifted her to one side to put her behind him.

Correctly reading Preacher's intention to fight, the Cheyenne raised their weapons. Preacher tensed and drew both of his Walker Colts. His intention was to weaken the Cheyenne enough to crash through and make a run for it. The fight was about to begin.

Then, at the last moment, an older warrior drifted down the shallow bank. He raised his right arm in a commanding gesture and called to his fellow Cheyenne.

"Hold! Do not attack this man. I know him well. He is a friend."

He trotted forward then and greeted Preacher. "Ho, White Ghost, it seems that you are always helping little children."

Preacher recognized him at once. "Cloud Blanket, you look the same as when I last saw you."

Cloud Blanket turned in his saddle so the other Cheyenne could hear his words. He spoke in his own tongue. "I made you my brother when you rescued my little son and daughter from that bison stampede on our hunting grounds that summer long ago."

Preacher smiled and replied in the same language. "I remember it like it was yesterday."

Cloud Blanket gestured to the five warriors. "These men scout for my band. I am moving far to the east because of the unrest among our people."

"If you are talking about the fightin' at the fort, I can understand. What's your fix on what's gotten the tribes so stirred up."

Cloud Blanket scowled. "It is the doing of one man. Iron Shirt. I will come and talk about it with you over coffee."

It all started with a misunderstanding at the main gate. Private Masters, on sentry duty, saw Preacher approaching with an Indian at his side. He drew the obvious conclusion.

"Corporal of the Guard, Post Number Two. Chief scout returning with a prisoner. Looks like he's found the girl, too."

When Lieutenant Colonel Danvers received word of that, he left his office hastily and went to meet Preacher. Two privates and a nervous Corporal Penny stood around a mounted Indian, weapons leveled. Before Preacher could explain, Danvers burst onto the scene.

"Corporal Penny, escort the prisoner to the guardhouse."

"Yes, sir."

Preacher protested at once. "Now, hold on a minute. This man is my friend. He's not a hostile."

"He's an Indian, isn't he?" Danvers replied.

Eve Billings, tears of relief on her face, came up then to relieve Preacher of Anna. She stopped short, astonished at the figure who sat his horse in front of her. "Why, that's the Indian I told you about, Preacher. He's the one who watched us from a distance." To Danvers, she added, "He's friendly right enough. He smiled and waved to me every time."

It was time for introductions, Preacher felt. "His name is Cloud Blanket. This is Miz Billings. An' this is . . ."

Charlie Billings came forward and raised his right

hand in the sign of greeting and peace. "*Heyota*, Cloud Blanket."

Shock registered on the face of Eve Billings. "Charles Ryan Billings, you . . . you *know* this Indian?"

"Oh, sure. He's my friend, but it's supposed to be a secret. Back in the other mountains he came to me and taught me how to track game. That's why I always done so good."

"Did so well," Eve corrected automatically.

"He gave me these moccasins, too." Charlie beamed with pride in his friendship.

Lieutenant Colonel Danvers interrupted the domestic scene. "He is still a hostile prisoner, and I want him removed to a secure place at once."

Preacher's dander rose. "An' I say hell no. 'Fore you lock anyone up, Colonel, we'll all jist ride out of here and leave you to the mercy of the real hostiles."

"You can't do that. It's desertion in the face of the enemy. I'll have you shot for that."

Eyes narrowed alarmingly, Preacher pinned Danvers with a burning gaze. "You may try, Colonel, but you'll have a damn hard time doing it." He raised himself in the saddle. "Antoine, Three Sleeps, grab yer gear. We're gettin' out of here," he shouted.

After two tense minutes, the mountain men appeared with their horses loaded. The Arapaho warriors came with them. Without another word, Preacher and Cloud Blanket in the lead, they left the fort by the open main gate. After they departed, Danvers looked around and spotted BSM Muldoon.

"Sergeant Major, take a horse and follow them. I want to know every detail of what they are up to."

"Yes, sir."

Beyond the ridge that overlooked Fort Washington, Preacher halted the small party and made a fire for coffee. While it brewed, he listened to what Cloud Blanket knew of Iron Shirt. His conclusions, arrived at over the first cup of heavily sweetened brew, surprised Preacher.

"I believe that there is more behind this than a moon-struck holy man. There are three white men who go wherever Iron Shirt goes. They do not have kind faces. They are the ones who bring the rifles."

"I'll have to look into that. A while back I thought I had run into the whites that was supposed to be runnin' with Iron Shirt." He went on to relate the run-in with Blake Soures, including a description of the outlaw leader.

Cloud Blanket nodded thoughtfully, then brightened at the portrayal of Soures. "That is the man who brought the wagons with the rifles. He is like the rattlesnake."

"*Was*, Cloud Blanket. I killed him."

"He will not be missed by me or any of my band."

"I'm gonna have to go get a look at these other whites you tole me about."

"You are not going back to the soldier lodges?"

"No. Let that damned pompous Danvers sweat a bit. The others can go back in a couple of days, if they want. That'll help some."

"While you are gone, my braves and I will not be able to protect the foolish soldiers, but we will try."

They drank another cup of coffee and Cloud Blanket described to Preacher how to find the war camp. They parted as friends.

BSM Terrance Muldoon and his three-man detail returned to Fort Washington to report. They remained unaware that they had been allowed to get close enough to hear what was being discussed. Nor, after hearing Preacher speak in Cheyenne, did Muldoon wonder why the conversation had been in English. Doubtless he would have been furious to learn that it had been done that way for his benefit.

"So, Mr. Preacher is going off to look for some nonexistent white renegades who are supposed to be aiding the hostiles that attacked us? Do you suspect, Sergeant Major, that he intends to join them?"

BSM Muldoon bristled. "Certainly not, sor, an' that's a fact. Preacher may be a lot of things, dependin' on how ye see him, but he's not disloyal, not a bit, sor."

"I want a detail sent off to trail our Mr. Preacher. Lieutenant Judson will lead it. I know how you dislike garrison duty, Sergeant Major, so I am sending you along as ranking noncom."

"And the purpose of our going after him, if I may ask, sor?"

"I want you to bring him, and the others who deserted us, back here."

Muldoon raised an eyebrow. "To be punished, is it, sor?"

"No, to tell us what we need to know to defeat these hostiles."

"Ye think they'll be comin' back, do ye, Colonel, sor?"

"You can count on it, Sergeant Major. As soon as they lick their wounds and get in a proper frenzy." Then he turned his attention to a dispatch he had to write to his superiors back East.

After a three-days fast, hard journey, Preacher and his friends, none of whom seemed eager to return to the fort, reached the war camp deep in the Bighorn Canyon region. It had been up and down mountains all the way. Mostly up, as Preacher saw it. At noon of the last day, Preacher reined in and pointed to the crisp-edged imprints of iron wagon wheels.

"There's no question that there's white men with that biggest Blackfoot band. They're close, too. I think we need only get close enough to take a peek, then git on back."

"Sounds right," agreed Three Sleeps.

Antoine cast one eye at an odd angle. "You reckon the colonel will thank us for what we find out?"

Preacher ran long fingers through his long, dark, sandy hair. "I doubt he knows the words, Tony. We'll ease up on these-here hostiles after dark and see what we can see."

Late that night, what they saw, though they had no names for them, were Praeger, Gross and Reiker. Preacher watched their activity for a while, then came to the conclusion that the Blackfoot and their allies were making preparations to return to Fort Washington. He nudged Three Sleeps in the ribs and whispered in his ear.

"I think we got what we came for. We'll ease our way out of here and head back in the morning."

Except for Lieutenant Judson and BSM Muldoon, the detail that followed Preacher consisted of men so inept that they made their presence painfully obvious. So lulled did they become, that they had not the slightest awareness of being watched. Early the next morning, they blithely walked their horses directly into imminent danger.

When the large war party of Blackfoot attacked, they took the Dragoons entirely by surprise.

27

Arrows flew in a dark cloud out of the grass along the trail left by Preacher. Three Dragoons died before a one could fire a shot. The hostiles, who had left early to return to the fort, had come across the sign of white men and decided upon an ambush. The sight of the Dragoons had been entirely too tempting.

Lieutenant Judson acted correctly and promptly. "Dismount. . . . Form a circle with your horses. Every other man, return fire."

The only trouble was they saw nothing to shoot at. Another flight of deadly shafts rose from the conceal-ment of waving grass and thick brush. Instinctively, the Dragoons aimed at the places where the arrows first appeared. Several cries of pain rewarded them. Mounted warriors came from a tree line along one ridge and charged toward the circle of horses. Had the Blackfoot waited only a short while longer, they could have caught all of the birds in their nest.

It turned out not to be so. From a distance, Preacher and the men with him heard several muffled reports.

The mountain men cocked their ears and concentrated a moment.

"It sounds like carbines to me," opined Preacher, who pronounced the word *car-bines*.

Three Sleeps agreed. "That it does. Now, what you suppose?"

"Figger Colonel Danvers sent some people after us."

Antoine joined in. "An' they got theyselves in trouble." He ended with a cackle.

Three Sleeps Norris turned to Preacher. "Should we go help 'em out?"

Preacher pretended to ponder that a moment. "I don't see why not."

The Arapaho in their wake, they set off at a brisk canter. From the faintness of the sound, Preacher reckoned they had a good twenty-minute ride.

A lot can happen in twenty minutes. Terribly outnumbered, the eighteen-man patrol died by ones and twos. Blackfoot swarmed around the improvised shelter, the horses targeted indiscriminately, along with the Dragoons. One beast, shrieking in pain from a neck wound, broke the grip of the soldier holding it and ran out among the charging hostiles.

That opened a gap which allowed a dozen Blackfoot to dash through. With lance and tomahawk, they began to slash at the Dragoons from terribly close quarters. BSM Muldoon saw Lieutenant Judson go down, a lance rammed through his belly. The unfortunate Private Mallory died a second later, his body draped over that of his officer.

"Poor, stupid lad," Muldoon said aloud as eulogy for them both.

Then his ears heard something he could not believe. Gunfire! And coming from beyond the press of savages. It could only be Preacher and those he had taken with him. Relief flooded Muldoon as he shot a screaming Blackfoot full in the face from two feet away. Another of the Dragoons died while he cocked the hammer to take out a hostile.

Three mountain men and six Arapaho warriors charged down on the backs of the triumphant Blackfoot. Their rifles cracked at the best possible range and nine Blackfoot died. Preacher unlimbered one of his Walker Colts and shot two more before the hostiles could react and turn to face this new threat.

Wounded, one of them thrashed in the grass. Preacher aimed at a fourth target. He knew his chances to be good; he hadn't missed yet. His evaluation of his marksmanship proved accurate. His .44 ball slammed into the skull of a warrior who swung a war club at the head of BSM Muldoon.

Preacher's action did not prevent Muldoon from being hit, but turned the strike into a hard, glancing blow. Believing the spirits had turned on them, the surviving Blackfoot fired a few final arrows, those without mounts were hoisted up by comrades on horseback and the warriors streamed off over a notch in the ridge to the south.

Stunned by the rap on his head, Muldoon looked slowly around himself to discover he had come out of the fray as the sole survivor. "Jesus, Mary an' Joseph, sure an' I'm glad to see you, Preacher, that's a fact."

Preacher also totaled the grim score. "How'd this happen to you?"

"Devil take it, lad, they got us entirely by surprise, they did. Didn' know there was any heathen about 'til they shot arrows at us from the grass, an' then more of the spalpeen bastids come out of the trees, shootin' better rifles than we have. It was a terrible slaughter, it was."

Preacher tried for understatement. "I can see that."

"All me poor lads. Even lame-wit Mallory, an' our darlin' lieutenant. The colonel's not going to like that, he's not."

"No doubt. Tell me something, Muldoon, you seemed to put a note in your voice when you mentioned the colonel. Was it the knock you got on your head, or something else?"

Muldoon's grimace of pain turned to a sour expression. "You've got the heart of it, Preacher, sure an' you do. I've not seen nor heard anything certain, but I do have some worries about the darlin' colonel, I do. He's been writin' a lot of dispatches of late. Only they aren't to Gen'ral Ferris, or the War Department. I've yet to see to whom he addresses them, but it's certain sure it's not anyone in our chain of command."

"There's more?" prompted Preacher.

"Aye, that's the big an' little of it. It's about his attitude toward the men, Preacher. The way he sent us out here, an eighteen-man patrol into hostile country, with not a fare-thee-well. An' orderin' that counterattack back when the heathens had the fort surrounded. It's almost as though he wants us to get killed off to the last man jack of us, it is. But, a commander leads his men, inspires them, an' protects them, too. It can't be."

That awakened dark suspicions in the mind of Preacher, although he had to put them aside for the present and look into it all later. Muldoon had suffered a hard, messy blow to the head, which cut his scalp and raised a knot. Time that was taken care of.

"You know about those things more than I, Sergeant Major. Now, let me get a good look at that wound of yours." After some gentle probing and prodding, Preacher satisfied himself the skull remained intact and pronounced his verdict. "You'll recover. But with your patrol wiped out, and no way to get back alone, it might be best for you to ride with us."

BSM Muldoon's eyebrows elevated. "Yer not goin' direct to the fort?"

"Nope. This ambush tells me we haven't finished our business here. We need to get a look at this Blackfoot messiah, Iron Shirt, up close and personal. Find out what hold he has on these Injuns."

"When will that be?"

"Tonight," promised Preacher.

Preacher's little band made careful observations of the routine engaged in by Iron Shirt. In this case, two large bands of Northern Cheyenne, won over by news of the near success at the fort, prepared for the ritual. Late that night, after the immersion, fire-walking, feasting, drumming and singing ended, would be ideal for what Preacher had in mind, he told the others.

Once they had pulled back far enough from the camp, Preacher revealed his intentions. "Antoine an' me are gonna go in there and stir 'em up some. Leave some real scary things for Iron Shirt. If we're lucky, he'll begin to doubt his own medicine."

"Such as what?" BSM Muldoon asked.

Preacher brushed off the question. "Oh, some things we gathered up earlier today."

The hearty band had ridden west of the ambush scene to avoid any contact with hostiles that might happen by. Preacher and Antoine had hunted during part of the afternoon, using bows with all the skill of an Indian. Part of what they took, they ate. Some portions of the animals had been put away for later use. Preacher knew exactly what he wanted, and had used the last hours of daylight to paint plains-Indian pictographs on strips of rawhide. He took those, and the animal parts, with him when he and Antoine slipped away to the Blackfoot encampment at around two o'clock in the morning. A heavy overcast made the ground a pool of ink.

They entered the sleeping war village silently. Only the soft scuff of moccasins on hard soil indicated their movement. Preacher worked his way to the center of camp, then located the ideal spot.

With Antoine standing guard in front of the entrance to the lodge of Iron Shirt, Preacher placed a headless skunk on the ground. Next came a fresh deer heart, to which he affixed one of the pictograph strips. Those were the symbols for Iron Shirt's name, he had explained when he painted them. Beside that, he left the severed testicles of the same deer, with signs on the rawhide for White Wolf takes these from Iron Shirt.

Satisfied with his nocturnal display, Preacher signaled to Antoine and the mountain men slipped out of camp. Once beyond any chance of apprehension, they both threw back their heads and made the wailing sounds associated with the spirits of those who had been blinded and mutilated and could not journey to the Other World. Not too surprisingly, no one stirred in camp until daylight.

Shortly after the uproar that heralded the discovery of Preacher's handiwork, the hostiles broke camp and rode off to the southeast, in the direction of Fort Washington. Preacher's stalwart band followed at a discreet distance.

Over the next several nights, Preacher continued to pay ghostly, taunting visits to the band of warriors. On the fourth night, he edged in close to two teenaged boys, along as apprentice warriors and assigned as herd guards. After a round of ordinary talk about which girl in their village they thought the most beautiful, one lad brought up a subject that Iron Shirt's fury prohibited from being talked of openly.

"My older brother has seen the bad medicine that appears in camp these last nights. This White Wolf has powerful medicine. My brother thinks maybe more

strength than Iron Shirt. Men have tried to kill White
Wolf before, yet he lives, while our warriors die by the
white man's bullets. My brother is thinking of taking me
and returning to our village."

The other boy agreed. "Yes, that is a wise thing."

From his careful observation of the furtive glances the
warriors made in all directions when they left their low
war lodges, and now this indication of unrest, Preacher
decided that an aura of bad medicine and even fear
hung over the entire camp. His work had been well
done.

A quick count of those in the war camp the next morning informed Preacher that some twelve or more had
abandoned the cause. Earlier that day he had watched
the three white men in camp set off southeast with
Cheyenne guides, well ahead of the rest. Cloud Blanket
had been right, and Preacher would tell him so. A big stir
came when Iron Shirt learned of the defections.

He called the warriors together, most of them already
mounted to continue the ride. "They are women! They
shame the name Blackfoot. I have had a vision. We will
make a mighty raid on the soldiers we have fought before
with our Cheyenne and Sioux brothers. This time we will
be victorious! I have strengthened the medicine that
protects you. Nothing of the white man's can harm you."

From his vantage point, Preacher grinned at the crafti-
ness of this fraudulent medicine man. As if he did not
plan all along to go back to the fort. He decided upon
one more visit to this uneasy war camp that night.

They came in the darkest part of the night. Preacher
and his companions burst into the gathering of lodges
from ten different points of the compass. Whooping
ferociously, a torch spluttering in one hand, Preacher

bent low to set fire to a six-foot-high lodge. Then he made for another one.

Not far away, one of the Arapaho, Gourd, overturned another and shot the occupants. Three Sleeps Norris trampled mounds of supplies and set them ablaze. Antoine Revier hurled cases of ammunition and bundles of arrows into the central fire. The enemy swirled all around them, unwilling to fire their rifles for fear of hitting a friend.

In the mad gyration of the swift raid, Preacher eventually came face-to-face with Iron Shirt. Preacher's right-hand Walker Colt bucked first and the ball smacked into the chest of his enemy. Iron Shirt went down in an eyeblink. Elated, Preacher signaled for the others to leave. They had accomplished much more than he had expected. Firing their weapons behind them, the mountain men, Arapaho, and BSM Muldoon quickly faded into the dark.

28

To Preacher's astonishment, the warriors did not disband after the death of Iron Shirt. Nor did they take time to mourn the loss of their leader and elect a new one. Rather, some set out immediately, with Cheyenne braves acting as guides, in search of those who had done the damage. The rest continued toward the fort.

Preacher soon learned the reason. Iron Shirt was alive! Obviously sore as hell, he moved slowly and sat his pony warily. Surrounded by a hundred Blackfoot warriors, the medicine man was unreachable. Knowing where the hostiles were headed, Preacher urged all speed to the fort. Muldoon concurred.

Mid morning remained markedly cool two days later, when the sentry's voice rang out from the gate. "Corporal of the Guard, Post Number Two. Visitors at the gate."

Bustling over on sore feet—he'd joined the Dragoons to ride, not to walk—Corporal Collins found three men confronting the guard. They were dressed like dandies. Nevertheless, he addressed them politely enough. "Good morning, gentlemen. May I inquire as to your business at Fort Washington today?"

Quinton Praeger took the lead. "We must see your commanding officer at once."

Collins blinked. "What about?"

"It is a matter of great urgency."

Following regulations, Corporal Collins did not give an inch. "If you tell me what it is, I can convey the information to Colonel Danvers."

His patience growing short, Praeger put heat in his words. "It is a matter of life and death."

Amused by the man's pomposity, Collins let his eyes go wide. "Oh, that's what it is, eh? The colonel will want to hear that, I'm sure."

Praeger flared. "Damnit, man, the country west of here is full of roving bands of hostiles. Tell him that, and tell him that Quinton Praeger and two associates are here to see him at once."

Corporal Collins scratched one ear. "I reckon you fellers didn't see the bullet scars on the wall. We've done whipped the savages and sent them running."

Praeger regained his control and fixed the insolent corporal with a frigid stare. "No you didn't. Because all the Indians we saw were headed this way. Tell that to your Colonel Danvers."

"Uh . . . yes, sir, right away, sir."

When Lieutenant Colonel Danvers learned of their presence, he had the three men ushered into his office. He waited a moment to insure that no prying ears lingered beyond the door then turned on Praeger, Gross and Reiker with a face suffused by hot fury.

"What in the name of God are you doing here?" he demanded.

Praeger took a step forward, asserting his control. "The whole thing is coming apart. Preacher is alive."

"I know that. But he's gone now, I dismissed him and he went away."

Praeger's words struck Danvers like lead pellets. "He went right to the war camp of Iron Shirt. He's worked some sort of savage mysticism that's nearly driven Iron Shirt out of his mind. He told me after the first little gifts were left that Preacher wants his balls. It's true what I told your corporal. The Blackfoot, Cheyenne and Sioux are on the way here. But if we don't get a war started soon, it will all blow up in our faces."

Danvers fumbled for words. "That's . . . terribly disturbing. What do you expect me to do?"

"I want you to have these Dragoons attack the peaceful Cheyenne at once, the ones who did not join Iron Shirt. That's sure to bring about the desired reaction and satisfy our friends back East." He paused, looked around the headquarters and at the palisades beyond.

"Apparently you did too good a job on this fort. By now I expected to find all but you dead. The troops are in much too good shape. Looks as if they could fight their way through any number of Indians."

Instinctively Danvers stood up for his men. "My Dragoons had to fight their way out here. Naturally they gained experience."

Praeger closed with Danvers in two rapid steps. He tapped a long forefinger on the colonel's chest. "Let me remind you that *they* are the ones who are supposed to lose. The whole program is poised to fall into place. But . . ." He raised the finger and tapped Danvers again. "It will take a massacre and an Indian war to clear the land of the savage vermin."

Choking on his anger, Lieutenant Colonel Danvers turned partly away. Why had he ever thrown in his lot with these insufferable scoundrels? Desperately he tried to disassociate himself from this distasteful part of their plot. "I am only taking orders. I am not a participant in anything beyond the military involvement, of which, I'll remind you, I took no part in the planning. I suggest you leave forthwith, before any fighting begins, if you value your hides so much." With that, he showed them out of his office.

* * *

Preacher's valiant band arrived at Fort Washington the next day. The Blackfoot, Cheyenne and Sioux came right behind. Once more, the fort was very active. From the round-top knoll where he had made medicine, Iron Shirt observed the frantic activity within the walls through a brass telescope given him by Quinton Praeger. He could not mask his surprised reaction when he recognized three particular faces. He lowered the glass and turned to Two Moons.

"The Great Spirit smiles on us. The man Praeger and his nurselings are inside the fort. We can now sweep all of our enemies away in one battle. Then all the plains will burst out in flame."

For his part, Two Moons would have preferred to be spared Iron Shirt's rhetoric. Cunning and intelligent, Two Moons had long ago accepted that the great medicine of Iron Shirt was a fake. Men died at the hands of the whites not because they had lost faith, but because they had been shot. What sat foremost in the mind of Two Moons was the swiftness with which Iron Shirt had turned against their benefactors. Praeger, who wanted to be called Star Child, had brought them the fine new rifles, the barrels of powder and boxes of caps. For that he deserved praise, not death. He kept all that to himself as he replied to his leader.

"We have them trapped right enough. Why have they come here?" Two Moons inquired.

"Why do the white men do many stupid things?" Derisive laughter followed that suggestion.

"Iron Shirt, since they know of our plans, it cannot be for protection. It may be they came here to betray us."

Iron Shirt's face darkened at that. "Then they shall die slowly."

* * *

Quinton Praeger withdrew into a dark rage when he learned of the death of Blake Soures. He took his fury to the saloon in the sutler's store only half an hour before the Indians swarmed down the length of the narrow finger of land to the stockade that surrounded Fort Washington. There he observed the three, buckskin-clad men who had ridden in earlier in the day. They gulped down prodigious drafts of beer and wiped their lips with the backs of their hands. When the Blackfoot and their allies appeared, the sutler spoke from behind the bar to one of them.

"Well, Preacher, looks like you brought us more company than we wanted."

"I coulda told ya they were on the way, if you'd've asked," came the reply. "Boys, we'd best be gettin' to the walls. Those Injuns ain't here for a bison feast."

Jolted by this revelation and driven by a blind desire for revenge on Preacher, Praeger went in search of Heck Driscoll, one of Soures' lieutenants, who managed the wagons. He found him near the stables.

"Driscoll, I have a job for you. I've located this troublemaker, Preacher, and I can point him out to you. I want you to kill him. Do it up on the wall, so it will look like the savages did it."

Driscoll hitched his belt and produced a confident grin. "I can handle that all right." With that, they set off to find Preacher.

Like a cataract's roar, gunfire greeted them as they approached the wall. From outside came the challenging reports of Praeger's nice new rifles. Praeger winced involuntarily at the thought of being shot at by them. He quickly located the lean, broad-shouldered man in buckskin and pointed him out to Driscoll. The renegade gave a curt nod and moved off toward the access stairs.

* * *

Preacher first became aware of Driscoll when the mountain man moved abruptly and a tomahawk blade swished past his ear. The haft struck his right shoulder and Preacher turned, expecting to find a warrior had scaled the wall.

Not so. He faced another white man, one he vaguely recognized. His carefully planned blow gone astray, Driscoll sought to recover. Before he could lift the 'hawk, Preacher hit him in his exposed gut. Driscoll dropped the tomahawk and bent double. Air rushed from Driscoll's lungs, to be quickly stopped when Preacher kneed him in the face.

Dazed, Driscoll went to one knee. The fighting around them had grown so intense that no one noticed as Driscoll slid a knife from its sheath. Concerned with holding off the Indians, Preacher did not have time to play by the rules. He simply drew a .44 Colt and blew a hole through the head of his assailant. Heck Driscoll did a backward half gainer off the parapet.

Then enlightenment settled on Preacher. The dead man had been with the others in the Blackfoot war camp. He'd handed out rifles and ammunition from the rear of a wagon. That meant the other whites must be here. He knew them by sight, and vaguely recalled that someone had given him names: Praeger, Gross and Reiker. Behind him, the firing slackened and the first assault by the hostiles broke off. Preacher went in search of the men behind this uprising.

He found Quinton Praeger with surprising ease. Shunning the hypocrisy of fighting his Indian allies, Praeger had returned to the saloon. Preacher came upon him there.

Arctic chill coated the words Preacher spoke in a slow drawl. "I reckon you're the one they call Praeger. You're responsible for stirrin' up this Injun ruckus. An' I reckon you know who I am. For what it's worth, yer errand boy didn't get the job done." Preacher's lip curled in contempt. "I hate a stinkin' white renegade more'n I hate a Pawnee. Are you going to do it the easy way an' give up?"

From outside they heard sound of renewed attack. This time it came from the west. Praeger responded with a bravado he did not feel. "That'll be the day."

Preacher had come willing to oblige. "Do you want it inside or out?"

Praeger did not reply. Instead, he fired with a concealed pistol from under the table. The sneak's aim was off because of the extreme angle, so all that hit Preacher was a shower of splinters. The flattened ball moaned past. Responding in a manner totally unexpected by Praeger, Preacher dove over the table at him.

They spilled out of the chair together. Preacher rammed Praeger's head against the floorboards repeatedly until a small cloud of dust hung around the battered renegade. Drops of blood from Praeger's split scalp formed a halo around his head. His eyes glazed and Preacher eased up, came to his feet.

He soon found that Praeger had more than one card up his sleeve. Lightning quick, Praeger grabbed for the butt of another of his short-barreled .60 pistols. He found himself not fast enough.

Preacher filled his hand with a Walker Colt and shot his enemy in the right shoulder. The Deringer went flying. His gun hand made inoperable, Praeger made a try with his left. To his surprise, he got the pistol free and fired a shot that creased the outside of Preacher's right thigh. That did not prevent Preacher from shooting the corrupt land speculator through the heart.

Hyman Entermann stared at Preacher a moment. "There's another of them out back in the chicksale."

Preacher nodded his thanks and left the saloon. He found Morton Gross at the outhouse. The chubby renegade fumbled to button his fly as he exited the small building. Preacher's words froze him.

"I killed Praeger not a minute ago. I'd gather you are the one called Gross. It sorta fits," he added parenthetically.

"I . . . I don't know who you mean. My name is Pembrook." His slight hesitation over the name put the lie to his words.

Preacher took note of it. "I don't care what you call yerself. You rode in with a piece of renegade white trash named Praeger, who's been stirrin' up the Blackfoot, Cheyenne and Sioux. I'm here to take you to justice in front of Colonel Danvers, or bury you. The choice is yours."

In the next tense second, Morton Gross made the biggest mistake of his life. Instead of surrendering, he grabbed for his pistol. He cleared it of his coat and had the hammer back when Preacher drew and fired his Walker Colt. The .44 ball struck Gross in a rib, which flattened it and deflected it from his heart, though it did terrible damage to his left lung. Eyes wide, he blinked slowly and sagged to the ground. Preacher stepped close and kicked the gun away.

"Where will I find Reiker?"

"I . . . don't know. You must be Preacher, right?"

"That's what they call me."

"I know . . . I'm going to die. I . . . just want . . . to do something . . . on the plus side of . . . the ledger . . . before I do."

"Go on, I'm listenin'."

Blood bubbled in pink froth on the lips of Morton Gross. "Watch out . . . for your Colonel Danvers, Preacher. He's in on . . . this thing of Praeger's."

Preacher bent close. "You're sure of that?"

A breathy word answered him. "Yes." Then Morton Gross shuddered and died.

"Dang. That went too fast. I sure would like to know where Reiker is," Preacher said over the dead man.

"He's right here." The voice came from behind Preacher, like the crack of a whip.

A violent crash and a rumble came from beyond Aaron Reiker. Unlike the previous time, the Blackfoot warriors did not try to scale the wall. Instead, they rode forward, attached several ropes to a series of spike-topped lodge-pole pines in the palisade and rode fast away from the wall. With as many as eight horses per upright, the log barricade strained and at last gave away. The rammed earth behind cascaded down from sheer gravity.

Preacher tensed and made ready to spring to one side. He fully expected to get a bullet in the back at any second. Instead, Reiker started toward him, talking as he came.

"I saw Quinton's body. And now I see you have disposed of Morton as well. Saves me the trouble, I suppose. I should be grateful and let you go. Our Indian friends will finish you readily enough." Reiker paused and sighed. "But then, coward that he was, I imagine Gross told you more than you should know. You've more lives than an alley cat, Preacher, and you might get away from the Blackfoot. So, you see, I don't have any choice."

While the overconfident Reiker rambled, Preacher's expectations soared. Braced for evasion, he used flexed knees to power his next move. With a loud, piercing yell, he jumped straight into the air and spun, bringing a Walker Colt ahead of him. Lacking the precise position of Reiker, his first shot missed.

Lithe as a cat, Preacher came down on the balls of his moccasined feet as he eared back the hammer. Reiker's ball caught Preacher by surprise, and burned like hell's fire along the left side of the rib cage. Had he been standing still, he would have died. It put Preacher's second shot off so that it only cut a chunk off Reiker's right hip-bone.

Reiker stumbled to his left, to the protection of the outhouse. A stench came from the interior that told of much frequent use. A fastidious man in dress and decorum, Reiker wrinkled his nose. Over it all, though, hung the coppery odor of violent death. Cautiously he peered around one corner.

Surprise puckered his lips when he saw no sign of Preacher. Where could he have gotten to so quickly? Reiker searched the entire area behind the sutler's with his eyes. Confident that Preacher had left, there being no hiding place, he came from behind the small structure and started back toward the saloon. The door to the outhouse creaked on leather hinges at his back.

"Behind you, Reiker."

He made a valorous try, spun from left to right, so his pistol would come in line first. Preacher let him complete his turn before he pumped a .44 ball into the center of Reiker's chest. Gagging, Reiker sank to his knees. His pistol discharged. The ball punched through the door of the toilet. Feebly he reached for another pistol.

Preacher shot him again. This time the ball put a black hole at the top of the bridge of Reiker's nose. Preacher stepped into the clear.

"Got to remember to tell Entermann to do something about that smell," he muttered. He sighed and set to reloading his Walker Colt. With this accomplished, all he had left was Iron Shirt and the aroused Indians.

29

With the wall almost breached, Preacher busied himself in an effort to get some of the young Dragoons to pull the three-pound cannon to the top of the dirt platform. Lieutenant Colonel Danvers confronted him there.

"Do you mind telling me where Mr. Praeger and his associates happen to be?"

Mincing no words, Preacher told him. He concluded with a fateful remark. "An' before one of them died, he told me you are mixed up in this dirty little business."

Danvers' eyes went wild. Froth formed at the corners of his mouth as, heedless of his condition and surroundings, he drew his Dragoon revolver. "That's a damned lie. Soldiers! I'm arresting this man as an Indian sympathizer. Disarm him and lock him up in the guardhouse."

Moving swiftly, Preacher knocked both privates aside and pulled his Walker Colt. Danvers had already triggered his Dragoon pistol. The shot went somewhat wild, to punch a hole through Preacher's left shoulder, which caused him to drop his Colt. Danvers took aim again.

In the next instant, a Cheyenne lance split the heart of Lieutenant Colonel Danvers. It had been hurled by Cloud Blanket, who dropped from the roof of the headquarters building to land beside Preacher. They embraced in the Cheyenne manner.

"Now all we have to do is kill Iron Shirt and this first-cousin-to-a-skunk alliance will fall apart."

Cloud Blanket appeared saddened. "Yes. I always knew it would come to that. Though I will not be the one to spill his blood. Here, that shoulder needs caring for."

While Cloud Blanket bound Preacher's shoulder, he offered advice on the best means of finishing Iron Shirt. Preacher listened intently. Around them, the battle raged on. Once the cannon had been moved into place, as Cloud Blanket packed the wound with a poultice, the assault on the weakened portion of the wall ended quickly.

Little respite came for the defenders. No sooner had the Blackfoot withdrawn from the west stockade than the Cheyenne and Sioux flung themselves at the north face. They used the same tactic of tearing down the wall. Another section broke away and the dirt buffer rumbled into a loose ramp. Up it plunged the Sioux warriors.

With the fortifications about to fall, the desperate young Dragoon gunners manned the cannon, firing in a flat trajectory now. When they ran out of prepared grapeshot, they dumped loose balls down the barrel and double wadded it. Preacher reappeared on the parade ground with his French Le Mat sporting rifle. Aching from wounds in both shoulders, he fought his way through a group of Sioux who had breached the wall and now swarmed onto the parade ground. BSM Muldoon saw him coming and helped clear a path with some well-aimed shots. After a solid smack to the kidneys of one warrior, which sent torrents of pain through Preacher's body, he gained the parapet.

Eyes straining against the haze of smoke and dust, Preacher at last located the Blackfoot prophet. This was going to hurt him almost as much as it would Iron Shirt, he thought as he knelt and put the buttplate of the rifle to his shoulder. True to his word, Iron Shirt made medicine on the little round-top knoll. His body twisted and jerked in the gyrations of his ritual dance around a blazing fire. Taking careful aim, Preacher touched the set trigger, then put a fingertip on the release tang.

The Le Mat let go with a terrible bark at the front end and a ferocious bite at the back. Preacher's face screwed up in a response he could not suppress. Two long seconds passed; then Iron Shirt looked up sharply as the ball cracked over his head. Moving like an aged weakling, Preacher reloaded. Again he took aim.

With another punishing report, the Le Mat fired again.

Iron Shirt staggered, sagged, toppled. He hit the ground and lay there, his limbs twitched in agonized reflex for three long minutes, then he lay still. A gusty sigh of relief came from Preacher.

It had worked as he'd expected. Although much smaller, the .36-caliber ball had markedly more velocity and better sectional density than a .54 round so that it cut through the links of chain mail and pierced the heart of Iron Shirt. Word of the messiah's death traveled fast. Suddenly, the allies fell silent on the battlefield. Cloud Blanket appeared at Preacher's right. He raised his bloodied lance to command attention.

"My brothers, your false prophet, Iron Shirt, is dead. His medicine was not good against the long gun of White Ghost, who took his life. Stop the fighting and go home. Live there in peace with the white men, who will leave this place in the Moon of Painted Leaves. There will be no fort in this place."

Slowly, his message sank in. Their heads bowed in perceived defeat, the warriors turned away from Fort Washington and began to leave the area in small groups. Within an hour they had all passed out of sight.

* * *

After the warriors had left the field and order had been restored, Eve and her children came with some of the others to where Preacher sat under a single oak that had been spared by the builders, deadening the ache of his wounds with a jug of good rye.

Not one to defer to any man, Eve spoke what they had on their minds. "Preacher, we were wondering what you had in mind for the next few months?"

Preacher took a long pull and smacked his lips. The liquor probably was not good for the healing process, he knew, but by the time he got well into the second jug, he wouldn't give a damn. "Well, I'm gonna write a report on what happened here, to go with that Captain Dreiling. You know, the one whose gonna lead these soldier-boys back come September. My friends, Antoine an' Three Sleeps, will scout for them."

Eve pushed him further. "Yes, but what about you?"

"Me? I'm gonna take myself off somewhere quiet, where I won't see no Injuns or pilgrims or soldier-boys for a long, long time, an' jist plain heal up."

Eve's expression revealed that he had just slammed a door on what she wanted so desperately to know. Gathering her resources, she relented for the moment. "Actually, I wanted to ask you about a more immediate future. I would be pleased if you would take supper with my children and myself."

Preacher beamed up at her. "Well now, I think that could be managed. I'm tired of all this backslappin' that's gone on over me shootin' Iron Shirt. A little quiet supper sounds fine."

After the meal, with Charlie and Anna asleep for the night, Preacher and Eve talked earnestly and quietly for a while. Then they took a stroll to the small cabin set aside for Preacher.

* * *

Early the next morning, Preacher emerged from the low log structure. He yawned and stretched as much as his wounds would allow, then glanced back through the open door as he made his way to the nearest cookfire and pot of coffee.

He had a big grin plastered on his face as he made an announcement to the unseen person within. "Well now, I'll allow as how I jist might find that quiet place I want to rest up in somewhere in the Northwest Territory."